P9-CFJ-475

DEATH
in a
DESERT LAND

Also by Andrew Wilson

Fiction

The Lying Tongue

A Talent for Murder

A Different Kind of Evil

Nonfiction

Alexander McQueen: Blood Beneath the Skin

Mad Girl's Love Song: Sylvia Plath and Life Before Ted

Shadow of the Titanic: The Extraordinary Stories of Those Who Survived

Harold Robbins: The Man Who Invented Sex

Beautiful Shadow: A Life of Patricia Highsmith

DEATH
in a
DESERT LAND

A NOVEL

Andrew Wilson

ATRIA BOOKS
New York London Toronto Sydney New Delhi

An Imprint of Simon & Schuster, Inc.
1230 Avenue of the Americas
New York, NY 10020

This book is a work of fiction. Any references to historical events, real people, or real places are used fictitiously. Other names, characters, places, and events are products of the author's imagination, and any resemblance to actual events or places or persons, living or dead, is entirely coincidental.

First Atria Books hardcover edition July 2019

ATRIA BOOKS and colophon are trademarks of Simon & Schuster, Inc.

Manufactured in the United States of America

1 3 5 7 9 10 8 6 4 2

ISBN 978-1-5011-9744-4
ISBN 978-1-5011-9745-1 (pbk)
ISBN 978-1-5011-9746-8 (ebook)

To M. F.

DEATH
in a
DESERT LAND

Prologue

Dearest Father,

I can hardly believe the words that I am about to set down. It sounds ridiculous, quite preposterous, but I am in fear of my life.

There have been many occasions where I have been forced to confront the prospect of dying. The terrifying ascent and descent of the Finsteraarhorn, when I was convinced I was going to slip into a glacial crevice or, in the midst of a ferocious snow storm, be swept off the edge of a precipice and fall thousands of feet to my death.

I remember too the time when I traveled across the desert sands to Hayyil, a perilous journey that many have not survived. When I finally reached the feared city I was taken prisoner. There I heard it said that in that place murder was considered so normal, it was likened to the spilling of milk. There are those, many of whom were born in Arabia, who seemed offended by my spirit of adventure, as if I was an affront to the female sex. Indeed, in Hayyil I was told that a woman should only leave her house on three occasions: to marry her bridegroom, on the death of her parents, and in the event of her own death.

And then there was that no-man's-land of the soul that I inhabited after Dick's death. I have never been so low as then, when it felt as though I had nothing left to live for, when I had been tempted to put an end to it all. The shock of the news of his shooting at Gallipoli almost stilled my heart. I was at a lunch party in London when one of our number casually mentioned how sad it was that Dick Doughty-Wylie had been killed in action. How were they to know of my attachment to him? Afraid that I was going to be ill, I excused myself from the lunch, my head reeling. I learnt later that Dick had left his pistol behind on his boat and witnesses told me that he strode into village houses—which conceivably could have been packed to the rafters with Turkish soldiers—holding nothing more than his cane. As he reached the top of the hill, a swell of Hampshires, Dublins, and Munsters behind him, he was shot in the head and buried where he fell. What a terribly sad end to a glorious life.

The only conclusion I can come to as to why Dick would advance unarmed is that he could not face the situation back at home: a wife who threatened to commit suicide if he were to leave her, a woman—me—whom he loved but knew he could never marry.

I must resist the urge to get swept back into the past. But there is a reason why I cite these occasions, moments when I have faced the possibility of nonexistence.

I believe, and have done so since I was a girl, that there is nothing that lies beyond the here and now. When I am gone I know that I will know nothing, be nothing. I don't expect to meet dear Dick, or my darling brother Hugh, in some paradise of an afterlife.

So you see, it is not death that frightens me. It is the thought—quite natural and justifiable—that someone may want to wrest my life away from me before I am quite ready. I have lived a good life, a great deal fuller and richer than many women on this earth, but am I ready to die? Lately, I have become weak, I have suffered from illness. But not to see that rare bloom of a daffodil in my garden in Baghdad? Not to walk through the date palms on a spring day or take a swim in the waters of the Tigris on a hot summer's evening? Not to sit under the shade of a tamarind tree and eat a ripe fig? Never again see the delights of my little museum that houses the treasures of the past? And this is nothing compared to the important work still to be done with King Faisal and the continuing improvements in an independent Iraq. No, I am not ready to go just yet.

It could be my fancy, but I have become convinced that someone wishes to do me harm. An uneasiness of spirit has come over me. I feel as though I am being watched, studied, but when I look up there is no one in the room. In the early hours, when I have been in bed reading, I have noticed how Tundra suddenly stirs, the dog's ears pricked, her bright eyes turning on some invisible enemy, a low growl beginning to form in the back of her throat. I have gone to the window, looked out into the purple night, but I have been unable to see or hear anything beyond the stirring of the palms in the breeze. I have taken to sleeping with my gun under my pillow. I need to be ready, prepared. As someone once told me, "Every Arab in the desert fears the other."

Ever your affectionate daughter,
Gertrude

* * *

Dearest Father,

I cannot write very much because my hand is trembling so; I apologize if you cannot read my words.

Enclosed is a drawing that I received this morning. As you can see, it shows a grave at Ur, which has recently come to light during the dig overseen by Mr. Woolley and his team. Next to a stick figure you will see a set of initials. They are my own: G.L.B.

If the missive's purpose was to unnerve me, then it has worked. I feel shaken to the core. My hope is that this was the only function of the letter, that it was designed to unsteady me and nothing more.

In my previous letter, I spoke of my irrational fears that someone wants me dead; now I am afraid that this is indeed the case. You know that I do not have a melodramatic streak. I do not strive to create drama where there is none. I have always borne my miseries with fortitude. I am of a practical bent and not prone to fancies. I wish I did not have to set the words down; to see them written before me gives them a certain reality that makes me tremble. But set them down I must.

If I were to be found dead—and if there was an indication that my death was not due to the onset of some terminal illness—then it is safe to assume that I was murdered. And my murderer? I suggest you look no further than Ur.

Ever your affectionate daughter,
Gertrude

1

"So, what do you make of it?" asked Davison as he took the two letters from me.

I did not answer immediately. Too many questions were crowding my head. I took a sip of iced soda water and gazed across the terrace of the hotel to the Tigris below. A lonely boatman was singing a queer, discordant song that brought back to me the ghosts of the past.

"And the handwriting is definitely that of Gertrude Bell?"

"It seems so," said Davison, peering at the scrawl again. "Someone who knows about these kinds of things has compared the letters to others she wrote to her father and stepmother, and although it's difficult to say for certain, there are particular elements of style—such as the distinctive way she formed her *d*'s, for example, with a curious backwards slope—that suggest they were indeed written by Miss Bell."

"I've always understood that she died of an illness—pneumonia or something bronchial," I said, remembering the obituaries I had read of the famous adventurer and Arabist when she died in July 1926. At that time I had been in the midst of my own troubles, drowning in a sea of grief after the death of my mother, valiantly trying to hold together a marriage that was falling apart at the seams, battling a creative block that was driving me to the edge of reason.

"Yes, that was the story put out by the family," said Davison. "But according to the doctor who examined her, Miss Bell died from barbiturate poisoning. A bottle of Dial tablets was found by her bedside at her house here in Baghdad. Of course, no one wanted to draw attention to the fact that her death, or so it was thought, was a suicide."

"And tell me again how these letters came to light."

"It had been thought that her family had taken possession of the bulk of Miss Bell's archive, diaries, numerous photographs, documents relating to the archaeological museum she founded, letters, and so on. Indeed, as I'm sure you know, her stepmother published two volumes of Gertrude's letters only last year. But then, just last month, these unsent two letters were discovered in a tin box that served as a place to store seeds. It was only when one of Gertrude's former servants, Ali, a gardener whom the family continued to employ, started to look for a particular type of seed that he came across them. Of course, he couldn't read the contents—he's a local, and Miss Bell was always proud of the fact that she communicated with her servants in Arabic—but Ali knew that they had been written in his mistress's hand. And he knew enough English to realize that the initials G.L.B. were those of Miss Bell. He did the right thing and took the letters to our man in Baghdad. Apparently, the drawing distressed him a great deal. He thought it represented some kind of curse."

"I can imagine it would have that effect," I said. Although I had missed the British Museum's *Treasures of Ur* exhibition earlier in the year, I had seen a similar drawing of dozens of stick figures reproduced in the *Illustrated London News*. Reading about the discovery of the skeletons—which were thought to be victims of human sacrifice that dated to 2,500 years before the birth of Christ—had sent a chill through me. "Do you know if Miss Bell had any enemies?"

As Davison smiled, his intelligent gray eyes sparkled mischievously. "Plenty, I would have thought. She was hardly the easiest of women to get along with. Headstrong—independent if one wants to be polite, bloody infuriating if one is speaking plainly. Sorry, I—"

"Davison, you know I always prefer plain speaking. Did you know her well?"

"We only met a few times, once out here in Baghdad, another time in Egypt, and then, of course, in London."

"And is there anything I should know about her background? Her work for you at the Secret Intelligence Service or for any of the other covert government departments, for instance?"

Davison looked away from me, his gaze settling on a cluster of black rocks on the other side of the riverbank. "Now, is that a sacred ibis down there?" He started to raise himself out of the wicker chair to take a closer look. "I do believe it is. You know what, I've never seen one of those. Fascinating, of course, especially if you're interested in Egyptian mythology. Venerated and mummified by the ancient Egyptians, you know; a representation of Thoth."

I could feel my cheeks begin to color with frustration.

"But, on closer inspection," he said as he squinted down at the river, "it could be a northern bald ibis, said to be one of the first birds that Noah released from his ark, that bird being a representation of fertility. Anyway, whatever it was, it's gone now."

As he turned his head to me, Davison assumed a pose of the utmost seriousness. He managed to freeze his features into a mask of implacability before the skin on his cheeks started to turn pink, his eyes sparkled once more, and he burst into a loud fit of laughter.

"I'm sorry, Agatha," he said, taking up a starched linen napkin to wipe the beads of sweat from above his upper lip. "It was too good an opportunity to miss to tease you. I know it's not really a laughing matter, but you should have seen your face! You looked like you wanted to slap me—or at the very least walk out of the hotel and take the first Orient Express back to London."

"You can laugh as much you like," I said, fighting the urge to smile, "but there was a time, not too far in the past, when you didn't trust me enough to provide me with all the information I needed to help you. Remember?"

"But Tenerife was different," he said, lowering his voice to a near whisper. "You know the reason why I was so reluctant to share certain details of my life with you."

"That may be so," I said. Although it would have been easy to do so, I decided not to embarrass Davison, and instead turned the conversation back to the current case. "Now that you've had a jolly laugh at my expense, why don't you tell me what you know?"

"Very well," he said as he crossed his legs. "Yes, you're right. Miss Bell did work in secret intelligence during the war."

"In what capacity?"

"She was stationed in Cairo, where it was her mission to provide us with evidence about the links between the Germans and the Turkish Empire, particularly in eastern and northern Arabia. Because she had done all this traveling, trekking across the desert, gossiping with sheikhs over strong coffee, she had an unparalleled insight into certain alliances which would otherwise have remained obscure. She wrote reports for the *Arab Bulletin*, which I'm sure you know provided the British government with a stream of very helpful secret information."

I thought back to my own time in Cairo, where I had lived with my mother for three months during the winter of 1907. What a stupid girl I had been. At seventeen years old I had only been interested in romance—endless flirtations with dashing men in the three or four regiments stationed out there—and my appearance.

"Miss Bell sounds like she was an exceptional woman," I said, feeling distinctly unworthy in comparison. "Am I right in remembering that she took a degree from Oxford?" My education could be described as patchy at best—for great swathes of my childhood I did not even go to school—and, the more I heard from Davison, the more I was beginning to feel envious of Miss Bell's extraordinary achievements.

"Yes, the first woman to take a first—and a brilliant one at that—in Modern History. And in two years instead of the usual three. She always seemed the most intelligent person in the room. That had its benefits, particularly for the department, but of course she was not the most subtle of individuals. I remember once, at some grand dinner, sitting opposite her and hearing her describe one of the diplomat's wives, in a dismissive voice, as a "nice little woman." That was always her insult of choice for women she deemed her inferior, which was the majority."

In that instant I felt a certain relief that Miss Bell was no longer with us—I doubted she would have liked me—and then, almost immediately, I felt ashamed for thinking ill of the dead.

"But why do you think she believed someone at Ur wanted to kill her? Did she know anyone there?"

Davison took out two photographs from the inside pocket of his jacket and passed them over to me. "This is Leonard Woolley, of whom you've no doubt heard, the man in charge of the dig down at Ur." I studied the image of a man dressed in shorts and a jacket, a man with a puckish face, who was sitting cross-legged on the ground, peering intently at a clay slab in his hands. "Woolley and Miss Bell knew each other during the war when he was head of intelligence at Port Said and she was stationed in Cairo. From all accounts, they seemed to get on well. The only thing we've managed to dig up is a possible suggestion that the two did not see eye to eye in regards to the dividing up of the treasures at Ur."

"What do you mean?"

"Well, in Miss Bell's role as head of antiquities in Iraq, it was her duty to decide which objects she should set aside for her museum here in Baghdad, and which ones she allowed the team at Ur to transport back to Britain and America. Apparently, Woolley was upset that Miss Bell insisted on keeping for the museum an ancient plaque showing a milking scene. I've been told that Woolley valued it at around ten thousand pounds. She also managed to secure a gold scarab which experts believe is worth one hundred thousand pounds."

I could not disguise my astonishment. "Really? As much as that?"

"Yes, and she won it on the toss of a rupee."

"I can imagine Woolley would be annoyed. But surely nobody is suggesting that's the reason why he might want her dead?"

"We both know that murder has been done for an awful lot less."

"Indeed we do," I said, taking a moment to pause to look at the river, with its traffic of *gufa*s and other vessels. "So, what do you have in mind? You told me something of your plan before we left London, but I'm assuming there is something more specific you want me to do."

"Yes, there is," said Davison, all traces of his former joviality now erased from his face. "We need to know for certain whether there is any truth in Miss Bell's suspicion that she was going to be murdered. For that, I'm asking you to travel down to Ur. I've already discerned that you would be welcome there. There is a Mrs. Woolley, you see, and she normally dislikes other women on site. She is the queen of the camp and likes to be treated as such. She cannot endure the prospect of competition from other members of the female sex, but I am told that for you she would make an exception. The reason why you are most suitable for this assignment—the reason why your name was mentioned to me by the head of the division, Hartford—was because of Mrs. Woolley's enthusiasm for *The Murder of Roger Ackroyd*. Something of a literary snob by all accounts, but her passion for that book is—"

"I see," I said, feeling uncomfortable with the prospect of further praise of my work. "Can you tell me any more about Mrs. Woolley?"

Davison did not say anything for a few seconds. As he began to form his thoughts I noticed a pair of horizontal lines crease his forehead, making him look a good deal older.

"Perhaps it's better if you forge your own opinion of her," he said, draining the last of his brandy. He raised his hand to call over the waiter. "But know this: Miss Bell told various acquaintances that she believed Mrs. Woolley to be a dangerous woman."

"And is this Mrs. Woolley, in this photograph here?" I asked, gesturing towards an image of a woman who, although middle-aged, still possessed a certain striking beauty. The photograph showed her sitting on the desert floor, examining a shard of an old pot.

"Yes, that's her all right," said Davison. "From what I've heard of her, Katharine Woolley is a Jekyll-and-Hyde character, charming one moment, cold and cruel the next. There is also some mystery surrounding the death of her first husband, Lieutenant Colonel Bertram Keeling, whom she married at St. Martin-in-the-Fields in March 1919. Six months later, Keeling, who was only thirty-nine, shot himself at the foot of the Great Pyramid of Cheops."

"And did Keeling work in intelligence, too?"

"As a matter of fact he did—during the war, in Cairo. But at the time of his death he was director-general of the survey of Egypt and president of the Cotton Research Board."

"A good cover for espionage if ever I heard one. Do you know if he had any dealings with Miss Bell? Had they a history I should know about?"

"Not as far as we know. But the very nature of these things means that a great deal of what occurred during the war remains a secret."

"But doesn't it seem odd to you that Keeling and Miss Bell, both of whom worked in Cairo in intelligence during the war, went on to die as supposed suicides?" I asked. "What if someone wanted them dead and made the murders *look* like suicides?"

"It's a possibility, of course. But we've never thought about connecting the two cases because—"

"Because the suggestion is that your own government, or an agency acting on its behalf, may have something to do with their deaths?"

"I wouldn't put it quite in those terms," Davison said dismissively.

"I'd rather know the whole truth, if you have access to it," I said.

"Yes, of course, but I promise on this occasion there is nothing else I can tell you. I'll put out some feelers, see what I can come up with, but at the moment there really is nothing to link their deaths."

"That's not quite true," I said, taking up the photographs of the archaeologist and his wife. "There is something that links them together: the Woolleys." I tried to picture a sequence of possible events, the scenes flashing through my mind like a series of imagined tableaux. "Why would a man kill himself six months after getting married? That doesn't seem right to me, as he would surely still be in the first flush of romance. Of course, he may have realized that he had made a terrible mistake, or he could have faced the prospect of ruin. Perhaps he had saddled himself with debt or embroiled himself in an impending scandal in his personal life. Those need to be ruled out. With suicide, there are so many factors one needs to take into account, but there's something about that case that strikes me as odd. And then, seven years later, Miss Gertrude Bell, at the peak of her achievements, takes her own life by an overdose of barbiturates. That too doesn't ring true. These letters written by her to her father just before her death—there is something very queer about them. Why weren't they sent? How did they end up in that seed tin? Why have they just turned up now?"

Davison was looking at me with a mix of admiration and bafflement. "I'm at a loss to know what to say," he said. "I'm afraid I don't have any answers."

"The 'suicide' of Colonel Keeling, Katharine Woolley's first husband, in 1919," I continued. "The 'suicide' of Miss Bell in 1926, whom we know had dealings with Leonard Woolley and who described Katharine as dangerous. Then the recent discovery of these letters—letters written by Gertrude Bell in which she directs us to Ur to look for her killer. Could the murderer be either Leonard or Katharine Woolley?"

"But what could be their motive?"

"Something that is hidden out of sight, at least for the moment," I said. "It could be connected with their intelligence work. We know that Colonel Keeling, Miss Bell, and Leonard Woolley all served in secret operations during the war. Perhaps that's something you can look into."

Davison nodded and scribbled in his notebook. Although we were sitting in the shade of the terrace, the breeze had dropped and the heat was becoming unbearable. I shifted in my seat and took another sip of my soda water, which was now lukewarm. "Of course, there is another possibility."

"There is?"

"Oh, yes," I said, pausing for a moment. "The Woolleys, the husband and the wife, could have been responsible for both murders."

"What do you mean? As if they had some kind of pact?"

"Perhaps," I said. "People have done stranger things for love—or some warped version of it." I thought back to the case in Tenerife and the mess Davison had got himself into over his feelings for a young man, whose partly mummified body had been found in a cave. And I thought of my former husband, Archie, and the scandal surrounding my disappearance for ten days at the end of 1926.

"Yes, indeed, but best not to dwell on that," said Davison as he noticed the cloud of melancholy that had started to steal over me. "So, what do you think? If I stay here in Baghdad, are you happy to travel down to Ur? See what you can dig up? As I said, I'm certain you're the perfect person for this."

As Davison continued to talk—about what an extraordinary job I had done in Tenerife, how I had brilliantly applied my skills as a novelist to the business of solving crimes—I thought of my old life as a conventional wife and mother. Archie's affair with Miss Neele, followed by the nasty rash of newspaper headlines that followed my disappearance, the ridiculous rumors that Archie was somehow responsible, the allegations that I had staged the whole thing as some cheap publicity stunt, had taken their inevitable toll. And then there was the interview I had been persuaded to give to the *Daily Mail* earlier in the year which was designed, in that dreadful phrase, to "put the record straight." Little did anyone know how much I had drawn on my skills as a novelist during that meeting.

I often wondered, when I woke in the middle of the night and was unable to get back to sleep, whether I could have saved my marriage. If I had been more attentive to Archie . . . if I had been a better wife . . . if I had never taken up writing and had simply devoted myself to him and his concerns, and laughed at the inane jokes of his golfing friends and never had a complicated thought in my head. Would that have made any difference? Of course, it was all too late now. The divorce had gone through. We were no longer man and wife. But if I was no longer a wife, who was I? A mother, of course: yes, always. An author? After that awful period of writer's block following my mother's death, I had produced a couple of books of which I was not proud. But I hoped I was back on track now. After all, I had no option: writing was the way I earned my living. But what else?

"Agatha . . . are you all right?" It was Davison. "Did you hear what I was saying?"

"Sorry, it's this heat," I said, feeling a little dizzy. "I'm not sure Baghdad entirely agrees with me."

"Yes, you do look a little pale. I say, why don't I walk you back to your room?"

"That would be very kind, thank you," I said as Davison took my arm. "I really do think it's best if I lie down."

But I had no intention of taking a rest.

2

After Davison had safely seen me into my room—and arranged to meet me for breakfast at the hotel the following day in order to say goodbye—I took a quick bath and changed into a silk blouse. I walked out onto the balcony and watched the sunset turn the Tigris red. In the distance I could hear the call to prayer echo around the ancient city.

I had been in Baghdad for only a day, and everything about it seemed so exotic, so wonderfully oriental. Even though I had traveled the world, or a good deal of it, during my 1922 tour with Archie, I had never visited anywhere like this. I was desperate to explore on my own and so, armed with my guidebook, I ventured downstairs, through the cool of the lobby with its marble floor, and out into the street.

The contrast between the hotel and the world outside could not have been greater, and for a moment I had to steady myself by a palm tree as I took it all in. The main thoroughfare, Rashid Street, which ran along parallel to the Tigris, was full of a pulsating mass of people, all touting goods for sale: a cacophony of voices proclaimed fish squirming in barrels; partridges squashed together in undersized cages; pots and pans of every description; goods made from reeds (brushes, baskets, mats, even shoes); cheese and yogurt from the milk of buffaloes; spices of every description, most of which I had never seen or even heard of; tables piled high with strange vegetables and odd-looking fruits; tailored clothes for the discerning Arab gentleman; cheap-looking garments clearly more suited to the servant classes; items of jewelry that shimmered with delicate mother-of-pearl and startling lapis lazuli; a stall that sold a range of oddly shaped musical instruments that I wasn't sure could be blown, plucked, or rattled; and tools for the land and garden, some of which looked like they could inflict a nasty head injury.

As I walked, my sense of smell was assaulted by aromas sweet and foul, and at times I had to take my handkerchief from my handbag to cover my mouth and nose. I had been warned about this before leaving England. It had been one in a litany of objections raised by my family and some friends when they heard that I intended to travel to Baghdad. Sewers in the streets, pestilence and the threat of disease, the danger from the natives, the unstable political situation, the awful climate, the insects, the length of the journey—all had been used in an effort to dissuade me from traveling to the Near East.

Of course, I could tell no one about the real reason for my visit: my work for Davison and the Secret Intelligence Service. My sister, Madge, and Carlo, my secretary and friend, had all been in favor of me taking a holiday—after all, my daughter Rosalind was away at boarding school in Bexhill—and had approved when I had popped into Cook's, the travel agents, and booked a passage to the West Indies. Then, just a few days before I was due to leave, I received a message from Davison. The letters surrounding the mysterious death of Gertrude Bell had come to light and he needed someone to investigate further. Although I was initially reluctant, as soon as he mentioned passage on the Orient Express, and then the chance of visiting Ur, famous for the exquisite treasures that I had seen featured in the press, I told him that I would cancel my holiday. The West Indies could wait.

"You're going where?" screeched my sister when I told her of my change of plan.

"To Baghdad, via Damascus, traveling on the Orient Express as far as Stamboul and then the Express."

"You must be out of your mind," Madge continued, before launching into a tirade of a dozen reasons why such a journey was not only unwise but dangerous. "You must be unhinged, Agatha. Please tell me you're not having another one of your queer episodes."

"I'm perfectly well, thank you," I said. "You know what the doctors told me."

"I know, but I'm just worried for you, that's all," she said. "What if anything were to happen to you out there? What about Rosalind? Don't you think you owe it to her not to do anything foolhardy? Of course, James and I would look after her," she said, referring to her husband, "but even so, it would be beastly for her to lose you after all that's happened. And what's wrong with the West Indies? They would be so much more restful." She paused. "And why have you gone and altered your plans? I just don't understand what's behind all of this."

"Don't worry, I'll be extremely safe," I said. I had already prepared a story to explain why I had changed my mind. I told her—and Carlo—of how I had met a naval officer and his wife at a dinner party and how they had enthused about the delights of Baghdad. It was perfectly civilized, they had said; in fact, Mesopotamia was the birthplace of civilization, the area where the cuneiform script had been invented, the oldest form of writing in the world. That had seemed to silence Madge, and she retreated in a sulk.

"All by yourself?" said my faithful secretary Carlo, when I told her of the trip. "But you don't know anyone there, or anything about it."

"You're right, but it's about time I did something a little more exciting," I replied. "After all, Rosalind is happy at school. You can go and take that trip to stay with your sister. I'll only be away for a matter of weeks. I'll be back for Christmas."

As I gazed up at the turquoise and gold dome of the Haydar Khana Mosque and heard snatches of Arabic all around me—a language I could not understand—the thought of an English Christmas seemed like an impossibility.

I continued wandering along Rashid Street until I came to the Souk al-Safafeer, full of men hammering copper into pitches and pots, but did not stay long as the deafening noise was bringing on a headache. The dizziness I had first felt on the terrace of the hotel had also returned. I felt breathless and in desperate need of a glass of water. I made my way out of the first exit I saw, into a side street, but instead of walking in the direction of Rashid, I must have taken a wrong turning, because I found myself in a darkened alleyway that ran between the backs of run-down houses. I looked around. There was no one to ask for directions to the main street. I tried to take a deep breath to calm myself, but I could feel my heart beating, a fast rhythm that only made me more afraid. The stench from a nearby trough was overwhelming, and I tasted bile in my mouth. In that instant, even though I could see no one, I was sure that I felt someone's eyes on me.

As I walked down the alley, back towards what I thought was the direction of the copper souk, a door in one of the houses opened and a figure appeared. He was a boy on the verge of manhood. He exclaimed something in a guttural language I could not understand, but within a matter of seconds it was clear what he wanted as his long, bony figures started jabbing at my handbag. I told myself that it would be unlikely he would grab my bag; I knew there were extremely severe penalties for even minor crimes. I felt a sweaty hand encircle my wrist, soon followed by a sharp pull on the bag.

"No, I'm sorry, I'm not going to give it you," I said loudly, in the grandest voice I could muster.

The boy replied with an obscene-sounding flow of invective.

"I'm not carrying any money and there is nothing of value inside," I said, relieved that I had left my poisons safely locked up inside one of my cases in my hotel room. It was clear that he couldn't understand a word of English, but I persisted. "The handbag only contains items of sentimental value," I added, pleading with my eyes. "Photographs of my daughter, back in England. My dog, Peter."

The boy was standing close enough now for me to feel his breath on my skin and see the light line of down across his upper lip. It was obvious he was not yet old enough to shave. But there was something in his eyes—fear, hesitancy, kindness, even—that told me he didn't like what he was doing.

"Your parents wouldn't be very proud of you, would they?" I said. "What would your mother think?" Perhaps he did understand something of this, as his eyes widened at the mention of the word *mother.* But instead of loosening his grip as I had hoped, his hands tightened around my bag.

"Help!" I shouted. "I'm being attacked. Help!"

Even before the words were out, I heard the sound of footsteps behind me. The boy let go of my bag and ran down the alley, turned a corner, and disappeared. I fell back against the wall and clutched my handbag to my chest.

"Are you hurt?" The voice was that of an American.

I turned to see a tall, slim man dressed in a light linen suit. He was about my age and impossibly handsome, with dark, slicked-back hair, and a mustache.

"That swine didn't hit you, did he?" he said, looking for any signs of injury.

"No, I'm all right, just a little shaken," I said.

"You've got to be careful around here in the evenings. There are some unpleasant types walking the streets." He paused. "What are you doing back here?"

"I was wandering around the copper souk and took an exit into an alleyway, and the next thing I knew, I was lost," I said, knowing that I sounded rather foolish.

"Well, there's no need to worry now," he said kindly. "You're safe, and that's all that matters." He looked down the alley. "I've half a mind to go after that kid. Show him what it means to feel scared." He took another look at me and decided against it. "Let's get you back to your hotel—you *are* staying in a hotel?"

"Oh, yes, the Carlton," I said.

"I'm sorry, I should have introduced myself," he said, and we started to walk down the alley. "My name is Harry Miller."

"Miller?" I said. "Why, that's my maiden name. My father was Frederick Alvah Miller from New York. You're not part of the same family?"

"No, we're from Philadelphia," he replied as we stepped into the copper souk. "And your married name?"

"Mrs. Agatha Christie," I said, my words getting lost amid a thousand hammer blows.

"Sorry, this damnable noise! I can't hear a thing. Follow me."

He led me out through a maze of stalls, tiny compartments filled with a variety of pots and pans and metal-beating equipment, staffed by men who looked exactly alike to me.

"How do you know your way around?" I asked.

"I've been coming here on and off for a while," he said when we reached the relative quiet of Rashid Street. "Now, first things first. I wouldn't advise it—knowing it wouldn't get you very far—but I must ask: Do you want to report the incident to the police?"

"Oh, no, the boy didn't take anything, and it was silly of me to wander off like that."

"Well, what do you say we go and have a drink? It will help steady your nerves."

I thought his approach rather forward. "I'd much sooner just return to my hotel, the Carlton, if you don't mind, Mr. Miller."

"Very well, but let me at least walk you back, Mrs. . . . ? I didn't catch your name."

"I'm Mrs. Agatha Christie."

"Well, how do you do, Mrs. Christie," he said with an amused glint in his dark eyes.

"I'm feeling much better now. I must thank you for rescuing me back there. I really don't know what would have happened if you had not come along."

"Yes, it could have turned nasty," said Mr. Miller. "And what brings you to the 'God-given' city?"

"I'm here on holiday," I said as we continued to walk in the direction of the hotel. "I wanted to see something of the world, something out of the ordinary."

"You'll certainly get that here. Have you done much traveling before?"

"A little. South Africa, New Zealand, Australia, Hawaii, and Canada. But that was back in 1922."

"Sounds wonderful. And you're traveling alone?"

Mr. Miller obviously wasn't wasting much time. "Yes . . . yes, I am," I said. "I did make one acquaintance on the train journey here, a Mrs. Clemence, who lives in Alwiyah. She keeps asking me to go and stay with her, but I am rather keen to get down to Ur."

"You're going to Ur? That's where I'm heading, too. I've been picking up some supplies in Baghdad but I work down there, on the archaeological site, as the photographer."

"How extraordinary," I said. "Actually, would you like to come into the hotel for a drink after all?" There were a few questions I wanted to put to Mr. Miller.

"I'd be delighted," he said.

A few minutes later we settled ourselves in the comfort of the library, Mr. Miller with his Scotch and me with a lime and soda water.

"I really must thank you once again for what you did earlier, Mr. Miller," I said.

"It was nothing—only what any passing gentleman would do. And call me Harry, please. But I hope you won't let this incident put you off Baghdad. It's a wonderful city in many respects. Still has something of the mystique of the *Arabian Nights* about it, even after all the recent troubles."

"Yes, you're right. I won't let it warp my view."

"By the way, I'm intrigued," he said. "What brings you to Ur?"

"After reading about the site in the newspapers, I was so keen to see it for myself. All those beautiful objects dug up from the desert sands."

He leant a little closer to me. "How did you manage to secure an invitation to Ur? Mrs. Woolley usually turns down most requests for visits from other women."

"With the help of a mutual friend—and also the fact that I believe she is a fan of one of my books."

"You're a writer?"

"Yes."

"What kind of books?"

"Detective fiction. Light thrillers. Short stories. Nothing serious, I'm afraid."

"Would I have heard of any?"

I reeled off the titles, but Mr. Miller looked none the wiser.

"Sorry, but I'm not a great fan of having my nose in a book," he said, coloring slightly. "Never have, even as a boy. I'd always much rather look at the world through a camera lens. You probably think me very stupid."

"Not at all. If we were all the same, then the world would be a very dull place indeed," I said, regretting the words as soon as they were out of my mouth. I was sounding like one of the old maids who used to congregate at my grandmother's house. "Tell me, Mr. Miller"—I

couldn't bring myself to call him Harry; not yet, at least—"it must be fascinating to work as a photographer with the team at Ur. How long have you worked there?"

"This will be my third season," he said. "I keep telling myself that this year will be my last, but something keeps drawing me back."

"I can imagine: it must be quite magical to see those objects appear out of the sands, after thousands of years buried underground." I recalled some of the photographs I had seen in the *Illustrated London News*.

"Oh, yes, it is. And it's just as extraordinary—I'm talking about the darkroom now—to see the images emerge out of nowhere and form themselves on photographic paper. Sometimes, in that darkroom, in the house in the middle of the desert, I feel I've had the equivalent of a religious experience. I know that may sound silly, but . . ."

"It doesn't sound silly in the least," I said.

"I said the same thing once to Father Burrows—he's a Jesuit priest and the man in charge at Ur of reading and translating the cuneiform tablets—and he looked at me with the strangest expression on his face. Like he was hearing a phrase in a foreign language he couldn't understand."

"Who else is there at Ur?"

"There's quite a crowd at the moment, which is unusual," said Miller. "Of course, there are the people who work on the dig, Mr. and Mrs. Woolley. There is the epigraphist, Father Burrows; the secretary, Cynthia Jones; then there's the architect, Lawrence McRae, and his nephew, a young boy, Cecil. One has to pity him, really: he's not quite right in the head, if you get my meaning. Lost his parents in an accident, and so McRae took him under his wing. He'd be in some institution if it weren't for his uncle's kindness. And then there are the current visitors, the Archers: Hubert, a railway millionaire from the Midwest, and his wife, Ruth, and daughter, Sarah. The only reason Mrs. Woolley tolerates their presence, especially that of the wife and daughter, is the fact that they promise to invest in the dig to the tune of what could be thousands of dollars. Archer is thick with the directors of the Penn Museum in Philly and, in addition to the sponsorship of the dig, promised them even greater riches in the future. The guy's one of those hangovers from the last century who believe in the word—the literal word—of the Bible."

"I see. So it's the lure of the Old Testament that brought him to Ur."

"Yes, and Mr. Woolley is convinced that he will soon find evidence that Ur was indeed the birthplace of Abraham."

"It sounds like a fascinating group of people," I said. I did not, of course, mention the fact that one of the party could be the murderer of Gertrude Bell. "And I hear Miss Bell did a great deal to help the preservation of the treasures here in Baghdad. I believe she drafted the antiquities law in Iraq and held an important position to that effect in this country."

Miller had fallen silent.

"King Faisal must have thought very highly of her," I continued. "And then there's the archaeological museum here in Baghdad, which she set up and which I believe houses some objects discovered at Ur. It was so sad to hear the news of her death. I hear that she had been ill, but still, such a tragic loss."

Tears had formed in Miller's dark eyes, and as he bit his top lip, he reached out for his glass and drained it of the whisky.

"I'm sorry; I didn't realize," I said. "You must miss her a great deal."

He nodded and then coughed, choking back the emotion. "Yes, she was very dear to me," he said, blinking. "Excuse me. You must think me a fool. I'm fine most of the time—I lose myself in my work, have a few drinks in the evening—but then it steals up on you when you least expect it and floors you. Grief, I mean."

"I know exactly what you mean," I said, remembering my chaotic state of mind after the death of my mother and then the way I went to pieces after I had discovered the truth of Archie's love affair. Losing him had been a kind of bereavement. At times I wished that he had died instead of finding happiness with that other woman, a thought which then made me feel wicked and full of shame.

"I think it's admirable you can talk about it," I said. "So many of my fellow countrymen wouldn't dream of talking about their feelings in this way, and it does them no good whatsoever." I wasn't totally in favor of men—or women, when it came to it—unburdening themselves of their emotions, but it was clear that Mr. Miller needed to hear something reassuring. "Was she a very close friend?"

"I just don't understand it," he continued. "Her death, I mean. She had so much to live for. Not only her work here in Iraq, seeing the fruits of her labors, enjoying the friendship she had built up with the king, her delight at witnessing the museum come to life. But also she had her personal happiness, something she richly deserved." He looked completely lost and broken. "Why would she throw that away? No, it doesn't make sense."

"What are you saying, Mr. Miller?"

Anger fired up his eyes now. "What I'm saying is that there is no way she would have committed . . ." He didn't want to say the words. "There's no way she could have died . . . in that way, like the doctor said."

"I thought she died of natural causes."

"That was just a story put out by her father and stepmother to stop unseemly speculation in the press," he said. "The doctor who attended her, Dunlop, discovered a bottle of pills by her bed. Sedatives. I know she had problems sleeping—all of us do, sometimes—but there's no way she would have taken an overdose. It just wasn't in her nature." He stared into his empty glass and fell silent for a few moments. "Anyway, there's nothing that can be done now; it's all in the past." He caught the eye of the waiter and signaled for him to pour him an extra-large measure of Scotch.

"Could there be another explanation?" I asked.

"Yes, I suppose that must be it—an accidental overdose. She had lost a good deal of weight, I believe, in the last few years. Her system was weakened; she'd suffered an attack of bronchitis, and then pleurisy. Perhaps she took a couple of pills to sleep and forgot she'd taken them and so took a couple more. And that was too much for her . . ."

It was obvious he had not thought of the possibility of murder—or, if he had, he was keeping that to himself. Had he heard about the existence of the two unsent letters, and the sinister drawing, that had been discovered in Miss Bell's house in Baghdad? Davison had told me that the servant who had come across them had been sworn to secrecy on the issue—the man would be severely punished and his family would suffer if he so much as breathed a word of what he had unearthed—but often these things leaked out. I decided it would be wise to keep the contents of the letters to myself, at least for the time being.

"And when are you traveling down to Ur, Mr. Miller?" I said, changing the subject.

"In a couple of days' time," he said, grateful that we had left the death of Miss Bell behind for now. "I'm just waiting for some chemicals to arrive and some supplies for the team, and then it's back to work. From what Woolley tells me, we should be in for an interesting season."

He looked at me as if seeing me for the first time, his eyes assessing my hair, my skin, my clothes, and as his gaze finally came to rest on my figure, I felt myself blushing. "And it sure will be fascinating to see what Mrs. Woolley makes of you." He nodded his head as if to confirm a thought he chose not to articulate before he added, "Yep, there could be fireworks there. Mark my words. Fireworks."

3

This was certainly no Orient Express, I said to myself as I sat in the stifling heat of a shabby compartment in the rackety train that would take me from Baghdad to Ur Junction. I fanned myself with a newspaper, but I still felt as though I couldn't breathe. The train hauled its way out of the station, passed through the ugly outskirts of Baghdad, and began its slow journey across the desert. I had a compartment to myself—perhaps I was the only person stupid enough to travel like this?—so fortunately no one had to see my reddened neck and face and the sheen of perspiration that was quickly spreading across my skin.

In order to try and cool myself, I closed my eyes and pictured the grandeur and elegance of the train that I had boarded at Calais. Saying the name Simplon–Orient Express silently to myself was enough to transport me back. The glass and silverware, sparkling so brightly it hurt one's eyes. The soft touch of the mahogany in the dining car. The soothing voices of the uniformed men, so attentive that they seemed blessed with second sight. I recalled the deep sense of pleasure I enjoyed, sitting in the wagon-lit, opening up my brochure from Cook's (a document I had gazed on more than a dozen times already) and seeing the planned route ahead: Calais, Paris, Lausanne, the Simplon Pass, Milan, Venice, Zagreb, Belgrade, Sofia, Stamboul. I was sure nothing in life would give me more pleasure than the anticipation I felt when I first stepped onto the train. I didn't even mind the fact that I was due to travel second class; Davison's office, which had arranged the tickets, had informed me that all seats in first had been taken. Yet my heart did sink when I entered my compartment to find that I had to share with a talkative and somewhat overfamiliar woman.

"Hello," she had said, standing up and stretching out a plump hand. "I'm Elizabeth Clemence, but you can call me Betty. Everyone does."

As soon as I introduced myself, she seized on the fact that I was an author. Was I that writer who had caused a stink a couple of years back by disappearing? I had to admit that, yes, that had been me. Had it been true that my husband had been suspected of my murder? Nothing more than the speculation of a sensational press, I told her. So why had I disappeared? Could I really not remember anything of those ten or eleven days? My doctors had warned me not to dwell on the issue, I said—to do so could only bring about another episode—so I brought that line of inquiry to a close.

After a few minutes' silence, Betty Clemence started up again by asking me where I was traveling to. Was I going to Italy? No, I replied, a little farther than that. But where exactly? Well, I told her, I was going to Baghdad. At this she simply exploded. What a coincidence! She couldn't believe it! Oh, she couldn't wait to tell her husband! Why, she lived there, and I had to stay with her. It would be simply criminal if I were to pay for a hotel. But what was I doing in Baghdad? I could not, of course, tell her the real reason—that I was traveling to Iraq at the request of the British Secret Intelligence Service to investigate the suspicious death of Miss Gertrude Bell—and so I related the story about meeting a naval officer who had recommended Baghdad to me. And, she asked, what was his name? I could not remember, I said. Was it Rogers? Fletcher? Aylesbury-Eyreton? The name had escaped me, I said. Surely, if he has passed through

Baghdad—and he sounded like a person of some importance—then he would have made himself known to her or her husband, Geoffrey. And what were my plans once in Iraq? I reeled off a list of things I had read about in my guidebook before Betty Clemence started to inform me of the delights of the city: the tennis and lunch parties, the gardens, the wonderful people (all of whom were English, of course, many of them having retired from the higher ranks of the military or diplomatic service). I got the distinct impression that, to her, Baghdad was nothing more than a slightly more exotic Bournemouth.

"And did you ever meet Miss Gertrude Bell?" I asked when she finally paused for breath.

"Oh, yes, an awful woman," she said, puffing out her cheeks. "So rude. Some of the things that came out of her mouth. Do you know she once had the audacity to suggest that my life out in Baghdad was superficial? That I was wasting my time flitting from lunch party to tennis party without a thought in my head. I had half a mind to tell her what I thought of her—some of the circles she would mix in you would not believe, my dear—but propriety and good manners prevented me. She was obviously unbalanced—unhinged, yes, that's the word. Sad, of course, what happened at the end, but I can't say I was surprised."

"You weren't?"

"No. She had no husband, no children. What had she made of her life? What had she to show? Nothing but a few dusty artifacts clustered together in a museum."

"But what of Iraq? Surely she did something there to—"

"Better if she'd never bothered—that's what my Geoffrey says. She should have left well alone. And I have to say I agree. Who knows what all this meddling will do? It's like opening a can of worms. Better to let the British take charge, just as we do in India. After all, these people have no idea how to govern themselves. Don't you agree?"

Before I could answer, she had launched into yet another line of inquiry. She wanted me to tell her my exact route to Baghdad. Was I not getting off the train at Trieste and then taking a boat to Beirut? That was her preferred itinerary; it was, of course, the best method, tried and tested. When I told her I was taking the Orient Express as far as Stamboul, from where I would get another train via Damascus, she informed me that that would be a disaster. Surely I could change my ticket and accompany her on her journey? When I told her that I could not, she went on to outline the exact and innumerable ways in which my journey could and would go wrong.

"I expect it will be awful, but never mind; it's too late now," I said. "But I *am* looking forward to my travels, particularly Ur. Have you been there?"

Her eyes, fat currants set within her generously proportioned face, lit up at the mention of the name, and she proceeded to tell me all about it. How she believed Mr. Woolley's discoveries would change the world of archaeology forever. How there was every possibility that Leonard would find evidence that Ur had indeed been the birthplace of Abraham. And how thrilling—and also quite disturbing—it must have been to uncover those bodies. "Just think how lovely it must have been for the king and queen to believe that their servants were going to accompany them after death. Their every need catered for, even in the afterlife. Woolley told me that there were no signs of struggle, suggestive of the idea that the servants went to their deaths willingly. So wonderfully romantic."

There was nothing romantic about death, I wanted to tell her, but held my tongue.

"And what of Mr. Woolley himself?" I asked.

She outlined some facts I already knew: how Leonard Woolley had been born in London, the son of a vicar; how he had worked with T. E. Lawrence at Carchemish, the archaeological site that lay about sixty or so miles north of Aleppo; and about how he had been imprisoned by the Turks during the war. She had heard him give a couple of lectures in Baghdad and, yes, she had been greatly impressed by the vitality with which he talked, his ability to conjure up the past as if it were something real and concrete.

"What is his wife like?" I asked.

Betty raised her eyes in unspoken disapproval. "The less said about Katharine Woolley, the better," she sniffed.

"What do you mean?"

"She's an odd woman. Strange."

"In what way—or ways?"

"You'll see for yourself when you arrive at Ur," said Betty. "Like Geoffrey always says, no good ever comes from being a so-called independent woman." I could have taken offense at this; after all, now that Archie had abandoned me and I was forced to support myself, this was the category I fell into. "Look at what happened with poor Miss Bell."

"Did they know each other—Miss Bell and Mrs. Woolley?"

"They were not the best of friends."

"I wonder why not. You would think they would have so much in common."

"I wouldn't be surprised if there's something wrong with her."

"With Mrs. Woolley? What do you mean?"

"She's not all there."

"You mean she's mad?" I asked.

"Let's just say it's Len I feel sorry for." Mrs. Clemence took up a book with an air of finality, a gesture which served as an indication she had nothing more to add on the subject. An uncomfortable silence—something I had not experienced since first stepping onto the train at Calais—settled over our carriage, and I turned to my guidebook.

At that moment a knock at the compartment door roused me, and my thoughts returned to my current journey through the desert.

The bearer informed me that we were about to stop for something to eat, and, sure enough, within a matter of minutes the banshee cry of the train's brakes sounded all around us. I was ushered out onto a deserted platform and into an isolated restaurant, where I was presented with a series of dishes drowning in fat. As I ate I again thought back to the conversation I had had with Mrs. Clemence on the Simplon–Orient Express. What she had chosen to keep from me was just as interesting as—no, it was much more interesting than—the information she felt free to part with. I opened my notebook and jotted down a series of key points about what I knew of the case so far.

> July 1926: Gertrude Bell (GB) found dead in her bed in her house in Baghdad. Dial poisoning. Overdose? Family kept suicide quiet, made out she died of natural causes.
>
> October 1928: Discovery of two letters by GB, and one drawing sent to her, in her house in Baghdad. Letters point to her fear that someone may be about to murder her. Why didn't she send the letters to her father? Drawing is an illustrated plan of one of the graves at Ur. Initials G.L.B. added next to one of the bodies. At the time of her death GB believed her future murderer would be found at Ur. What if the murderer is no longer there? After all, it is now two years since her death.
>
> Possible factors that could have a bearing on the case:
>
> Suicide of Lieutenant Colonel Bertram Keeling; killed himself at the base of the Great Pyramid of Cheops, Cairo, September 1919. Did he know GB? Was the death really a suicide? Could he have been murdered?

Intelligence connection? Keeling, Gertrude Bell, and Leonard Woolley all worked in British Intelligence during the war.

The personality of Mrs. Katharine Woolley. Clash between KW and GB?

The treasures of Ur and their division between London/Philadelphia and Iraq. Clash between LW and GB? Relationship between GB and photographer Harry Miller?

Enemy of GB, identity unknown.

By the time I stepped back onto the train, I had a clearer idea of what I needed to find out. I would watch, listen, and ask the occasional question. Just as Mr. and Mrs. Woolley and their team excavated the past, so I would do my own spot of gentle digging. In the course of their work they had uncovered treasures of exquisite beauty, but they had also unearthed the unmistakable signs of human sacrifice. Darkness was falling across the desert, and in the distance I could hear the scream of what sounded like a wounded animal being hunted, most probably to its death.

4

I made the final part of the long journey across the desert by car. As soon as I stepped out, I was assaulted by a great torrent of enthusiasm. "Welcome to Ur!" I immediately recognized the impish face that greeted me as that of Leonard Woolley. His blue eyes sparkled with life, and, dressed in shorts, long socks, a jacket, and an open shirt, he looked more like an adolescent than a man of middle age. He gestured to an Arab boy to take my bags.

"It's such a pleasure to have you here, Mrs. Christie," said Woolley, shaking my hand. "I can't tell you how much my wife is looking forward to meeting you. She has a hundred questions to ask you about your writing, particularly that book about the doctor. Very clever, yes, very clever indeed. But she's indisposed at the moment, having one of her headaches." His face seemed to freeze for a moment before he began again. "But never mind. I'll give you a tour around the site, then I really must get back to work and leave you to settle in your room. Terribly basic, I'm afraid, but better than nothing. Then later, just before sunset, I'll take you up to the ziggurat," he said, pointing to an enormous baked-brick structure that dominated the skyline. "And then we can have dinner. Meals are usually quite a simple affair here, but we try our best."

Woolley led the way down a dusty path towards a single-story brick house with a veranda built for shade at the front.

"How was your journey?" he asked as we walked.

"Long, and hot, but—"

"You survived the food?"

"Yes, just about," I said, smiling. Then the smile froze on my lips as we passed through a gate surrounded by a barbed wire fence that encircled the enclosure. I felt like I was stepping inside a prisoner-of-war camp.

"It's a shame about the wire fence, but it can't be helped," said Woolley. "The desert is full of marauders and thieves. As you no doubt know, we are digging up a great deal of precious and semiprecious stones, as well as beautiful objects crafted from gold and lapis lazuli. Some of the finds have been valued in the thousands of pounds, if not the hundreds of thousands. Out here life is cheap, I'm afraid."

I thought about the death of Gertrude Bell. Was that why she had been killed? Because of some dispute over a piece of ancient jewelry or precious metal?

"But don't worry, you will be perfectly safe," said Woolley, misinterpreting the expression on my face as concern over my own safety. "There's a jolly group we have with us at the moment. You'll meet them all at some point I'm sure, but look—over there is Father Burrows and our secretary, Miss Jones. Let's go over and I'll introduce you."

I trailed behind Woolley as he continued to talk—about the climate, the ferocious heat of the summer months (which meant that, in effect, the season of the dig ran only from October to March), the terrible rainstorms in the autumn, and the extraordinary power of the sands. One spring he had returned to find a whole wing of the house buried up to the roof in sand, something that took three days to shift. "But what we've uncovered makes up for the slight discomforts we experience, wouldn't you agree, Father?"

"Yes, indeed," said a tall, spindly man wearing round, wire-framed glasses and a white clerical collar.

"Father Burrows, this is Mrs. Christie, the famous author I'm sure you've heard so much about."

"I rather think not," I said, feeling myself blushing.

"And this, Mrs. Christie, is the person whom we all rely on—the one who makes the operation run like clockwork. The indispensable Miss Cynthia Jones."

"Mr. Woolley, how you flatter so," said Miss Jones, a kindly looking spinsterish type with lank mousy hair and large brown owl-like eyes. She turned to me and smiled sweetly. "How do you do?"

"I'm a little tired and dusty after the journey, but thrilled to be here," I said.

"I know," Woolley interjected. "Miss Jones, why don't you show Mrs. Christie to her room and we can have a tour of the site once she's settled in."

"I'd be delighted," said Miss Jones.

"I'll go and check on Katharine," said Woolley. "Poor thing, she's been forced to lie low again. These damnable migraines are the bane of her life. And then I must get back to the dig. Please excuse me, Mrs. Christie."

Woolley and Father Burrows retreated amid talk of cuneiform tablets, royal cemeteries, and seams of clay.

"You must forgive us if we appear rather caught up in our work, Mrs. Christie," said Miss Jones. "Because the dig is confined to such a short season, in effect less than six months, it means that there is always so much to do. And with the richness of the finds, we never seem to have enough time."

"I completely understand," I said. "It must be absolutely fascinating. I don't know much about archaeology—although last year I was on the island of Tenerife, where I saw at second hand something of the work of Professor Wilbor. Have you met him?"

Miss Jones said she had not, but she had read something of his work on the Guanche culture of the Canary Islands. A memory flashed into my mind of a man's crumpled body at the bottom of a dry riverbed, a nasty smear of blood on the rocks, a bird-of-paradise flower spiked through his eye.

"That journey from Baghdad to Ur Junction is exhausting," said Miss Jones. "I don't know why the train has to take so long—and all through the night. Come with me. I'll show you to your quarters."

As we stepped under the shade of the veranda I noticed a well-fed ginger cat curled up in a round basket fashioned from reeds. He had that look of unknowability so peculiar to cats, a quality that I found frustrating; it was one of the reasons why I preferred dogs.

"Look, there's Tom," said Miss Jones.

I bent down to stroke him, but before I could do so, I felt a light slap on the back of my hand.

"Best not to touch him," said Miss Jones. "The only person he seems to like is Mrs. Woolley. Anybody else who tries to get close to him is rewarded with a vicious scratch or a nasty bite. We've tried to get rid of him several times, but Mrs. Woolley will not have it. And her word is the law around here."

"Oh, I'm sorry," I said.

"You weren't to know," she said as we stepped into an open courtyard. "On the left here is the room of Mr. McRae, the architect, and his nephew, Cecil. I'll tell you about them later. And on the right is the antiquities room, where the treasures are studied and stored. That's always locked, of course, as one cannot be too careful. Mr. Woolley has a key for that and I have a spare. There is a darkroom for Mr. Miller, the photographer, who is in Baghdad for another day or so." I didn't tell Miss Jones that I had already met him. "And ranged around the courtyard are the other bedrooms."

A number of Arab servants busied themselves with household

tasks, carrying containers full of water, clearing up plates and dishes from breakfast, and sweeping up what seemed like an insurmountable amount of dust and sand. We passed into a large living room with apricot-colored walls and a floor made of burnt bricks partly covered in rush matting. In the corner there was a makeshift library, mostly stocked with books on ancient history and archaeology, and in the center of the room stood a long, rectangular wooden table and several chairs.

"All this won't be what you're used to, but it might provide you with some colorful material if you were ever to write a book set in the Near East," said Miss Jones.

I did not reply; instead I asked, "How long have you been here?"

"A few years now," she replied.

"And what do you do?"

"You mean the reason why Mr. Woolley finds me so—what was it—indispensable?" She smiled as she said this. "I'm just a glorified dogsbody, really. I don't do any of the transcribing of the tablets, but I type up Father Burrows's notes. I make sure every new find is logged and described, together with the appropriate reference numbers. I deal with the correspondence between the staff here and the museums in London and Philadelphia. And also I'm rather good at making tea."

"That's a relief! I was worrying that all I would find out here is that peculiar brand of coffee everyone seems to drink," I said.

"The kind that keeps you up all night—it's like tar, isn't it?" she said. "Or something you'd find at the bottom of a rather dirty bucket."

The comment made me laugh, but at this she shot me a look of warning. "Shh—best keep your voice down," she said in a whisper. "We're about to pass by Mrs. Woolley's room. She can't be disturbed when she is having one of her attacks."

"I'm sorry," I said again. I thought about what Mrs. Clemence had said to me on the Orient Express. "What exactly is wrong with her?"

Miss Jones did not respond. Either she had not heard me or she had deliberately chosen to ignore the question. "Here's your room," she said, opening the door. "Very basic, but you should be comfortable enough."

As I stepped into the darkness, my heart immediately sank: it was nothing like the splendor of the Carlton. The walls and the floor, constructed with baked bricks, were bare of decoration apart from an old print of Baghdad and, by the side of the single bed, a threadbare Persian rug. In the corner there was a desk and chair, together with a bowl and jug for washing, and by the window, which looked out into the courtyard, was an old basket chair that had clearly seen better days.

"The whole house was built from reused bricks found on the site, some of which are twenty-five centuries old, or so I'm told," said Miss Jones, her eyes taking on a misty, dreamlike quality. "So for all intents and purposes we live just like the people who settled in Ur in ancient times. At night, when the house is quiet, you can almost feel like you're stepping back in time. I'm not a superstitious person, Mrs. Christie, but even I can feel the ghosts of the past here." Her owlish eyes blinked, a gesture which seemed to bring her back to the present. "I'm just across the courtyard, so if you need anything, please just ask," she added. "Now, where are your bags? That stupid boy's probably put them in the wrong room. Excuse me, I'll go and see where he is."

I walked over to the open window and looked out at the dusty courtyard. The sound of voices drifted over the hot air, and then two figures—those of a handsome middle-aged man and an awkward-looking adolescent—came into view.

"I just don't understand," I could hear the boy say. He seemed on the verge of tears.

"Women—one of life's greatest mysteries," said the man in a lilting Scottish accent, his pale face and auburn hair shaded by a hat.

"It's not funny, Uncle," the boy replied. "How would you feel if your heart was always being broken?"

"I'm sorry, Cecil, but as I've said before, women can be extremely cruel. Best to avoid them if you can."

"Sarah says she could never love me. Do you think that's true?" The boy's face was covered in spots, his dark hair had been plastered down on his head with grease, and his elongated frame reminded me of a large, ungainly bird. "She said I was ugly. That I was stupid. That I should never talk to her again."

"I think it's best if you put Sarah out of your mind. You know she won't always be here, don't you? Her mother and father will move on soon and then no doubt return to America. Of course, you could always write to her, but—"

"I don't want to write to her, I want to . . . ," he began, his face coloring.

"Now, now, let's not get upset. Try to see—"

"If I can't have her, then no one will. I can make sure of that."

"Cecil, you're talking nonsense now. Let's go and have a cup of tea."

The older man, whom I took to be Lawrence McRae, the architect, placed a hand on his nephew's shoulder and led him across the courtyard and into the house. The voices quietened and a moment later Miss Jones returned, followed by the Arab boy and my bags.

"Sorry about this, but for some unfathomable reason Sahid left your bags outside Mrs. Archer's room. She's staying here with her husband, Hubert, and daughter, Sarah. I'm sure you'll meet them later when they've returned from their excursion to Eridu. Have you heard of it?"

"No, I'm afraid I haven't."

"It's supposed to be the oldest city in the world. One of the five cities built before the great deluge."

"Are they the visiting Americans?"

"That's right," she said. "He's very interested in sponsoring the expedition. Made his money from the railroads. He's here because he wants to see evidence that Ur was the birthplace of Abraham."

"And has Mr. Woolley uncovered such evidence?"

"Not yet, but he's determined that he will."

"And what of Archer's wife and daughter?" I asked. "What are they like?"

"Ruth is a lovely woman—hasn't a bad bone in her body. Her daughter, Sarah, meanwhile, is another matter."

"What do you mean?"

"She is beautiful—blond hair, blue eyes, alabaster skin, alluring figure. A vision of perfection. I suppose she can't help the way she looks, but when she's out of sight of her father, you should see the way she teases some of the men on the site. It's not fair. A man has—well, he has certain appetites and urges. I've told her she should be more careful, the way she leads the men on. And then there is the upset she causes poor Mrs. Woolley. It's obvious to everyone they don't like each other; I think Katharine is jealous of the girl's youth and beauty, and Sarah can't abide the way that she tries to steal male attention away from her. I'm sure Katharine would have got rid of the girl had it not been for the fact that she knows they need Archer's mountain of money. So, if you notice an odd atmosphere at dinner tonight, you'll know what it's all about."

"I see," I said, slightly at a loss for words.

"I suppose we should be grateful for the fact of Mr. Miller's absence. He's the photographer I mentioned earlier."

"In what way?" I asked as I sat down on the hard mattress.

"He plays them off, one against the other. One minute he is fetching and carrying for Mrs. Woolley, the next flirting with the young girl. I wouldn't be surprised if he tries a spot of lovemaking with you when he returns."

I tried to stop myself from blushing at the memory of our encounter in Baghdad.

"So life in the camp is rather the opposite to what I was imagining," I said. "I brought a number of novels with me in case I might get bored. But it looks as though there will be little chance of that."

"We'll keep you entertained, that's for certain," said Miss Jones with a sardonic smile. "What with the treasures from the site, the history, the personnel and our visitors, I doubt you'll have a dull moment."

I seized the opportunity. "Talking of visitors, you must have had a fascinating mix of people coming to see the site."

"Oh, yes, plenty. But most of them come just for the day."

"Did you ever meet Miss Bell?"

Cynthia Jones blinked at the mention of her name. "Gertrude? Yes, of course. We were great friends." Tears came into her eyes and she steadied herself against the wall. "Such a sad loss."

"I'm sorry I brought up her name," I said. "If you'd rather not talk about her, I understand. It's just that she sounded like such a fascinating, unusual woman."

"I never met anyone like her and doubt I ever will again," she said. "Of course, she wasn't everyone's cup of tea. She couldn't bear empty-headed women; she simply loathed the type of woman who used her husband's position to do nothing more than take tea or read novels or gossip. She had a desire to really live; it was quite frightening sometimes, almost as if she knew that she didn't have long in this world."

"Yes, I had read about her illness in the newspapers," I said, feigning ignorance of what I knew of the manner in which she had died.

"Oh, that business about passing away in her sleep was just a piece of nonsense."

"You mean that . . . that she took her own life?"

"Suicide?" she said. "I don't believe Gertrude would ever have done that. She had too much left to live for."

"If not suicide . . . then what?"

Miss Jones paused, walked over to the window, and stared out into the courtyard before turning back to me. "I'm not sure I should say anything."

"What are you suggesting?"

She looked nervously around her, as if there were people—invisible to us—who might be listening to our conversation.

"Miss Jones—"

"Please, call me Cynthia."

"Cynthia . . . if you feel you want to say something in confidence to me, then please unburden yourself. It's clear that something is worrying you."

"You must promise that you won't say anything," she said, making sure the bedroom door was closed. "This must be strictly between us."

"Yes, of course. I promise."

Cynthia bit her lip, took hold of my hand, and led me towards the bed. "It's funny we've only just met, but it's as if I've known you for years," she said, smiling, as we sat down. "I feel I could tell you anything."

"That's good," I said, not entirely comfortable in my role as Miss Jones's newfound confidante. "Please feel free to tell me anything you wish."

"Thank you," she said, a troubled look in her eyes. She took a deep breath and clasped my hand. "I always thought it was odd the way that Gertrude died. I can understand, of course, the way her death was hushed up. That's entirely natural, as the family didn't want any scandal. But what I never understood was that the doctor found some pills by her bed; sedatives, I think they were. I don't know. To me it seemed a little contrived, almost as if it were staged." She looked at me for encouragement.

"Yes, I understand. Go on."

"When I heard the news, I was terribly upset. It was such a big loss. I realized how much I would miss her. I used to go to Baghdad to stay with her in her house. She would come down here to visit and argue over the finds. We had so much to talk about: our families back in England, our love of travel, of history, of the old Mesopotamia and the new Iraq. And I think I was one of the few women whom she could tolerate."

"But what of her death, Cynthia?"

"That's just what I was coming to. You see, a few months before she died, I was in Baghdad, ready to return to Britain. The heat was already too much for me then. I don't know how Gertrude could stand the summers out here. Anyway, while I was there we were talking about the season at Ur. I noticed that she had turned pale and had started to tremble. I made her sit down and tell me what was bothering her."

Miss Jones lowered her voice to a whisper. "She told me that she was afraid that she might be killed. And if she were to die, she was sure that her murderer was one of the team. Here on this dig. I couldn't believe it when she told me. I thought she must be talking nonsense, but she was adamant. There was someone here who wanted her dead."

"Why did she think that?"

"She said she had received some threatening letters, together with a drawing, I'm not sure of what, which made her fear for her life."

"Did she give you a name?"

She looked around her as if she were half expecting to see someone standing in the corner of the room.

"Take another deep breath," I said, squeezing her hand. "Cynthia—did she give you a name?"

She nodded, her eyes haunted by the memories and secrets of the past.

"Who was it? Who did Miss Bell believe might murder her?"

"You promise not to say anything? I could get into a great deal of trouble. I don't want to lose my position here."

"Yes, I've already given you my word."

"Very well. It was—"

5

"Tom! Can someone please bring Tom to me?" The voice sounded high-pitched and strained and was coming from a room nearby. It had interrupted Miss Jones just as she was about to give me a name.

"Oh, that's her now," said Cynthia, jumping up with a look of terror in her eyes. "Mrs. Woolley. I must go to her."

"What do you mean? Was it Mrs. Woolley that Miss Bell was afraid of?"

"She must have woken up," she said, turning away from me. "I have to see to her."

I accompanied Cynthia Jones out of the room, following her like a shadow until we stood outside Katharine Woolley's bedroom.

"Oh, where is that damned cat?" asked Cynthia, turning to an Arab boy to whom she asked something in Arabic, presumably the same question.

"This headache is simply killing me," said Mrs. Woolley from inside the room. "The least someone can do is to bring me Tom. Len! Where are you?"

"Could you just stay there while I go and try and fetch the cat?" Cynthia asked me. "Hopefully he'll still be in his basket." She tapped on the door. "Katharine, it's Cynthia. I'll go and find him. I won't be a minute."

"Do please hurry up," Mrs. Woolley said from behind the door. "You know he's the only thing that can bring me comfort when I'm feeling like this. And don't scare him like you did last time. You know what happened then—you got a nasty bite."

A moment or so later the door opened to reveal a pale-faced Katharine Woolley, dressed in a white nightgown. Before I could say anything she took one look at me—her dark eyes seemed tortured, haunted somehow—and then closed the door. Through the partition I could hear the sound of strange mutterings, snatches of conversation she appeared to be having with herself. Perhaps the woman really was as unstable as people had suggested.

"Mrs. Woolley," I said, gently knocking on the door. "There's no need to distress yourself. If you let me in I can help. It's Mrs. Christie. I think you are expecting me."

There was no response. "I believe you suffer from terrible headaches. I might be able to provide you with some relief. I was a nurse during the war, you see. I came across a number of cases such as yours." Still no answer. "Mrs. Woolley? Can you hear me?"

The door opened again and Katharine Woolley gestured for me to step inside. The shutters on the windows had been closed and the room was cool and dark. In contrast to the stark interior of my room, Mrs. Woolley's quarters seemed feminine, tastefully decorated, and quite beautiful. In addition to the bed, the room was furnished with an old-fashioned desk made from dark wood, its surface covered with sheets of paper. There was a wardrobe with clothes spilling out, a table with a gramophone, and a messy dressing table complete with various pots of lotion and jars of cosmetics. The walls had been decorated with a number of exquisitely worked sketches, some in pencil, some in charcoal, many of which hung at awkward angles as if they had been disturbed.

"Yes, all my own work," she said as she caught me looking at the drawings.

"They are very good," I said. "Not that I know much about art."

"You have your own métier," she said. "Sorry, it's so rude of me not to properly welcome you here. It's these beastly headaches; they are driving me insane." Katharine raised her hand to her temples and sat back down on the bed. "You must excuse me."

"I completely understand," I said. "And I'd rather not have a special welcome. But I must say I am very excited to be here."

"You've met Len at least?"

"Mr. Woolley? Oh, yes," I said. "He was full of enthusiasm for your work here. I can't wait to see more of the dig and, of course, the ziggurat. He said he would show me that later, when he's returned."

"And who else have you met? Father Burrows, I expect."

"Yes. He seems an interesting character."

"That's one way of putting it," she said. As she smiled to herself she winced. "Oh, dear, it seems to be getting worse. I thought a nap would help, but I'm afraid it's only made the pain more intense." Her long, bony fingers gripped the sides of her head, and her mouth formed itself into an unpleasant grimace. In that moment she looked nothing like the photograph I had seen of her; features which I knew to be elegant and refined had been transformed into something careworn, even a little ugly. "Did you say you knew of a way to relieve the pain?" she asked as she reached out to grip a bedsheet. "Anything you could do, I'd be most grateful."

"Yes, of course," I said.

"And where's that girl got to? Why isn't she back with Tom yet?"

"Don't think about that for the moment," I said. "If you can take some deep breaths. Would you mind if I placed my hands on your neck and shoulders?"

"No, please do," she said, closing her eyes.

"Could I wash my hands first? They are still a little dusty from the journey."

"Of course. There's a bowl of water over there," she said, pointing towards the dressing table. "I'd show you, but I can feel my vision blurring."

I walked over to the dressing table, briefly stopping by the writing desk as I did so. I cast a quick look towards Mrs. Woolley to check she wasn't watching me before I examined the sheets of paper that I had noticed on her desk.

"It's a work in progress, nothing more," said Mrs. Woolley from the bed. "Don't be embarrassed. I know I would probably have done the same."

As I poured some water into a bowl I could feel myself blushing in the dark.

"It's just a silly story I'm working on," she continued. "Notes towards a novel. I'd love to talk to you about the craft of writing at some point."

"I'm not sure if I'm the right person."

"Don't be so modest," she said. "But we've got plenty of time for that."

"Now, when did the headaches start?" I asked after drying my hands and returning to the bed.

"A few years ago," she replied. "But they seem to be getting worse."

"Do you have any other symptoms? Tiredness? Nervousness?"

"Yes, both of those," she said. "Sometimes I feel as though I'm going quite mad. I think the headaches make me say certain things . . . And I see people doing such odd . . ."

Her voice died away as I laid my hands on her head, drew her dark hair back from her face, and began to massage her temples and then the muscles in her shoulders. I could feel the stubborn knots of tension under her skin resisting the pressure exerted by my fingers and so pressed harder and deeper into the tissue.

"Does that hurt?" I asked.

"Yes, but please continue. I think I can just bear it."

After working on her neck and shoulders, I placed my hands over her eyes and started to gently manipulate the muscles around the sockets. Mrs. Woolley fell silent, and as I worked and the tension started to melt away from her, I took the opportunity to study her in more detail. Her face was perfectly proportioned and refined, with high cheekbones and a clearly defined jawline. I estimated her to be more or less the same age as I was, in her late thirties, or forty at the very most. She had a kind of dark, almost exotic beauty that struck me as quite unusual, not the sort one normally found among the English. Had she some foreign blood in her? Could she have some Jewish ancestry?

"Does that feel better," I said as I ended the procedure by gently stroking the skin on her temples.

"That feels marvelous," she said, opening her eyes. "Whatever you did, it's cleared the headache completely."

"I'm pleased it worked." I moved around to stand in front of Mrs. Woolley.

"Len tries to help—he really does—as do some of the others, but his touch is nothing like yours." She smiled. "Now, what do you say to a cup of tea? It's the least I can do after welcoming you in such a rude and beastly manner."

"That would be very nice indeed," I said.

Mrs. Woolley walked to the door and clapped her hands. A moment later the boy I knew as Sahid appeared and was issued with the appropriate orders. As she moved to open the shutters I noticed a dark sparkle had returned to her eyes.

"I'm sure the last thing you expected to do when you arrived was give a massage to a strange creature like me."

So Katharine Woolley had a sense of humor; yet murderers, I had to remind myself, could be as capable as the next man—or woman—of making self-deprecating comments. "I was a little surprised, I must admit, Mrs. Woolley," I said, "but it was clear you were in some pain."

"Please call me Katharine," she said. "Pull that chair up and come and sit down. You must be exhausted after your journey."

"Thank you," I replied, taking hold of a wicker chair and drawing it a little nearer towards the bed. "I'm grateful that you've allowed me to visit. I know that you've got more than your fair share of visitors at the moment."

"You mean those ghastly Americans? Oh, please don't look shocked. You'll see what I mean later. The man, this millionaire and his wife and daughter—don't get me started on that thing—are only here because of the depth of their pockets. Len needs them to provide the necessary funds for the continuation of the dig. It takes everything in my power to keep me from telling them what I really think of them."

I was rather at a loss to know how I should reply, and so I said nothing. There was a knock at the door and the boy appeared with the tea, which he set down on a low table between us.

"You, on the other hand, are in a different category altogether," Katharine said, dismissing the boy with a wave of the hand. "When I heard that there was a prospect of you coming to visit here, I could not believe it. You must realize, Mrs. Christie—"

"Agatha, please," I interrupted.

"You must realize—Agatha—that what you have achieved is something quite out of the ordinary. I'm talking about *The Murder of Roger Ackroyd*, of course."

Despite my initial reluctance, we continued to talk about that book and the subject of detective novels in general before it was my turn to ask her a few questions. I told her that I had been lured to the Near East not only by the fascinating series of articles I had read about Ur but also by the enigmatic figure of Miss Gertrude Bell. On mention of the name, Katharine lowered her head so I could not see the expression in her eyes.

"Did you know her?"

"It was impossible not to know Gertrude," she replied.

"Such a tragic end," I said, deliberately vaguely in the hope of provoking a response. "But her achievements were so varied. I suppose one must remember her for the part she played in helping make this country, her dealings with the king, and, of course, her role as head of antiquities. She must have been a great deal of help."

"Help? No, rather the opposite, if you must know."

"In what way?" I asked.

"Let's just say that Gertrude and I didn't always see eye to eye."

"You weren't friends?"

"No, we were decidedly not friends. That's not to say I was not sad when I heard of her death." She said the words without any trace of emotion, almost as if she were saying them by rote.

"I've heard that she took her own life. Is that what you think happened?"

"I suppose it must have been the case. I didn't realize she had so many tragedies in her life. I think she'd lost a man she was close to and, of course, there was the death of her brother a few months before and then various illnesses—pleurisy, bronchitis. I think she was very weak at the end. I believe she'd found it difficult to sleep. Perhaps she took too many pills without realizing it."

"You don't believe she could have been murdered?"

"Murdered?" Katharine's voice jumped at the word. "Whatever gave you that idea?"

I decided I would keep the existence of the threatening letters to myself; neither did I say anything about the drawing. "I don't know," I replied. "There are just a few details about her death that don't quite add up."

"Such as?"

I hesitated a moment before I began to tell her something of what I had learnt. "Did you know, for instance, of the relationship between Miss Bell and Mr. Miller, who I believe works as the photographer here at Ur? It seems unlikely for her to have committed suicide if she had someone like Mr. Miller in her life."

"Whatever he saw in her I just don't understand," she hissed before she could stop herself.

So that relationship had been a source of rancor, after all. Had Mrs. Woolley formed some kind of attachment with the handsome Mr. Miller, too? Was it jealousy—that age-old motive for murder—that lay behind all of this?

"Do you know how old she was?" she continued. "She was nearly sixty! She was old enough to be his mother, if not his grandmother. It was almost indecent. And the way she treated poor Harry was completely unacceptable. Oh, I can't think about it any more; I feel that headache returning." Her hands flew up to her temples once more and she began to pace the room like a cat confined in a space against its will. She suddenly stopped and looked at me with suspicion. "And how do you know about that? About what happened between Gertrude and Harry?"

"I met Mr. Miller in Baghdad," I said, deciding to tell the truth. "He told me a little of his friendship with Miss Bell and his sadness on her passing. He couldn't believe that she would take her life."

"And did he think that she had been murdered?"

"No, I don't think so," I answered. "I believe he thinks her death was a tragic accident."

Katharine Woolley walked over to the dressing table, sat down, and looked at herself in the mirror. "I look an absolute fright. Have you seen my complexion? So tired and drawn and gray. Can you see the lines?" she asked as she squinted into the glass. "Look—here and here." She pointed at her forehead and the corner of her mouth. "And as for these shadows under my eyes . . ."

Mrs. Woolley reached out for one of the jars on the crowded surface and began to massage some white cream deep into her skin.

"It's all this talk of Miss Bell. It's making me age by the minute. After all, I don't want to end up looking like she did."

I thought the comment unnecessarily cruel, but I let it pass. "Let's not dwell on it any more," I said. "Why don't you take some deep breaths. And here, drink this." I poured out a tumbler of water from a carafe for her and watched as she drank it. "Let's talk about something else. What about your writing? Can you tell me about that?"

After she had calmed down she went on to tell me a little of her novel, which was about a young woman who disguises herself as a man in order to have various adventures in Iraq. She then went on to reveal how she had first met Leonard Woolley—she had arrived at Ur in the spring of 1924, keen to do something different with her life—but she made no mention of the first husband who had shot himself (or so it was said) at the foot of the Great Pyramid of Cheops in 1919.

The war continued to cast a shadow over the shared past of our generation; it was a perennial subject that often needed to be addressed when strangers first met. I told her about my time as a Voluntary Aid Detachment nurse working at the Town Hall Hospital in Torquay, and she, in turn, confided in me a little of her service in a prison camp on the Russian-German border. Some of the horrors she had seen when she had tried to care for the army of Ukrainians who had been imprisoned there could never be adequately described. I knew exactly what she meant. It was time to change the subject and so I asked her about her background. She had been born in Kings Norton—her father had been a merchant in the Midlands—and she had spent two years studying history at Somerville College, Oxford, before she had been forced to leave due to ill health.

"What a curse it is to have this body," she said, her face darkening with a sudden melancholy. I felt saddened that a line of questioning which had been designed to brighten her state of mind had the opposite effect on her. "Actually, would you mind if I had some time to myself? I'm feeling so terribly drained after that massage." She did not look tired, however; rather, her eyes flashed with a manic quality that frightened me. It was clear that something that had been said during the course of our conversation was still distressing her.

"Of course," I said, feeling more than a little embarrassed. I stood up and moved towards the door. "It's probably a good idea for you to get some more rest."

"Look at me—I'm a wreck!" she gasped. "I can't let the others see me like this. And still in my nightdress at this hour of the day! You must think me quite insane."

I did not answer.

"Now, where is that stupid girl with the cat? Why is it taking her so long?" She opened the door and shouted, "Cynthia! What are you doing?"

A moment later a red-faced Miss Jones appeared running behind the cat. "I'm sorry—you know what he's like," she said. "He took one look at me and fled. He led me a merry dance all around the courtyard." She knelt down and guided the cat towards Mrs. Woolley's open door. "Go on, Tom. Look, there's your mistress."

Katharine pursed her lips and the cat came running towards her. She made a series of clicking noises in the ginger tom's ear. The animal responded immediately with a loud purr. She ran her fingers up and down its long tail—a tail encircled by markings that reminded me of those on a rattlesnake—before she bent down and scooped it up into her arms. That unmistakable expression particular to a person strongly bonded to a domestic pet—a mix of utter devotion, pure joy, and unconditional love—melted away any signs of anxiety, pain, or mania from her features. It was clear that, in that moment, Katharine Woolley was happy.

Unfortunately, I had a feeling she would not remain so for long.

6

After a rest I emerged from my room refreshed, ready for Mr. Woolley's tour of the site. As I stepped into the living room I was met by Lawrence McRae and his nephew, Cecil, who sat drawing at the table.

"Hello," said Mr. McRae, standing up as he saw me. He introduced himself and his nephew, who refused to meet my eye. "Have you met everyone on the site yet?"

"I think so—apart from the Archers, who I believe are returning later."

"And what about 'she who must be obeyed'?"

I pretended not to know who he was talking about.

"Come off it," he said in his Scottish accent. "If you've met Katharine Woolley, you must know what she's like. I mean, she's hardly what you might call a shrinking violet."

"She's suffering from one of her headaches at the moment."

"Oh, is she now? That's very convenient," he said with a note of bitterness in his voice. "Just when we could do with her help to document the new finds."

On the table before him were a number of pencil drawings of earrings, tools, cosmetic jars, robe pins, necklaces, bracelets, rings—and a beautifully realized image of a dagger.

"Are these yours?" I asked.

"Yes, and some are Cecil's—some of the best ones, in fact," he said, smiling at his nephew, who had started to blush.

"I thought you were the architect here?"

"I am. But I'm also called upon to help out with some of the drawings when Mrs. Woolley is . . . indisposed."

"Does that happen often?"

"With more and more frequency, I'm afraid," he said, placing a pencil behind his ear. He was a tall man, with serious gray eyes, striking auburn hair, and pale skin which had a tendency to freckle.

"Is she ill?"

"I doubt it very much," he said. "I don't want to sound cruel, but I think most of Mrs. Woolley's problems exist in her head. I know you've just arrived here, and of course you must make up your own mind, but let me give you one piece of advice. Don't let yourself be bullied by her. She is an arch manipulator and will flatter and cajole—say anything, in fact—to get what she wants. I've witnessed it first hand. I've also learnt it's better to speak one's mind. Of course, she hates me for it with a vengeance, but I didn't come to Ur to make friends."

"What *did* you come for, Mr. McRae?"

He turned his head towards his nephew, who was concentrating on a drawing. "Him, mostly," he said. "It was important that we make a new start, away from . . . from everything that had gone before."

I nodded in silent agreement. Harry Miller had told me that Cecil had lost his parents in an accident, and I knew that any further discussion on the subject would only distress the boy. Just then Cynthia Jones entered the room and informed me that, if it was convenient, Mr. Woolley was ready to show me around the dig. She said that she would be happy to accompany me.

"The way Mr. Woolley brings the past to life, it really is quite extraordinary," she said. "I've heard him dozens of times on the subject, but I learn something new on each occasion."

As we walked towards the veranda, where we were due to meet Mr. Woolley, I stopped and gestured for Miss Jones to step to one side.

"I wanted to ask you something about what you said earlier about Mrs. Woolley."

"What do you mean?"

"About Miss Bell and what she had told you about Katharine."

"I don't know what you are talking about," she said. Cynthia looked around her, terrified someone might overhear our conversation.

"I just got the impression that it was Mrs. Woolley who—"

"I can't say any more," she hissed. A figure appeared at the door. "Look, here's Mr. Woolley," she said, her voice sounding a little strained as she tried to regain her composure.

"Are we ready for our grand tour?" he asked, his blue eyes shining.

"Would you mind awfully, Mr. Woolley, if I didn't accompany you on this one?" Cynthia asked.

"My dear Miss Jones, of course not. Is something the matter?"

"No, just that I realize I'm rather behind with my correspondence with Philadelphia."

"Yes, we don't want our American friends to feel they are not being kept up to date. Now, Mrs. Christie, where would you like to start?"

I looked at Cynthia Jones, whose eyes darted back and forth as if she were seeing some invisible enemy.

"Are you going to be all right?" I asked in a low voice.

"Yes, why shouldn't I be? I'll be perfectly fine. I really must get back to my desk. If you'll excuse me . . ."

After Miss Jones made a hasty retreat, Leonard Woolley whisked me away. As he began to tell me about the history of Ur and the civilization of the ancient Sumerians, I began to feel worried for Cynthia. It was clear that she regretted what little she had told me and was anxious that someone had overheard our conversation. Perhaps Lawrence McRae and his nephew, Cecil, had heard snatches of the encounter? And earlier, when Miss Jones had first related to me what Gertrude Bell had told her—about how she believed her life was in danger—had anyone been listening then? Certainly there had been no one in sight, and we had kept our voices low, but that did not mean anything in a house such as this. Privacy was in short supply—I had worked out that eleven people, including myself, shared the space—and there were many dark corners where people could stand unobserved and eavesdrop on a conversation.

"You see, many people have assumed that Egypt is the oldest civilization in the world," said Mr. Woolley as he led me out of the compound. "I mean, Tutankhamen was all very well, but it was rather showy, don't you think? When historians come to write the definitive account of archaeology in the twentieth century, they will realize that this—this!—was the most important find of the modern age," he said, gesturing towards the land around him and the great ziggurat.

I nodded and pulled my hat farther over my head to shield my face from the intense sun. Woolley's little legs carried him forwards at great speed, and as he dashed towards the site, he continued his lecture about Ur. He was nothing if not passionate about his subject.

"As I was saying, what you are about to see here, the tombs and suchlike, date from between 3500 and 3200 BC, the same time the Egyptians were nothing but barbarians. And when Egypt does manage to forge itself into something like a meaningful civilization, guess where it gets many of its ideas from? Yes, here! From the ancient Sumerians, a great civilization, one that flourished here, in old Mesopotamia, the land between the two rivers—the Tigris and the Euphrates."

He stopped on a barren mound and, with his stirring voice, his flashing eyes, and his hands like a magician's, began to conjure up the past.

"Imagine if you can this place not as a desert, dry and parched, but an island full of greenery," he said. "Water was plentiful then, and the sophisticated irrigation channels directed it in an ingenious way. Trees, fruit, vegetation—nature was in bountiful supply. Imagine too that on this spot Abraham—the Abraham of the Old Testament—once walked." He took my hand and led me towards a section of land that had been excavated, a series of low-lying walls that looked like many ruins I had seen in the past. "This indeed is a house built at the time of Abraham. One can see, as a result of the excavation, that it was a two-story structure, with thirteen or fourteen rooms, all arranged around a central courtyard. In fact, it could be the very house where Abraham lived, the great Hebrew patriarch from whom all Jews are descended, a man who was ordered by God to leave Ur of the Chaldees and journey to a place that would be shown to him."

"How fascinating," I said, but I'm afraid I did not quite believe my own words. "And have you found evidence that Abraham actually lived here?"

"The place is mentioned four times in the Old Testament," Woolley said sharply by way of an answer. It was obvious that I had touched a raw nerve. I wanted to believe in the story, but the cynic in me whispered a snakelike suggestion only I could hear: perhaps Mr. Woolley needed to show his belief in Ur's link to Abraham so as to obtain that extra funding from those rich Americans.

"Your guests, the Archers, must be thrilled by your discoveries," I said.

"Oh, yes, they are," he said, his mood revived by my more positive comment. "So you've heard of them?"

"Only from what I've picked up since I arrived," I replied.

"I think Mr. Archer's input will make an enormous difference to the excavation," he said. "We can take on more people, make the site more secure, perhaps even stage another exhibition, a joint one, organized by the British Museum and the Penn Museum in Philadelphia."

"That's wonderful," I said. "It seems as though you have a very talented team here already."

"We've been fortunate, yes. Of course, we're missing Max—Max Mallowan, my assistant—but that can't be helped. Appendicitis."

"And I hear you also received the great support of Miss Bell."

At the mention of the dead woman's name, the light faded from Leonard Woolley's eyes. "That was a very sad business," he said quietly.

"She must be greatly missed," I said. "Particularly here in Iraq, where she did so much good."

"Indeed," he said, looking across the desolate plain. "We didn't always agree—I think she found me quite tiresome at times—but we did go back an awfully long way."

"Really?"

"Oh, yes, we knew each other during the war. In Egypt. But those days are best forgotten." He turned from me and scanned a dusty horizon. "From looking at it, at this desert, you'd never believe that such treasures could be found underneath the sands. But some of the most beautiful—the most precious and exquisite—objects that I've ever seen in my life have been unearthed here."

"Yes, I saw some of them featured in the pages of newspapers and magazines back in England. That's one of the reasons why I wanted to come here."

He turned to me, squinting in the sunlight. Was there also a look of suspicion in his eyes?

"What do you make of my wife, Mrs. Christie?"

For a moment I was lost for words. He clearly knew that I had met her. "She seems like a remarkable woman," I replied. "She is talented: I saw the sketches on the walls of her room. She is very beautiful, too. But I think it's obvious that her headaches give her a great deal of distress."

"Do you think they're genuine? The headaches, I mean."

"I'm sure they are. Why?"

"It's been suggested to me by certain individuals on the dig—I won't name them—that Katharine suffers not so much from a physical illness as a psychological one. They believe her presence here to be quite damaging. They accuse her of . . . of poisoning the atmosphere here. I've tried to explain: Katharine has her headaches and, yes, she has her moods, too. But she contributes so much: her drawings, her models, the re-creations of the headdresses. But above all—and this is what people tend to forget—she is my wife. My wife." He had to stop himself for fear he might break down. He took a deep breath. "However, I am worried about her. Her problem seems to be getting worse. She's started seeing things, hearing things."

"What sort of things?"

"Faces at the window. Voices."

"That does sound worrying."

"I don't want to bring the doctor in; he's two hours from here and it will only cause further upset in the house. It will give ammunition to the people who think that I should send Katharine back to London." He turned to me and, with pleading eyes, continued, "I know you're not a doctor, Mrs. Christie, but I believe you worked as a nurse during the war. Would you do me a favor? While you are here, would you mind spending some time with her?"

"Of course. It would be a pleasure. As long as you realize I'm not at all qualified in these sorts of matters."

"Yes, I understand. She told me she already likes you a great deal—and that's something she doesn't say about many women," he said, a touch of humor coming back into his voice now. "Between you and me, she thinks most women are fools. That's one thing she had in common with Gertrude—with Miss Bell."

I knew the answer to the question I was about to put to Mr. Woolley already, but experience had taught me it would be worth asking: the way someone answered was just as valuable as what they had to say. "They must have been good friends—your wife and Miss Bell."

"Friends?" Woolley exclaimed. "Katharine would have scratched Gertrude's eyes out, given half the chance."

"I see."

"And Gertrude had no time for Katharine. No, they couldn't bear the sight of one another."

"Was there a reason for their enmity?"

"I couldn't work it out myself. On paper they were so similar. They both went to Oxford, read History, shared a passion for the Near East and for archaeology. But they really couldn't stand being in the same room with one another. It was almost like a chemical reaction, I think. Something you read about in novels—a clash of the personalities. That's all I can think. Perhaps there was more to it, but whatever that was remains a mystery. When I asked Katharine about it, she chose not to illuminate me."

"That must have put you in a difficult position, the fact that your wife and Miss Bell didn't get on."

"You could say that, yes," he said, striding forwards through the sand.

As we moved nearer to the excavation then under way, I heard a strange chanting, followed by the sight of two hundred or so men digging, sifting, clearing, all singing as they worked. The image reminded me of a colony of ants who worked not singly but together to achieve their aim. Woolley noticed the expression of wonder and admiration on my face and went on to outline the system under which the Arab men operated. They were overseen, he said, by a foreman, Hamoudi, or, to use his more formal title, Mohammed ibn Sheikh Ibrahim, whom Woolley had first met on the archaeological site of Carchemish.

"I wouldn't work anywhere in the Near East without Hamoudi," he said. "He taught me the most important lesson there is here: in order to be loved, one must also be feared."

It was not a motto I subscribed to, but perhaps it was the nature of things here, in this foreign land.

"We've had no trouble with the men as a result—no thieving, no insolence. They rise in the middle of the night, walk across the desert from their homes a few miles away, and work all day shifting sand, bricks, and stones in the heat. Of course, we pay them well and give them baksheesh if they find anything of value; that's only fair. But Hamoudi keeps a careful watch over them." A smile broke over his impish face and his blue eyes twinkled with mischief. "The funny thing is, the person who keeps Hamoudi in check is none other than my wife. The Arab is in awe of her, as are all the servants. There's no doubt that she is the one who strikes fear into their hearts."

After passing through one of the gates of what he said was the temenos wall—a divider between ordinary land and something approaching royal or sacred territory—Woolley led me towards what looked like an enormous hole in the ground. He helped me as we walked down a series of steps dug out of the earth, and with each step I felt as though I were descending into an underworld. I knew before Woolley told me that I was passing into a burial site. The hairs on the back of my neck rose ever so slightly, and although it may have been my imagination, it seemed as though the temperature dropped a few degrees. This was a site I felt should never have been disturbed.

"What is this place?"

"We're calling it the Great Death Pit," he said. "A rather melodramatic name, but it will certainly capture the public's imagination."

"Indeed it will," I said, remembering the relish with which I had read of Woolley's discoveries. As I saw the partly excavated site, robbed of its treasures, I felt guilty for regarding the unearthing of the tomb as a source of entertainment. I should have known better. This was a burial site, a sacred place. My very presence here was questionable.

"You are one of the first people, outside the team here, to actually see this," said Woolley, looking more like a boy than ever. "When we dug down we discovered the clean-cut earth sides of a pit, sloping inwards and smoothly plastered with mud. As we worked down we discovered the largest death pit in the cemetery, measuring twenty-seven feet by twenty-four feet at the bottom."

"And what did you find in the pit, Mr. Woolley?"

"There were the bodies of six male servants, who lay along the side by the door, as well as sixty-eight women, all closely laid together, found with their legs slightly bent and their hands brought up near their faces. We also discovered four musical instruments, including a silver lyre, and two statues of rams in a corner. But what was fascinating—as we discovered in the tombs of Queen Shub-ad and her husband—was that there was a total absence of any signs of terror or violence."

"Which suggests that . . ."

"Yes, that the men and women walked down into the pit of their own accord. They were willing victims of human sacrifice. I think it's likely that these men and women took their places in the grave and then ingested some drug or poison—perhaps something like opium—which induced sleep and then death before the pit was filled in."

Despite the heat from the late afternoon sun, the image made me shiver.

"We've made a map of the pit, showing each of the bodies in situ."

The comment reminded me of the drawing Gertrude Bell had received just before her death.

"Is this mapping something you do yourself?" I asked.

"Well, it's a group effort. No one single person. Katharine and I noted down the exact position of the bodies, our photographer Harry Miller took some snaps, while Lawrence McRae and his nephew helped with some of the final sketches."

I thought of the fragment of conversation I had overheard between Mr. McRae and Cecil earlier: "If I can't have her, then no one will. I can make sure of that." The boy had been referring to Sarah, the daughter of the rich American I had yet to meet. But if he harbored thoughts such as these, who was to say what he was capable of?

"As you can see, we're still in the process of excavation, but we've already unearthed some treasures. I'll show you when we get back to the house. They're safely locked up in the *antika* room, and then they'll be securely shipped back to London, Philadelphia—or Baghdad, of course."

"How do you go about deciding which items stay in Iraq and which ones go to the museums?"

"An interesting question. When Miss Bell was alive, she and I would hold regular meetings and we would just argue our respective cases. Occasionally it would get heated, and I seem to remember once we had to toss a coin over who would take possession of an extremely beautiful—and valuable—gold scarab. Much to my annoyance, Gertrude won that one."

However, Woolley did not look that upset, and the idea that he might have killed Miss Bell over such a thing seemed unlikely. Or could Leonard Woolley be that very dangerous thing: a master dissembler?

"Of course, it's only right that certain objects remain in Iraq, but also I have a duty to the trustees of the British Museum, and to the British public," he said. But, as I had heard from his own lips, he also had a duty to his wife, who he believed was suffering from some sort of mental condition. Was he covering up for something she had done? "Look," he said, pointing at the horizon, "the sun will be going down soon. Shall we walk up to the top of the ziggurat? The view from up there is magnificent."

"That sounds like a splendid plan," I said.

"This is the courtyard of the Temple of Nannar," said Woolley. "The whole complex was devoted to the worship of a moon god. We know this because of certain inscriptions found on cylinder seals here."

"Are they awfully difficult to read?"

"What? Cuneiform? Yes, quite tricky. Of course, they have to be cleaned first, using a diluted solution of hydrochloric acid. If you're interested, I'll ask Father Burrows to give you a crash course."

"Yes, I'd like that very much," I said.

As we walked up the steep incline of one of the structure's three staircases, Woolley explained a little of the history of the building. The ziggurat was built, he said, by King Ur-Nammu in around 2100 BC. The people who built it wanted to erect a structure so they could feel themselves nearer to the sky and to the god they worshiped. By the time I had reached the first level I was out of breath, but Woolley, as nimble and lithe as a mountain goat, skipped ahead. I took a moment to look out across the empty, desolate desert plain.

"It's extraordinary," I shouted so that Woolley could hear. "There's absolutely nothing here for as far as the eye can see."

Woolley turned and retraced his steps so that he stood by me. "But there, Mrs. Christie, you are quite wrong," he said, smiling. "Come with me and I'll show you what I mean."

A few minutes later, and now considerably out of breath, I stood at the top level of the ziggurat. The setting sun was creating its magic across the sands, casting the desert in an ever-changing palette of colors, one moment mauve, the next apricot or rose pink.

"You may think there is nothing, but as with all things it's a matter of adjusting one's perception. In the east," he said, gesturing for me to turn around, "one can see the dark tasseled fringe of the palm trees at the river's bank. Of course, the Euphrates has changed its course since the ancient days. Can you see?"

I squinted until I could make it out. "Yes, just about," I replied.

"And there, in the distance," he said, pointing to the southwest, "you should just be able to see the ruins of the staged tower of the sacred city of Eridu."

"That's where the Archers have visited today?"

"Yes, that's right. I'm sure they will be full of enthusiasm for it when they return." He shifted his position so that he was facing northwest. "And there, although it's difficult to see, you can just discern the low mound of Tall al-'Ubaid, which I excavated a few years back. But, yes, apart from this there is nothing but the empty desert."

I stared across the vast plains that stretched for miles before me. The thought of being so cut off from the world thrilled and terrified me in equal measure. Perhaps I should have listened to the advice of Madge and Carlo when they had told me not to venture to the Near East. And of course neither my sister nor my secretary knew anything of my real purpose in Iraq.

A series of images came into my mind. Gertrude Bell's terror on receiving those threatening letters and the map of a grave pit with her initials. My nasty encounter with the boy in the backstreet in Baghdad, an incident which could have ended in violence. The mania that haunted Katharine Woolley's eyes, a look suggestive of madness. The fear that gripped poor Miss Jones when she had realized she had said too much. The unsettling, queer song of those Arab workers who sifted through the rubble for signs of a past civilization. And the dread I had felt when I had descended those steps into the "Great Death Pit."

My feelings of unease were not helped by what Woolley said next. "Do you know the original Sumerian meaning for the Great Ziggurat at Ur, Mrs. Christie?"

I shook my head, unable to speak.

"It went by the name of 'Etemennigur,'" he said, hesitating for a moment. "Or 'Temple Whose Foundation Creates Horror.'"

7

By the evening Katharine Woolley's spirits seemed to have improved. In fact, she looked an altogether different woman. Her hair was shining and tidy, combed into a neat bob, and she was wearing a stylish dress of a shade my mother would have called *vieux rose*, complete with gloves of the same color that ran up to her elbows.

She had taken it upon herself to direct a special supper to welcome me to the site. She oversaw the cooking, frequently dashing into the kitchen to supervise the Arab chef and watch the progress of our meal of food I had never tasted before: cheese pastries, fried chickpea balls, a spicy salad, skewers of meat, a rice and aubergine casserole, and cooked lentils. She smoothed a white linen cloth over the table and in the center she placed a small vase filled with yellow chamomiles. Then she set the table for ten with a makeshift collection of plates and not-quite-matching knives and forks, but she did so with such style that in the end it looked charming.

She had delegated various tasks to Miss Jones, who busied about the sitting room sweeping and rearranging the furniture, but Katharine seemed to find fault with virtually everything she did.

"Do you really think that the armchair should be placed quite so near the far wall?"

"It seems you've missed a good deal of dust under that side table just there."

"I can see some smears on those glasses, dear. Would you mind cleaning them once again, just to make sure?"

Miss Jones met each of these requests with grace and as much good humor as she could muster, but I still felt sorry for her. Yet, whenever I tried to help Cynthia, Katharine would send me back to my chair with the words "You are our guest here; you must do nothing but try and enjoy yourself."

At six o'clock Leonard Woolley appeared, dressed in a dark suit and tie, and at his wife's request started to mix drinks. Gradually the rest of the party arrived. There was Father Burrows, who I noticed behaved awkwardly in company, still wearing the clothes I had seen him in earlier; Lawrence McRae and his nephew, neither of whom had made much of an effort to dress for dinner; and, the last to join us, the Americans, Mr. and Mrs. Archer and their daughter, Sarah.

In contrast to Father Burrows and the McRaes, the Archers had pulled out all the stops. Ruth, a small, rather overweight woman, had donned a dark silk dress which unfortunately did her no favors. But she had made up for this with a dazzling array of jewels: a diamond-and-emerald necklace, complete with earrings to match, and a beautiful diamond-and-platinum brooch. Her daughter, a slight figure with blond hair, blue eyes, and the face of an angel, was wearing a shimmering silver-beaded dress—which she later told me was Lanvin—and a long string of pearls. The father, Hubert, a huge haystack of a man with a bald head, graying mustache, and prominent sideburns, had dressed in a dinner suit and stepped into the room with the confidence and swagger typical of the very rich.

After making sure that the Archers were served with soda water and lemon—the father said that none of them touched alcohol—Leonard Woolley brought the family over to me to be introduced.

Hubert, on hearing that I was a novelist, proclaimed that he didn't believe in works of fiction. The only book he and his family read, he said, was the Lord's book—the Bible.

"That is the only truth I need to know," he said, puffing up his chest. "Sorry, Mrs. Christie, I don't mean to embarrass you or slight you in any way. But I think it's worth setting out one's principles, don't you?"

"Oh, yes, I do indeed," I said, not quite telling the truth.

I listened as Hubert Archer proclaimed his views on religion and the sorry state of the modern world. I shared his opinion on certain subjects—the very real threat that came from evil, for instance—but we differed wildly on others, such as the creation of the world in seven days.

"You may not choose to support my view, but I believe that every word—every word, mind—of what is written in Genesis is true," he said.

"And we've come to Ur to find proof, isn't that right, Hubert?" said Ruth Archer, beaming, her eyes shining as brightly as her jewels.

As the couple continued to talk about original sin and the biblical flood, I noticed that their daughter, Sarah, seemed to show more interest in Lawrence McRae than our conversation about the Old Testament.

"Mr. Woolley has found evidence of a flood that he thinks could be linked to the flood of Noah's time," Ruth said. "That's right, Leonard, isn't it?"

"Without a doubt," Woolley replied without hesitation as his wife announced that it was time for dinner. "As I've told you, we know that the Flood as related in the book of Genesis is based on the older Sumerian legend and that—"

"What tosh," whispered Father Burrows to me as I moved away from the group.

"I'm sorry?"

"That nonsense about Woolley finding traces of the Flood here," said the clergyman, pushing his wire spectacles back up the bridge of his nose. "He's just saying that to get hold of their money."

"I see," I replied.

"Of course there was a flood, but a local one, nothing to do with Noah at all," he said, his voice still low. "And I doubt we'll find evidence of Abraham ever living here. But those fools will believe anything they're told."

I looked at Miss Archer as Lawrence McRae held the chair back for her. As she sat down, a look of triumph came into her eyes. Across the room, sulking in the corner, Cecil McRae watched his uncle, his face burning with anger, his eyes dark with jealousy.

"Yes, please sit anywhere you like," said Katharine. "We're very informal here."

Leonard Woolley sat at the head of the table, with Hubert Archer and his wife next to him; Lawrence McRae took a place next to the American millionaire and opposite Sarah; and I pulled out a chair next to the girl.

"I was admiring your dress," I said as I sat down. "It looks so lovely in the candlelight."

"Thank you," said Sarah, pleased that I had commented on her appearance. She told me a little of a recent shopping trip to Paris and her love of art and music, topics which, she said, were dismissed as frivolous, if not out and out sinful, by her father. In turn, I shared a few memories of my own time in the French capital when I had been a girl. Of course, I had been without her considerable resources, and my time at Mademoiselle T's school was a miserable one. I remembered the raw gnawing in my stomach which I gradually came to realize was homesickness: I had never really been away from my mother before and to be parted from her caused me to suffer. Gradually, however, I came to enjoy my time in Paris—oh, the opera, the music, the fashions! I had improved my French—my grammar was awful, but my accent not so bad—and some basics of arithmetic, history, and deportment.

"You must have had quite a time there, in Paris," said Sarah.

"It was wonderful, and I made many friends with girls from all over the world," I replied. "Particularly American girls, like you. I always enjoyed their breezy way of talking, so refreshing after the rather stuffy drawing rooms of England."

"Not all Americans can talk quite so freely," she said, casting a quick glance at her parents. "The only reason I'm allowed to wear this dress tonight is because I'm about to come into my own money."

"Your own money?"

"Yes. You see, I'm about to be wealthy in my own right," she said. "I know the English think it's terribly vulgar to talk about such things, but, yes, I will soon have my own money, nothing to do with father or mother. My grandmother on my mother's side left her entire fortune to me, due to be made over to me on my next birthday. It drives father crazy, because I know he'd like to threaten to cut me off without a cent."

"So that makes you—"

"Yes, quite the catch," she said, her eyes sparkling. She turned her attention to the man sitting opposite her and said, "Mr. McRae, would you please pass me the salad?" while I started talking to Cynthia Jones on my right and Katharine Woolley at the foot of the table.

"The food's not too bad tonight: nothing's burnt, nothing's too salty or too spicy," said Cynthia, smiling at Katharine. "Usually I have to take a glass of water with me when I go to bed. A good decision of yours to supervise Abdul in the kitchen."

We talked of cooking and the ingredients you could buy in Iraq, and the ones they had shipped in, and various disastrous meals that they had eaten since arriving in the country. Mrs. Woolley made us all laugh by telling us how at one dinner she had been presented with a congealed broth made from sheep brains and on another occasion she had taken a mouthful of a dish so rich in chili spice that it had made her nose stream. The conversation was light and pleasant—jolly, even. From Mrs. Woolley's demeanor—her eyes were now bright and clear—you would never guess that, only a few hours before, she had been laid low with a terrible migraine.

During a break in the conversation I expressed my gratitude to Mrs. Woolley for going to such trouble with the dinner. It was the least she could do, she replied. After all, I had given her hours of pleasure. She looked down the table and addressed her guests.

"I'm sorry to interrupt," she said, lightly tapping a fork against her glass, "but I wanted to welcome our guest tonight, the distinguished author Mrs. Agatha Christie."

As the room quietened and all eyes turned to stare at me, I felt myself beginning to blush. I was not keen on being the center of attention. Katharine saw the look of consternation on my face and she leant over and whispered, "Don't worry, I won't ask you to make a speech." She raised her voice and continued, "Many of you may know that I have—how shall I put it?—particular tastes in literature. I only read what I consider to be *la crème de la crème*. And I can tell you, without a doubt, that Mrs. Christie's work is that rare thing, the very best. I'm not going to embarrass my friend any further—for all her genius, she is an extremely modest woman—but please could I ask you to raise your glasses to our very welcome guest, Agatha Christie."

The assembled guests stood up from their seats and toasted my name. The whole thing was ghastly, but I told myself that it would soon be over and that it had been done with the best of intentions.

"Thank you," I managed to say. "That's most kind. Please sit down." I turned to Katharine and, in order to try and deflect attention away from me, asked her about the digging season.

"Yes, I'm confident it's going to be our most productive yet, don't you think, darling?" she asked, calling down the table for her husband's opinion.

"What's that?" replied Leonard.

"Mrs. Christie here was just asking about our hopes for the season. And I told her that we have every confidence that it's going to be extraordinarily productive."

"Indeed," he said. "In fact, after dinner I'll show you, Mrs. Christie—and of course you, Mr. and Mrs. Archer—some of the treasures we have already unearthed. Needless to say, a few of the very best artifacts have already been sent to Baghdad, London, and Philadelphia, but we still have things of wonder here. To see them by candlelight is a most magical experience."

"I'd like that very much," I said.

"Is there anything that once belonged to Abraham?" asked Mr. Archer.

For a moment the question flummoxed Woolley, but he quickly regained his composure. "Not yet—but as I said, I'm sure it's only a matter of time. We've dug up so many other beautiful things: lyres, gold cups, headdresses, necklaces—"

"Finery doesn't interest me," Archer replied. "What I want to see is something concrete that once belonged to the great patriarch. As you know, it could be worth a good deal to you. We're talking thousands of dollars, Woolley."

"That's most kind of you, Mr. Archer. In fact, I have one object that should interest you a great deal and which I think may have a connection to Abraham himself."

"Really?" said Archer, his eyes lighting up.

From across the table Father Burrows leant over to Cecil McRae and whispered something into the boy's left ear. The adolescent, who had remained silent and sullen for most of the meal, snorted at what Burrows had said. All eyes fixed on him.

"Do you find something amusing, young man?" asked Archer,

a man who believed his fortune should protect him from mockery. "Would you like to share it with the rest of the table?"

The boy squirmed in his seat. "N-no, sir," he stuttered, his pimpled face reddening.

"Perhaps you find God a subject of humor, is that it?" There was an unpleasant, bullying tone to Archer's voice now. "Let me tell you, there's nothing funny about it."

"I think you've made your point, sir," said Lawrence McRae, who was sitting between the millionaire and Cecil. "My nephew meant no harm."

Archer continued to glare at the boy and was about to say something to McRae but was prevented from doing so by his wife's pleading look, an expression which I assumed she must have perfected over the years through constant practice.

"I believe you were in Paris recently, Mr. Archer," said Woolley, desperate to ease the tension in the room.

"Indeed," said Archer. "A place full of sinners."

"Father—you can't say that!" said Sarah.

"Why not? It's what I believe. Some of the people I saw in that city, well—" He stopped himself. "I couldn't begin to tell you, not with ladies in the room." He looked at his daughter's bare shoulders with disgust. "And you, young lady, should learn to cover yourself up."

Sarah was about to answer her father back, when her mother placed a gentle hand on her wrist.

"Why don't we do that tour of the artifacts now?" said Woolley, dabbing his lips with a white napkin and standing up. "Mr. and Mrs. Archer? Mrs. Christie? Would you like to join me? We could have coffee when we return."

As we stood up from the table, all of us breathed an audible sigh of relief. Woolley took a key from the inside pocket of his jacket and led our little group towards the *antika* room. I cast a backwards glance to the table and saw that Sarah continued to flirt with Mr. McRae while Cecil remained silent. Katharine Woolley excused herself and Cynthia Jones walked over to talk to Father Burrows.

Woolley turned the key in the door of the *antika* room and the four of us stepped inside. The light from his candles immediately caught the gold of an exquisitely crafted cup that he said had been used to store cosmetics. "Not dissimilar to the kind of stuff my wife uses at night on her face," he joked. Archer managed a half smile. "She has a seemingly infinite amount of jars; I've no idea what's in them." From a trestle table in the center of the room Woolley picked up a cylinder seal fashioned from lapis lazuli, together with its impression, which had been transferred onto a flat piece of clay. "As you can see, this shows a banquet scene—again not dissimilar to the kind of feast we have been enjoying tonight." Woolley pointed out the figure of what he said was a queen or a princess drinking wine from a beaker.

"What's that?" asked Ruth Archer as Woolley's candle passed over a horrible devilish face complete with horns.

"Oh, yes, a very curious find," Woolley replied. "It's a copper pin, the kind of thing they used to fasten tunics. But I'm at a loss to know why it's got horns; maybe its owner had a mischievous sense of humor. Can you see the work that's gone into this?" Woolley picked up a gold dagger. "Look how it's been formed, how it's been crafted with such love and attention to detail. Of course, gold wasn't mined at Ur. Rather it was imported from Persia and—"

His words were interrupted by a piercing howl. Each of us momentarily froze, as if the horrible noise had paralyzed our nervous systems.

"It's my wife—it's Katharine," said Woolley, running from the room.

Everyone had been drawn to the source of the disturbance, which seemed to have come from Katharine's bedroom. A circle had formed around Mrs. Woolley, necessitating Leonard to push his way through.

"What the hell has happened?" he shouted. "Katharine? What's wrong?"

Katharine Woolley stared down at the bed as if in a daze. I followed her gaze and there, by the pillow, was Tom, her adored cat. It wasn't moving, and there was a small pool of clear liquid mixed with blood on the pillow case by its mouth. Leonard strode forwards, bent down, and gently took hold of the animal's front paw. He lifted it with no resistance. He then opened the creature's eyes; all signs of life had been extinguished.

"I'm afraid to say Tom is dead," said Leonard, turning to his wife. "He must have died in his sleep. I doubt very much he suffered."

Tears formed in Katharine's eyes, and the pain she felt was visibly etched on her face. She tried to speak, but the words refused to form themselves in anything but an animalistic moan.

"Darling," said Leonard, taking his wife in his arms, "I know it's an awful shock, but I'm sure it's for the best. He was probably getting on a bit, and he didn't seem to like anyone but you."

Katharine looked up in confusion at her husband's clumsy attempt to comfort her. She pushed him away and came to sit on the bed next to the limp body. She placed her head right down against the cat's stomach and nuzzled the poor creature's fur.

"Tom, dear Tom," she whispered.

The rest of the party turned their backs and, with a few polite, well-meaning words—"I'm so terribly sorry," "It's always such a shock, losing a pet one has loved"—the guests made their way to the main room. I remembered all too well the deep sorrow I had felt after losing each of my dogs—to recall them brought a lump to my throat—and so I went over to Katharine, sat on the bed, and took her hand. I knew that there was no need to utter commonplaces at this time. Woolley himself looked embarrassed at this show of feminine feeling and slowly edged his way out of the bedroom with the words "Yes, good to have some time to come to terms with it. Poor old Tom."

Katharine continued to sob, her tears coating the cat's fur with a fine sheen, until finally she could cry no more.

"Thank you," she said as she wiped her eyes with a handkerchief.

"It's the least I could do," I said. "I know it's no comfort, but I do know what it's like."

"What I don't understand is why—why now? Despite what Leonard says, I don't think he was that old. Of course, we don't know exactly, as we found him as a stray in Baghdad."

"Perhaps he had been ill?" I suggested.

"He hadn't shown any signs of illness," said Katharine, taking one of his paws in her hands and cradling it as if it were the hand of a baby. "After getting ready for tonight, I left him sleeping there, on the bed. I gave him a stroke and he started to purr." At the memory, tears began to appear in Katharine's eyes once more.

"Think of all the lovely times you had together," I said, squeezing her hand. "All the pleasure he gave you—and you gave him."

"Thank you, Agatha," she said, tears rolling down her cheeks now. "If you would just give me a few minutes . . . to say my goodbyes."

"Of course," I said, standing up. "And just think what a wonderful life he had."

The grief consumed her and I quietly made my way out of the room and rejoined the others at the table. Even though the cat had not been popular—I remembered Cynthia's words about how some of her colleagues had tried to get rid of it before, much to Mrs. Woolley's distress—there was a funereal atmosphere in the room. Woolley had poured out generous measures of brandy for those in the party who consumed alcohol, and most of the group sat in respectable silence. Hubert Archer was engaged in a conversation with his wife, and as I passed them I heard the millionaire say, "I don't know what all the fuss is about. It was only a cat! I'd understand if it had been her child," closely followed by Ruth's words: "I think it's best if you keep your own counsel, Hubert."

"How is she feeling?" asked Cynthia.

"She's in shock, of course," I said.

"She may need a glass of brandy," said Woolley. "Yes, that will do the trick." He poured a generous measure of cognac into a glass and was about to take it into his wife's room, when Katharine appeared at the door. There was something unreal about her, and she stepped into the room with the air of an actress making her final appearance at the end of a tragedy. All traces of tears were gone now, but her face had a deathly pallor to it, almost as if she were wearing a mask.

"Thank you all so very much for coming," she said in a brittle, artificial voice. "It was a lovely evening and your company was as charming as ever."

Woolley walked towards her with the glass of brandy. "Darling, I think you should drink this," he said, passing the glass to her.

"No, I couldn't possibly," she said, waving away the brandy. "I need to keep a clear head. I'll start on the washing up now. There's no point in putting it off."

Each of the guests stared at Katharine Woolley with incomprehension and embarrassment. A few minutes before she had been reduced to tears, and now here she was, pretending to play the part of the hostess to perfection.

"My dear, you've had a terrible shock," said Woolley, placing a hand gently on her shoulder. "Why don't you come and sit down?"

Katharine brushed him off and walked over to the dining table. She reached for a plate to take to the kitchen to wash up but stopped herself.

"If I am to do the washing up, I must take off my gloves," she said.

"Let one of the servants do that, darling," said Leonard.

"No, it won't take long," she said as she started to peel back a glove. "It's no trouble, no trouble at all."

"Oh, my . . . ," said Ruth Archer, her voice trailing off. Her gaze was focused on Mrs. Woolley's lower arms.

Underneath each of Katharine's arms, on the soft flesh that ran between elbow and wrist, ran a series of bloody lines that looked like scratches from a cat. It appeared as though the wounds were fresh and no more than a few hours old.

"What in God's name has she done?" asked Lawrence McRae.

The question did not need to be answered.

It seemed there had been a struggle and Mrs. Woolley had killed the cat she said she loved.

8

I took Katharine's hand and led her back into her bedroom. Leonard Woolley followed us.

"What about the clearing of the plates?" she asked. "The washing up?"

"That can wait," I said, guiding her towards her dressing table. I glanced over at Woolley; understanding at once, he nodded and went to fetch a blanket. While I tried to distract Katharine with talk of her cosmetic lotions and cleansing creams, he undertook the unpleasant business of removing the body of the dead cat from the bed. Once he had done that—and stripped away the pillowcase with its nasty stain—he left us alone to talk.

"Katharine, may I ask: What do you remember about earlier this evening?"

"What do you mean?"

"If anything . . . particular sticks in your mind."

"Well, I sat here in front of the mirror and then I dressed for dinner."

"Do you remember putting your evening gloves on?"

She looked down at the gloves, which were curled in her lap like a pair of strangely colored exotic snakes. Something stirred within her—a fragment of a memory, perhaps—and then she gazed in amazement at her arms.

"What happened? Did something happen to Tom?"

"Yes. I'm afraid he's dead. Don't you remember?"

Katharine clutched at me with a desperation I had only seen in some of the men I had treated in the war. They had lost their minds on the front and had returned as empty shells haunted by the violence of their own actions and the violence done to them.

"Dead? But how?" she asked, her hand trailing up to her forehead. "Where is he? Why is he not on the bed?" Her voice rose in a panic as she stood up and looked for her cat. It was a pitiful sight. "I left him on the bed, sleeping. He was purring when I left him. Where is he? Where's Tom? What have you done with him?"

"Katharine, you must calm yourself," I said, placing a hand on her shoulder. "You've had some bad news. You're in shock. Try to take some deep breaths." She looked down at her arms again. "Why do my arms hurt? How did I get these scratches?"

"You can't remember anything of what happened?"

"I don't know what you mean. Why do you keep asking me what I remember?" Her voice had risen to a fevered pitch.

"Please, you must try and stay calm."

"What happened? What?" The horrible look of panic haunted her eyes; her breathing had quickened and she had started to perspire. The signs told me that unless she was sedated, she could be on the edge of a nervous breakdown.

"I'm going to leave you for a minute, but I am going to return," I said. "Everything will be all right."

I left her and went to fetch Woolley, who was talking to Father Burrows. I explained the situation and told him that I thought it would be best to sedate his wife.

"But, as I told you, the doctor is over two hours away," he said. "Will that be too late?"

I informed him that I had a supply of a medically prescribed sedative which I could administer if he agreed. He nodded vigorously and I returned to my room to retrieve the drug. I opened my trunk and, with my special key that I always carried with me, unlocked the case inside. From there I extracted my precious poisons. I quickly found what I was looking for—a simple barbiturate, similar to the one involved in the death of Gertrude Bell—locked up my case, and went to the kitchen for some tea. I returned to Katharine's room, where she was pacing the floor like a caged animal.

"I've got something here which will help you," I said, stirring the grains of the sedative into the hot liquid. "Please drink some of this."

Her eyes were full of fear. "Are you trying to poison me?" she said, pushing the cup away.

"No, of course not. What gave you that idea?"

"People have been doing strange things to me. Horrible things."

"Who? And what things? What do you mean?"

She looked like a sullen child. "You wouldn't understand. You wouldn't believe me."

"Here, please try to take this," I said, offering the cup to her once more. "You can trust me. I can assure you that this will not harm you."

I had some suspicions about Katharine Woolley, but I met her accusatory stare with kindness. It was obvious that she was very ill indeed. She took the cup and sipped its contents. "That's right, a little more of the tea," I said. "Now let's get you into bed." I helped her undress, pulled back the covers, and made sure she was comfortable. "You'll feel better in the morning," I said, not convinced at all that this was the truth. I cleaned the scratches on her arm and sat with her as the drug started to do its work. Her eyelids fluttered, closed, and soon she was asleep.

When I returned to the sitting room, I discovered that everyone except for Leonard Woolley had gone to bed. He was sitting in a leather chair, nursing a large glass of brandy.

"How is she?" he asked, gesturing for me to come and sit by him.

"She's taken the sedative, so at least she'll get some sleep," I replied.

"I can't believe it—she loved that animal. You should have seen her with it; it was like her own baby. I thought the attention she showed it was a bit pathetic at times. Surely she wouldn't have done anything to harm it?"

But he—like all of us—had seen the scratches on Katharine's arms. "I suppose it must have been done in a fit of madness. She must not have known what she was doing," he admitted.

"Have you seen her like this before?"

Woolley's eyes clouded with painful memories. "I suppose you might as well know the truth," he said, taking a large sip of the brandy. "I'm at a loss to know what to do. I'm not sure if I can endure it much longer."

"Do you want to tell me what's been troubling you?"

"You've seen what she's like. I've been trying to pretend to everyone here that Katharine suffers from nothing more than terrible migraines. But over the last few weeks I've begun to worry about the state of her mind."

"Have you witnessed things that warrant such a concern?"

"I have," he said, sighing. "So many, I don't know where to begin." He stood up and checked the doors to make sure no one was listening. "I've been trying to keep it from the rest of the team here, but that has not been easy. A number of people came to me; poor souls, I should never have asked them to put up with it. Anyway, they felt that Katharine's behavior had started to become not only eccentric but erratic. They said that . . . that they no longer felt safe around her. Well, after tonight's incident, who is going to blame them?"

"I think it's best if you tell me everything, Mr. Woolley," I said. "I'm not sure I'm the right person, but I will do my utmost to help."

"You will?"

"Why, of course."

"Would you care for . . . ?" he asked, proffering the brandy. "No, I forgot: you don't drink," he said, pouring himself another measure. "Well, I may as well start at the beginning. I'm correct in saying that's what you writers would do?"

I nodded encouragingly. "That's right."

"It's not a pretty tale, I'm afraid, but it is one that you must hear if you are to understand anything about my wife. And you are sure you won't be shocked?"

"As you know, I was a nurse in the war, Mr. Woolley. There is precious little in this world that shocks me."

"Very well," he said. "When I first met Katharine—Mrs. Keeling, as she was then—in the spring of 1924. She was already a widow. She was a beguiling creature, a beauty . . . well, she's still that. She came out here as a volunteer and almost immediately I spotted her talents. She had a wonderful eye for capturing the essence of an object, almost as if she had a real affinity with the artifacts that we were digging up from the ground. Of course, she suffered from headaches then, but we managed to work around them. Her presence, however, caused some consternation with the heads of the sponsoring museums, and the director of the University of Pennsylvania Museum, George Byron Gordon. He's dead now, by the way; had an unfortunate accident at the beginning of last year at the Racquet Club in Philadelphia."

"So he was against Katharine's presence here?"

"Yes, and he wrote a letter to me outlining his position. There had been some talk—there's always talk, isn't there?—about the propriety of having a single woman on the excavation site, here in the middle of nowhere, thrown together with a number of men. It was beginning to bring the expedition into disrepute. Gordon said that he would hate to think that Katharine might become the subject of 'inconsiderate remarks' and that her reputation would be sullied."

"And what of Miss Jones? Was Mr. Gordon not concerned about her presence?"

"Apparently not. I think he assumed she was the spinster type."

"And so you married Katharine?"

"Yes, we were married by my brother, in fact. In Hampshire, in April 1927. But I want you to know that was not the only reason why I asked her to marry me. It wasn't as if I was forced, if you see what I mean. No, I found her a bewitching woman. She could be vivacious, funny, charming. But she was mercurial."

That word sounded like a euphemism to me. "*Mercurial*?"

"Yes, I suppose that's what I found so attractive to begin with." He stood and checked again that the doors to the room were closed. "I'd hate this to get out. You won't say anything, will you, Mrs. Christie?"

"I promise I will be discretion itself."

"Very well. It was on my wedding night that I got a taste of . . . well, of Katharine perhaps not being like other women."

"In what way?"

"We had arranged to spend the night at a hotel in London. I don't know what I thought would happen—I was a very inexperienced man; I'd devoted my life to my work, I suppose—but I was shocked and, yes, a good deal upset."

I let Woolley talk in his own time, as I could tell that he found discussing this intimate subject difficult and embarrassing.

"She'd already made it known that she didn't want anything to do with my family. That hurt me, but I understood she wanted to start a new life after the death of her husband."

It was interesting, I thought, that he chose not to share with me the manner in which Colonel Keeling had died.

"And I had certain assumptions . . . because she had been a married woman."

"Assumptions, you say?"

"Yes. I thought that she would have a certain knowledge and experience of these things."

"I see," I said.

"B-but," he said, blushing. "That . . . that night, our first night together, she made it clear that she wanted to have separate bedrooms. I told her that this could be arranged. But she meant it in a more permanent sense, if you see what I mean. I pointed out to her that we had just got married, that this was our honeymoon night, but she got more and more upset. I couldn't see any sense in what she was saying, but in hysterics she locked me in the bathroom and refused to let me out until I had promised that I would not make love to her. In the end, what could I do? Of course I gave her my word. Later, we tried to talk about it, but she was adamant. She did not want that from a marriage."

"Oh, dear, that must have been extremely difficult for you."

"And since then that is how it has been. I did seek out the advice of my sister, Edith, and, if the truth be told, I even considered divorce. But I decided that it would be unseemly to cause a scandal. And my family believed that divorce might well bring about the end of my career."

As I thought about my own divorce, I felt myself beginning to blush.

"I'm sorry if I've shocked you, Mrs. Christie, I didn't mean to—"

"No, not at all," I said. Even though it pained me to say the words, I thought it right that I share my own experience with Woolley, so as to reassure him that he wasn't the only person in the world to have experienced marital problems. "You see, my own marriage broke down and before I came out here I agreed to divorce my husband, Archie."

"I'm sorry to hear that. I had no idea," said Woolley.

"He fell in love with another woman," I said.

"I don't think Katharine has fallen in love with another man. Perhaps she just doesn't care for those kind of feelings—with anyone."

"Yes, perhaps that's it," I said. "Some women—and men, I believe—are like that."

"But I just wish she had told me before we'd married!" There was anger in his voice now. "I might well have thought otherwise. I could have chosen someone else, or perhaps nobody at all would be better than this." He paused to reflect on what he had just said. "Listen to me; you must think me an utter beast, talking like this about Katharine. No, I made my vows and I'm going to stick to them. 'For richer for poorer, in sickness and in health, to love and to cherish, till death us do part.' " He fell silent and pensive. Had his final phrase struck some deeper resonance within him?

"Has your wife shown any signs of violence?"

Woolley looked appalled at the question. "What do you mean?"

"I wondered if you had seen her inflict harm on others . . . or herself."

"No, she's not like that at all. I don't know what you could be suggesting."

"I think we both know that Katharine killed her cat, don't we? And I wondered whether there could have been other occasions when she might have lost her temper."

"She is headstrong, yes, and can be cruel at times. I think tonight was just an isolated event. She must have momentarily lost her mind."

"Did she ever mention Miss Bell to you?"

"Gertrude?"

"Yes."

"No, not really. But as I've told you, my wife and Gertrude didn't get on."

"Do you know when the two women last met?"

"I've got no idea. I last saw Gertrude in March, I think it was, when I went to Baghdad. Oh, yes, Katharine did accompany me then because we were on the way back to England. I spent a few days with Gertrude at the museum, working on the classification of some artifacts."

"So that was March 1926? And Miss Bell died in July."

"That's right, but I don't see how this has got anything to do with Katharine. We were both in England during that summer."

My mind was running ahead with possibilities. Could Katharine have sent those threatening letters and that drawing of a death pit to Miss Bell from England? Did Gertrude Bell know something about Katharine Woolley that might have prevented her marriage to Leonard? Perhaps Miss Bell had some knowledge of what happened to Katharine's first husband.

"I'm just trying to get a few things into some kind of order, that's all," I said. "You say your wife was a widow when she met you."

"Yes, she was married to a Lieutenant Colonel Keeling. That marriage, I'm afraid, was not a happy one."

"Do you know how Colonel Keeling died?"

"A very sad case. He took his own life, I'm afraid. Katharine told me he shot himself in Cairo only a few months after their marriage."

I did not say anything. The silence forced Woolley to fit together the pieces of the puzzle himself. "You're not . . ."

"What?"

"You can't possibly believe that Katharine . . ."

A look of horror filled his face as he slowly realized the seriousness of the implication.

"Could she have killed her first husband?" he whispered.

"I don't know . . . Is that something you believe she could be capable of?"

"No, not Katharine. She's not that kind of woman. But . . ."

Doubtless the events of the night played through his mind. "But if she could kill Tom, then perhaps she could have done that, too." The articulation of that thought drained the color from his face. "No, I refuse to believe it. It's too ridiculous for words!"

"Yes, quite ridiculous," I said.

But both of us knew it wasn't so far-fetched at all. In fact, it would fit the pattern. The question was: Would Katharine Woolley kill again? And if so, who would be her next victim?

9

I was dreading the gloomy atmosphere at breakfast the next morning, but it was enlivened by the return of Harry Miller from Baghdad. The American photographer was full of tales of the exotic city, but thankfully he chose not to regale everyone with how he had saved me from a street urchin. With him he brought back all the supplies. There was typing paper and carbon sheets for Cynthia Jones, new blocks of clay for Father Burrows, a nice set of pencils for Lawrence and Cecil McRae, and some religious pamphlets for Hubert Archer, who had set out on an early morning walking excursion with his wife and daughter.

"Where's the queen?" asked Miller with a mocking tone. "Is she still in bed?"

The room went quiet except for the scrape of a knife across a piece of toast.

"What's the matter? Why are you all looking so odd?"

I had been to see Katharine earlier that morning. She was still extremely drowsy, but it looked as though her symptoms had dissipated. However, I advised her to spend the day in her room. I said I would check on her at regular intervals, and Woolley, who was still sitting with her, was extremely grateful for all my help. However, I could tell that he was guarded around Katharine, mindful perhaps of the conversation we had had the night before.

"She's not feeling too well," I said.

"What? Again?" replied Miller. "Don't say we're going to have to get the leeches out."

"Leeches?" I asked.

"Sure. She likes the little bloodsuckers. Says they help relieve tension or something. Sounds like a load of—"

"Well, I'm sure anything that can help Mrs. Woolley at the moment can only be a good thing," I said.

"What—like that time she made Len sleep outside her room with a string attached to his big toe?" said Lawrence McRae in an unpleasant tone of voice. "So that she could pull it if she needed him in the night?"

"Is that true?" I asked.

Miller nodded and poured himself another cup of coffee. "She's got that man where she wants him all right," he said. He looked around the table, studying each of us in turn. "But, seriously, has something happened?"

Cynthia Jones told the story of what had occurred the night before.

"I don't believe it," said Miller. "I know Katharine's a bit odd, she has her moods, and some of the things that come out of her mouth can be cutting, but to kill Tom? She loved that cat."

"What else can we think?" said McRae. "We saw the scratches on her arms. She could pick up Tom, but obviously there had been a struggle when she began to hurt him."

"So what do you think happened?" asked Miller, still mystified.

"The only logical solution is that she must have killed the cat in her room, where it scratched her," said McRae. "She finished it off, put on those long gloves of hers to cover up the marks, got ready for dinner, and came in here."

"Would the cat not have made an almighty noise?" asked Cynthia. "We've all heard it at times making that awful yowling."

"Did you hear music coming from Katharine's room last night?" asked McRae.

"Yes, now you come to think of it, I think I did hear the sound of her gramophone," said Cynthia.

"Perhaps that drowned out the cries of the cat," said McRae.

"But to be so heartless?" said Miller.

"She may not have known what she was doing," I said.

"She was out of her mind? Is that what you're saying?" asked the photographer.

"By all accounts, it seems as though Mrs. Woolley has been under a tremendous amount of strain," I said. "She may have carried out the attack under the delusion that the cat presented some kind of threat. And she could have blocked out all memory of it."

"Is that really possible?" asked Miller.

"Yes, I'm afraid it is," said Father Burrows, who had been silent up to this point. "Once, just after the end of the war, I saw a case of a poor man who had been convinced that his wife was a German soldier. When he came back from the front he attacked her—he came at her with a hammer—and as a result he had to be taken into hospital. After he'd come round from sedation, he had no memory of the incident. Luckily, the wife survived the attack, but of course the gentleman had to be locked away."

"So she's . . . ?" asked Cynthia.

"Mad, yes," said McRae, finishing the sentence for her. "I always said she was unstable. But now it seems as though she might be dangerous." Gertrude Bell had used the same word to describe Katharine Woolley.

"What are you saying?" Cynthia asked, clearly frightened now.

"I'm just wondering whether . . . whether it's safe to be here, in the middle of nowhere," answered McRae. "Who knows what she might do? I'm not concerned for my safety so much—I'm sure I can defend myself against a woman—but for those less able to protect themselves. We've got women to think of—girls like Sarah. And then there's Cecil."

"You don't need to worry about me," said Cecil, finishing off his toast and brandishing a knife. There was something unpleasant in the way in which he smiled as he did this. "I can look after myself."

"I think it's far too early to jump to any such conclusions," I said, trying to calm everyone. "After all, we don't know exactly what happened. I'm going to try and speak to Mrs. Woolley again today. Perhaps we'll know more after that."

Father Burrows stood up from the table and started to clear away his breakfast things. "Perhaps the woman needs some religious guidance," he said. "I could talk to her if you think it would help."

"Yes, I think that's a very good idea," I said.

"What utter tosh, Eric!" exclaimed McRae. "I don't think that's going to make much difference. I don't know if you've noticed, but God is no longer with us, if he was ever with us at all."

"McRae, really, I think that's taking things too far," said Burrows.

"Let's all try and keep our heads here," said Miller.

"Yes, I'm sure there's a perfectly good explanation for what happened," said Cynthia. "Perhaps Tom was already ill or injured and Mrs. Woolley had to put him out of his misery."

"That sounds most unlikely," said McRae, checking the pot on the table for coffee. "Where's that servant boy? Why can't he—" He stopped, as if something had just occurred to him. "Now I think of it, what was that story I heard? About Mrs. Woolley. Yes, it was something to do with her time during or shortly after the war. Now, who told me about it? I can't remember now, but it may have some bearing on this."

"What do you mean?" asked Miller. "What story?"

"Something to do with the death of her first husband," said

McRae with fire in his eyes. "Yes, that's right, it was about a servant in Cairo. You see, the servant discovered something about Katharine—I don't know what it was—and he threatened to tell her husband. What was the husband's name?"

"Keeling, I think," said Cynthia.

"Yes, that's right, a Colonel Keeling. The next thing, Keeling is found dead at the base of the Cheops pyramid, apparently having shot himself. But it doesn't take a genius to work out what really happened."

"What really happened?" I asked.

"It's obvious, isn't it," said McRae. "Katharine shot him and made it look like a suicide. And if she can do that once, it's my opinion she can do it again. Wouldn't you say that's true, Mrs. Christie? What do they say in works of detective fiction? Murder is a habit?"

"Well, I—"

"That's all hypothesis and conjecture," said Miller. "I mean, do you know that for sure?"

"That Colonel Keeling died?" said McRae, enjoying the attention. "That he shot himself? Of course. That's a statement of fact."

"No—that other thing you said," Miller clarified. "That Mrs. Woolley killed her own husband. You said it was a story, something someone told you."

"Yes, but—"

"But nothing," said Miller, walking up to McRae with an aggressive swagger. "I want to know who told you this."

"I don't know. I can't remember. But I'm sure it was someone—"

"I thought better of you, McRae, I really did," said Miller, stopping a couple of inches away from the architect's face and looking at him with disgust. "Unless you've got concrete proof of Mrs. Woolley's guilt in the matter, then—"

His words were cut off by the entrance of Leonard Woolley into the room. "Mrs. Woolley's guilt in what matter, Mr. Miller?" The room fell silent. "I'm sorry, I seem to have interrupted the flow of your conversation. Please carry on."

"We were just talking about Mrs. Woolley and Tom, the cat," said Miller, thinking quickly. "Whether she was responsible for . . . for . . ."

"For its death?" asked Woolley coolly.

"Well, yes," Miller replied.

Woolley appraised the group, casting his eye over each of us in turn. Had he been standing at the door for long? What exactly had he heard?

"Really, all this fuss over the death of a stray cat," he said, laughing. "It's really quite ridiculous."

"But if she did kill Tom, then how are we—" said McRae.

Woolley cut him off quickly. "Let me stop the rumors and the speculation right now," he announced. "My wife didn't kill the cat. I did."

The confession sent ripples of confusion through the room. "If you'll just let me explain," he said, holding up his hand. "You see, Tom had not been quite himself for some time. I'm sure most of you had noticed it. He'd become increasingly bad-tempered. He wouldn't let anybody pick him up or stroke him even at the best of times. But last night, when Katharine tried to stroke him, he went for her and injured her badly. You saw for yourself the marks on her arms. And so I did the kindest thing possible: I put him to sleep."

"I don't understand . . . ," said Cynthia, her face the color of ash. "Sorry, I—"

"I think what Miss Jones is trying to say is: Why did you let Mrs. Woolley find him like that?" I asked. "Why didn't you tell her what you'd done?"

"I did," said Woolley, looking taken aback that I had dared to question him in this way. "But I think Katharine didn't want to face up to the truth. She adored that cat. But she knew that as soon as it attacked her, then it would have to be put down. I told her last night, before dinner, but she pretended not to hear or understand what I was saying."

This version of events did not correspond with what Woolley had told me only the night before, and I suspected this story to be a lie designed to protect his wife. "But to leave the cat there on the bed like that for Mrs. Woolley to find," I asked. "Was that not terribly cruel?"

"Again, Mrs. Christie, that's not quite how it happened," replied Woolley. "After the cat was dead, I covered it in some sackcloth and moved it into one of the storage rooms. I thought I would dispose of its body the next day. But Katharine must have found it and brought it back into her bedroom. She told me she couldn't bear to live without it—even after what it had done to her."

Each of us stared at Woolley, none of us quite sure about what to say in response to his bizarre explanation. Finally it was Harry Miller who walked over to Woolley and shook his hand.

"I wasn't here to witness any of this, but by the sound of it, you handled a difficult situation well," he said.

"I wouldn't say that exactly," replied Woolley. "I really should have told you all about it last night, but Katharine was in such a state, I wasn't sure how to deal with it. Anyway, I apologize for any upset I caused."

I had some questions that I still wanted to put to Mr. Woolley. Cynthia Jones too looked confused, while McRae seemed possessed by a mix of embarrassment and anger.

"Now, do you think we can get on with some work," said Woolley. It was not so much a question as a statement. "Burrows? What's the latest on the inscription of that damaged cuneiform tablet that you've been studying? Can you read any fragments of it yet? McRae, I'd like to take a look over the latest batch of drawings, if you don't mind. Miller, I'm interested in looking again at those photographs of the two sets of gold and lapis lazuli beads, if that's not too much trouble. And, Miss Jones, I need to send a memo to the directors of the museum in Philadelphia." It was clearly business as usual for Woolley, and soon the director of the expedition had restored, for the moment at least, a sense of order and confidence in his team.

I slipped away and gently knocked on Katharine's door.

"Come in," she said.

I entered to find her sitting up in bed, the shutters to the windows still closed. When she saw me she smiled awkwardly; it was clear from her expression that she regretted the scene that she had caused the previous night.

"How are you feeling?" I asked.

"A little tired," she said.

"That's only to be expected," I said as I came to stand near the bed.

"Agatha, I'm terribly sorry about what happened," she said, gesturing for me to sit down next to her. "You must think me such a fool, and as for the rest of the team . . . I know how they view me, how I must come across. I can hardly bear to show my face today."

I needed to find out the truth about the cat. "Don't distress yourself further," I said. "It was obviously very upsetting for you. I think everyone understands what must have happened."

She looked blankly at me. "What do you mean?"

"Leonard explained everything," I said, giving her a kind smile. "About how he had put the cat down."

There was a long silence during which time I began to feel more and more unnerved.

"Leonard didn't kill Tom," Katharine said finally.

"But he just came in and told everyone how—"

"Yes, about how Tom had turned on me and how he discovered me covered in scratches? That was just a story Leonard made up to try and protect me."

So I had been right. Automatically I shifted my position to sit a little farther away from her on the bed. Katharine noticed that and also the subtle change in my eyes. I tried not to look afraid, but the more I concentrated, certainly the more frightened I appeared.

"It's not what you think," she whispered.

"But if your husband didn't kill the cat, then who did?"

There was a pause before she asked, "Do you think I did it?" There was a coldness to her voice now. "Is that what you think I'm capable of?"

"I'm just trying to make some sense of what happened," I replied.

She studied me as if I were an object, a lifeless piece of sculpture in a gallery or a mannequin in a shop window.

"I had higher hopes of you," she said at last. "From reading your books, I thought you would be cleverer than this."

"I'm sorry, Katharine, I don't understand what it is you're trying to say."

She took a deep breath as if she were a teacher in the presence of a particularly stupid child.

"So you're saying Leonard didn't kill Tom?" I asked.

"Yes, that's right. And I know I didn't kill him either."

"You didn't? But what about the scratches on your arms?"

"I can't explain those."

Was Katharine to be believed? Was this just a game she was playing?

"Don't you see someone else is behind all of this?"

"Someone else? Who?"

"I don't know," she said, looking around the room as if there might be someone hidden in one of the corners. "I've seen things. Heard things." Was she in the grip of another horrible delusion? "I can't explain."

"Perhaps you need another sedative," I asked, but I was wary of giving her more. After all, she couldn't spend her life on the drugs.

"No, I need to keep my wits about me," she said, panicking. "What if someone wants to kill me? Or they might try to murder Leonard."

"You're scaring me now, Katharine," I said. "Why would anyone want to do that?"

"I don't know; it's just a feeling I've got," she said. "I know you don't believe me," she snapped, looking at me with resentment in her eyes. "You may as well go."

"I'm not going to leave you until I understand what it is you are afraid of," I replied. "Because I can see that you are frightened. Very frightened indeed. I know—let's have some tea."

"It won't have a sedative in it?" she asked, her voice rising. "Please, I told you: I can't afford to go to sleep."

"No, I promise. Nothing but good English tea."

"Very well." She nodded.

I called the servant boy, and as we waited for the tea to come, we talked of other matters, such as the weather, the shifting nature of the desert sands, the social scene in Baghdad, and, finally, the things the Woolleys missed about England.

"Do you have any family back at home?" I asked as I poured the tea. There was no response. "Someone mentioned to me that you were married before. Is that right?"

"Who told you that?" she asked with an accusatory look.

"I think it might have been your husband," I said.

"Why were you talking about that? What's that got to do with you?"

"I know it was quite presumptuous of me, but I was asking Mr. Woolley about you, the state of your health, your headaches and so on, and he must have mentioned it. I'm sorry if I've offended you in some way."

Katharine fell silent. "Yes, I was married," she said finally. "It didn't last long."

"I'm sorry to hear that," I said, then told her a little of the breakdown of my own marriage and my recent divorce. I explained how my husband had left me for a younger woman. "You see, I've had rather a hellish time of late," I concluded.

Something akin to pity came into Katharine's eyes, and she began to warm to me again. "That does sound most unpleasant," she said. "What a beast of a man."

"No, not a beast," I replied. "Just utterly, utterly selfish."

"At least with Bertie I never had to worry about that sort of thing," she said.

"Was that your first husband? Bertie?"

"Yes, and he was devoted to me," she said.

I didn't ask the next question that sprang to mind, but instead I let her tell me something of the history of their marriage.

"He was always a very sensitive man, and I think he was left disturbed by the things he had seen in the war. Who wouldn't be? He was in the Royal Engineers, and so terribly brave. He was wounded in France in 1916 and sent home, but then returned the following year. He was at the Somme and the Battle of Cambrai, and survived both."

"He sounds like an extraordinary man," I said. I noticed she said nothing about the intelligence work Davison told me Keeling had done. Perhaps she had not known about that, or was she keeping something secret?

"He was so very clever: he loved the stars, astronomy, and mapping and lots of technical things, triangulation and things like that. Did a lot of work in Egypt, which he loved. He'd just got this new job in Cairo when . . ." Her voice faltered. "When he fell ill and died."

"I'm so terribly sorry," I said. "Did he require a lot of nursing at the end?"

"No, his death was rather . . . sudden," she said, taking a deep breath. "I suppose you may as well know: Bertie took his own life."

"Oh, my," I said, pretending to be shocked.

I watched her closely as she related the sad story to me: how she had said goodbye to her husband one morning as he left their home in Cairo for his position as the director-general of the survey of Egypt. The next thing she knew was that an official arrived bearing the bad news that her husband had died. It seemed that the colonel had shot himself. She did not appear to be lying. In fact, it seemed as though her emotions were genuine. However, I knew that people who worked in intelligence, like some murderers, possessed that frightening ability to lie so convincingly that even trained observers were taken in. Perhaps Mrs. Woolley was both things: a spy and a killer.

"But why did he do it? Were there any signs?"

"Not that I could see," she said, blinking. There was something incomplete about her answer, as if she was holding something back.

"I'm sorry I have to ask you this, Katharine," I said gently, "but did you see his body?"

"But why do you ask that?" She looked at me with deep suspicion. "I don't understand. What do you suspect me of? What have you heard?"

"I wondered whether you had actually identified him?"

"No. The head of the police in Cairo told me that it would be too distressing for me," she said, with tears in her eyes. "Even though I didn't see him, I could just imagine the scene . . . the blood, the—"

"Let's not think of that," I said. "It's my fault for asking. I'm terribly sorry."

She got out of bed, opened a shutter of one of the windows, and looked out. "I've seen things out of this window," she said, straining her neck, patterned by red blotches, and peering upwards. "Faces. Horrible faces."

"Please calm down," I said. "I didn't want to upset you."

"Why did you ask about Bertie?" she asked, turning away from the window and walking towards me. "What do you know? And why did you ask all those questions about his body?" She blinked, and the expression on her face changed, as if she had just realized some awful truth. "Oh, no, please God, no."

"Katharine—what is it? You've thought of something, haven't you? What's occurred to you?"

"No, it couldn't be—it can't be true."

"Tell me. What can't be true?"

She was shaking now. "What . . . what if Bertie isn't dead?"

"What do you mean?"

"You asked whether I had seen his body. I hadn't. I believed the police who told me that Bertie had died—that he had shot himself."

"But surely there was a death certificate. You had that?"

"Yes, but Bertie could have substituted a body to try and fake his own death."

This was like something I might dream up for a plot in one of my own books. "That couldn't be possible, could it?"

"All he needed to do was find a victim, shoot the poor man in the face so he was unrecognizable, dress him in his clothes, substitute his identity papers for the victim's, and then disappear."

"But why would your husband do that?"

She stared at me with eyes full of terror. "A week or so before he died, we had an argument. A terrible row. Awful things were said on both sides, and I confess I expressed certain sentiments I now regret. But during that brutal argument he said something to me. He said, with a cold tone of voice I'll always remember, 'I could kill you. You know, one day I may just do that.' "

10

The next few days passed without incident. Katharine locked herself in her room, convinced that her first husband was still alive and that he might want to kill her. Woolley told the rest of the group that his wife was suffering from one of her headaches, and although it seemed that most people believed his story about the cat, an air of suspicion still hung over Katharine. Lawrence McRae continued to feel a certain level of antipathy towards her and, while Woolley wasn't looking, did everything in his power to turn others against her.

I wrote to Davison in Baghdad asking him to find out more about Colonel Keeling's past and who had identified his body. I also wanted him to dig out reports of other deaths of men of a similar age in September 1919. I kept Davison up to date about the events at Ur—adding a number of character sketches—and voiced some of my own suspicions. Was Keeling still alive? Could that really be possible? Had he taken over the identity of the man he had killed and dressed in his own clothes? Even if that was true—and it sounded so unlikely—that did not explain what had happened to Gertrude Bell. I had to remember that I was here to find out who had killed her, and so far I was no nearer the truth. Had Katharine sent those letters to Miss Bell? But if she had, why would she go to the trouble of telling Gertrude Bell that her future murderer was based at Ur?

Or had Colonel Keeling sent the letters in order to cast suspicion on his wife?

I told Davison that there was no need for him to venture south to Ur just yet; his presence, or that of another official, would only raise more questions. After all, no crime had yet been committed here save that of the suspicious death of a cat. There was something about the demise of that ginger tom that unsettled me, but I couldn't quite put my finger on it. Had Woolley killed it so as to try and drive his wife insane? Was he subjecting her to a subtle form of psychological torture?

It was no surprise that, after the events of the last few days, an air of melancholy descended over the expedition. Despite the best efforts of the seemingly eternally cheerful Harry Miller and the youthful exuberance of Sarah Archer, the group's spirits could not be raised. Breakfast was mostly a silent affair, while the evenings seemed to stretch on for eternity, with endless conversations about cuneiform tablets, the minutiae of the archaeological process, and the lineage of Abraham. Finally, one night, after a particularly depressing dinner, Woolley declared that, as he knew it would soon be Miss Archer's birthday—she would be twenty-one on the following Saturday—he thought it would be a good idea to celebrate it with a picnic at the top of the ziggurat.

"What a swell idea," said Miller, slapping Woolley on the shoulder. "We could all do with something to look forward to."

"Thank you, Mr. Woolley," said Sarah. "I was beginning to wonder how long you British could carry on with your long faces."

"Now, don't be rude, dear," said Ruth Archer, giving Woolley an apologetic smile. "What would your father say if he heard you?" Luckily for Sarah, Hubert Archer had stepped outside with Father Burrows for some night air.

"No, Sarah is quite right," replied Woolley. "We've been down in the dumps for too long. It should be a jolly event. Your father has given his approval, and I've started planning it with the chef and the servants already. There will be food, a nice fruit punch for those of us who partake, and a fresh lemonade with mint too for Mr. and Mrs. Archer and you, Mrs. Christie."

"And will Mrs. Woolley grace us with her presence?" asked McRae, barely trying to disguise the sarcasm in his voice.

"I've yet to hear from Katharine on that point," said Woolley. "As you know, she has not been quite herself since Tom died. But I hope she will come; she needs cheering up, as do we all. This will give us an opportunity to put that unpleasantness behind us. Then we can go into the season with a renewed vigor."

* * *

On the Saturday of the picnic, Woolley announced that Katharine was feeling a great deal better and had decided that she would, after all, join us on the outing. On hearing this news I went and knocked on her door.

"Come in!" she called from inside.

I opened the door and stepped into what seemed like a different room to the one I had seen a few days before. Mrs. Woolley had thrown open the shutters and light streamed in, bathing everything in a delicate yellow glow. She had taken the trouble to order her desk: there was no sign of the papers that she had been working on. The floor appeared to have been swept, the clothes that had previously spilled out of the wardrobe had been tidied away, and the pots that had cluttered her dressing table had been arranged neatly. Like the room itself, Katharine appeared to have tidied herself up. She had washed and brushed her hair, her neck seemed free of the blotches that had plagued her complexion, and she was dressed in a striking lavender blouse, skirt, and jacket, with shoes, gloves, and a hat to match.

"Isn't it a beautiful day?" she said brightly, taking a gray silk scarf from the wardrobe and tying it lightly around her neck. As she did so, I noticed that she had painted her nails a vibrant red color and was wearing an elegant gold dress watch.

"Yes, it is," I replied. "And you're looking a great deal better."

"I thought it was about time I faced the world again," she said.

"I'm very pleased to hear that."

Katharine walked over to the window and looked out. "I can't imprison myself in here any longer. And I refuse to continue to be afraid. I told Leonard about my fears regarding my first husband and he convinced me that I had nothing to worry about. In fact, looking back, I'm sorry I said such silly things to you. I don't know what came over me."

"It was understandable after—"

"After what happened with Tom. Yes, I remember now Leonard telling me about what he had done. Yes, the cat did scratch me and my husband took it away to put it down." There was something artificial about her delivery, as if she were reading an over-rehearsed script. "Best, really. One cannot have an animal like that around. Leonard did me, and everyone else, a favor."

I knew she was not telling the truth but I decided not to voice my suspicions, as I didn't want Katharine to suffer another relapse.

"And as regards my own safety," she continued, "as Leonard said to me this morning, what can happen to me? I'm going to be surrounded by him and the other men, you, all my friends on the dig. Then there are the servants. I've nothing to worry about at all." She said this as if she were trying to convince herself. "After being cooped up in here for days, I can't tell you how much I am looking forward to the picnic, even though Sarah Archer is not exactly my favorite person."

"Yes, I don't quite understand her," I said.

"Oh, good. I was worrying that she and you might become as thick as thieves."

"No, not at all. She's very young," I said. "And also, she's too rich."

"Too rich? Surely no one can be too rich."

"You know what I mean," I said, smiling. "She's got different values, different ideas about the way life should be. All that money—imagine! And she told me that she will be soon be very rich in her own right. Independently wealthy, quite apart from her father."

"I know. Aren't some people lucky?" Katharine said. "That's not to say I have any regrets in marrying a poor archaeologist. There are other benefits, it must be said."

I recalled the conversation I had had with her husband. The couple, or so Woolley had told me, had never been intimate. Perhaps Katharine was referring to the simple joys of companionship; that was, I knew, enough for many people. It would have been enough for me, but never for Archie. During the dark days leading up to my divorce, I had even suggested that Archie continue his relationship with Miss Neele as long as he remained married—in name only, of course—to me. Thank goodness Archie had had the good sense to reject such a proposal.

"Oh, please don't say anything about my aversion to Sarah," pleaded Katharine, suddenly realizing the implication of what she had said. "If it got back to her or her father, the Archers might think twice about pledging their financial support. And Leonard would be furious with me."

"I'll keep it just between the two of us," I assured her.

"Anyway, I must get going," she said. "I promised Leonard I would supervise the picnic. I don't know why he suggested to the Archers that we have it at the top of the ziggurat. What's wrong with the courtyard? Anyway, it's done now. But it does mean an awful lot more work."

Katharine was not exaggerating. The chef had to draft in extra help from his sons, and throughout the day Leonard had even been forced to requisition some of the Arabs from the dig to carry things from the house up to the top of the ziggurat. As was their custom, they sang as they worked, that strange sound that was not so much a song as a monotonous chant. However, by four o'clock they had erected various tents, a couple of tables, and a selection of chairs, cushions, and rugs, and an hour later they finished bringing all the supplies of food and drink to the top of the ziggurat. We left the house all together in a group, and to outsiders it would have appeared as though none of us had a care in the world. The conversation was superficially light, and a delicious sense of anticipation hung in the desert air. Harry Miller took snaps of us all as we walked—he said he wanted to give a selection of the resulting photographs to Sarah Archer as a birthday present—and he made us smile and laugh with his seemingly endless supply of jokes.

"Do you know why photographers can be so nasty?" he asked, a mischievous sparkle in his eyes.

"Nasty? I don't know. Why?" asked Sarah, twirling her parasol around in her hands.

"You really can't work it out?" teased Harry.

The girl shook her head. Clearly there was a spark between them, something that both McRae and his nephew pretended not to be bothered about.

"Well, here we go. First we frame you, then we shoot you, and finally . . . we hang you on the wall."

"That's a terrible joke!" said Sarah, laughing.

"It amused you, though," said Harry. "You can't deny that."

"Only because it was so awful," she replied.

It did not amuse me, however. I also noticed that it failed to raise a smile from Leonard Woolley. Perhaps he was too worried about the smooth running of the picnic, and as we walked he busied himself with last-minute arrangements, talking to various Arab servants in snatches of conversation I did not understand. I could not fail to be impressed by the sound of the language—rich guttural tones that seemed to be wrenched up from the very back of the throat—but there was something quite alien and unnerving about it, too.

By the time we had reached the top of the ziggurat, climbing steadily up one of the three staircases that led to the pinnacle, we were all out of breath. However, we were met by a glorious sight: a series of tents had been erected in one corner of the enormous plateau and a number of servants were ready with trays of drinks. The lemonade was tart but delightfully refreshing, while the fruit punch was, according to those who sampled it, both delicious and quite potent.

"Just think, Sarah, you could be celebrating your twenty-first birthday in one of the best restaurants in Paris, London, or New York," said Ruth Archer, "and here you are at the top of an ancient temple in the middle of a desert. Who would have thought it?"

"I couldn't think of anything nicer," said Sarah, flashing a smile first at Miller and then at McRae. The girl—who was out of earshot of her father—was playing a very dangerous game with this flirtation. Ruth cast a concerned look at her daughter and tried to engage her in conversation with Miss Jones, but the girl's eyes kept returning to the two men. She never once looked at poor Cecil, who stood by himself in a corner of the tent with a brooding expression on his face and a large glass of punch in his hand.

"Don't you think this is just splendid?" asked Katharine, coming up to me.

"Yes, it was a lovely idea," I said.

"I feel so much better," she said. "How could one not, standing up here, with this view?"

I looked across the desert plain, the setting sun turning the sands the color of blood. The sound of Sarah's laughter drifted across the ziggurat. She had made her way over to talk to Miller, who said he wanted to take some photographs of her standing at the edge of the ancient structure.

"Be careful, Sarah," said Ruth. "There's a terribly long drop there."

"Don't worry, Mrs. Archer," said Miller. "She's in safe hands."

Sarah changed her pose with each click of Miller's camera, clearly enjoying the attention from her fellow American. As she kicked her heels she dislodged a few small stones, sending them over the edge of the ziggurat. Her black net dress, embroidered with chenille, made the near-translucent whiteness of her skin stand out, giving her the look of a ghost.

"I'd really like to have a suntan," she was telling Miller, "as it's the fashion now on the Riviera. But Daddy would be furious."

"Well, I think you look swell just the way you are," replied the photographer.

"In fact, he would not be at all pleased by some of these pictures," said Sarah. "He can be such a prude at times. By the way, Mommy, where is he?"

"Father Burrows is showing him some inscriptions on one of the temple walls," said Ruth. "And you're right, your father would most definitely not approve. So I'd make it quick if I were you, Mr. Miller."

Although Woolley was trying to persuade people to sit, as the food was ready, Sarah Archer and Harry Miller were reluctant to move away from the precipice. Harry asked Sarah to turn her back to him so he could photograph her silhouette set against the sky.

"Just look at this light!" exclaimed Miller. "The shadows are something else."

McRae mumbled something to Cecil and both of them glared in the direction of the photographer. As Sarah pirouetted around, she caught sight of her father approaching and signaled to Miller to stop.

"I get the message," said Harry Miller. "But I think we got something special there."

The two walked over and took their seats under the tent as the servants began to plate out the food. The group fell silent as we began to eat a thick tomato stew made with meat which I think was lamb but may have been goat. Woolley took out a bottle of wine and offered it to the group.

"Yes, I think I would like a glass of that too, if you don't mind," said Katharine.

"Do you think that's a good idea, my dear?" asked Leonard. "After all . . ."

"What?" said Katharine under her breath.

"Just that it may not be wise, that's all," he said gently, trying to prevent the conversation from escalating into a row.

"I think it will do me a world of good—just like this party," said Katharine, holding out a glass.

Husband and wife locked eyes, and finally, after a few moments, a defeated Leonard poured out the wine for Katharine.

"Thank you," she said.

Miller, glass in hand, stood up and proposed a toast to both Mr. and Mrs. Woolley for hosting the picnic and to Sarah Archer to wish her happy birthday. We all sang along, and even Lawrence and Cecil McRae roused themselves from their black humor and joined in.

"Thank you," said Sarah, coming to sit by me. "I can't believe I'm twenty-one."

I thought of myself at that age. What had I achieved by then? Absolutely nothing of consequence. "And what do you have planned when you return to America?" I asked. "I suppose you must have a great many suitors waiting for you at home."

"There are some young men who have been picked out for me as being eminently suitable, yes," she said. She cast a flirtatious glance over at Harry Miller. "But whether or not I will accept them is another matter."

As the servants lit a series of long torches, enclosing the group within a circle of fire, Sarah began to tell the story of how, aged eighteen, she had endured a proposal from a man she considered old enough to be her father. Mr. Adams, the man in question—whom she regarded as really quite ugly—had taken great pride in outlining what he thought were his considerable financial resources. Sarah had sat and listened patiently to his list of assets: his properties scattered across New York and Philadelphia, his portfolio of stocks and share certificates, his savings and investments. "So you see, Miss Archer, it would be greatly in your interest if you were to accept me," proclaimed Mr. Adams, "as I can offer you a personal sum in excess of two hundred thousand dollars." She told everyone how she had made a pretense of amazement, thanked him for his offer, and told him that, as she would only have five hundred thousand to her name, she was sure that he would find her too poor for his consideration. "Also, I fear that you are too handsome for me, sir," she added with extra spite.

Although the group laughed at the story and her punch line, I thought Sarah's comment to be ill-judged. Her aspiring suitor had been crass, yes, but that did not—in my opinion—permit her to be so cruel. It was obvious that her father thought so, too.

"You don't do yourself any favors by telling that story," said Mr. Archer. "In fact, it's not at all Christian of you."

"Papa, you know as well as I do that Mr. Adams would have been wrong for me."

"That may be so, but—"

"I think you should listen to your father," said Katharine, interrupting the girl.

Sarah looked astonished that someone outside her family had dared to contradict her. "Excuse me, I didn't quite hear what you said."

She was giving Katharine the chance to retract her comment, but it was obvious from what Mrs. Woolley said next that she had no intention of doing so.

"I think at times it is wise to listen to those who know better," said Katharine. "Those with a little more experience of life."

Sarah Archer looked around at the startled expressions of some of those in the group and, emboldened by what she took to be support, placed her fork back on her china plate and said, "And those who think they know better should sometimes keep their own counsel."

Katharine's eyes burnt with a dark fury. Leonard reached over and placed a hand on his wife's arm, but she brushed it off.

"In fact, the kind of advice I get from people never ceases to amaze me," continued Sarah, pausing for full effect, "especially from those who are not quite all there."

"How dare you," said Katharine, standing up.

"Sarah!" hissed Mr. Archer.

"What? I'm only voicing what we all think, aren't I?" She looked around for someone to try and back her up. "Or am I the only one brave enough to say the unsayable?" She turned to Katharine and addressed her directly. "Very well. Here goes. The truth is everyone thinks you're cracked. That you're crazy. Unhinged. There are plenty of words to choose from—take your pick."

Mr. Archer took hold of his daughter's wrist in an effort to stop her. "What's gotten into you today, Sarah? I know it's your birthday, but there is no need to—"

"There's every need!" said Sarah, her voice rising. "We've all been pussyfooting around, pretending everything is fine, when we're living with—I'm sorry to say this—a madwoman. Someone who could be dangerous. After what happened to that poor cat . . ."

"But Mr. Woolley explained what happened to Tom," said Cynthia Jones. "That he had to put him down."

"It was obvious he was just covering up for her," said Sarah. "Weren't you, Mr. Woolley?"

Leonard, who looked mortified by the scene playing out before him, did not answer. How could he?

"Are you going to stand there and let this girl talk to me in this way?" Katharine asked her husband. "Leonard?"

"I—I think it would be best if—"

"Yes, it would be best if Miss Archer here found it in her soul to behave in a more Christian-like way," said Katharine. "But perhaps her parents were more interested in studying the good book than in instilling some basic good manners."

"Excuse me," said Mr. Archer, reddening in the face. "I really don't think that is called for."

"Now, Katharine, why don't we all try and calm down," said Woolley.

"Well, this sure is a birthday I'll remember," said Sarah as she flung down her napkin. Before anyone could stop her, she took a torch from one of the servants and dashed from the tent, across the ziggurat's plateau, and into the darkness.

"Sarah!" shouted her father. "Don't be a fool, now. Come back. It's pitch-black out there."

"Yes, the sun does seem to just drop out of the sky," said Woolley. "Don't worry, I'll go after her."

"I'll come with you," said Miller. "If we use the light from her torch to guide us, we should be able to catch up."

"So will I," said McRae, who was followed a few minutes later by his nephew.

"Honestly, what a ridiculous scene," said Katharine to the rest of us sitting in the tent. She seemed completely oblivious to the part she had played in the drama. "Had the girl been drinking on the sly, do you think?" she said to me so the Archers couldn't hear. "I know her father said the family didn't touch alcohol, but I wouldn't be at all surprised if she'd had some of that fruit punch. The men did say it was awfully strong. What else could have caused such an outburst?"

"Birthdays can often lead to tension," I said diplomatically. The real issue was, of course, the rivalry that existed between the two women. It was clear that Katharine was jealous of the attention Sarah had been receiving from both Harry Miller and Lawrence McRae. And, like a younger sibling who resents the flow of birthday gifts to an elder brother or sister, she had been determined ruin the day for her. Unfortunately, Sarah was not the kind of person to be silenced, and she had struck back with a vicious verbal blow.

"Well, I think it's time we got back to the camp," said Mr. Archer, somewhat stiffly. "And then tomorrow we can think about leaving."

"Leaving?" said Katharine. "What do you mean?"

"Well, you don't expect us to hang around here and let ourselves be insulted, do you?" he said.

"But what about—"

"And of course the additional money I talked to your husband about is quite out of the question now. Come on, Ruth." Mr. Archer signaled for two servants holding torches to accompany him and his wife down from the ziggurat. "We've got an early start tomorrow."

"Please, I know I may have spoken out of turn, but . . . ," Katharine said as the Archers disappeared into the night. "Oh, dear," she added, turning to me. "What will Leonard do when he finds out? He was depending on the Archers' money. He had so many plans."

"I'm sure Mr. Woolley will find another rich donor willing to sponsor the expedition," I said. "After all, the project has had so much publicity."

"Leonard would kill me if they withdrew their support now," said Katharine. "No, I'm going to go after them and see if I can change their minds." She too took a torch and ran across the plateau with a plea for the Archers to stop.

"If you and Father Burrows are happy to make your own way down, I'll go with her and make sure she doesn't come to any harm," Cynthia said to me.

"Yes, good idea," said Father Burrows. He called for the remaining servant men to provide us with some more light and ordered them to clear up as best they could; if they took the food and drink back down to the house that night, then they could dismantle the tents the following day. "Well, I'm sorry you had to witness that, Mrs. Christie."

"Yes, it was most unfortunate," I said. "But I suppose Mrs. Woolley could not endure it for much longer."

"Endure what?"

"The behavior from that silly girl."

Father Burrows looked at me blankly. "What on earth do you mean?"

"Didn't you notice the way Sarah was flirting with those two men, one minute with Mr. Miller and the next with Mr. McRae? And then there was that awful thing she had said to poor Cecil."

"What thing?"

I related what I had overheard that day I had first arrived: how Sarah Archer had told Cecil that he was ugly and stupid and that he should never talk to her.

"It seems as though you've got it all worked out," he said. "But perhaps I've deliberately made myself blind to such things. Only way if one wants to cope out here."

"Yes, I can imagine you're right on that score," I replied as I took Father Burrows's arm and two servants, holding torches, led us across the plateau towards the ziggurat's staircases. The sky was covered by a blanket of cloud, eclipsing the stars and the moon, and although it was not yet cold I nevertheless felt a chill at the back of my neck. Just as I pulled my shawl around my shoulders a scream split the night air. Was it the noise of the animal I had heard when Woolley had taken me up to the ziggurat that first day? No, this was unmistakably a human cry, the cry of a woman.

"What on earth . . . ?" said Father Burrows.

"I think that's Mrs. Woolley," I said.

Father Burrows pressed the servants—who were wide-eyed with fear—to accompany us as fast as possible down one of the staircases to the source of the cries.

"Quickly," I said. "Each moment of delay could make all the difference." But Father Burrows, for all his slim form, was unsteady on his feet, and as we rushed he tripped a few times, nearly dragging me down with him. "Please, let me go on ahead," I said. "Can you ask one of the servants to accompany me and also to let me have a torch of my own?"

He looked dumbly at me. "Please, Father Burrows," I pleaded. "It could be a matter of life or death." Fighting to regain his breath, he gave the appropriate orders in halting Arabic and I hastened down the stone steps of the ziggurat, the flames from my torch casting a series of grotesque shadows onto the ground. As I approached the bottom of the structure I heard cries of alarm and then the screams of another woman. I saw the backs of Lawrence McRae and Cynthia Jones, who were peering at something on the ground, and then Ruth Archer, lifeless as a rag doll, being supported by her husband.

"What's happened?" I asked, breathless from both the exercise and the fear that was rising within me.

Cecil appeared out of the darkness, his face white with shock, and pointed at something on the ground, a shape that seemed to be even darker than the black night. I stepped closer to see that there were in fact two figures: Katharine Woolley on her knees and a strange unnatural configuration before her on the ground.

"Don't look," said Lawrence McRae, trying to stop me. "It's not—"

I pushed past him. "It might not be too late," I said. "I was a nurse. Let me see if I can help."

I thrust the torch nearer to the scene before me. The glistening form illuminated by the flames was like something from an unholy nightmare. Katharine Woolley stared at her palms, covered in blood, as if her hands did not belong to her. In front of her, in the ancient sands, lay the lifeless body of Sarah Archer, the back of her skull crushed. Nearby lay a rock covered in blood. Without much hope of finding signs of life, I took her pulse, but there was nothing.

The noise of footsteps diverted our attention for a moment. Leonard Woolley and Harry Miller appeared out of the darkness. "We couldn't find her—she must have gone down one of the other staircases, but we saw some other—" said Miller, stopping himself as he took in the shocked expressions on all our faces.

Leonard Woolley stepped forwards and, as we parted to let him through, he saw for himself the horrors of the scene: his wife with her bloodied hands, Miss Archer's dead body . . .

"Oh, my God, Katharine," he whispered. "What have you done?"

11

There was a moment not so much of calm but of near silence, when no one spoke and it was possible to hear the cry of birds down towards the river and the whispers of the dry wind across the desert. Then everyone began to speak almost at once.

"Katharine . . . get up and come with me," said Woolley, stretching out his hand.

Ruth Archer looked up from her husband's shoulder and tried to break away from him. "What have you done to my daughter?" she asked, her voice full of rage. Luckily, Hubert Archer managed to restrain her, otherwise there was a danger she might try to scratch out Mrs. Woolley's eyes.

"Sarah! Surely she can't be . . . ," said Cynthia.

"I'm afraid it's too late," said McRae, checking Sarah's body.

"But . . . I don't understand," said Miller. "She had only been gone a minute. We were following her torch and then it disappeared from sight."

"It must have been a terrible accident," said Father Burrows. "She must have slipped and hit her head on a rock."

"Does that look like an accident to you, you damn fool?" said Hubert Archer. "Sorry for my language, but the evidence is right in front of us. We can see it with our eyes as plain as day."

The only person who did not speak was Cecil McRae, who had turned his back on the scene. His uncle went to place a hand on the boy's shoulder, but Cecil brushed it off and ran back towards the camp.

"It's understandable he's in shock," said Lawrence. "He worshiped that girl. As I'm sure many of us did."

Mrs. Woolley tried to stand, but as she did so she caught sight of her bloodied hands and fell back onto the sand. She opened her mouth to speak, but no words came out.

"Here, let me help," said Woolley. He took out a handkerchief from the top pocket of his jacket and offered it to his wife. But, still paralyzed by shock, she did not know what to do with it, and so let the white square simply drop to the ground. Woolley bent down beside his wife and supported her as she stood up.

"If a crime has been committed," said McRae, looking first at Mrs. Woolley and then at the body, "then nothing should be touched or removed."

"McRae's right: we need to get hold of the police," said Hubert Archer, fighting back tears. He was the kind of man who did not like to show signs of grief in public.

"Let's not jump to any conclusions," said Woolley.

"It's obvious what's happened," replied Archer. "How long does it take to call in the authorities here?"

"If we sent a servant now to the nearest town, there still wouldn't be anyone here before the morning," replied McRae.

Archer looked down at his daughter, the blood from her head collecting beneath her like a sinister, dark pool. "But we can't leave Sarah out here all night," he said. "No, we'll sit by her side, won't we, Ruth?"

His wife did not respond but continued to stare at Katharine Woolley with hatred in her eyes. Woolley gave orders to two servants to ride to Nasiriya, from where they would fetch a doctor and a policeman.

"I can't believe it," said Cynthia. "It seems so unreal."

"I'm sure there's some explanation for what happened," said Woolley.

"But you more or less admitted it yourself, man!" exclaimed Archer. " 'Oh, my God, Katharine—what have you done?' you said, unless I misheard you."

"Yes, but I'm sure it's just a case of—"

"Cold-blooded murder, yes," said Archer. "I don't think the authorities look kindly on killers out here, do they, Mr. Woolley? And I would advise that you lock up your wife tonight—just as much for her own safety as for the rest of us."

Woolley refused to be drawn into an argument and instead turned to practical matters. "I suggest all of us make our way back to the house. We need some strong, sweet tea or a spot of brandy. I'll send some over to you and your wife, Mr. Archer, together with a couple of camp beds and blankets. Obviously a couple of servants will stay with you all night. Then, in the morning, when the authorities arrive, we can try and make some sense of this."

Woolley led his wife away from the body, the rest of us trailing silently behind them. Back at the house, after making sure Katharine was safe in her bedroom, Leonard took me to one side and asked me to talk to her. "She's saying nothing to me," he said, carrying a chair and placing it outside his wife's door. "I'll sit on guard here all night. I'll make sure she doesn't get out—and that no one else gets in."

I knocked on the door, gently turned the handle, and stepped into the room. Katharine was standing at a wash bowl, scrubbing her hands with soap like a real-life Lady Macbeth. She stared down at her palms, which were now nearly clean of blood, but the water was a reddish-brown color. A cup of tea, untouched, sat on the dressing table.

"Here, let's get you into bed," I said. "You've had a nasty shock."

I helped undress Katharine and tied a silk dressing gown around her slender form. There was a deadness to her eyes, as if a part of her too had perished out there at the base of the ziggurat. Once I had managed to persuade her to get into bed, I fetched her a small glass of brandy and urged her to drink it.

"Now, that's better, isn't it?" I said as she sipped the dark liquid.

Slowly she turned her head to me, blinked, and said, "No, nothing will make it better." She brought up her hands to her face. "I can still smell the blood. It's seeped into me. I'll never be free of it."

I took her hands. "But you've almost rubbed them raw," I said. "Why don't you try to sleep and we can talk about this in the morning?"

"You're not going to leave me? Please don't leave me."

"No, I'll stay with you as long as you like," I said. "And Leonard has stationed himself outside your door, so you are quite safe."

"Do you still have those sedatives?" she asked.

"Yes, I do."

"I know I said I didn't want them, but now, after this . . . well . . . if I could just forget about it for a few hours?"

"Of course," I said. "I'll go and measure some out for you."

Outside the door I found Leonard playing the sentinel of sorts; he was sitting in a chair, a candle by his side, making some notes about the dig. When I told him of his wife's request, he looked concerned. "Will you be careful with the dose?"

"What do you mean?"

"Well, after tonight's terrible events, we don't want . . ."

His voice trailed off, but I understood his meaning. "You think Katharine might take an overdose?"

"Well, there is that possibility. After all, she's been under an awful lot of strain. What happened tonight could push her over the edge."

"I see. Can I ask you a question, Mr. Woolley?"

"Yes, of course," he said. We stepped away from the door and walked across the courtyard so that Katharine couldn't hear our conversation.

I looked Woolley straight in the face and asked, "Do you believe your wife was responsible for the death of Miss Archer?"

The question clearly pained him. "She's not that kind of woman: she abhors violence of any kind. I know what I said before, but . . ." He turned away from me, unable to finish the sentence. "No, I refuse to countenance any suggestion that she was responsible for this. It must have been a tragic accident."

"If you're so certain of that, why would you be worried about your wife taking an overdose?"

"I know her character. She's terribly high-strung, as you've seen for yourself. Her mental state has never been strong."

There would be time for more questions tomorrow. "Very well," I said. "Anyway, I must fetch that dose of sedative. A good sleep is what she needs. And don't worry, I'll be very careful how much I give her. Could you please order some tea for me? I find that's a good way of taking the drug."

I collected the barbiturate from my room, nodded to Woolley on my return, and entered Katharine's quarters again. As I prepared the sedative, Katharine, lying on her bed, studied my every move: the careful measurement of the dosage, the addition of the sedative to the tea, the gentle stirring action as I made sure the grains were evenly dispersed in the liquid. Then she started talking in a strange, trancelike fashion.

"How wonderful it would be just to forget everything," she whispered. "Just to go to sleep knowing that all one's worries had slipped away. Do you ever think that, Agatha?"

"I must admit I have on a number of occasions," I said. "Now, here's the sedative. If you drink this, it will help. It won't provide a permanent solution to your anxieties, but it will guarantee you a good night's sleep."

Katharine took the cup in her hands, and although the tea was hot, she gulped it down as if she was greedy for unconsciousness.

"I can't stop thinking of the blood—all that blood," she said as she laid her head back on the pillow. "I was rushing down the steps of the ziggurat, trying to find Mr. and Mrs. Archer, who must have taken one of the other stairways, when I slipped and fell. I could feel a warm stickiness on my hands, but I didn't know what it was at first. There was a torch on the ground, casting its sideways light onto . . . and then I realized what it was. Blood. And then I saw Sarah. I reached out to try and lift her to her feet, but it was no use. Then I saw that, where the back of her head should have been, there was . . ."

"That's enough. You've had a horrible shock. We all have. We can speak of it tomorrow."

The drug had started to have an effect. Her eyelids drooped and her breathing slowed.

"But then everyone gathered round," she said. "The things people said. Mr. and Mrs. Archer, Mr. McRae—Leonard, even. And the look in Cecil's eyes frightened me. They were all standing there, accusing me of killing Sarah." She paused as a horrific thought possessed her. "Maybe everyone is right. I know I was angry with her. I felt like putting my hands around her neck and strangling her until she was blue in the face. Perhaps it was me after all . . . Perhaps I am guilty of murder. But I don't remember doing it. Am I going mad?"

As Katharine's arm went limp I took the teacup from her hands and made sure that she was comfortable. She would sleep soundly for at least eight hours, I hoped. I watched her as her eyes closed, thinking over not only the events of the night but of the days since I had arrived in the camp. There was so much evidence that pointed to the fact that Katharine Woolley was, as Gertrude Bell had said, a truly dangerous woman. Although I knew she was not in Iraq at the time of Miss Bell's death, she could have sent the threatening letters and that drawing from England to an intermediary in Baghdad. Perhaps she was guilty of sending a poison pen letter but nothing more? But what of the suggestion that she had played some part in the death of her first husband? And what was I to make of the dreadful sensations and events since my arrival at Ur: of the awful atmosphere, the thick scent of suspicion that hung in the air, the demise of Katharine's cat, and then the horrible death of Sarah Archer? Yes, Katharine seemed to sit at the center of it all. And yet . . . there was something not right.

As I sat there gazing at Katharine's quietly beautiful face, I did not feel any fear. Despite what I had witnessed tonight—the sickening image of Sarah Archer with her skull smashed in, the sight of Katharine Woolley with the girl's blood smeared across her hands—I realized that I was not afraid of her. Mrs. Woolley probably suffered from some sort of mental illness, but my instinct told me that she was not a murderer.

I walked over to her desk and picked up the incomplete manuscript of Katharine's novel, which she had entitled *Adventure Calls.* I sat down and read for half an hour. It was a strange tale of a girl called Colin who disguised herself as her twin brother to undertake a dangerous secret service mission in Iraq during the early 1920s. It was an entertaining if unlikely story, but then I thought of some of my own novels and short stories, whose plots required leaps of the imagination, too. One paragraph from Katharine's manuscript, about the law of the desert, jumped out at me.

> In England, if a man is killed, the murderer is pursued by the far-stretched arm of the law; both the detection of crime and its punishment are the duty of the State alone. But tribal law is different. There the family of the murdered man takes upon itself the duty of pursuit and punishment, and the guilt extends from the murderer to every

> man of his house. There is no jury and no judge, only the avenging kinsman's bullet fired at the first member of the blood-guilty family caught unawares. The feud, a chain of murders, may be drawn out for generations, till the original crime is forgotten and the alternate slaughter goes on senselessly.

As I read this, Katharine's words sent a chill straight through me. What if she was playing an elaborate game? I had been taken in before by the surface sheen of appearances, and, despite my best efforts and past experience, I could certainly be deceived again. Of course, I knew that one should not use literary criticism as a form of detection. After all, how would I feel if strangers started looking into my novels and short stories for clues to my own inner life? Yet there was something about the words that Katharine had written that made me suspect she was drawing from something very close to home. My imagination started to turn over. Could Katharine be using the mask of insanity as a cover? Could she simply be pretending to be unhinged in order to carry out murders in cold blood? Was she enacting some perverse form of justice that she had dreamt up in her twisted mind, setting herself up as judge, jury, and executioner of people who had offended her? If not that, then what was her motive? Was there a pattern? I read the passage again, and one phrase in particular jumped out at me: "a chain of murders." I knew what she meant by that; after all, one death often sparked off others, like some awful kind of catalyst.

I feared that the death of Sarah Archer was not an isolated event. In fact, I had a terrible premonition that this was just the beginning of a cycle, one which could be long and bloody.

12

Katharine woke with a start, jolting me from my slumber. My neck was sore from the awkward angle at which I had been sleeping in a wicker chair by her bed.

"Sarah's head . . . something in the dark . . . all sticky," she said. "All covered in blood." She looked down at her hands, as if surprised to see that they were clean. She looked at me like a confused child. "What happened?"

"There was an accident with Miss Archer," I said. "What do you remember of it?"

After taking a few sips of water she began to tell me something of the incident. As she spoke I was conscious of not taking her word as the gospel truth. Her version of events would, I knew, have to be compared to the evidence gathered by the authorities. I assumed that, once the local police had been informed, the message would be relayed to the high commissioner in Baghdad and thence to Davison. I surmised that it would not be long before my friend arrived at Ur.

"I think I said something unfortunate, something that upset Mr. and Mrs. Archer," said Katharine. "They said they would be leaving—that they would be pulling their funding for the expedition. I wanted to explain, and so I ran after them. It was dark, but I followed their torches. But then I think I must have lost them. I saw another light and I started to walk after that, and as I came down the steps I heard what sounded like a girl's cry. I ran towards the noise. I couldn't make out what it was at first; I thought it was a doll, a life-size one, on the ground. But I realized it was Miss Archer. I think I collapsed, and as I reached out, that's when I felt something wet on my hands. I screamed, and the next thing I knew, I was surrounded by the rest of the group, all with horrified expressions on their faces. Then the accusations started. I think listening to those—hearing what people thought I was capable of—was worse than the discovery of that body. Even Leonard thought . . ."

"And did you hear or see anything before you heard the cry?"

"I'm not sure," she said. "I might have heard the sound of footsteps or some sort of scuffle. And it was so very dark, wasn't it? I was finding it difficult enough to find my way with a torch." She sat upright and grasped my hand. "You do believe me, don't you? You're not one of those traitors who would try and get me to hang for something I didn't do?"

"I'm sure it's not going to come to that," I said, trying to disguise the fact that I wasn't quite sure what I believed. There was a gentle knock at the door. "Excuse me," I said, relieved that I could turn my back on Katharine so she could not see my ambivalent expression.

It was Woolley. "How is she?" he whispered as he ushered me outside the room and gestured for me to shut the door. "Has she said anything about last night?"

I informed him of what his wife had told me: that she might have heard footsteps or a scuffle, soon followed by a cry.

"So it may not have been an accident, then?" he said, his face darkening.

"No, I don't believe it was," I replied.

"Just that we've heard from Nasiriya and they won't be able to send anyone over here until tomorrow at the very earliest," he said. "Minor uprising or something along those lines."

"I see," I said.

"I just told the Archers the news and they blew up in my face," he said. "They demand I get someone higher up from the Baghdad police. I've told them of course we will try, but the police are not going to get here any sooner, what with the journey." He collapsed back down on the chair, looking exhausted. "Normally, I don't mind not getting much sleep." He stared at me. "You probably didn't get much either, eh?"

"No, but it doesn't matter. I thought it was important to sit with your wife."

"And now Hubert Archer is demanding that I keep Katharine locked up in here. He says that it would be too much of a risk to let her out—that she would be a danger. I've tried reasoning with him, but he's not having any of it." He ran his hands through his hair and exhaled deeply. "I suppose if my daughter had been murdered I would feel the same way."

"I don't mind staying with her," I said.

"You're not . . . afraid?"

"Should I have cause to be?"

He did not reply.

"Mr. Woolley, if there is anything you have kept from me—for example, anything relating to your wife—I think it's only fair that you tell me."

"Well, I—" Just as he opened his mouth to say something—something that I was sure would prove to be important—Katharine opened the door.

"Excuse me, Leonard. If I could just have a word with Agatha for a moment . . . ," she said. She spoke as if she were at a village tea and she wanted to talk to me about the minutes of the parish meeting or to ask me about a recipe for a particularly delicious sponge cake, not about the ramifications of a brutal murder in which she was the chief suspect. Had she been standing behind the door listening to our conversation? Was she fearful that her husband would say something that would implicate her?

"Of course," he said with a strained smile.

Inside, Katharine rushed me away from the door and immediately started to talk in whispers. "I heard what Leonard was telling you," she said. So she had been eavesdropping after all! "That monster of a man, Mr. Archer. I wish he'd never set foot in this camp, the moralizing idiot. Sorry, but to suggest that I should remain locked up here in my bedroom like a common criminal . . . It's preposterous!"

"It does seem rather extreme, but then, often after a sudden shock, some people's reactions can be quite uncompromising," I said.

"I know the police are delayed and I don't want a cloud of suspicion hanging over me for longer than is necessary," said Katharine, color rushing into her face now. "So this is what I want you to do. I'd like you to go around to everyone here and interview them about what exactly they saw and what they were doing last night. It's only what the police would do and you may as well get on with it, don't you think?"

"Yes, but—"

"How would you persuade people to talk to you? I've thought of that, too. People will be open to you; you've got that kind of face. And if they aren't, you can say that the police have sent a message asking you to do some groundwork for them in preparation for their arrival, or something along those lines. What do you think? You'll do it, won't you? Please say you will."

Strangely enough, I had already thought of such a plan, as I was sure I could get Davison's retroactive backing to carry out some initial investigations.

"If you think it will help, then yes," I said.

Katharine threw her arms around me. "Thank you," she said. "I can't tell you how grateful I am." I remained as stiff as a board and extracted myself from her embrace, looking at her with a serious expression.

"What's the matter? Why are you looking at me like that?"

"Katharine, you must realize that if I'm going to do what you ask, I have to remain impartial."

"Yes, of course, but—"

"Which means that, if it wasn't an accident, I have to regard you as being just as much of a suspect as anyone else," I said.

"Oh, I see," she said quietly. She fell silent for a moment or two before she said, "Well, you may as well start with me, then. Ask anything you like."

Once again she went over her movements of the previous night: how she had followed the Archers, how she had lost sight of their torch, how she had heard the sound of footsteps and then a cry, and how she had found Sarah's body at the base of the ziggurat. Katharine made it seem all very plausible, but how did I know that she wasn't lying? Now was the time to ask her some more searching questions—questions relating to her past. This line of inquiry did not come naturally to me—I would have preferred more subtle measures—but I needed to gauge her reaction. The only way I could get through this would be if I imagined myself to be a detective character from one of my own novels.

I took a deep breath and began. "Have you ever committed a crime, Mrs. Woolley?"

Katharine looked startled, appalled. "What do you mean?"

"Your first husband, Bertie, the one you told me shot himself." I paused. "Did you kill him?"

"How dare you!" she exclaimed, her eyes full of fire.

"You said that I could ask you anything."

"Yes, but I meant about last night, not something that happened years ago."

"But as you know, the events of the past often have a bearing on the present," I said, trying to swallow, but my throat was dry. "I must ask you again: Did you murder your first husband?"

"Have you lost your mind? Of course I didn't kill Bertie!"

"And what about Miss Gertrude Bell?"

"What about her?"

"Did you play any part in her death?"

Katharine looked at me as if I were playing some cruel practical joke, almost as if she expected that at any moment my mask would slip. "I don't understand where this is all coming from," she said. "Leonard and I were in London when Miss Bell died."

"Did you send her any kind of threatening letters or drawings?"

"No. What makes you think I did?" She stopped and looked at me as if seeing me for what I really was: a false friend who had won her intimacy by not wholly honest means. "I see. It's all beginning to make sense. How could I have been so foolish as to trust you."

"Katharine, if you'll allow me—"

"Mrs. Woolley to you," she said with ice in her voice. "And to think that I confided in you. You who came here under false pretenses. Who sent you? I wonder. It doesn't matter, but whoever it was had something they wanted to find out. I'm right, aren't I? They suspected me all along of . . . what? Killing Bertie? And driving Gertrude Bell to her death? And now you think I'm the one behind Miss Archer's death, too."

"Please, if you—"

"Don't waste your breath," she hissed. That manic look had returned to her eyes. "A snake in the grass, that's what you are, or rather something more deadly: a snake in the sands." She stood up and looked towards the door, a clear sign that I should leave. "There are other less polite names for your kind, but I wouldn't lower myself by saying them."

I opened my mouth to speak, but there was nothing left to say. Katharine Woolley was right. I was a snake—yes, worse than that.

She had every right to be angry. I had handled the situation badly. I had assumed one could act like a character from a novel. What a fool I had been! It had been wrong of me to accept Davison's offer. I should have stuck to what I knew: sitting at my typewriter, writing stories, spinning tales from the rich swell of my imagination. What had possessed me to think that I had the talents for anything but that? I opened the door slowly, stepped through it, then turned back to her, feeling the sting of tears in my eyes.

"I'm sorry," I managed to say before Katharine slammed the door behind me.

"Oh, dear," said Leonard, who had already jumped from his seat outside the room. "Are you all right? You do look terribly pale."

I nodded, unable to speak for the moment.

"Did Katharine give you a piece of her mind?" he said. "Yes, we've all been subject to her sharp tongue, I'm afraid. Here, why don't you sit down."

I took Woolley's chair as I tried to compose myself. "She—she asked me to help by taking everyone's statements about their movements last night."

"Yes, a very good idea in the circumstances, I would have thought," he replied.

"She said I could ask anything—anything at all. I thought she wouldn't mind a few probing questions. But I'm afraid I was wrong."

"Oh, I see," he said.

"It was my fault entirely," I said. I recalled the crazed look in her eyes, a look that frankly frightened me. "I was too clumsy in my line of questioning. I'd like to apologize to her, but she's so angry that she won't hear me out."

"What we've all learnt—those of us who are close to Katharine—is that she has a temper, a temper so strong that it can burn. She can be charm itself one moment and turn on you the next. She can say the most vicious, the most unforgivable things. Some people have it in their hearts to forgive her. But there are others—such as Mr. McRae, for example—who refuse to have anything more to do with her. I do hope you decide you are of the former type, not the latter."

I didn't know which camp to place myself in. I only knew that I had seriously misjudged a very delicate situation. As I returned to my room I thought of the blood that had been spilled at the base of the ziggurat and Miss Archer's lifeless body. I feared I had made an enemy of Katharine Woolley. I did not want to be the next victim.

13

When I returned to the living room, I was informed that Mr. Archer had called a meeting to discuss how to proceed following the death of his daughter. Everyone, apart from Mrs. Woolley, who was locked in her room, and Ruth Archer, who was still with Sarah's body, had taken a seat around the table.

It was obvious that Hubert Archer, in an effort to cope with the tragedy, had clicked into automatic mode, playing the part of the American businessman and millionaire to perfection. By doing so, it was obvious that he was attempting to deflect the shadow of grief that loomed over him.

"Now, top of the agenda as I see it is to decide what to do about the police, or rather their absence," he said. "I can't believe that there is no one around who could help with this matter. Burrows? McRae? Do you know any alternatives?" The men shook their heads. "Miller?"

"Sorry, but I'm afraid Woolley is right when he says the man from Baghdad will take just as long as the chap from Nasiriya," replied the photographer.

"So, what do you do when there's an emergency?" asked Mr. Archer.

"We just wait," said Woolley dryly. "It's one of the hazards of being out here, I'm afraid."

Mr. Archer stared at Woolley in disbelief. "The next thing we need to decide is what to do about . . . about the body," he said. I surmised that he was using deliberately clinical language so as to distance himself from the awfulness of what had happened to his daughter. "Obviously we can't leave it out . . . there," he said, glancing towards the ziggurat. "Ruth is with her now, but she can't do that all day. And even though it's winter, the heat of the sun would still . . . well, it wouldn't be ideal. I'm sure all of us can agree on that."

The room was filled with an echo of murmurs and agreement, as if we were voting on the implication of a new card system at the local library or a particular planting scheme in the municipal gardens.

"I'm wondering which is the coolest room in the house," said Woolley. "I suppose it must be the pantry. Is that correct, McRae?"

"Yes, indeed," replied the architect. "A good few degrees cooler. Of course, we would need to move out the supplies."

"The pantry?" asked Mr. Archer. "It hardly seems suitable."

"No, but I'm afraid it is the best place," said McRae. "After all, we wouldn't want—"

Hubert Archer cut him off with a nod of the head before clearing his throat in preparation for the most difficult question on his agenda. "And then there is the problem of what to do with Mrs. Woolley."

"In what regard?" asked Woolley.

Archer's reply came as quick and as deadly as a rapier. "Well, I know my wife for one would not be comfortable sleeping under the same roof as a murderer. I'm sure the same could be said for most of you around this table."

The statement—articulated and declared with the conviction of a man of standing and means—forced many in the group to acknowledge what they had only been thinking. Cecil, clearly distressed and red in the face, tried to talk but was stopped from doing so by his uncle, who placed a hand on his nephew's shoulder. Father Burrows looked like the saddest man on earth, an Adam being given the news that there was no place for him in paradise. Miss Jones had gone pale and looked as if she were unable to raise her big brown eyes from a dirty mark on the table, a stain that seemed to hypnotize her. All traces of jollity and optimism had been wiped clean from Mr. Miller's face. And Woolley himself appeared inscrutable, for once unable to interpret or predict.

Finally he stood up and addressed the group, talking quietly at first. "I know that you all have very grave concerns about what has happened," he said. "And I must express my deep sadness and condolences to Mr. and Mrs. Archer. Although my wife has not been well—many of you have witnessed that—this does not mean that she is the one responsible for . . . for what befell poor Miss Archer."

"How can you stand there and say that?" said Cecil McRae, standing up with such force that his chair nearly fell over. "There's only one of us who was found with blood on our hands: Mrs. Woolley."

"That's enough, Cecil," said Lawrence, trying to calm the boy.

"Everyone's thinking the same thing," said Cecil, shaking with anger. "We more or less saw it with our own eyes. First the cat and then this. She clearly took a rock and smashed it on Sarah's head. How could she do that?" The boy's voice broke, and tears had started to stream down his face. "Maybe she's just mad or evil or a bit of both, I don't know. But I think she couldn't bear the thought of anyone prettier than her getting more attention. And Sarah was younger, much younger, and much more beautiful, too. I'm sorry, but if you've snuffed out a life, that means, by my reckoning . . . well, that she's got what's coming to her."

"Cecil, control yourself!" commanded Woolley. "I will not have such talk in my camp."

The boy looked at Woolley with a mix of anger and self-loathing and, unable to bear the contradictory impulses which were raging inside him, dashed a water tumbler to the floor and ran out. The impact sent shards of glass across the hard floor.

"Cecil! Come back!" shouted McRae. He bent down to pick up the pieces of the glass and, in the process, cut his thumb.

"You're bleeding," said Cynthia.

"It's nothing; don't worry," said McRae, taking a handkerchief from his pocket and wrapping it around the wound. "And, Woolley, I'm sorry about that. He's young and headstrong, and you know how much he thought of Sarah."

"Never mind," said Woolley. "Now, where were we? Yes, the question of what to do about my wife."

Just as Mr. Archer was about to launch into another speech, I thought it best if I tried to calm things down a little.

"May I venture a suggestion?" I said. All eyes turned to me, astonished that I had an opinion on the subject.

"Yes, Mrs. Christie?" asked Mr. Archer.

"I can see that we are all getting rather heated about the matter," I said. "And I can comprehend the very strong feelings. But I do believe it is important to stick by the English principle of innocent until proven guilty." I said this although I was quite uncertain of Mrs. Woolley's innocence in the matter.

"A very noble idea, but in this instance—" said Mr. Archer in a rather condescending manner.

"In this instance, I think it's all the more important we don't let tribal instincts take over," I said. I thought of the paragraph in Mrs. Woolley's manuscript relating to tribal law. "We can't let ourselves be swayed by outmoded notions of justice. Even though many of us might consider the judicial system in Iraq to be, well, not quite what we would find at home, it's good to remember something of the country's contribution to the history of the law."

"Indeed, but with the police so far away, and—"

"Exactly so, Mr. Archer," I said, trying to disarm him with a smile. "With the police so far away, we cannot allow this to degenerate." An image of an ancient relic, an enormous tablet from a bygone age, came into my mind. Something I had been taken to see in the Louvre all those years ago when I had been a carefree girl in Paris. "Correct me if I am wrong, Mr. Woolley—as you will know so much more about this than I—but is there not something called the Code of Hammurabi?"

"You mean the ancient Babylonian law code? Discovered by Jéquier in 1901 at the ancient site of Susa. Translated a year later by Father Scheil."

I had no idea of the history, but I knew to trust Woolley's expert knowledge. "Yes, I'm sure that's right," I said. "Does that code not lay down what later became the precept of a presumption of innocence?"

" '*Ei incumbit probatio qui dicit, non qui negat*'?" he replied. "Which roughly translates as 'The burden of proof lies upon him who affirms, not he who denies.' "

"Yes, that's right," I said. "It's up to those who are doing the accusing to find the body of evidence."

"Hold on there, my dear," said Mr. Archer, addressing me as if I were a child. "I'm sure you can get away with this kind of thing in your books, but unless I'm mistaken, you aren't qualified in the law."

I could feel myself blushing. "No, I'm not, but I do think—"

"And if you'll forgive me, you're not the only one acquainted with the Code of Hammurabi," he continued. "While we were in Paris, I went to the Louvre to see the famous stele for myself. As a scholar of the Old Testament, it was only natural that I wanted to study an ancient relic that spoke of the *lex talionis*. My view, like young Cecil's, is very much 'An eye for an eye, a tooth for a tooth.' "

Leonard Woolley interjected, "I can understand that in a state of shock you may feel like this, but surely it's more Christian to think of the Sermon on the Mount: 'If anyone strikes you on the right cheek, turn to him the other also.' "

"Woolley, Mrs. Christie, I'm not here to have an argument about the finer points of theology," snapped Archer. "Let me outline the facts as I see them. My daughter has been murdered. Her corpse is lying outside, being watched over by my heartbroken wife. The police aren't due until tomorrow morning. Under this roof there is a murderer. A murderer who has been discovered with blood on her hands. A murderer who is none other than Mrs. Katharine Woolley."

"But Mrs. Woolley told me—"

Mr. Archer cut me off. "Told you what? That she was innocent?"

"Yes, that she heard the sound of footsteps or a scuffle, and the next thing she knew, she stumbled upon your daughter's body."

"And you believe her?"

"Well, I . . ."

"Why the hesitation? From the look in your eyes, it's obvious that you're not completely sure of Mrs. Woolley's innocence."

It was true. I couldn't stand up before Mr. Archer and tell him that Katharine had not killed his daughter. Yet neither was I certain of her guilt in the matter.

"Just as I thought," pronounced Mr. Archer. "Now, what I propose is this." He began to outline his scheme for dealing with the immediate aftermath of his daughter's death. "Don't worry, I'm not suggesting that we try Mrs. Woolley in some kind of kangaroo court. I'm not that ignorant or barbaric; just that I think it would be best if we removed her from the house. That we contained her somewhere under lock and key while we wait for the authorities to arrive tomorrow. Woolley, is there any such place here?"

Leonard turned his head away from Archer so he could not see the resentment burning in his eyes.

"Woolley, did you hear what I said?"

"Yes, I know a place," interrupted McRae. "There's a storeroom just by the outer fence that is used to keep spare tools, building materials, and the like."

"Are you out of your mind?" shouted Woolley. "You cannot expect my wife to spend the night in that shed?"

"Perhaps we could make it comfortable for her. Could a mattress conceivably be brought in for her?"

"Yes, but . . . ," said Woolley, the color draining from his face.

"And it's lockable from the outside?" asked Archer.

"Yes, there's a padlock on the door," answered McRae.

"There's no way Katharine will agree to this," said Woolley. "No way at all."

"Well, I'm afraid she won't have much choice in the matter," said Archer. "As far as I'm concerned, she gave away her rights when she smashed that rock down on my daughter's head. Ideally, I would have her removed from the compound altogether, but as the police will want to question her first thing, this is the most appropriate compromise, don't you think?"

Archer looked around the group as if he had just won a particularly tricky game of cards. No one had the energy or the courage to argue with him any more. Even though I was not totally convinced of Mrs. Woolley's innocence, I felt that the plan was a mistake. What if Katharine was right and someone wanted to do her harm? Even if she was locked up in that shed, she would still be terribly vulnerable. The phrase *lamb to the slaughter* came to mind.

"But is this really the best course of action?" I asked.

"What do you propose, Mrs. Christie?" Archer's tone of voice was withering now. "That we all carry on as if nothing had happened? Should we all sit down and enjoy a nice cup of tea? Yes, that would be very English, wouldn't it?"

I ignored his sarcasm. "Why don't I stay with Katharine in her room as I did last night? You can lock it from the outside if you like. That way Mrs. Woolley will continue to be comfortable and you will feel safe knowing that she is . . . contained."

"You're prepared to spend hours locked up with a woman who

could be a killer?" whispered Miss Jones, her eyes shining with the anticipation of future horrors to come.

"I don't think you need be quite so melodramatic, Cynthia," I said, trying to lighten the mood with a smile. "I'm sure I will be quite safe, as will the rest of you."

"No, that's completely out of the question," said Archer.

"But—" said Woolley before Archer cut him dead.

"Your wife will sleep in the storeroom, which will be locked. And I'm saying this for her safety as much as ours." Archer walked over and whispered something in Woolley's ear, then turned to the rest of us and added, "I'm sure you do understand now that this plan would be for the best, don't you, Woolley?"

"Yes, I suppose under the circumstances you're right," said Woolley. He no longer had the energy to fight. "I'll go and talk to Katharine now."

What had Archer said to Leonard to make him change his mind? Perhaps he had dangled the prospect of not withdrawing the funding from the dig after all. Before Archer excused himself, he said that he would go and talk to his wife and tell her about the arrangements for the body of their daughter to be moved into the pantry. His face was inscrutable, as expressionless as an ancient carving; I wondered at what point Mr. Archer would allow himself to grieve for his dead daughter. If he was so ardent in his Christian beliefs, then the thought of everlasting life would at least give him some comfort. But was there not also a danger in such an attitude, too? Did his fundamentalism not blind him to the very real joys and sadnesses of the concrete world in which he lived?

"Thank goodness Mr. Archer is taking charge of the situation," said Cynthia to me after Archer had left the room and the rest of the group began to disperse.

"I only hope he knows what he is doing," I said.

"What do you mean?" she asked. "Surely everyone will sleep

more soundly knowing that Mrs. Woolley is locked away in that shed."

"Perhaps," I said. "But there's something not right about this—something not right at all."

"In what way?"

"I'm not sure yet," I said.

"You're beginning to worry me, Agatha," said Cynthia. Her eyes searched the room for signs of danger. "When the police arrive, they will take away Mrs. Woolley, and then we can get back to normal, can't we?"

"I hope so," I said.

"You're not telling me something," she said, her hands beginning to tremble. I could sense the difficulty with which she formed her next question. "Y-you think someone else is in peril, don't you?"

"Yes, I'm afraid I do."

"But who?"

"It's Mrs. Woolley herself. I fear someone means to do her harm. I think someone wants her dead."

14

Back in my room, I took out my notebook and scribbled down the events leading up to the death of Sarah Archer at the base of the ziggurat.

There she was, the young girl full of life, celebrating her twenty-first birthday, kicking up her heels at the edge of the ziggurat as Harry Miller took his photographs. Her mother told her not to go too near the edge, warning her of the long drop. Harry Miller replied that the girl was in safe hands. Then we all sat down to eat. Sarah told her story about that inappropriate proposal, cruelly describing the man as old and ugly. Her father told her off, which then gave rise to the awful clash between Sarah and Katharine Woolley.

The atmosphere had changed from jovial to something more unsettling in a moment. Sarah had grabbed a torch and stormed off into the night, quickly followed by Leonard Woolley and Harry Miller, then Lawrence McRae and Cecil. Mr. and Mrs. Archer, disgusted by Katharine's behavior, left the picnic, soon followed by Mrs. Woolley and Miss Jones, leaving Father Burrows and myself. Then the night air was split by that unholy scream and we all clustered round that horrible sight, the figure of Katharine Woolley, her hands covered in blood, kneeling by the body of Sarah Archer.

As I finished reading through what I had written, I heard the sound of wailing. I opened my door to see two servants carrying the shrouded body of Sarah Archer on a bier. Behind her trailed her father and mother. Ruth Archer's pale face was a mask of misery like that of a painting I had once seen of Mary after the death of Christ. The sad parade made its way across the courtyard to the pantry, where Harry Miller stood at the door. As the servants maneuvered the body into the room, the photographer bowed his head in respect, leaving the Archers to kneel by their daughter's body.

"That was the saddest thing I think I've ever seen," said Miller, catching my eye and walking over towards me. "I can't believe one moment there she was, happy as anything, standing on the top of the world, with everything to look forward to. Then the next minute her life had been snuffed out. It doesn't seem right somehow."

"No, it doesn't. There's something very evil at work here," I said. "Mr. Miller, would you mind coming into my room? I'd like to ask you something."

"Not at all," he said, running his hand through his hair.

"I'm just trying to build up a picture of what happened before and around the time of the—of Miss Archer's death," I said as I closed the door behind us. "And I wondered whether it would be possible for me to have a look at some of the photographs you took. Just to see if they might provide some kind of clue."

"To the murder, you mean?"

"Well, yes," I said. It seemed that there could be no other explanation for the girl's death.

He shuffled uneasily on his feet, and a certain nervous quality came into his eyes. Was there something he wanted to hide? "I would need a couple of hours to develop the film."

We stepped out of my room to hear an almighty row coming from Mrs. Woolley's quarters. Obviously, Leonard had broken the news to his wife of her proposed imprisonment within the confines of the shed.

"I will not agree to it!" shouted Katharine. "I refuse to be treated like an animal!"

"But Mr. Archer insists," replied Leonard.

"And why didn't you stand up for me? It's always the way with you."

"If we want the—"

"You're weak, Leonard. You've always been weak."

"But it's only for one night, until the police arrive tomorrow. I'm sure they'll be able to clear everything up, and once you've talked to them, you'll be free to—"

We heard the sound of something like a vase smashing against the wall, and I suggested to Harry Miller that we take a walk around the compound while we waited for the argument to finish. We continued to talk about what he had seen last night before Sarah Archer's death. He told me once more of how he had accompanied Woolley down from the ziggurat and how they had lost sight of Sarah Archer's torch. Did he remember which staircase he had used as he had made his descent? He said he thought that he and Woolley had used the one that ran down the left side of the ziggurat.

"Would you mind showing me?" I asked.

"Of course," he said.

We strode out of the compound and across the dry landscape towards the great ziggurat. The digging had been stopped for the day—the men had been told not to turn up for work because of what had happened to Sarah Archer—and instead of the queer low chanting of the Arabs, all I could hear was the sound of the wind as it passed across the desert sands. I recalled Mrs. Woolley's fears about her first husband being alive. Here, in this vast open plain, there was nowhere for him to hide. And yet . . . what if Colonel Keeling had disguised himself as one of the Arabs? After all, no one in the household actually paid any attention to the workmen, apart from Hamoudi. I made a mental note to ask Woolley whether it would be possible to have an interview with the foreman to ask if he had noticed anything unusual among his men.

"I can't believe Mrs. Woolley would do such a thing, can you?" asked Harry Miller as we approached the ziggurat. "I know the two women didn't exactly get along, but even so. To smash the girl's head in with a rock seems unbelievable."

"Indeed, it does seem hard to comprehend," I said. I was careful what I said next. I didn't want to offend Mr. Miller the way I had offended Katharine Woolley. "May I ask you a . . . delicate question, Mr. Miller?"

"Go right ahead. What do they say about Americans? 'Nothing embarrasses us.' "

"I think you were friendly with both Miss Archer and Mrs. Woolley."

"Yes, that's right." I did not say anything, and luckily Mr. Miller picked up my meaning exactly. "I see: you want to know whether anything serious was going on between us?" He broke into a smile, and at that moment he seemed more handsome than ever. "No, it was nothing like that. Sure, Miss Archer and I enjoyed a little flirtation here and there, but it was just a bit of friendly banter."

I gave him an inquisitive stare.

"Nothing more, I promise!" he exclaimed. "What do you take me for? Some kind of gigolo?"

The comment made me smile, but I tried not to show that he had amused me. Harry Miller was charm personified—and he knew it—but I didn't want to give him the satisfaction that he had won over yet another woman.

"And I suppose Mrs. Woolley did get a bit jealous—not that anything had ever happened between us. Lord, no!" he said. "I hope you don't think that. Just that her nose was put out of joint by the fact that I was showing Sarah a little attention. Katharine—Mrs. Woolley—had been used to having me to herself."

"I see," I said.

"But you don't think that's why Mrs. Woolley—" He broke off, unable to finish the sentence. "I refuse to believe it."

"It does seem unlikely. Let's go and have a look where it happened," I suggested.

As we walked, I ran through the list of possible killers in my mind. The question a detective would ask would be: Who benefits from the death? In this case I had to assume that the only people to be made substantially richer from Sarah Archer's murder would be her parents. But surely neither Mr. nor Mrs. Archer would kill their own child so as to increase their wealth. Or would they? When Davison arrived—as I was sure he would when he had learnt of what had happened—I would ask him whether his department could check on the existence and contents of Miss Archer's will.

If money was not the motive behind the murder, then what else could it be? Desire? Certainly, there were a number of men at the site who were infatuated by the girl. There was Cecil McRae, whom I had overheard saying that if he couldn't have her, then he would make sure no one else could. And what about Lawrence McRae and even Harry Miller? They were men with appetites. What if Sarah had led them on and then had withdrawn her attention? Would they have felt so angry and full of frustration that they would have been prepared to kill her? Yet Harry Miller had come down from the top of the ziggurat with Leonard Woolley, and the two men could each verify the other's movements. Could they be working in tandem? But what motive could they possibly have for wanting Sarah Archer dead? Or could Harry have murdered Miss Archer on Leonard Woolley's behalf? Could the archaeologist have a reason to be blackmailing the handsome photographer?

When we arrived at the spot where Miss Archer's body had been found, we bowed our heads in a moment of silent respect. Then, when I opened my eyes, I knelt down and examined the ground, a patch of earth still reddish-brown from Sarah's blood. I saw something glinting in the sunlight. Using my handkerchief, I eased away the sand. It was Mrs. Woolley's gold watch, its face cracked and smeared with blood. Perhaps, just as Katharine had said, she had tripped over the body and in doing so had fallen over, smashing her watch in the process. But the other, darker possibility seemed more likely: she had indeed murdered Miss Archer and the watch had slipped off and been damaged in the process.

"What's that you've found?" asked Harry.

"It's a watch—one that I think belongs to Mrs. Woolley."

His face looked grave. "What should we do with it? Do you think you should leave it there for the police to look at when they arrive tomorrow?"

"Yes, I suppose we should," I said, letting the watch drop back into the sand.

Next I turned my attention to the rock that appeared to have been used to kill Sarah Archer. It was a large piece of pink sandstone, so substantial that one would need two hands to lift it. Half of it was still covered in Miss Archer's dried blood, and on one of its jagged edges I could make out a small clump of blond hair attached to a bloodied patch of skin. Although I had seen some true horrors during the war when I was working as a VAD nurse, the sight of the bloody rock turned my stomach. As I tried to stand I felt myself feeling faint, and for a moment I thought I might pass out.

"Are you all right?" said Harry. "Oh, my, no, you've gone pale. Here, let me help." He took hold of my arm and led me away from the spot where Miss Archer had been killed. Gently and protectively, he helped me lower myself onto a boulder. His touch lingered a little longer than necessary, and I could feel myself blushing at the way he made me feel.

"Thank you," I managed to say. "It must be the heat."

"And the sight of all that . . . mess," he replied. "I should never have allowed you to come up here. I thought you wanted to see the layout of the ziggurat, not the actual spot where it happened."

"I'm feeling much better now," I said. "Really I am. Sorry for being such a nuisance." Using my hat as a protection against the sun, I looked up towards the ziggurat. Then I took a deep breath, raised myself to my feet, and walked back to the spot where Miss Archer had died. I strained my neck as I tried to work out where the rock could have fallen from, if indeed it had been an accident—something which seemed increasingly unlikely.

"Let's walk up there," I said.

"What is it you want to see?" asked Harry as he took my arm. The lightness of his touch thrilled me. After all, I had been without physical contact of this sort for years now. Of course, I had felt my daughter Rosalind's soft skin against mine and enjoyed the occasional kiss on the cheek from my sister, but nothing—no, nothing—like this.

"Just in case it was an accident, there might be a trace," I said, coughing, pretending I had a frog in my throat, but of course this was just a ruse to mask my real feelings.

While Harry guided me up the ziggurat's staircase, I concentrated on counting the steps in front of me, studying each stone and brick before me as a way to distract myself from his attentions. The heat stimulated my imagination, and I had to blink away the inappropriate images that floated through my mind: his mustache set against his rather full and fleshy lips; his sturdy shoulders that looked as though they were strong enough to carry half a ton of stones; his large and powerful hands, one of which now rested on my arm—hands capable of taking hold of a woman and lifting her towards him.

When I reached the top of the staircase, I paused for a few moments to recover my breath.

"Are you sure this is a good idea?" asked Harry. "Why don't we go back to the house and have a glass of water?"

"No, I'll be all right," I said. As I looked across the desert, the heat beat down onto the plain. I stepped forwards along the edge of the precipice to the point which was, by my estimation, situated directly above the spot where Sarah Archer's body had been found. I kicked the ground around me to see if the action would dislodge any rocks, but nothing more than a couple of handfuls of sand cascaded down. Just as I peered over the edge of the ziggurat I felt the periphery of my vision begin to darken. My legs started to sink from beneath me. Was this how I was going to die? Death from a broken neck or a terrible head injury, my body twisted and broken after falling off the edge of the ziggurat? What was it Woolley had said to me about the etymology of the name? "Etemennigur . . . Or 'Temple Whose Foundation Creates Horror' "?

I tried to step back, but my balance had deserted me. I had begun to fall now and I couldn't stop myself. I closed my eyes, hoping that the impact wouldn't be too painful, that my death would be quick. But then, just as I collapsed, just as I saw the ground disappear from beneath me, I felt the strong hands of Harry Miller around my waist.

"What the—" he said before pulling me back from the edge. "It's my fault: I knew we shouldn't have come up here. Don't worry, I've got you now." I felt something soft and cool across my forehead. I opened my eyes to see him fanning his hat across my face. "Does that feel better, Agatha?"

For a moment I couldn't speak. I stretched out my hands and my fingers felt the sharp ridge of a rock and then the softness of the sand. I took in Harry's face, really the most pleasing face imaginable, and I was conscious of the fact that I was smiling. He had saved me: yet again he had been there when I had been at my most vulnerable. Without him . . . well, I knew what my fate would have been. "Thank you," I said.

"You must have fainted," he said. "Let's get you back to the house." His powerful hands raised me upwards and he led me slowly and gently down the staircase. "That's right: just one step at a time. You're doing great."

Even though my body was weak, my mind was still working. I was certain now that Sarah Archer's death was not an accident. There were no loose rocks on the ridge of the ziggurat that lay directly above where her body had been found. I had seen traces of blood and strands of hair on the rock by the place where she had died. Miss Archer had been murdered. Yet there was something that still troubled me.

What if the intended victim had not been Sarah Archer but Mrs. Woolley herself? Could the murderer have mistaken the light from Sarah's torch for Katharine's? Certainly, Mrs. Woolley had seemed terrified of something or someone. What if her "delusions"—the voices she claimed to have heard, the horrific faces at her bedroom window that she said she had seen—were real?

I was about to share my thoughts with Harry Miller, but as we passed the scene of the crime, I thought better of it. I still had quite a few things to work out, and I was not certain whether I would be able to express myself clearly.

"You must have had a shock up there," said Harry as he led me into the compound.

"Yes, I did," I replied. "Thank goodness you were there. I don't know what would have happened otherwise."

"We don't need to dwell on that. Look. They don't hang around, do they?" he said, pointing towards the shed, which was being cleared out by two servants. "I suppose they'll have Mrs. Woolley locked in there by sundown."

I walked up to the store and inspected the door, which, as described, had a padlock attached. "Do you know who holds a key to this?" I asked Harry.

"Woolley has one for sure, and I think McRae, and I've got one too, as at one point I stored some chemicals here," he said. "To be honest, I'm not exactly sure how many keys there are. It's only been used for holding tools and supplies, nothing valuable. There's never been any need to worry about that before."

His answer made me worry a good deal, however. Miller told the servants to make themselves scarce for a moment and we stepped inside the shed. The shifting of the tools to the outside had disturbed a great amount of dust, and within seconds both of us started to cough. There were no windows that could be opened, and the floor was nothing but bare earth.

"Do you think this is a fit place for Mrs. Woolley?" I asked, placing a handkerchief over my mouth.

"Clearly not, but it's what the Archers want," Harry replied. "Since they arrived I've learnt that the will of that couple rule. Anyway, you can't worry about that now. We need to get you inside, into your room, where you can lie down."

"But what if—"

"What if you don't go and lie down as I say? Well, I couldn't be responsible for my actions," he said, with a mischievous twinkle in his eye. "No, seriously, Agatha, you really do need to rest."

"I'm just worried about the keys. You see, if—"

"I know: Why don't we make a deal? Why don't I go around and ask for everyone's key to the store? I'll track all of them down, and then we can decide on the safest place to keep them. How does that sound?"

"That would be something," I said as we entered the courtyard. "And could you go and fetch your camera? We need to think about developing the film—just in case any of the photographs give us a clue to what happened."

"I'll go and get my trusty Leica now," Harry said as he accompanied me to my room. "Once that is done, you must take to your bed. I wouldn't be surprised if you had a touch of heatstroke."

"Very well," I replied, and we parted.

Inside my room I still felt light-headed—not so much from my fainting spell as from the feel of Harry Miller's arms around my body. I poured myself a glass of water. As I passed the looking glass on the wall, I caught a glimpse of myself. What a sight! Even though I had been wearing a hat, my hair had become loose and was hanging around my head, making me look like a disheveled fishwife. My dress was dirty, my skin looked all red and blotchy, and fine lines of perspiration had formed under my arms and around my neck and breasts. What a fool I had been to think that Mr. Miller could be interested in me! A divorced woman with a child, a middle-aged woman who was on her way to becoming an old maid. I had made the mistake once before with Archie, forming an attachment with a man who was too handsome for me. What a disaster that had been. No, I couldn't—I wouldn't—let it happen again. Not that Mr. Miller had any intentions in that direction. He was probably just being kind to me. Yes, he had taken pity on me; that was it. I blushed as I thought of my girlish behavior.

A moment later there was a furious knocking at my door. "Agatha—Agatha!" It was Harry Miller. "Let me in."

In that instant everything I had just told myself slipped from memory, my resolve melting as I felt my heart race.

"What's wrong?" I said as I flung open the door.

Harry Miller stood there with a pale face and open hands. It took me a while to work out what lay in his palms: a mass of broken, shattered metal, together with a spool of spoilt film.

"It's my Leica," he said, his voice flat. "Someone's destroyed my camera and everything that was on it."

15

"Who could have done such a thing?" I asked as Harry Miller stood dumbfounded before me. He continued to gaze down at the fragments of what had been his camera with a look of sadness so profound, it almost broke my heart. "When did you last see your camera?"

"It was j-just before we heard that argument between Mr. and Mrs. Woolley," he said, blinking. "I put it on my desk in my room and left it there. How long had we been gone? An hour at most?"

"Someone must have gone into your room and smashed it to pieces while we were at the ziggurat."

"I guess so," he said. "But why would anyone want to do that?"

"I can think of one very good reason," I said. "The person who did this must have believed that you had captured something on your camera that could have implicated them in some way. It seems very likely that the man—or woman—who did this is the very same person who was responsible for the death of Sarah Archer."

He turned away from me, walked over to my desk, and dropped the pieces onto the surface. He took the crumpled reel of film and lifted it towards the light, then flung it across the room, swearing under his breath as he did so.

"Is there really nothing that can be done?" I asked.

"No. They're all ruined," he said.

"Do you remember what photographs you took? Besides those of Sarah?"

"There were some photos of the various artifacts here: pots, earrings, cuneiform tablets. And I took some of the grave pits, too."

"Casting your mind back to when you took the pictures of Sarah, do you remember seeing anything that struck you as unusual?"

He fell silent for a moment, then shook his head. "I don't think so. It was such a jolly occasion to begin with, wasn't it? Everyone in such good spirits. I took some shots of us strolling towards the ziggurat, people chatting, the food, the servants."

I thought back to Mrs. Woolley's wild theory regarding her first husband and the incredible suggestion that he might actually still be alive. "Can I ask: Have you noticed any of the Arabs behaving in a peculiar manner recently?"

"In what way?"

"I don't know; perhaps a man who seemed out of place or one who looked like he might be in . . . disguise?"

"Disguise? What do you mean?"

"I know it sounds extremely unlikely, but when I was talking to Mrs. Woolley, she mentioned her fear that her first husband might not be dead—that he could be here, on this dig, perhaps disguised as one of the workers."

"But that sounds absurd!"

I had to agree. "I wanted to mention it in case you had seen anyone acting strangely."

"Sorry, but no, nothing springs to mind." Harry returned to the desk and looked down at the shards of his Leica. "What I want to find out is who is responsible for smashing up my camera. I don't know what to do." He gazed at some pieces of metal in the vain hope that they might meld together and somehow miraculously form a camera once more. "Do you think we should go and ask the others if they saw or heard anything suspicious?"

"Yes, it might help," I said. Although the culprit was unlikely to declare himself, perhaps it might be possible to gauge the reactions and pick up traces of guilt. I told Harry that if he broke the news of what had happened, I would watch the faces and the bodies of the rest of the group for any hints or clues. He picked up the remains of his camera, together with the ruined spool of film, and walked into the main room, where he threw everything onto the table.

"Oh, my, what's happened?" asked Cynthia Jones. She was about to lay the table for lunch.

There were similar cries of astonishment from Father Burrows and Lawrence McRae, while Cecil remained sullen and silent. Harry explained how he had found his broken camera and voiced his suspicions about a possible motive behind the destruction. And as I thought, no one admitted they had seen or heard anything untoward.

"And no noise at any time?" asked Harry, staring at each of the group in turn. "Nothing? It seems extraordinary that none of you heard the sound of smashing from my room while I was gone."

"Perhaps you need to inform Mr. Woolley," suggested Cynthia.

"Don't you think he's got enough on his plate at the moment," sneered Cecil, "what with having a wife for a murderer?"

We all ignored the boy's blunt remark. "Yes, I'll ask him if I can have a word," said Harry before he left us in uncomfortable silence. I studied the figures in the room in earnest; none of them seemed to be showing any sign of guilt. But then, when did those with a criminal bent ever show signs of culpability? They were, I knew, masters of deception, well practiced in the art of duplicity.

A minute or so later Harry Miller returned with Woolley. The photographer had already explained what had happened, but Leonard wanted to see the evidence for himself. He walked over to the table and picked up the shattered pieces of Harry's camera.

"Damn shame," said Woolley, turning the fragments over in

his hands. "Nice piece of equipment it was, too. I used to own one similar—an older model, though."

"Do you think Mr. or Mrs. Archer heard anything?" asked Harry. "Where are they now? In their room?"

"No, they're still with their daughter's body," replied Woolley. "I don't think now is the best time to ask them."

"How is your wife?" I asked.

"As well as can be expected," he said.

"She didn't take the news of her imminent move well, I imagine," Lawrence McRae ventured.

Woolley ignored the remark and encouraged the group to get on with their lunch as normal. Soon he would accompany his wife out to the shed, which he believed should now be ready for her.

"Mr. Miller and I were just talking about the keys to the padlock," I said. "We were wondering how many copies exist and who has them."

"Yes, it's something I was thinking about, too," he replied. "Probably a good idea to gather all of them together, considering what's happened." He turned to address the group. "If you could search through your things and see if you have any small keys that might fit a padlock, I would be so very grateful." It was difficult to know whether Woolley was being sarcastic or whether he really was apologizing to his colleagues for putting them to this trouble.

The group started to check their pockets, and some of them went off to their rooms to search their drawers and desks. A few minutes later three people—Leonard Woolley himself, Harry Miller, and Lawrence McRae—returned to the main room and placed their keys on the table.

"That's all of them?" asked Woolley. "Miss Jones? Cecil? Father Burrows?" All three shook their heads.

"And who is going to guard the keys?" asked McRae.

"Well, I thought I might," said Woolley.

"But what if the desire to liberate your wife suddenly came upon you?" persisted the architect.

"What would you suggest, Mr. McRae?" said Woolley icily. I could tell he was doing his very best to keep his temper under control.

"Perhaps Mr. Archer should keep them."

"Oh, no, I don't think that would be a very good idea," I said. All faces turned to me.

"Why ever not?" asked McRae.

"I was thinking that we shouldn't place that burden on his shoulders at such a difficult time," I replied. The truth was that I did not trust him or his wife with the keys.

"Yes, that's a good point, I suppose," said Woolley. "So why don't we let Father Burrows take charge of them?" He turned to the emaciated priest, who had taken his spectacles off and was in the process of cleaning them with his handkerchief. "Eric, what do you think? Would you be prepared to do that?"

The Jesuit paused for a moment, looked through his glasses, placed them back on the bridge of his nose, and nodded. "Yes, I don't see why not. I've got a strongbox in my room. They'll be safe enough there." He was indeed the best choice for the job; after all, I knew that he had not killed Sarah Archer because father Burrows had remained at my side as he accompanied me down from the top of the ziggurat.

"Well, then, what are we waiting for?" said McRae, addressing Woolley. "You may as well take her over there."

The archaeologist began to protest. "I think she should be allowed to enjoy a few more hours in her room. After all, lunch—"

Just then two pale figures appeared like ghosts in the corner of the room. Mr. Archer's demeanor, once so confident and impenetrable, seemed to have crumbled: his eyes were red and raw from grief and his shoulders had slumped forwards as if all life had been sucked from him. His wife looked almost deranged: her hair hung about her swollen, tearstained face and it was clear that she had not changed her clothes from the day before.

Mr. Archer cleared his throat. "I think it's best if she went into the shed straight away, don't you?" he said weakly.

How could anyone argue with a parent who had just spent hours sitting next to the body of his murdered daughter?

"Very well," said Woolley in a quiet voice. "I'll take her in there myself."

Woolley left the room and we fell once more into silence. Cynthia Jones went over to Mr. and Mrs. Archer and tried to encourage them to eat some lunch, but the couple refused. I suspected that none of us had much of an appetite for food at that moment.

"At least come and sit down and have a cup of tea," urged Cynthia.

"No, thank you," replied Mrs. Archer, her head angled towards the door and her eyes full of fury.

"But you must be feeling so weak," continued Miss Jones. "You have to keep your strength up. Mr. Archer, please try to persuade your wife to have something. We don't want you to—"

At this point Ruth Archer broke away from her husband and ran out of the room. A moment later we heard her screaming as though demented. Each of us sprang up from our seats and ran towards the courtyard, where a nasty scene between Mrs. Archer and Katharine Woolley was taking place.

"You murderer!" shouted Ruth Archer, her face red with rage.

"Please contain yourself, Mrs. Archer," urged Woolley, who had been leading his wife from the house.

"Why did you do that to my daughter?" Mrs. Archer shrieked, her voice breaking. "Just tell me why? What did she ever do to you?"

Katharine opened her mouth to say something, but Leonard pulled her towards him. "Try to ignore her. She's suffering; one must pity her," he said.

"It's you I pity," hissed Mrs. Archer as she lurched forwards.

"Ruth, that's not helping matters," said Hubert Archer, placing an arm around his wife and drawing her away.

"It's *you* I'd like to kill!" she shouted at Katharine.

"Ruth, now, that's enough!" continued Mr. Archer. "Try to control yourself, please."

At this, Ruth Archer burst into tears and ran back into the house; the sound of the slamming door echoed through the hot, dusty air.

"You can understand how distressed she must feel," said Mr. Archer.

"She's still in shock," said Woolley. "Totally understandable in the circumstances. I'm sure Katharine won't—"

Katharine Woolley stared in astonishment at the two men before she interrupted her husband. "Well, I'm pleased that you both feel able to talk for your wives. And, Leonard, if you were about to say that I wouldn't mind, well, you're wrong. I do mind. In fact, I'm not only angry but deeply hurt by the whole saga." She turned to the rest of us watching the drama unfold and with a deep and theatrical voice said, "As for you—all of you!—look at you gawping at me as if I'm some common form of entertainment you might see in some end-of-the-pier show. You should be ashamed of yourselves."

"Come on, let's get you into your new quarters," said Leonard, trying to calm her down.

"You make it sound as though I'm moving into a hotel. I don't know if it's escaped your notice, Leonard, but I'm being imprisoned against my will in a dirty, decrepit shed. Is that how little you think of me?"

"Let's not make another scene, now," he said. "I'm sure all this will be sorted out when the police arrive tomorrow. It's only a temporary measure."

Katharine was about to answer back but clearly thought better of it. Instead she sighed in frustration and allowed herself to be led by her husband down towards the shed. She cut a pathetic figure, with her smart lavender hat positioned so neatly on her head and her mauve scarf blowing in the dry wind, almost as if she had dressed in expectation of taking a pleasant jaunt in a motorcar. As she entered the hut she turned to the rest of us, her face full of dismay, hurt, and betrayal. It was the kind of look a sick horse might give you the moment before it was shot.

16

Nobody cared for lunch, and so all of us drifted back to our rooms. I went through my notes, assessing the case from the very beginning. Despite hours of reading and thinking, I could not find any link between the death of Gertrude Bell—which was, after all, the reason I had been dispatched by Davison to Ur—and the murder of Sarah Archer.

Were there two different killers at work here? It certainly seemed that way. After all, Miss Bell had died from an overdose in her bed at her home in Baghdad; even if she had a premonition that someone wanted to kill her, her death would have been a peaceful one. It looked as though Miss Archer, however, had been hit over the head with a rock—a nasty, brutal, painful murder. But could the two killers be working together? If so, what had they to gain from the deaths? Could Katharine have employed someone to murder Miss Bell? Leonard Woolley himself had told me that life was cheap in Iraq. What was it that Gertrude Bell had written in that letter to her father? Yes, she had been talking about a perilous journey to Hayyil, where she had been taken prisoner: "There I heard it said that in that place murder was considered so normal, it was likened to the spilling of milk."

Did Mrs. Woolley harbor a secret resentment towards other

women? Was it a simple case of madness? After all, if Katharine was that insane, then there really would be no need to examine the case for evidence of a complex motive. Perhaps, possessed by a blind rage or in the midst of some sort of maniacal frenzy, she had indeed taken that rock and bludgeoned Sarah Archer to death. I knew that it was also perfectly possible for such murderers, those classified as mentally unhinged, to erase violent acts from their memories. Maybe Katharine was guilty of the crime but believed herself to be innocent.

Yet, as I read my notes, the thing that struck me was how Mrs. Woolley had been regarded as an oddity from the very first, almost as if someone was trying to prejudice opinion against her. I had heard her described as everything from strangely attractive, demanding, manipulative, jealous, eccentric, and unreliable to hysterical, erratic, insane. After this, perhaps it was only natural to attach that other deadly label to her personality—that of a murderer—especially when she was discovered sitting next to a body with blood on her hands.

The more I thought about it, the more I became convinced that there was someone behind all of this—someone who was desperate to cast Katharine Woolley in the role of a killer. But could this be a case of a very clever double bluff? I remembered the way Katharine told me that she had admired my novel *The Murder of Roger Ackroyd*. I also thought back to the plot of my first published novel, *The Mysterious Affair at Styles*, which featured a killer who was the most obvious suspect. Sometimes it was better for a murderer to hide in plain sight.

And what was I to make of her wild surmise that her first husband might actually still be alive? It sounded preposterous, but nevertheless it needed to be ruled out. I intended to investigate this matter further by asking Woolley whether it would be possible to set up a meeting with Hamoudi. I doubted that the foreman spoke much English, and so Woolley or one of the other members of staff would have to be present to translate.

I found Leonard in the *antika* room studying a set of precious stones lying on a sheet of white paper.

"Come and take a closer look at these," he said, ushering me over. "They were found scattered in one of the death pits, and this set here belonged on one necklace, I believe."

"What are they?" I asked as I peered at the delicate beads, some colored a dull red, others a startling bright blue.

"A mix of carnelian and lapis lazuli, which would have been interspersed with gold using a delicate filigree technique. Can you see?" With a pencil he pointed out tiny fragments of the precious metal. "The carnelian may have come from India and the lapis from Afghanistan. The person buried in this grave wanted to look beautiful, even in death."

I asked after Katharine, but it was clear that Woolley did not want to talk about his wife. I then brought up Mrs. Woolley's suspicion that her first husband may not have died back in 1919 and her fear that he was the one behind the recent attack.

"But how could that be possible?" he asked. "And why would he want to do that?"

"I know: it sounds rather extraordinary, doesn't it," I said. "But I suppose Colonel Keeling could be out to exact some sort of revenge on his wife." I explained the possibility that he could have disguised himself in some way among the workers; then I asked whether it might be possible to put a few questions to Hamoudi. Although he acknowledged that the scenario seemed most unlikely, he agreed to send for the foreman.

"I think Keeling spoke good Arabic, but even so, I'm sure Hamoudi would have noticed if anything like that was going on under his watch," he said, when a look of alarm came into his eyes, shortly followed by disgust. "But that means . . . no, surely not." He could hardly bring himself to say the words.

I knew what he was thinking: if Keeling was still alive, that would make Woolley and his wife bigamists. "Don't worry, I'm certain it won't come to that," I said, not wanting to increase his fear by articulating it.

"I'll go and find him now," he said, placing the beads back in their box. "You're very welcome to stay here, though. I'm sure you're not going to run away with any of our precious treasures."

I told him that I would wait for him to return, secretly pleased that I had the opportunity to explore a room that I had seen only once before, in candlelight and only for a few minutes. As I stood in the dusty storeroom, the sound of Katharine's distress the evening when she had found the body of her cat seemed to echo through the air. The thought that the corpse of Sarah Archer lay only a few feet away, in the pantry, unsettled me. Despite feeling on edge and anxious, I thought it only right to search the *antika* room for any possible clues. After all, it was a locked room, out of bounds to most of the group.

Ranged around the room were a series of shelves on which lay dozens of brown boxes. A label had been attached to each one, but on close inspection these did not give me much of a clue, as they were written using a particular code of letters and numbers. I picked up a box at random, carried it over to the trestle table, and eased off the lid. The box had been packed with tissue paper, which whispered to me of secrets of the past as I searched through it.

At the very bottom of the box lay a small but beautiful dagger ornamented with gold. Delicately, I placed my finger on the very tip of the blade, which felt as sharp as if someone had whetted it the day before. I wondered who had been the last person to carry the weapon. Had it been used to kill? My imagination stirred, and I saw a man greeting his best friend, offering him a seat at his table, and asking him to consume the lavish feast his servants had prepared before walking behind him and stabbing his companion in the back. I saw it all play out before my eyes: a man who killed his friend because of the discovery of his wife's infidelity. Although culture and customs changed, I doubted human nature did; the same problems, desires, wants, and passions existed thousands of years ago just as they did today.

I packed up the dagger and took out another box. This one contained a group of exquisite small bowls and shells, each fashioned from bright gold, which looked as though they might once have contained cosmetic powders. The sight made me think of the array of jars and receptacles on Katharine's dressing table. Her husband had also made reference to them. What was it he had said? We had been standing in this room and he had been showing us a pot used for the storage of a primitive kind of makeup. Yes, that was it. "She has a seemingly infinite amount of jars; I've no idea what's in them." My mind began to work. *What if someone . . . yes, that would fit very nicely indeed. That would certainly explain it.* But I stopped myself. How did I know that this theory, hardly even formed in my brain, was not some half-baked product of my fancy? My imagination had already conjured a scenario around an ancient dagger. Supposition was one thing, evidence and proof quite another.

I covered the shells and bowls with tissue paper and replaced the lid of the box, but in doing so I knocked to the floor a pencil that had been sitting at the edge of the trestle table. As I bent down to pick it up, I noticed a small circle of wax on the ground. I picked up the disk and ran it through my fingers. I recalled the time when Leonard Woolley had given us a brief tour of the *antika* room. Yes, he had been holding a pair of candles, because he said the treasures looked even more magical in the soft light. Perhaps, in the panic and chaos that had followed Katharine's cries, Woolley had upset the candleholder and a spot of liquid wax had dropped onto the floor, where it then solidified.

I heard the sound of men's voices approaching, and a moment later Woolley walked into the *antika* room with Hamoudi. The foreman was an imposing character, a tall man with a long face, a pronounced nose, and a slightly protruding jaw; in fact, there was something animalistic about him. He was wearing a long, flowing tunic or *thawb* fashioned from a light fabric, together with an agal, or traditional head covering. His eyes were small and dark and shone with intelligence. Woolley talked to him in Arabic, and the foreman replied in a series of deep, harsh-sounding pronouncements.

"He's saying that he cannot believe that my wife would do anything wrong," Woolley said. "You see, he holds her in the highest possible regard." Hamoudi continued to talk over the archaeologist. "He thinks it is against Allah's will that she be locked up in the shed. There is talk among the men about it—even rumors of some kind of protest or rebellion." Hamoudi's voice quickened and rose in pitch. "Yes, Hamoudi, if you could just slow down, I will tell the lady," he said, addressing the Arab. "He wants me to tell you that the Shaytan has come to Ur. The devil. There is a force here that is like a poison festering and killing a healthy body. My wife is innocent and only greater evil can come from keeping her locked up like a prisoner."

When the speech came to an end, both men looked at me for a response. I started slowly, first of all asking Woolley to convey my thanks to the foreman for agreeing to meet. I too believed that no good would come from locking up Katharine Woolley in the storeroom. I then asked Woolley to put my question to Hamoudi: Had he seen anything suspicious among his men? At this the foreman looked at me with distrust.

"He wants to know what you are suggesting?" Woolley said. "He's not happy with the question."

"I'm sorry," I said to Woolley. "Let me try and rephrase it." I said that I was not implying that either he or his men had done anything wrong. Rather, I wondered if he had seen any of his workmen behaving in a way that might suggest something odd—that one of them might in fact be a European in disguise. The question was met with a laugh so loud, it reverberated around the room. Hamoudi's little eyes squeezed shut and his mouth revealed an array of broken and discolored teeth.

"What does he find so funny?" I asked.

Each time Woolley tried to answer, Hamoudi split the air with his laughter and soon tears were rolling down his worn, sun-spoilt face. Finally, the foreman explained himself to Woolley.

"He doesn't mean to be rude," said the archaeologist. "But it's the idea that a white man—a Westerner—could fool him or the other men by dressing up in that manner. He says the intruder would be discovered in a matter of hours. The man would stand out like . . . well, he uses an indecent expression that is probably best not translated. Better to say that the Westerner would indeed be discovered quickly."

"I see." I felt myself blush a little. It was best to bring the conversation to a close. "Well, perhaps you could ask him to keep his eyes open for anything suspicious," I added.

"Indeed," replied Woolley, dismissing the Arab in another guttural interchange. When he had gone, the mask of joviality worn by the archaeologist fell away and he slumped into a depressed silence; it appeared that the interview with Hamoudi had only strengthened the suggestion that Katharine was indeed losing her mind. He walked over to a canvas chair in the corner of the *antika* room, sat down, and put his head in his hands. He looked like a man broken by circumstance. I knew, from what he had told me, that his marriage to Katharine was not intimate. That was hard enough for any man to endure. But now he was being forced to acknowledge that his wife might, at best, be clinically insane and, at the very worst, be a murderer.

"Maybe it *is* better if Katharine is taken away tomorrow," he said. "Perhaps she *does* need some serious medical help."

"What do you think will happen to her?" I asked.

"I'm not sure," he sighed. "I suppose it depends on what the police decide. As you know, the rule of law is extremely unforgiving in the Arab lands."

"Would she not get any kind of special treatment? You must be able to appeal to the British authorities here for a certain amount of clemency."

"I'm not sure," he said again. "But I'm afraid to say that I fear the very worst."

As he said those words, a thought wormed its way through my mind: What if it was Leonard who was behind all of this? Could he be trying to drive his wife mad? After all, his marriage was a sham. Divorce would ruin him. If he could arrange for Katharine to be taken away to some discreet institution where she remained for the rest of her life, then surely that would solve all his problems. The marriage could be annulled. He could get on with his work without the burden of having a neurotic wife. He could be free to marry again. Was there another woman on the scene? I knew from personal experience that some men grew tired of their wives and hankered after younger models. And if he had been unable to enjoy personal relations with Katharine, then perhaps it was only natural for him to look elsewhere. Did Leonard have a mistress back in England? Or was there even someone in Iraq—in Baghdad, perhaps—or in the camp itself? I couldn't imagine that he would find Miss Jones very alluring, but one never knew. Or did he have another kind of secret?

"I see from your expression that you fear the worst, too," he said.

"Well, let's hope it doesn't come to that," I said, dissembling.

"It's bad enough to think of Katharine locked up in that shed, but . . . ," he said, his voice breaking. He swallowed a couple of times and then continued, "How will she cope with a prison cell in Baghdad? I'm afraid it would kill her."

"Don't think about that," I said, trying to sound as if I had his welfare at heart. "You need to remain strong, if only for Katharine's sake."

He coughed, ran his hands through his hair, and stood up. His mouth twisted into a smile—perhaps he hoped that the gesture would be enough to raise his spirits—but I noticed that his eyes remained devoid of any spark of happiness. "Yes, you're right," he said. "You know, I do wonder what people back at home would think if they really knew how we lived out here."

"What, the basic conditions? The dust, the heat, and so on?"

"Not just that," he said. "May I speak honestly to you?"

"Yes, of course. You know you can say anything to me."

He studied me for a moment as if assessing whether he could trust me. "There's something about the desert that strips away all the pretensions of human nature. It's a shock at first to find out what lies underneath the veneer of respectability."

I was careful what to say next. "Is that something you've experienced yourself?" I asked gently.

"I was just thinking about Carchemish," he said vaguely, as if his mind was beginning to travel back in time. I knew that he had worked on that site with T. E. Lawrence and Hamoudi. "Particularly Jerablus. I was there . . . it must be seventeen years ago, now. You see, the archaeological remains at Jerablus fell under the control of the *kaimakam*, or governor, of Birajik."

These other names meant nothing to me, but I nodded my head in encouragement.

"It was a place famous for the beautiful black ibis, which winters in Sudan and returns to Birajik to nest on the castle wall. We discovered a very fine mosaic floor, dating to about the fifth century AD, with an image of the glossy ibis—an indication, you see, that even in Roman times the bird always flew back to the Euphrates in order to nest."

As I was beginning to wonder what this had to do with his previous point, Woolley sensed my slight impatience. "Sorry to digress, but it's important that you understand what we were doing there," he continued. "There was some kind of mix-up about whether we were allowed to dig there. We feared there might be trouble, and Lawrence and I armed ourselves with revolvers, hoping that we wouldn't have to use them. But when we were refused permission by the *kaimakam* to dig, I felt so angry that I took my gun out and placed it against the governor's left ear. I was shocked when I heard myself say, 'I shall shoot you here and now unless you give me permission to start work tomorrow.' "

"And did you?"

He paused for a moment before he said, "Luckily the governor leant back in his chair and said, with a wintry smile, that he could see no reason why we couldn't start the next day. So you see, I believe many of us could be capable of murder, given the right circumstances."

"I don't doubt it," I said, thinking about some of my own terrible experiences.

"Indeed, a murderer can often be a bonus out here."

The boldness of the statement surprised me, but again the rules of the desert were very different to the ones that existed in the drawing rooms of England. "In what way?"

"The cook and general factotum employed on the dig at Carchemish was Hajji Wahid, a man Miss Bell found most charming, I believe," he continued. "But Hajji was also a murderer. Apparently he had been rather too keen on a local young woman and had ignored the requests of the girl's brothers to leave her alone. The situation got so out of hand that eventually Hajji killed four men in a skirmish. In due course, Hajji was sent to prison, but Campbell Thompson, who was in charge at Carchemish, thought that the man was just the sort of chap he was looking for. And so he proved. When he came out of prison, Hajji was the most loyal of employees. He never left Thompson's side, always standing by with a gun, guarding him. And later, when I took charge, he became my bodyguard. Anyone who set foot into the site without permission was risking his life, and for the most part it was a very safe camp, because everyone knew that Hajji would not hesitate to shoot them dead."

"Yes, I can see that," I said.

"It's a shame he's not here now," he said. "Hajji would not put up with any nonsense. In fact, I doubt any of this would have happened if he had been here."

There was something I wanted to know. "May I ask: Do you have a gun in your possession?"

"Yes, of course," Woolley replied. "It would be madness to live out here and not have any means of protecting oneself and also the very valuable treasures that we've dug up."

"And do you keep it on your person or in your room?"

"It's kept in a strongbox in my bedroom. Why do you ask?"

"I wonder if you'd mind checking to see if it's still there."

Woolley's eyes narrowed as he looked at me. "What is it you suspect?"

I did not, of course, tell him the whole truth. It was enough to reveal only part of what I surmised. "I'm worried that tonight, or at least before the police arrive tomorrow, someone may try to make an attempt on Katharine's life."

He couldn't quite take the words in, and his eyelids flickered as he tried to comprehend what I had just told him. "I'm afraid that your wife may be about to be murdered," I added.

As he contemplated the thought of losing his wife, a look of almost unimaginable grief crossed his face. If Woolley was the one behind the plot to drive Katharine mad—if that was indeed what was going on here—then he certainly was a very fine actor. He opened his mouth to speak, but uttered nothing except a low moan. Finally, he asked me to follow him to his room, where he would show me the gun. However, first he took his time to make sure everything in the *antika* room was safely stored away. As he turned the key in the door, I noticed that his hand was shaking slightly.

"I think I've just finally cracked the translation of that particularly difficult tablet we unearthed the other day," called out Father Burrows as we stepped into the bright light of the courtyard.

"Not now, Eric," replied Leonard.

"It's just that it is ever so exciting," the Jesuit persisted. "You see, I was reading it all wrong. I had been thinking that—"

But Woolley cut him off. "I said not now! For God's sake, man, can't you see I'm busy!" I had never seen Woolley lose his temper; he always seemed so composed, so controlled, even in the most stressful of situations. He pushed on across the courtyard with a determination and an energy that reminded me of an express train. He did turn around to see Burrows's puzzled and somewhat hurt expression.

A moment later we were in his room, which contained only a minimal amount of furniture: a rather sad single bed, a desk piled high with books and papers, and a wardrobe that contained barely a change of clothes. It reminded me of the quarters of a bachelor or a student rather than a married man.

"It's all kept under lock and key," he said as he bent down to retrieve his strongbox from underneath the wardrobe. His fingers reached out and took hold of the metal box, presenting it to me with something of a flourish. From the pocket of his trousers he took out a key ring and selected a key. "In fact, it's the same gun I was telling you about earlier, the one which I used—or at least I was prepared to use—when I was in—' he said, as he tried to turn the lock. 'What's this? Why is this open?"

His hands pushed into the box but seemed to turn over nothing but empty air. "I don't understand. Where the . . . ?"

I knew what he was going to say next.

"The gun's gone. Somebody's taken my revolver. And the bullets, too."

17

Each of us sat around the table trying to hide the suspicion in our eyes. Woolley had called the group into the main room and related the fact that his gun had gone missing. The news acted like a small explosion, sending waves of disbelief and confusion through the camp.

"But when did you last see it?" asked McRae as he stood up.

"I'm not certain," said Woolley. "I think it was when I—"

"You can't be vague about it," interrupted the architect.

"Let me see," said Woolley, blinking. "I remember going to look in the strongbox to check if there were any extra keys to the padlock on the shed. Yes, that was it."

"And the gun was there then?" McRae continued in his aggressively interrogative manner.

"Yes . . . yes, it was," replied Woolley.

"And you're sure you locked the box?"

"Well, I'm almost positive I would have done," Woolley answered, in a way that did not inspire confidence.

"Damn it, man—sorry, ladies," McRae said, addressing Miss Jones, Mrs. Archer, and me before he turned back to Woolley. "Can't you see?"

"See what?" said an exasperated Woolley.

"Couldn't Katharine have taken it?"

"I don't see how or why she—"

"But she may have had the opportunity!"

The interchange between Woolley and McRae had taken on the air of a compulsive and ghoulish spectacle.

"She can't have done," insisted Woolley. "She was locked in her room."

"How do you know for certain? Perhaps she picked the lock, crept into your room, and took your gun. You see, all of us, apart from Mr. and Mrs. Archer, were here in this room at the time. No one would have known if that's what she had done."

For a moment the room was quiet before Mrs. Archer, who had been twisting her fingers in her lap, started mumbling to herself.

"She killed my daughter; she killed Sarah, she murdered my beautiful girl," she said. "She took a rock and smashed her head in. Sarah was so proud of her hair, her lovely hair. Now it's all matted. I tried to make it look nice—I tried to smooth it out—but the comb got stuck. All that dried blood . . ."

Mr. Archer, who had reverted back to his steady, composed self, placed a hand on his wife's wrist. "Hush, now, dear. You've had a shock. We've all had a shock."

She broke away from her husband and turned to him, her voice full of venom. "A shock? Is that how you see it? Is that how you'd describe how you feel after the death of our daughter?"

"Ruth, please . . ."

Hubert Archer bent down and lowered his voice to say something the rest of us could not hear. She started to resist his quiet entreaties, when he took hold of her hand again and appeared to apply pressure to her wrist. Finally Mrs. Archer closed her eyes as she winced in pain.

"That's right, come with me," he said, leading her from the table. "Let's go and have a rest."

Just before she reached the door, Ruth Archer turned to the table and said, in a series of gasps, "Let me tell you something—all of you. If you don't do something . . . something about that . . . that woman"—it was clear Mrs. Archer wanted to call Katharine Woolley something else entirely—"you're all going to be . . ." She forced out the final word in one final exhalation: ". . . *murdered*!"

Mr. Archer bundled the weeping woman away, but her cries continued until she had reached her room.

"I feel so desperately sorry for her," said Cynthia Jones. "I can't imagine what it must be like to lose a daughter like that."

"Yes, it's awful to witness," said Woolley.

"Forgive me for saying, but what she says does have an element of truth," countered McRae.

"That's right," said Cecil, his face flushing. "Who's to say we won't all end up like . . ." The boy's eyes filled with horror as he recalled seeing Sarah Archer's body. ". . . end up being killed!"

"So what do you suggest?" asked Woolley.

All eyes turned to Lawrence McRae. "As I see it, there is only one option, and that is to search Mrs. Woolley and that shed to make sure she is not in possession of the gun."

"Very well," said Woolley with barely disguised contempt. "And who would you suggest as a suitable candidate to carry out such an investigation?"

McRae looked around the room before his eyes settled on me. "I don't know . . . What about Mrs. Christie here?"

There was no reason not to agree. The search would give me an opportunity to talk to Katharine—if she would let me. After all, the last time we had spoken, she had been so angry that she had dismissed me with contempt in her voice, calling me nothing but a snake, a deadly serpent that slithered through the desert sands.

"Now, you do know what it is you are looking for?" asked Lawrence McRae in a somewhat patronizing tone as he and Woolley led me out of the room.

"Yes, I think I do," I said. The sweetness of my delivery disguised my true feelings. McRae's insistence on Katharine's guilt had made me more than a little suspicious of him.

I followed the men to the Archers' room. After McRae knocked gently on the door, a shaken-looking Mr. Archer appeared. He was clearly in no mood to talk and simply nodded in agreement as McRae outlined the plan to search Mrs. Woolley's quarters. From there, we went back to the main room and retrieved a key to the shed from Father Burrows.

"I can assure you that my wife is not in the best of moods," said Woolley. "So pay no attention if she's rude to you."

I had an idea. I thought back to something Miss Jones had said when I had first arrived at Ur. "I know: Why don't I take her some coffee as a peace offering?" I suggested.

"If you like, yes," said Woolley vaguely. I left the two men and went into the kitchen. I made the strongest, most pungent, sweetest pot of coffee I could, the kind of thick brown liquid that could keep you up all night—which was just the effect I wanted to achieve. When it was ready, I took a sip of the dark, bitter brew. After a few moments my head started to spin and I felt adrenaline begin to course through my veins. *That should do the trick,* I thought.

As I carried out the steaming coffeepot on a tray, I asked the two men whether it might be possible to go by myself to the shed.

"But what if Katharine tries to attack you?" asked McRae.

"Nonsense. I doubt Mrs. Woolley will do anything of the sort," I said.

"What do you think?" asked McRae, addressing Woolley.

"Katharine might throw some cruel things Mrs. Christie's way, but I doubt that she'd hurt her," the archaeologist replied.

"If you feel afraid, you must come back to the house straightaway," McRae declared.

I left the men under the shade at the front of the house and proceeded on my own to the storage shed. After placing the tray on the floor, I eased the small key into the padlock. The lock gave a satisfying click. I picked up the tray and paused for a moment on the threshold. I strained my eyes to make out the shapes and forms before me. Katharine lay curled up on the mattress, completely covered with a white sheet, and as I stepped closer, I struggled to make out whether she was breathing. Was she asleep or . . . ? I felt panic rise in my chest, as if a small bird had got itself trapped inside my rib cage and threatened to push its way up through my throat. I put the tray down on the earthen floor and edged forwards, fearful of what I might discover. I turned my head to the half-open door and the line of light that partly surrounded its frame. It was tempting to rush out of the shed and call for Woolley and McRae, but I swallowed my fear, moved to the edge of the mattress, and knelt down. I extended my hand and, unsettled by the sight of my trembling fingers, steeled myself to pull back the top edge of the sheet.

"Katharine," I whispered, so softly that I wasn't quite sure whether I could be heard.

Just then the sheet moved and a hand shot out to grab me. I reeled backwards, but the grip on my wrist tightened.

"Katharine—it's me, Agatha," I said, trying not to raise my voice. After all, I did not want Woolley and McRae to come running.

She was sitting up and staring at me with wide, terrified eyes, the look of a woman who was in fear of her life.

"I'm not here to hurt you," I whispered. "I'm here to help. Katharine, please."

The grip on my wrist loosened and finally she fell back onto the mattress.

"Listen, we don't have much time," I said, taking a deep breath. "I've been told that I have to search you for a gun that has gone missing. I doubt very much you have it, but—"

"A gun?" she said, looking confused.

"Yes, Leonard's revolver."

"What do they think I would do with a gun?" she said, brushing her dark hair away from her face.

"I'm not sure," I said. "But the house is in a state of panic. People want to blame you for . . . well, for everything that has happened."

"But you know that I didn't do any of those things! I could never hurt Tom, my dear, dear Tom." Tears came into her eyes at the mention of the dead cat. "Lying here, I've been thinking about him. The way he used to curl up on my bed. The feel of his soft fur against my cheek. I wish he was here with me now. And although Miss Archer could be irritating, I would never do such a terrible thing as . . . as murder." She pronounced this as if she were fearful of the word itself. "You do believe me, don't you?"

That was the question. Did I? The situation was so very complex that I wasn't quite sure what I believed. Yet I did not have time to explain everything.

"Yes," I said, even though I wasn't quite sure of it myself. "Now, before we go any further, would you mind if I searched the room? For the gun."

Katharine responded with a shake of her head.

"It won't take long and then I'll explain what is going to happen next," I said. There were few places to hide a gun in the room, and after I had searched the floor and walls, looking for any recently dug holes or gaps, and then the mattress, there was only Katharine's person that needed to be checked. "I think this is why McRae chose me for the task," I said lightly as I related what I needed to do.

Her face darkened at the request. "That's completely out of the question," she snapped. "I'm not going to be frisked like—well, like a kind of woman I'd rather not mention."

Was she hiding something in her clothes?

"I understand that all of this must be terribly distressing," I said.

"But I really do have to know that you are not in possession of that gun."

Katharine stared at me, that dark energy burning in her eyes. "Very well," she said finally. She stood up and raised her arms as I ran my hands over her slim, boyish body.

Even though I discovered nothing, part of me wished that she had indeed stolen the gun, if only to protect herself.

"I hope you're satisfied now," she said.

"I'm sorry I had to do that," I said, trying to soothe her nerves. "I know it may not seem like it, but I'm actually trying to help you."

"Help me?" Her tone was sarcastic. "Somehow I can't see it myself."

I walked over to the door and looked outside to check that nobody was listening. I picked up the tray and brought it over to the mattress.

"Katharine, I'm going to tell you something that is going to alarm you," I said.

She turned her head to the wall like a small child who had decided to withdraw their affection from one of her elders.

"I am fearful that something may happen to you tonight," I continued. "I think someone may be planning to do you harm."

"Harm? What do you mean?" she said, turning back to look at me.

"I'm not certain, but I want you to make sure you stay awake," I said. "I've brought you a pot of very strong, very sweet coffee—not to drink now but to take later. It will be cold and not very nice, but it's important that you do as I say."

"I don't understand," she said.

"I need you to be on your guard," I explained. "I suspect someone will steal into the shed tonight and try to . . ." It was difficult to say the words.

"To what?"

I took another deep breath. "To make an attempt on . . . on your life."

Katharine looked around at the walls of her prison. "And you want me to stay here?" She immediately jumped up and tried to make a dash for the door. I grabbed her by the wrist. "Listen—please," I urged. "It's the only way we are going to find out who is behind it all. If you run now, you'll only put yourself at greater risk."

The muscles in Katharine's arms tensed as she considered what to do.

"If you want to discover the identity of your real enemy, then it's the only way," I said. "I know it's risky—I know that you'll be afraid—but I've got a plan. I'm going to stay awake too and station myself outside. At the first sign of any trouble, I'm going to come running."

"But what about the others? Wouldn't it be better if you shared your plan with them? At least then they might be able to protect me."

"I'm afraid I'm not sure whom to trust," I said. "If I revealed everything, then we might lose our opportunity. Waiting any longer would be a very bad idea. When the police arrive tomorrow, they will probably arrest you, after which anything could happen—perhaps the very worst. You see, I believe someone wants you out of the way. And I think someone has been trying to drive you mad." I was conscious that I was speaking too quickly, and so I made an effort to slow down. "Do you remember what you told me about the faces at the window? The voices you said you heard?"

"Yes, it was awful," said Katharine, the painful memories casting a shadow across her face.

"Well, I've got a theory about all of that. I can't go into it just yet, but I hope perhaps I can share it with you once tonight is over."

Katharine nodded. She looked at me with a certain amount of respect and admiration. "Very well. Now tell me," she said, taking a deep breath. "What do you want me to do?"

18

Throughout dinner we all tried to pretend that everything was perfectly normal, but it proved an impossible task. Our nerves were in a delicate state and jangled with each scrape of a plate or bang of a glass on the table. Conversation was a stilted affair, and we made an effort to avoid the subjects that preoccupied us: the body in the pantry, the destruction of Miller's camera, the imprisonment of Mrs. Woolley, and—most terrifying of all—the missing revolver.

When I had reported that I had found no trace of the weapon, either in Katharine's meager quarters or on her person, the room had fallen silent. The inevitable question hung in the air like a nasty gas: if she had not taken the gun, then who had? It had to be somebody in the house: Mr. or Mrs. Archer, Harry Miller, Lawrence or Cecil McRae, Father Burrows, or Cynthia Jones. Of course, I wasn't without suspicion, and at various points during the meal I caught sight of people casting dark glances in my direction. There was also the possibility that Leonard Woolley was not being entirely honest and remained in possession of the revolver after all. If so, he could be playing a very clever game of double bluff.

After the food had been cleared away, Father Burrows asked me whether it would be a good time for him to show me the basics of cuneiform. I was hardly in the mood, but it would have been rude to refuse, as Woolley had already told him that I was keen to learn. Perhaps it would provide a little distraction from the endless play of dark thoughts that continued to circle through my mind.

Father Burrows went to get a sheet of paper and a pencil and with boyish enthusiasm started to explain the principles of the ancient writing system. He told me how the Mesopotamians would use a stylus made from a piece of reed to inscribe what they wanted to say on a fresh piece of clay—clay which had been gathered from the banks of the Tigris or the Euphrates. It was not so much an alphabet, he told me, but an elaborate series of syllables and words. On the piece of paper he began to make a number of marks—there were, he said, vertical, horizontal, and oblique wedges—signs which he then asked me to copy onto my piece of paper. The lesson went on to take in more complex aspects of the system—it was, he said, impossible to write a consonant on its own, and certain sounds such as *j* or *c* simply did not exist—but, despite my best efforts, I could not concentrate, as my mind was shadowed by the horrors of the night to come.

"Now, why don't you try to copy this," he suggested, pushing a sheet of paper towards me. "After you've had a little practice, we can get a piece of clay and use that."

My handwriting was messy at the best of times, and no matter how hard I tried to copy the series of strange signs, my efforts were clearly disappointing.

"Don't worry: if you put your mind to it, you'll be a dab hand in no time." Burrows glanced across the room at Cynthia. "When I first met Miss Jones, she was a complete novice like you, and yet she picked it up very quickly. Quite the natural, weren't you, Miss Jones?"

"Oh, I wouldn't say that," said Cynthia, blushing and turning her back towards us. I suspected that, like me, she felt uncomfortable with compliments.

"It's fascinating," I said, "but I'm afraid I'm rather tired. Would you mind if we took it up again tomorrow?"

"Not at all," said Father Burrows. "Yes, it has been quite an exhausting day. However, I'm pleased that you'd like to learn more about cuneiform. Most people show no enthusiasm for it whatsoever. Once you've mastered the basics, then you can go on to read some of the great texts. Oh, the wonders of the library of Ashurbanipal! Do you know that?" He did not stop for an answer. "The last great king of the Neo-Assyrian Empire. A collection of thousands upon thousands of clay tablets discovered by Layard in the mid part of the last century. In fact, it was Layard's assistant Hormuzd Rassam—himself quite an intriguing figure—who unearthed the most famous ancient Mesopotamian text of all, the *Epic of Gilgamesh*, dating from the Third Dynasty of Ur. Yes, really quite fascinating."

I tried to say good night to Father Burrows, but even as I made moves to step away from him, he continued with his monologue.

"There are many parallels between Gilgamesh and the Bible, particularly when it comes to the great flood," he said. It was obvious that Burrows had no intention of drawing his lecture to a close, and although I did not want to appear rude, I also did not care to stand and listen to him for the next half hour or so.

"I could listen to you talk about this into the early hours, but I'm afraid I do have to go to bed," I said. "Will you forgive me if I say good night and you can tell me more tomorrow? I have the whole morning free, but only if you have time: I wouldn't want to take you away from your work."

Father Burrows's eyes lit up at the prospect of hours of uninterrupted discourse on the literature of the ancients. "I would be delighted," he said.

I doubted whether he would get the chance, as I was certain that the next day would be taken up with much more serious matters. I said my good nights to the rest of the group and, feeling relieved, retreated back to the quiet of my room. I knew I would have a long night ahead of me, and so, after using a match to light a couple of candles, I lay down on my bed and closed my eyes for a few moments. The events of the last few days flashed before me, unpleasant memories that, like bloated corpses in a river, refused to settle and disappear. The terrible sight of Katharine's cat, that stain next to him on the bed. The image of all those pale, shocked faces patterned by deep shadows cast by the torchlight, gazing on something unspeakable. The body of Sarah Archer, the girl's head smashed in. The horror in Katharine's eyes as she looked down at her hands streaked with blood. The hatred on Ruth Archer's face as she lashed out and tried to attack Katharine Woolley.

I felt too unsettled to rest, and so I took up my notebook in an attempt to make sense of it all. Davison had sent me here to look into the death of Gertrude Bell; yet, since my arrival at Ur, her murder seemed almost peripheral. There was something else at work at the camp, something dark and base and evil that did not look as though it had a connection to the death of Miss Bell. My mind started to work, teasing out the various possibilities, and as I tried to record the conjunction of myriad motives and hidden designs, my pen could not keep up with the fast flurry of my thoughts.

As the night drew on, I listened for the now-familiar sound of the occupants making their preparations for bed until finally there was silence. Before I left the room I made sure that I was sufficiently prepared for what might happen. I did not want to use my arsenal of poisons, but I felt a little more secure knowing that in my handbag was a syringe filled with a fast-acting drug that could put a man to sleep in minutes. I took a deep breath and quietly opened my door, hoping that I could slip out of the house without being noticed. If I were to confront anyone such as Mr. Woolley, who I knew did not need much sleep, then I would tell him that I was going to step outside to look at the stars, that I intended to refresh myself with a little night air.

I blew out the candles, picked up the box of matches, and let my eyes adjust to the darkness. I edged my way across the courtyard, stretching a hand out before me as I did so. I tried to keep my breath quiet and steady, even though the primitive instinct of fear did everything in its power to close up my throat. I felt my chest beginning to tighten. Was there someone watching me in the dark? The old terror of the Gunman—that nightmare I had had since childhood, the sense of an omen of ill fortune—threatened to return. I remembered how the specter of that figure had frightened me as a girl and how later, driven to the edge of despair by Archie's infidelity, I had thought it had stolen into my husband's body. How easy it was for someone you loved to turn against you; a face that you had once gazed upon with adoration became possessed by something else entirely, something unfamiliar and strange. I was certain there was someone in the house who had donned a mask of respectability but who, in effect, was the embodiment of evil.

I took a couple of deep breaths and tried to put such thoughts out of my head. I walked slowly and as inconspicuously as I could down towards the shed, making sure that I kept to the pockets of darkness not illuminated by the stars. I came to settle on a pile of sandbags hidden behind the store, from where I would be able to hear anyone trying to open the door of the shed. I thought of Katharine inside the wooden shack. I hoped that she had followed my instructions and had drunk the strong coffee which would keep her senses primed for any signs of an intruder. I didn't need such a stimulant; despite my deep breaths and my repeated mantra to calm down, my heartbeat was already racing.

I tried to make out the constellations, tracing imaginary lines in the sky in an attempt to bring some kind of order to the seemingly random pattern of stars. I loved the names that populated the celestial sphere, made up of mythological characters, animals, and objects, and as I tried to pick them out of the sky—where was Hercules?—I wondered how many people had sat here before me looking up at the heavens, unable to sleep or driven from their beds by thoughts of their own mortality. We were all so small, so insignificant; the thought was a well-worn one, something of a cliché, but still there was a reason why throughout history many of us, when gazing up at the stars, had pondered the nature of it all. We were all the same, I thought. Despite culture, background, status, and sex, each of us wept, each of us laughed, each of us, if cut or shot, would bleed; indeed, in the end, each of us would die. If this was the case, what was the point in me trying to prevent the death of Katharine Woolley? After all, I knew that the woman—whom I had only met quite recently—would die one day. The answer was that I believed in the sanctity of life; it was, I felt, something supremely important. Yes, I would do anything in my power to stop this murderer.

Just then I heard someone approaching. I dared not peek out from my hiding place behind the shed, but the sound of footsteps was unmistakable. I clasped my handbag closer to my chest and tried to ignore the rasp of my own quickening breath. The person approached the front of the shed and stopped. Then I heard the faint sound of a padlock spring open and the creak of a door. I knew that I would have to act. I eased myself slowly forwards and felt my way towards the front of the shed. My steps were slow and as soft as I could make them. As I turned the corner I noticed a dark shape surrounded by the frame of the open door. The figure's back was turned to me, but there was no uncertainty that it was a man and that he was raising his hand. I had not a moment to lose.

I moved quickly and took out a match and lit it. Although my fingers were trembling, I knew I had only one chance at this. I concentrated as I pressed down with the match onto the box. The touch, I knew, had to be firm and yet somehow graceful, a difficult combination to master when one was trying to prevent a murder.

As I struck the match a spark turned into a flame and the figure turned round. I lifted up the match and the small light was enough to illuminate the frightened face of a boy. Cecil.

"Stay away," he said, swinging around to look at me.

"He's got a gun!" shouted Katharine from inside the shed.

"Shut your mouth," he hissed, turning back towards Mrs. Woolley. "You've done enough damage as it is."

I had to think quickly. "Cecil, is this something you really want to do?" I said in as calm and as soothing a voice as I could manage. "What would your uncle say? Or your poor parents?"

"Don't you dare speak of them," he said as he continued to point the gun towards Katharine. "They have nothing to do with this. She's the one that has got to pay for what she did. For what she did to Sarah."

"How do you know for certain it was Mrs. Woolley?" I asked, conscious that my match would only burn for another few seconds. I knew that I could light another one, but in those moments of darkness that would inevitably follow, I had to acknowledge that anything could happen. Cecil might panic; he could shoot into the shed or fire the gun into the night. I or Katharine, or both of us, might get injured—or worse.

"Everyone knows it was her," said Cecil. "We all saw her. Her hands were covered in Sarah's blood."

I took a step forwards. "Now, why don't you put the gun down and we can—"

"Don't come any closer," he said, spitting the words out. "I warn you." As he swung round towards me I noticed that his hand was shaking from the way the glinting metal of the gun trembled in the starlight.

"I know that you were very fond of Sarah," I said, the match singeing the ends of my fingers. "It's terribly sad that she—" As the flame neared the end of the matchstick, the sensation of burning was too much and I had to drop it.

"That she was murdered by . . . by this . . ." said Cecil, his voice trailing off in disgust.

The sky may have been full of stars, but the loss of the light from the match seemed to plunge the scene into darkness. It took a moment or two before my eyes adjusted to the night. I quickly tried to light another match, but this time my fingers felt clumsy. I saw a spark, but it died as soon as it came alive. Then the second flared up too quickly, burning itself out in a moment. By the time I had successfully lit a third match, Cecil had moved inside the shed to stand over Katharine, who was cowering in the corner of the mattress.

"Please . . . please, no," she begged. "I swear to you I had nothing to do with—"

Cecil leant forwards and placed the gun on Katharine's right temple. Although it was obvious that the boy was nervous—the revolver continued to shake in his grasp—he would still kill her if he pulled the trigger. I had to act. With my free hand I unzipped my handbag, placed it on the floor, and took out the syringe. I moved quietly and stealthily toward the boy, ready to plunge the syringe into his back. But just as I was about to reach out, he turned towards me.

"What the . . . ," he said, as if he could not believe what he was seeing. He grabbed my wrist with his left hand and twisted my fingers, forcing me to drop the syringe and the box of matches. Again the match extinguished itself, again I felt the ends of my fingers burn, but this was nothing compared to the pain I felt in my other arm as Cecil forced my hand around my back.

"Are you in this together?" he spat. "Is that what this is all about?"

It was my turn then to feel the unmistakable cold caress of the gun against my temple. Fear closed up my throat, preventing me from speaking.

"If that's the case, I should finish you both off," he said, pressing the revolver harder into my skin. "Two sad old maids, jealous of our youth. Was that it?"

At thirty-eight years of age, I was far from old, but I knew in Cecil's eyes I was like an ancient relic. In that moment I thought of all the things I wanted to do with my life. I didn't want to die, not yet. I would never see Rosalind grow up, never see her children. And what about my books? After a rather dry spell, when I had suffered from that awful paucity of ideas, now I found that inspiration came easily. I had so many stories swirling about my head that I wanted to tell. One bullet dislodged by Cecil McRae would be the end of all of that—the end of me.

I took a deep breath, and although every cell in my body was telling me to fight back, to struggle, to do anything to stay alive, I closed my eyes and forced myself to relax. Perhaps if I went as lifeless as a dead fish, the boy might loosen his hold on me. I imagined myself as a child in my mother's arms. I was safe at my family home, Ashfield, in Torquay. Nothing could harm me. However, as soon as I opened my eyes, I realized the real danger which faced me. Was I experiencing my very last moments?

Just then, as I felt Cecil tighten his grip on me, I heard an almighty high-pitched scream. Katharine jumped up from the mattress and bore down on Cecil. She tried to stab the boy—she must have found the syringe on the floor—but as she reached out, Cecil grabbed her hand to stop her. In doing so, he had no choice but to free me and I fell back and away from him. Somewhere on the floor lay the box of matches that I had dropped. I moved across the ground like a crab, stretching out my hands in the hope of finding the box.

"Oh, no you don't," said Cecil as he bent back Katharine's fingers, forcing the syringe from her hand. "I'll take that."

"Agatha, help me," gasped Katharine, the pain audible in her voice.

"What's in here?" he asked. "What's in the syringe? Tell me!"

"Don't hurt her," I said. "It's a strong sedative, I promise, nothing more."

"If that's all it is, then I'm sure Mrs. Woolley here wouldn't mind a little something to ease her misery," he said. "I've always wondered about a gunshot wound to the head. How much pain you would feel. They say it's more or less instantaneous, but you must feel something. Although I don't like to think of it, I'm sure Sarah felt pain in the moments before her death."

As I made another large circular movement with my right arm, I felt the familiar rattle of the matches in their box on the ground. I grabbed it and, despite my shaking hands, managed to light one. Cecil had bent over Katharine: in one hand he held the gun, which he pointed at her chest; in another he brandished the syringe. It seemed as though Katharine's fate was sealed.

"You know Miss Archer was really quite taken with you," I said.

There was no response from Cecil.

"Yes, she told me that she liked you but that she was too shy to tell you," I continued.

"I—I don't believe you," the boy replied.

"Oh, no, it is true," Katharine managed to say, understanding what I was up to. "The girl more or less said as much to me, too."

"She had to pretend to be cruel to you because she didn't want you to know the truth," I said as I used a match to light a candle. The soft light cast its amber glow across the enclosed space of the shed, sending amorphous shadows across the walls.

"The truth?" His voice was soft now, gentle almost, and he lowered the gun slightly.

"That she loved you," I replied.

"Then why did she go and spoil it all, then?" said Cecil, the anger rising within him once more as he addressed Katharine. He aimed the revolver squarely at Mrs. Woolley's throat, his finger on the trigger.

"Cecil, I don't think Sarah would have wanted you to do this," I said.

"And what makes you such an expert all of a sudden?"

"She came from a Christian family, didn't she? Surely that must count for something. She wouldn't want you to suffer."

"Suffer?" he said, blinking as if seeing the gun in his hands for the first time.

"I'm not talking of the sweet—or not-so-sweet—hereafter, I'm afraid," I said. "No, I was referring to the here and now. As soon as that gun goes off, you're going to have everybody from the camp running from their beds to find out what has happened. Your uncle will see what you've done. I believe he's tried his very best to give you some stability since the deaths of your parents. And then it's a question of the police. You'll almost certainly be put to death for your actions. Is it worth all of that?"

In that moment Cecil looked like a confused child who had just woken up from a nightmare.

"If you put that gun down, I'm sure we can all agree that this was nothing but a boyish mistake," I said. "We needn't mention it ever again."

He looked from me to Mrs. Woolley. "Are you sure?"

"Oh, yes, quite certain. Aren't we, Katharine?"

Mrs. Woolley reluctantly nodded her head, but I could tell that she did not believe it for a second. She knew that as soon as the revolver was out of his hands we would raise the alarm and he would have to face the consequences of his actions.

"And if you felt like it, you could even help us find the real murderer of Miss Archer," I suggested.

He paused for a moment before he raised the gun again.

"It wasn't me, I tell you," whispered Katharine, trying not to show her fear. "It wasn't . . ."

I had tried everything I could, but it looked as though Cecil was determined to take his revenge on Mrs. Woolley. If I did anything to stop him, I knew he would not hesitate to turn the gun on me. I prepared myself for the very worst. I could not bring myself to witness the death of Katharine at such close quarters, and so I closed my eyes. I took the coward's way out.

However, instead of the click of the trigger and the blast from the gun, I heard Cecil's soft whimper. I opened my eyes to see the boy, now red in the face, throw the revolver and the syringe across the shed towards the door.

"Damn it!" he shouted as he stood up straight. "I'm pathetic. My father always said so and so did Sarah. They were right. I'm weak-willed. I can't even kill the person who murdered the girl I loved." He kicked the mattress and turned to go, but as he was about to leave the shed, he bent down and picked up the gun, hit the door with his fist, and disappeared into the night.

My immediate instinct was to run into Katharine's arms. We didn't say anything but just stood there silently as we replayed the terrible events of the last few minutes in our minds.

Finally Katharine stood back, looked at me, and in a low voice said, "Do you think . . . ?" I knew from her inference what she meant: whether Cecil might take his own life.

"I'm not sure," I said. "He may do so. He's in an awful state. I'll go back to the house and see if I can find his uncle."

"Don't leave me," she said. "I'm not sure whether I could stand it."

"I'll only be a few moments. And then I promise I'll come back and I'll stay with you."

"You won't lock me in, will you?"

"I think it's best, if only for your own safety," I said. "You never know: Cecil might be lurking outside, waiting for me to leave."

Katharine looked at me with an expression of utter misery. "I just don't understand. How long can this go on? I don't think I will be able to endure it." She raised her hand to her head. "Everything feels so . . . I don't know. I can't explain."

"You can tell me," I said gently.

"I'm scared, Agatha. Even more frightened than before. Not so much for my own life. After what happened, I feel that could be taken from me at any moment. It might come as a blessed relief."

"Don't say that," I said, placing a hand on her arm.

"What happens if they put me away? I'd rather be hanged or shot than spend my life in some kind of institution. I've seen what goes on in those places."

"I'm sure it's not going to come to that."

"Maybe it's best if I confess to the crime." The look of mania that had frightened me so had returned to her eyes. "Yes, I could tell the authorities that I had taken a rock and smashed it over Miss Archer's head. That I relished the sound of the stone hitting her skull. That I did it over and over until she was dead. Would that do it? Would that convince them? They'd take me away, I would be sentenced without so much as a hearing, and put to death in some primitive, utterly barbaric manner."

"Don't talk like that," I said quite firmly. "Now, listen. I'm going to leave you for a moment or two. I'm going to lock the door. I will go and find Lawrence McRae and tell him what has just happened. Then I'm going to come straight back here with some extra blankets. I can sleep on the floor, next to your mattress. And then, in the morning, we will clear all of this up. Also, I have every expectation that my friend John Davison—he works in a division in the Foreign Office . . ." I thought it best to keep details vague. "Anyway, I think he'll soon turn up with the police. He's got a good head on his shoulders. He is the kind of man who can see clearly through a difficult situation. He'll make sure nothing untoward happens to you."

Katharine did not respond, but as I walked towards the door, I saw that her eyes were beginning to dart around the walls of the shed. She watched the shadows cast by the candle with a mix of fascination and fear. Had this later incident with Cecil finally pushed her over the edge?

I turned the key that Cecil had left in the padlock, then pocketed it. Pausing by the door, I listened for signs of the boy. With the light from a candle, I made my way back to the house and across the courtyard until I reached Lawrence McRae's room. I knocked on the door and a moment or two later heard the sound of the architect stirring from his bed.

"Who is it?" he said from behind the door.

"It's Mrs. Christie," I said.

"Is there something the matter?" he asked as he opened the door, fastening a paisley-patterned dressing gown around him.

"It's your nephew, I'm afraid," I said. I took a deep breath before I explained what I had witnessed in the shed. "I fear Cecil may do something . . . stupid. He took off with the gun, you see."

"Yes, you were right to come and tell me," he said. I turned my back as he quickly put on some clothes. "As you might have guessed, he's not been right since the death of his parents."

"What happened to them?" I asked.

McRae did not answer. Instead he picked up a flashlight and asked, "Where did you say he went?"

"I'm not sure," I said as I accompanied him out of the house. "He ran out into the darkness. I came as fast as I could. I left Mrs. Woolley locked up in the shed."

"If you could rouse a few of the other men and tell them that Cecil has gone missing," he said, "I'll go down and start searching for him now."

McRae started to call out the boy's name. I ran back into the house and knocked on the doors of Leonard Woolley and Harry Miller. Mr. Archer had been through too much already, and I thought Father Burrows would be more of a hindrance than a help. I gave a quick synopsis of how Cecil had threatened Mrs. Woolley before taking the gun and disappearing. Disturbed by the noise, the other occupants soon opened their doors to find out what was happening. Cynthia Jones appeared, looking an absolute fright in her old-fashioned nightgown and bed hat. Father Burrows emerged blinking, battling with his wire-framed spectacles. The Archers, the poor grief-stricken parents, stepped into the main room looking as though their spirits had been sucked out of them.

"Please, I think it's best if you go back to bed," I said.

"What happened?" asked Mr. Archer.

"Please . . . please, not . . . not that woman," said Ruth Archer, with fear in her voice. "She hasn't . . . escaped?"

"No, nothing of that kind," I said. I didn't want to add to their worries. "She's still locked up in the shed. It's Cecil. He seems a little . . . unbalanced."

"When will this nightmare end?" asked Mr. Archer. "There's something rotten about this place. In fact, I don't believe it's where Abraham was born after all."

"I wish we'd never come!" his wife exclaimed, then started to cry. "Why didn't we stay in Paris? Sarah was so happy there."

Miss Jones and I watched them walk arm in arm back to their room. Cynthia asked me what had happened to Cecil, and as I related what had occurred, she looked taken aback and more than a little shocked.

"But don't worry, I'm sure he's not a danger to anyone but himself," I said. "I must get back to Mrs. Woolley. I promised her I wouldn't be long."

"Please take care," she said, her eyes full of concern as she handed me her flashlight. "After all, I'd hate it if anything happened to you as well."

Miss Jones's words echoed through my head as I made my way first to my room to get some blankets and then back to the shed. Just as I was about to turn the lock and open the door, I heard a call from Lawrence McRae.

"He's over here, by the spot where . . . where we found Miss Archer!" the architect shouted.

I saw the beams of light from the men's flashlights change direction as they ran through the darkness towards the bottom of the ziggurat. I hoped they would be in time to save the poor boy's life. He was in a very bad way, close to complete nervous collapse. As I opened the padlock and stepped into the shed, I heard a gunshot split the night.

19

"Quick, push something against the door," said Katharine.

"But what about Cecil?" I asked.

"If the stupid boy wants to go and kill himself, I say let him," she replied. "After all, he hardly behaved like the perfect gentleman, did he?"

The statement was true enough, but I ignored her cruel remark and told her that I felt duty bound to see if I could help. My nursing training had not left me and I still felt a moral compulsion to relieve any suffering I might encounter. If Cecil had indeed shot himself, he could still be alive, and, if so, his life might be saved.

"Now, where's that syringe?" I asked. "From my reckoning it should be still in this corner where Cecil threw it." I bent down and, with the light from the flashlight, searched for the hypodermic needle. I looked in dusty corners, under the edge of the mattress, and even outside the door, but it was nowhere to be found.

"Perhaps Cecil took it as he went out, when he picked up the gun," said Katharine as she saw me scrabbling on the ground.

"Yes, I suppose he must have done," I said. "Anyway, I must go and see what I can do."

"And you'll lock the door, won't you?" pleaded Katharine. "I don't want that boy making a second attempt on my life."

I did what she asked and then, with the flashlight, ran through the darkness towards the men's cries and calls emanating from the base of the ziggurat.

"Who's that?" It was Miller's voice.

"It's Agatha," I said. "What's happened?"

I tried to make sense of what I saw. Cecil lay prostrate on the ground, on the exact spot where Sarah had died. In the sand by his right shoulder lay Woolley's gun. He wasn't moving, but as I ran my flashlight across his body—from his head, neck, torso, towards his waist, lower body, and limbs—I couldn't make out any traces of blood or any obvious wounds.

"Is he dead?" asked Miller.

McRae stepped forwards, kicked the gun out of Cecil's reach, and bent down. "No, he's still breathing," he said. "Cecil, Cecil, wake up," he said, shaking him.

"He's probably injected himself with a sedative," I said, crouching down by the boy and using my flashlight to illuminate the ground. There, half buried in the sand, was the syringe. I picked it up and, as I held it up to my flashlight, saw that it was empty. "He must have had the gun in his hand but quite wisely decided not to end it all. Instead he decided to use this," I said, showing the men the syringe. "And the gun must have gone off as he injected himself. He's just going to have a very long, very deep sleep, nothing more."

"But where the hell did he get hold of that?" asked McRae.

"It's mine," I said.

"And do you make it a habit to go around carrying drugs of this kind?" There was an unpleasant tone to McRae's voice. "I hope you haven't got anything else stashed away."

I did not reply.

"Let's get the boy back to the house," said Woolley. "We can take it in turns to watch him and then we can inform the police of everything when they arrive tomorrow."

"What do you mean?" asked McRae. "Surely we don't need to tell them—"

"I'm afraid they need to know everything that has gone on here," Woolley replied, cutting him off.

"But it won't look good, not with the boy's history," said McRae.

"His history?" I asked.

There was an awkwardness that hung in the night air. The flashlight that shone on McRae gave him an unhealthy, sallow appearance.

"I suppose you may as well know now," he said. "It's about the boy's parents. The reason why I've been so protective of him. I didn't want to say anything before." He fell silent before Woolley prompted him to continue. "You know that Cecil's father and mother died in an accident. That is true enough. But what you don't know is the manner in which they were killed. You see, one day Richard, my brother, was showing the boy how to use a gun. They lived deep in the Scottish countryside and they were going to hunt some rabbits. But that day—this was when Cecil was only fourteen—the boy . . ." He cleared his throat and continued. "We still don't know the exact circumstances of what happened, but Richard and his wife, Elizabeth, died by gunshot wounds."

"So you're saying that Cecil killed his own parents?" asked Miller.

"I'm sure it wasn't deliberate," replied McRae. "Well, the coroner seemed to be very understanding. He ruled accidental deaths. Of course, I had to pull a few strings. Luckily I had some contacts in the local force, and I had to promise that he would live with me until he came of age."

"And you brought him to this camp?" said Woolley.

"Yes, but I was sure that—"

"You do know you put everyone's life here at risk, don't you?" Woolley's voice was cold and full of anger. "How am I going to explain this to the directors of the museums? What will I say when I tell them the truth?"

"I don't see why they need to know."

"Are you insane?" said Woolley, his voice rising. "For all we know, Cecil here may be some kind of unhinged killer. What if he is the one responsible for Miss Archer's death?" His brain worked quickly as he tried to make sense of how this new piece of information fitted into the larger picture. "What if her rejection of him led him to bash her over the head with a rock? And then he planned on framing my wife for the death? Perhaps he was going to make the shooting of Katharine look like a suicide. After all, the facts are undeniable: he stole into the shed, armed with my revolver, with the aim of shooting her."

"That's nonsense and you know it," said McRae. "Cecil would never dream of hurting Sarah. He loved her. And as regards to what just happened in the shed, I suspect he was just blowing off a bit of hot air."

"Hot air indeed!" exclaimed Woolley. "Had it not been for Mrs. Christie's clever intervention, I suspect all of this could have turned out very differently. No, I'm afraid that there is no question: the police will have to be informed of all the circumstances. And if I have my way, the boy will be tried and found guilty. He'll certainly be taken away, and even if he does escape with his life, I can tell you that he'll never set foot within the camp again."

"But—"

"We've stood here in the dark long enough as it is already," Woolley continued. "There's nothing more to be said. We need to get Katharine out of that awful place and back into her own quarters. God knows she's suffered enough as it is. But first let's get this boy inside. Come on, Miller. Will you give me a hand?"

The men took Cecil by the shoulders and legs and carried him into the house, leaving McRae and me to trail behind. I was curious to know more about Cecil and his mother and father. I could understand how the boy might have accidentally shot one of his parents, but not both. Surely after he had seen a bullet go into one of them—say, his father—he would have realized what an appalling thing he had done and then dropped the weapon. But if he truly did not mean to carry out the act of murder, why would he then swing around and take aim at his mother? What was it that made him hate them so much? It did not make sense. Woolley's theory—that Cecil had killed Sarah and then intended to frame Katharine and, after shooting her, make that death look like a suicide—seemed much more plausible.

"I understand this must all be very distressing for you, Mr. McRae," I said.

"Yes, indeed it is," he said as he stared straight ahead, refusing to meet my gaze.

"I wondered if I could ask a question." I did not wait for his response. "Was Cecil a happy boy? As a child, I mean."

"Happy?"

"Yes. Was he a cheerful little boy, without a care in the world?"

"No, I don't suppose he was. But that doesn't make him a killer, Mrs. Christie."

I fell silent for a moment. "No, of course," I agreed. I was conscious of McRae's inference with regard to Katharine Woolley: murder was a habit, he had suggested. At the time he had been trying to persuade us that Katharine had killed her first husband and that, since then, Mrs. Woolley had been possessed by some kind of urge to murder again and again. But what if it was not Mrs. Woolley who had a taste for murder but Cecil? And what if his uncle had known this all along and was doing everything in his power to protect his charge? Did that make him an accessory to the crimes?

"I know it's none of my business, but I was just thinking . . . about the accident involving Cecil and his parents," I said.

"I'd really rather not talk about it any more, if you don't mind," he said.

"You see I can't understand why Cecil didn't drop the gun after the first shot went off," I said. "I must appear terribly stupid, but—"

"Yes," said McRae, implying that I appeared to be very stupid indeed.

"But it seems to me that if it was an accident, then the most natural thing in the world would be to throw the weapon from one's hands. Or to simply stop shooting."

McRae turned to me and put a hand on my shoulder. "I really don't think it's any of your business, do you?" In the darkness I could sense the anger burning in his eyes. "In fact, I would suggest that you stop this line of inquiry right now. Am I making myself clear?" I felt his fingers dig into my skin. "After all, I think we've had enough accidents for the time being." The pressure on my shoulder intensified for a moment before he released his grip and stormed away back into the house. McRae was definitely hiding something—something which would not remain in the shadows for long. I would ask Davison when he arrived if he could send off and request records of the case, including information about the beneficiaries of Richard and Elizabeth McRae's will.

I had so much to tell Davison that I didn't know where I would start. In truth, I couldn't wait to see him so I could at last speak freely of some of the things I had observed since I had arrived in Ur. The phrase *wheels within wheels* came to mind; I sensed that so much still remained obscured from me. But as I walked back to Katharine, I had to acknowledge that this was more like a case of "murders within murders." I pictured a Venn diagram of sorts, a series of interlinked circles, their edges outlined in blood.

20

"Mrs. Christie, Mr. Davison of the Foreign Office tells me he is already acquainted with you, is that correct?" asked Woolley as he led my friend into the room where we were just finishing breakfast.

"Yes, indeed," I said as I stood up and shook Davison's hand. The look we exchanged—a rather formal but courteous expression of recognition—concealed not only the real nature of our purpose in Iraq but also the depth of our friendship.

"And this is Captain Forster, a representative of the Baghdad Police, who has been dispatched to try and sort out this unholy mess," added Woolley as he introduced a sandy-haired young man who looked barely old enough to shave, never mind lead a murder investigation. Clearly he had been sent out as part of the British administration in Iraq, and I wondered how much he really understood about the country.

"I've told Mr. Davison and Captain Forster the details of what has occurred, but obviously both of them will want to interview each of you in turn," said Woolley, addressing the group at the table. "I hope that won't put you to too much of an inconvenience." Murmurs of agreement came from Mr. Miller, Miss Jones, and Father Burrows; Mr. and Mrs. Archer and Katharine Woolley were not present, as they had decided to take breakfast in their rooms. "First of all, they are going to question Cecil McRae, who remains locked in my room."

"The whole thing is bloody ridiculous," said Lawrence McRae under his breath.

"You may think so," replied Woolley, who had heard the architect. "But nevertheless the process is one that has to be followed."

"You know as well as I do that the boy would not hurt a fly," said McRae.

Woolley was implacable. News of Cecil's past had already circulated through the camp, and so Leonard felt able to speak freely. "I've informed Mr. Davison and Captain Forster of the boy's background," he said calmly, "and they will contact the relevant authorities back in Scotland to find out the exact circumstances of his parents' deaths."

McRae pushed his plate away from him and stood up from the table, finding it difficult to contain his anger. "I always suspected you cared more for the dead than for the living, but now I know this to be the case," he said.

"Mr. McRae, I do think that's quite—" said Woolley just as McRae stormed across the room towards him. The architect lunged at Leonard, and just as he was about to strike him in the face, Davison and Forster restrained him.

"If anything happens to that boy, I know who to blame," McRae exclaimed as he tried to free himself from the men's grip.

"Really, I think that's—" said Woolley.

"I think it would be best if you calmed down," said Davison. "Come on, Forster, let's take him outside for a breath of fresh air."

As the two men ushered McRae towards the door, the architect turned to Woolley and said, "If that boy dies for a crime he didn't commit, you're the one that should be punished."

An embarrassed silence descended on the room and was broken only when Miss Jones asked if anyone would like another cup of tea. "I do think it would help," she said.

"I'm sorry about that," said Woolley. "I suggest, if you're all in agreement, that we get back to work as soon as possible. Not only are we behind schedule, but we could all do with something to take our minds off . . . well, off the rather distressing events of the last few days."

"Indeed," said Burrows. "In fact, there was something I wanted to talk to you about." As Father Burrows moved over to discuss the intricacies of a certain cuneiform tablet with Woolley, Mr. Miller came over to take his place at the table.

Since the incident on the ziggurat, when I had half fancied that I felt a certain amount of tenderness towards the handsome photographer, I had deliberately tried to distance myself from him. I dreaded the rejection and couldn't bear to let myself be humiliated.

"I heard what you did last night to save Katharine from Cecil," said Harry. "It must have taken a great deal of courage."

"It was only what needed to be done," I said coolly, pretending to butter a piece of cold toast.

"Agatha . . . I hope I'm not speaking out of turn, but I wondered if, well, if I had done anything to offend you."

"No, not at all," I said.

"I know the Americans and the British have very different attitudes when it comes to friendship," he said. "You must think us Yanks are vulgar and overfamiliar."

"You're forgetting my father was from New York."

"Yes, I remember you saying," he acknowledged, trying to warm my spirits with a flash of his winning smile. "Anyway, whatever it is I've done, I'm sorry. Maybe someone here told you something about me and . . . well, if you want to believe them, there's not much I can do about it."

As Miller stood up to leave the table, I realized I had to say something. "I'm sorry. It's nothing you've done," I assured him, my resolve softening. "The truth is that I've been rather shocked by everything that's gone on here. Sarah's murder, the awful way in which she was killed, and then all that business with Mrs. Woolley and Cecil McRae . . . It's shaken me to the core."

"That's hardly surprising," he remarked. "So I've done nothing to upset you?"

"No, and I'm sorry if I gave you that impression."

He gazed inquiringly at me, as if to test the veracity of my words, and his look was so disarming that I had no choice but to smile back. It was at this point that Captain Forster and Davison returned to the room. As my friend entered, I noticed that he had observed the silent interchange between Miller and me, but of course he was too discreet and well-mannered to say anything. Instead he asked Woolley whether there was a room that he and Forster could use to carry out their interviews. Leonard ran through a list of spaces: the *antika* room was free but hardly suitable, as it contained some highly valuable objects; his own room was being used for the containment of Cecil, while Katharine, after her ordeal, really should not be disturbed.

"The other guest rooms really are too small, which leaves only this space, I'm afraid," he said, gesturing at the table, still laid with breakfast things. "We could get the servants to clear up and have someone stationed at the door so you won't be disturbed."

"How does that sound to you, Captain?" asked Davison.

Forster did not look impressed but agreed that it would have to do. "If I could ask all of you to return to your rooms, we will call you one by one so you can give us your statements," he said rather stiffly. "I need not remind you that this is a murder investigation. This is a very serious matter indeed." A few of the group bristled; they must be feeling that they did not need to be patronized in this way, and indeed the overall effect of the unfortunate Captain Forster was that of a head boy at a minor public school who was intent on giving orders to his superiors. "Where are the Arab boys?" he asked, clapping his hands. "Let's get this mess cleared up as soon as we can."

Our little group dispersed and a moment later Harry Miller and I found ourselves in the courtyard.

"Shall we take a walk?" he asked.

"Yes, why not," I replied. "I could do with some air."

"I suppose we can't go far . . . We don't want to get into trouble with the captain," he said, smirking.

We walked towards the ziggurat, where a chain of Arab men and boys had resumed their backbreaking work. Miller asked me about the events of the previous night. I went over the horrible scene once more.

"Do you really believe the boy's the one behind it all?" he asked as we started a gentle circuit around the base of the structure. "Woolley seems to think as much—that he killed Sarah out of spite, because she had rejected him, and then he tried to frame Mrs. Woolley for the crime."

"I'm not sure," I said. Since last night I had reassessed the situation.

"So you don't believe that he intended to shoot Katharine and then make it look like suicide?"

"I don't think Cecil has that kind of calculating mind," I said. "He's a hotheaded adolescent, not a cold-blooded killer. No, the person behind all of this is driven by something altogether different. It's the work of someone with an ability to schematize and plot."

"You mean somebody like yourself?" said Miller. We came to a stop at the bottom of one of the ziggurat's grand staircases.

"I beg your pardon?" I said, somewhat taken aback. "I'm sorry, but I don't think that's a very amusing joke."

"You don't?" said Harry, his eyes glinting with mischief. "I'm sorry if I offended the great lady novelist. But if I'm not mistaken, I suspect you and the killer share more than a few characteristics."

His comment was so outrageous that I had no choice but to laugh. "I do hope you're not being serious, Mr. Miller."

"Oh, but I am," he said, and moved a step closer to me. "In fact, I do believe, Mrs. Christie, that if I applied a little more pressure, you may actually confess to the crime."

I could feel my face reddening and my breath quickening. "Indeed?"

"Oh, yes," he said.

Just then, as his face moved an inch or so towards mine, I heard something or someone above me on the ziggurat. I looked up, but as I did so a few grains of sand fell onto my face. Harry followed my gaze and instinctively pulled me towards him. For a moment I thrilled to the feel of his strong arms around me, but then I came to my senses. I was about to object—how dare he presume to act in this way?—but then I realized that he was simply trying to protect me.

"Who is that?" he shouted, straining his head to look up towards the top of the ziggurat. "Who's there?"

We heard the scuffle of footsteps, but although Miller dashed from the base of the ziggurat towards the open ground, he said he couldn't see anyone.

"Whoever it was disappeared in a cloud of dust," he said upon returning to me. "Are you all right? Here." He passed me his handkerchief to clean my face. "Did you swallow any sand?"

"No, I don't think so. But my mouth does feel a little gritty."

"Let's get back to the compound, where you can have a drink of water," he suggested, turning his head as we walked in an attempt to spot whoever had been perched on the top of the ziggurat. "I wouldn't worry; I'm sure we weren't saying anything particularly revelatory. Probably just a couple of the Arab boys."

"Yes, perhaps," I said, biting the corner of my lip. I was sure that they found it all rather amusing, the sight of a middle-aged Englishwoman making a fool of herself with a handsome American man. I really would have to make sure nothing of the sort happened again. What had I been thinking?

We walked back to the camp in silence. I let Miller believe this was because of the disagreeable sensation of having sand in my mouth, but the reality was that I felt eaten up by shame.

"I'd better knock before I go in," said Harry when we stood outside the door to the main room. "I don't want to walk in on an interview."

"Come in," said Forster.

Both of us stepped into the room to see the captain seated at the long table studying his paperwork. Miller explained that he wanted to get some water for me.

"Go ahead; we haven't started yet," the young officer said, waving his hand in the direction of the kitchen. "Davison said he was going to go on a recce of the ziggurat to see where the murder took place."

"Davison's at the ziggurat?" I said, hoping that I had misunderstood Forster's words.

"I've been here before—one hot summer, when you lot were back in good old England—so I know the layout of the structure, but Davison said he would find it helpful to go and have a look," he explained, not looking up from his papers.

The revelation that it had been Davison who had evidently been spying on us left me feeling confused and a little dizzy. What had he seen? What had he heard?

"But . . . ," I said, gripping the back of one of the chairs.

"Here, sit down," said Miller. "Are you sure nothing hit you out there?"

"Just a few grains of sand, nothing more," I said, dropping into the chair. "I think I should go and have a lie-down."

"A good idea," said Miller. "You won't need Mrs. Christie right away, will you, Captain?"

The captain did not bother looking up from his papers. "No, no," he said, sounding distracted. "As soon as Davison gets back, we're going to question Cecil McRae. We'll let you know when we want to speak to both of you."

I pushed myself up from the chair, and although Harry tried to take my arm to accompany me, I brushed him off. I could not show him any further signs of encouragement. But just then I stumbled, either from the effects of dizziness or from a slight ruck in the rush matting, and Miller grabbed my arm, preventing me from a nasty fall. It was at that moment that Davison opened the door and walked into the room.

"Oh, dear, has something happened?" Davison asked, rushing to help.

"We've got everything under control," said Miller, holding up his free hand in a rather possessive manner. "Mrs. Christie just felt a little faint, I think, and I'm taking her back to her room."

As I stared into Davison's hardened eyes I saw a hint of something approaching . . . what? Jealousy? Surely it could not be that. Suspicion, yes, but not of me. Perhaps it was some kind of warning?

21

I waited in my room for the gentle tap on the door that surely must come. I ran across the room and opened the door to a grave-looking Davison.

"What was that all about?" I hissed as soon as he had stepped into my quarters. "Watching me from the top of the ziggurat? What were you thinking?"

"I know you're angry, but I can explain," he said.

"I do hope you can," I said.

"I see you're not wasting any time on being civil," he said.

The comment stopped me in my tracks. Although I was showing all the outward signs of anger, I realized that my behavior was very much a performance. I trusted that Davison would always have my best interests at heart. And if he had felt a need to spy on Miller and me, I suspected that there would be a very good reason why. However, that did not mean that I was ready to give him an easy time.

"Why should I be polite to you after what you've done?"

"If you let me tell you what I know, then perhaps you'll see," he replied.

"Very well," I said, looking at him with a frosty expression.

"It's clear that you've become friendly with Mr. Miller," he began. “I realize he’s a very attractive man, but you may not know the whole truth about him.”

“You mean that he’s got a reputation as something of a ladies’ man? And that he had a relationship with Miss Bell?”

“Yes, and certain other things, too,” he said.

I waited for him to go on. He walked to the window that overlooked the courtyard and made sure the shutters were closed.

“Well,” he said, clearing his throat, “there is the not-insignificant matter of his name.”

“What do you mean?”

Davison took a small notebook out of his jacket pocket and read from it. “ ‘Mr. Harry Miller, photographer, born in Philadelphia on the seventh of October 1889, died in an automobile accident in that city on the twenty-fifth of May 1925.’ ”

I understood the implications straightaway. I blushed as I thought about the intimate talks I had enjoyed with the man I knew as Harry. I remembered the way I had felt when he rescued me, first on that backstreet in Baghdad and then when I had been at risk of falling from the top of the ziggurat. “So if Mr. Miller is not who he says he is, then who is he?”

“I’m afraid we don’t know that at the moment” was Davison’s response. “It seems as though he assumed the identity of the dead man, a man who was without family. How he got hold of his papers and his passport, we’re not sure.”

My mind started to work quickly, and I began to wonder out loud. “But why would he bother to do that? What was he running from?” I paused as I forced myself to think the very worst. There was no use in being sentimental, of imagining of what might have been. Thank goodness I had forced myself to draw back from him before we had become too friendly.

“Perhaps he committed some crime in America and needed a new start,” I said. “But what if something—or someone—stood in the way of him achieving that? The man we know as Harry Miller enjoyed a close relationship with Gertrude Bell. What if she discovered his real identity? Perhaps he could not risk the exposure and so had no choice but to finish her off."

"Yes, my thoughts exactly," replied Davison. "Now, I think you'd better tell me everything that has happened here, don't you?"

Slowly, but with as much precision as I could, I related the events that had occurred since I had first arrived at Ur. Katharine's odd, paranoid behavior. The death of her cat. The strange atmosphere among the group. The rivalry between Mrs. Woolley and the young Miss Archer. That awful row at the picnic. The discovery of Sarah's body.

"And then there was the thing with Miller's camera," I said.

"His camera?" asked Davison.

"Yes. Harry Miller—well, the man pretending to be him—told me that he had discovered his Leica in bits. As if someone had deliberately smashed it. I thought that this was because someone had wanted to destroy the film inside the camera because it might contain a clue to the identity of Sarah Archer's murderer." I paused. "But what if 'Miller' broke up the Leica himself?"

"It seems highly likely," he said.

"I feel such a fool. To think that I was taken in by him." I told Davison what had happened that day in the alley off Rashid Street. As I did so, a possibility struck me with such force that it left me reeling. "Do you think that it all could have been staged?" I asked, even though I knew Davison could not give me an answer. "That this man pretending to be Miller paid that young boy to try to grab my handbag so that he could then ingratiate himself with me?"

"I don't know, but we may have to face up to that possibility," Davison allowed.

"But this—this impostor wasn't here when Tom, Katharine's cat, was killed. He was in Baghdad."

"Or so he told you," said Davison. "But he could have stolen into the compound and done that."

"So what do we do now?"

"Of course, we can't let this chap know we suspect anything," he said. "It may be hard for you, but it's important that you behave normally. Continue to enjoy your . . . friendship with him."

I knew exactly what Davison was implying. What was the best way of putting him right? "At one point I was foolish enough to believe something might come of our friendship, but fortunately pride and common sense told me otherwise. As you know, I have not had the best luck when it comes to such matters. And I doubt whether I will enjoy such a close relationship again."

"I see," said Davison.

"So you don't need to spare my feelings when it comes to Mr. Miller, or whatever his real name is," I added. "I didn't expect anything from him." This was not quite the whole truth, but by saying it I hoped to make the sentiment real. "I wonder what his game is. I'm sure it will come to light soon enough. Now, what else did you discover? Yes, what about Katharine Woolley's first husband, Colonel Keeling, who supposedly killed himself in September 1919? Did you find out who identified the body?"

"Yes. It was one of his work colleagues, Mr. Thurley," replied Davison. "He told the police that the man on the mortuary slab was Colonel Keeling."

"But how would this Mr. Thurley know for certain if the man substituted for Keeling had suffered extensive head and face injuries? And what about other men of a similar age who disappeared at the same time?"

Davison consulted his notebook once more. "Let's see . . . Albert Morrison, a civil servant, who on the eighteenth of September 1919 walked out of his house in Cairo after a row with his wife and who was never seen again. He was born in 1882, so that would make him two years younger than Keeling. And then there was Patrick Deller, a man of independent means, who disappeared from his home on the fifteenth of the month. He was older, forty-five at the time of the disappearance, and lived alone. There is some suggestion that he may have been linked with . . . well, with something unsavory."

"Such as?"

"Do you really want to know?"

"Yes, of course I do. My grandmother always said a true lady can never be shocked nor surprised. Now go on."

"Well, it seems as though Deller took an unhealthy interest in young girls."

"I see. So that disappearance could have been an act of revenge by one or more of the justifiably angry parents or relatives. And no trace of a body?"

"None," he said, beginning to close his notebook.

"And did you find out anything else about Colonel Keeling?"

"I'm still waiting on a few pieces of information to come through," he said. "If anything significant turns up, I've asked for it to be delivered here."

"Right. But it does seem strange that the whole thing could be linked to two separate cases of swapped identity—first Colonel Keeling and then Harry Miller," I said. "If Katharine Woolley believes her first husband may still be alive, we have to take that suspicion seriously, even if it does not sound at all credible. Unless . . . ," I said, almost under my breath. But it was best to keep my thoughts to myself for the time being. "And there are a couple of other things I wondered if you might be able to help with." I outlined what I needed to know: who in each case benefited from the wills of Miss Archer and Cecil McRae's parents.

"That shouldn't be too difficult to find out," said Davison. "I'll send a message to the department back in London." He looked at his watch. "Right, I'd better be getting back to Forster."

I raised an eyebrow. "He's very young, isn't he?"

"Yes, and between you and me he hasn't got a clue. It's a mystery how he got the job."

He asked what I thought of Woolley's theory.

"I doubt very much Cecil is the one behind all of this," I said, walking with Davison towards the door. "However, he may well be the key to it."

"What do you mean?"

"Would you mind asking Captain Forster to step inside for a moment?"

"What's going on, Agatha? I can see you've come up with some kind of scheme. What is it?"

As I outlined my plan, a real smile—one with verve and mischief and delight—began to form on Davison's face.

"I say, that's splendid," he said. "Highly risky, of course, and it remains to be seen whether Forster will go for it, but there's a touch of genius there. Yes, only you could have thought of that. I'll go and fetch the boy wonder."

A moment later Davison returned with an irritated-looking Forster. "Now, what's all this about?" he barked. "We really do need to start questioning Cecil McRae. I'm not in the mood for any idle chitchat."

"If you could just listen for a moment to what Mrs. Christie has to say . . . ," said Davison.

"About what?"

I did not have the time or the inclination to reveal everything I knew about the complicated case, and so I told Forster something of my suspicions relating to Cecil and how I did not believe that he had killed Sarah Archer. Then I outlined how he might be able to help.

"No, it's completely out of the question," said Captain Forster.

"It would be tantamount to interfering with the evidence. No, I couldn't allow it, I'm afraid."

"But can't you see Mrs. Christie's point?" said Davison in as calm a manner as he could manage.

The young captain looked at me and with a wave of the hand turned away from me. "To be honest, I cannot," he said, his face reddening. "I need to establish the facts of the case for myself. I can't have the evidence messed about with in this manner."

Davison tried to interrupt, but Forster cut him off. "I wouldn't expect a lady to know the correct protocol of such an investigation," he said, addressing me. "To be honest, I'm rather surprised at you, Davison. You really should know better. In fact, I may even have to mention this to my superiors back in Baghdad."

Would Davison reveal his hand and tell the pompous young fool of his real status—that, instead of being a mere civil servant in the foreign office, he worked for the Secret Intelligence Service?

"I'm sorry you think that," said Davison, remaining composed. "But perhaps you're right. Maybe it was an oversight on my part."

"We've got to do this by the book," said Forster, checking his watch. "Let's get on with it. That boy should have come round now."

"Indeed," said Davison, taking a small card from his inside jacket pocket. "But before we go and question him, there is something I should show you."

"What is it now?" snapped Forster. "Really, Davison. My chief said he was sending someone with me who would help and assist me, not bother me with all these unnecessary details. It really is quite—"

The sight of what was written on the card—Davison's name and title at the service—stopped Forster in his tracks. He coughed in a halfhearted attempt to swallow his words. "Well, I—I mean," he blustered. "If I'd only . . . then, of course, I—"

"Not to worry," Davison, smiling gently, assured him. "You weren't to know. And I'd appreciate it if you kept that information to yourself. Now, why don't you listen carefully as Mrs. Christie here explains what's going to happen."

Forster blinked back his astonishment as I turned towards him and began to outline in more detail what I wanted him to do.

22

We had all been told to wait in our rooms until we were called for questioning. My own session with Forster and Davison was done very much for show, as we had discussed certain aspects of the case earlier in my room. The interrogations continued until four o'clock, when we were informed that we were invited to return to the living room to take tea with Captain Forster, who wanted to share with us some important information. I was the first to arrive, and as I entered, Forster jumped up and found a chair with a thick cushion for me at the table.

"Are you sure you are comfortable?" he asked, fussing around me like an old maid. "Would you like some tea? And how about a cake?" He snapped his fingers and a servant brought over a little plate of Arab delicacies. He lowered his voice so nobody else could hear. "If you do get a moment to talk to Davison, I would be enormously grateful if you could extend my apologies for earlier. Really, I had no idea. If I had known, obviously I would never—"

At that moment the door opened and Father Burrows entered with a nervous-looking Miss Jones, soon followed by Lawrence McRae, the man who went by the name of Harry Miller, Mr. and Mrs. Archer, Leonard Woolley, and then Davison. All of them took their places at the table and helped themselves to tea, the ritual accompanied by the familiar sounds of the clink of teaspoons on china and the low murmur of polite conversation. On the surface the occasion appeared an utterly civilized one, but underneath the sheen of respectability there was something ugly, something evil.

"Now, who is it we are waiting for?" asked Forster, looking around the table. "Oh, yes, Mrs. Woolley."

"Katharine still hasn't recovered from her terrible ordeal," said Leonard Woolley, taking a sip of tea. "I'm afraid she won't be joining us."

"Mr. Woolley, I thought I made myself clear that everyone had to attend the meeting this afternoon."

"Is that strictly necessary?" Woolley's eyes glinted.

"I must insist: there can be no exceptions," Forster maintained. "If you'd be so kind as to go and request her presence . . ."

Woolley placed his teacup on the table, stood up, and with as much grace as he could muster walked out of the room. The conversation resumed as if nothing had happened. Father Burrows started speaking about the intricacies of certain cuneiform tablets with Miss Jones, who did not seem to be paying him very much attention. Harry Miller informed Lawrence McRae of his intention to go to Baghdad as soon as he could to order a new Leica camera—the question now was which model he should order—but the architect remained silent and preoccupied. Without doubt he was worried about the fate and well-being of his unfortunate nephew. Mr. and Mrs. Archer talked quietly together, so softly in fact that I couldn't make out their words.

A few minutes later Woolley returned with Katharine trailing behind him. At her entrance, all heads turned towards her as if she were some kind of lodestar. She was dressed smartly not in her customary shade of *vieux rose* but in black. She held herself with a dignified posture—her expression spoke of stoicism and unspoken suffering—and as her husband pulled out a chair for her, she reminded me of one of the great classical actresses of the stage. Ruth Archer opened her mouth to speak—was she about to apologize for some of the awful things she had said?—but her husband placed a hand on her arm.

"Let's wait to hear what the captain has to say," he said, then looked up and addressed Forster. "The sooner we get this over with, the better. We have a funeral to organize. A daughter who needs to be buried."

"Yes, I understand," said Forster. "And I do appreciate the fact that you've delayed your departure. As I said, we can help with any arrangements regarding the body and so on."

The captain's reduction of Sarah Archer to a mere "body" startled Ruth Archer, and quite understandably she took out her handkerchief and pressed it to her mouth. I only hoped that the inexperienced officer would not make any more blunders.

"Now, as I suggested, we have some important information that I would like to share with you," he continued.

A silence descended on the group as we waited for the captain to impart his news.

"As you know, on Saturday night the body of Sarah Archer was found at the base of the ziggurat. She had sustained a number of serious—in fact, fatal—head injuries." Again Mrs. Archer winced at Forster's words. "It looks as though she had been hit with a rock." The captain must have caught a glimpse of Mrs. Archer's appalled face and, after clearing his throat, began again. "I must thank Mr. and Mrs. Archer for their patience and for their help at this most distressing of times. And I would like to thank each of you for your cooperation. I know it must not have been easy to relate the details of what you saw and heard."

Mr. Archer shifted impatiently in his seat. "Thank you, Captain Forster," he said. "And we are grateful to you too for coming down here. However, I'm conscious that time is of the essence. I don't want to appear rude, but we do need to sort this out as soon as possible so as to make the necessary arrangements."

"As I was saying, we have concluded our investigation into the death of Miss Archer"—Forster puffed out his chest slightly—"and I am satisfied to tell you that we have secured a confession from—"

A low, excited murmur ran around the table.

"—Cecil McRae, who—"

At the mention of his nephew's name, Lawrence McRae stood up, tipping over his cup of tea as he did so.

"Oh, my, dear me," said an agitated Miss Jones, taking out her handkerchief and dabbing the table.

"That wicked, wicked boy! How could he have done that?" exclaimed Ruth Archer.

"This is absurd!" shouted McRae. "Cecil is the last person who would have hurt that girl."

"If I can ask you to sit down, Mr. McRae," said Forster, "I can explain to you—"

"No, I will not sit down. I demand that you take me to see him."

"All in due time," said Forster.

"What did you do?" said McRae. "Beat a confession out of him?"

"I can understand why you feel distressed," said Forster, "but, really, that's quite unnecessary."

"Please, Mr. McRae," said Davison, coming to stand by the architect. "If you could let the Captain explain . . ."

McRae glared first at Davison and then across at Forster; he must have been thinking that he'd very much like to punch them both, before he audibly dragged his chair back across the floor and sat down. "I won't believe a word of it—not until I hear it from the boy's mouth myself," he said.

"Thank you, Mr. McRae," said Forster. "As I was saying, we have obtained a confession from Cecil, a confession that was given voluntarily and entirely without duress." He took out a notebook from his pocket. "This is not strictly proper procedure, but I can see how the crime has distressed you all," he said, watching the stricken faces of the Archers and the nervous hands of Miss Jones flutter across the table as she continued to blot up the last traces of the spilled tea. "In order to put all your minds at rest, I can supply you with a few more details in Cecil's own words."

He cleared his throat once more and, from his notebook, began to read out the boy's statement:

> I wasn't looking forward to the picnic. I didn't want to go and I thought the whole thing was a stupid idea. As soon as I saw Sarah flaunting herself in that black dress, I felt my blood begin to boil. Part of me wanted to tell her to go and change into something more modest. Another part of me—well, let's just say I wish she could have been nicer to me. None of this would have happened if she had been a bit kinder. Not so cruel. Why did she have to go and say those things? That I was ugly and stupid? Why did she tell me that I couldn't talk to her?
>
> After walking to the top of the ziggurat, I helped myself to a couple of those fruit punches. I suppose they must have gone to my head. I was watching Sarah and Harry Miller laugh and joke about. He was taking her picture and she was standing at the edge of the ziggurat. You should have heard them. It made me sick to my stomach. And then the next thing I knew, she was looking at my uncle in the same kind of way. She never once cast a look in my direction. I saw her dancing on the edge, kicking her heels up, in that dress, a dress that was nearly transparent. If she'd never worn it, things might have been very different.
>
> My uncle saw the way I was looking at Sarah and told me not to worry. One day I'd forget her, he said. I didn't

want to forget her. I wanted to be with her forever. Then Sarah's father came, everybody sang happy birthday, and she started telling that stupid story about the man who had proposed to her. She got into that horrible row with Mrs. Woolley and stormed off. "This is a birthday I'll remember," she said, or something to that effect.

I didn't mean to do it. It was a terrible accident. You've got to believe me when I tell you that I didn't mean Sarah any harm. I just wanted to go and make her feel a bit better. She was upset after that argument. So I went after her. I found her running down the path. I called her name, asked her to stop, but she told me to go away. I reached out and grabbed her. I just wanted to talk to her. But she got me all wrong. She said some cruel words to me and went to slap me, but when I reached up to protect myself, she fell backwards. It all happened so quickly. She must have banged her head. I shook her, told her to wake up, that I didn't mean her any harm. But then I thought what would happen if she did wake up. She would tell people that I had tried to attack her. What happened with my parents would get dragged up again. I would get locked away, or worse. And so I took hold of a rock and hit her over the head. I know it was a bad thing to do. I can see that now. But I wasn't thinking right.

That's when I heard footsteps. I suppose it must have been Mrs. Woolley. I didn't meant to hurt Sarah. I hope that one day Mr. and Mrs. Archer will forgive me.

This completes my statement.

—Cecil McRae

Captain Forster looked up from his notebook to a sea of bewildered faces. Mrs. Archer wept into her handkerchief and her husband's face looked ashen. Lawrence McRae seemed as though he was on the point of storming out again, and Miss Jones stared at her tear-stained handkerchief with something approaching horror in her eyes.

"We should pray for the boy," said Father Burrows.

"I may be a Christian man, but I refuse to pray for him," said Hubert Archer. "In fact, I'm going to see that boy hangs for what he did. Come on, Ruth." He stood up and held out his hand for his wife. He turned to Captain Forster. "We don't want to bury Sarah out in the desert. We'd like to take her back to Baghdad, if that's possible."

"Yes, of course," said Forster. "I'm sure that can be arranged, can't it, Davison?"

"Indeed, sir," said Davison, playing the role of the subservient civil servant. "I'd suggest the British cemetery. I know your daughter was an American, but it does seem the most fitting and distinguished place. After all, it's the same cemetery in which Gertrude Bell was buried."

The Archers seemed honored that their daughter had been compared to the famous traveler and archaeologist who had helped to found the new state of Iraq. The mention of the name had other effects, too: Harry Miller got up from the table and turned his back on the group; Leonard Woolley smiled in fond recollection and said that she was greatly missed, while his wife remained unmoved; and Miss Jones asked to borrow a clean handkerchief from Mrs. Woolley, which she then used to dab her eyes. I still could not work out whether the death of Miss Bell was connected in any way to the murderous goings-on at Ur. An image of an ancient pot lying in pieces flashed into my mind. I couldn't see how it would be possible to fit all the differently shaped shards back together.

"We've all had quite a shock," said Miller from behind me. I turned around to see the handsome photographer. "Who would have thought that Cecil was the murderer? Are you all right?" he asked me. "You look a little pale."

"I do feel a little shaken by the news," I said. I had to do everything in my power to stop myself from asking him to explain himself. If he wasn't Harry Miller, then who was he? What had he done that was so terrible that he had had to flee America? And what was the truth about his relationship with Gertrude Bell? "I think I'm still suffering from shock," I said instead.

"Why don't we take a walk?" Miller said in a gentle voice. "That might help calm your nerves."

"Very well," I said in a louder voice. "A little fresh air might be just the thing I need. Where shall we go? Perhaps to the ziggurat?"

When Davison saw us leave the room, he shot me a look of warning.

"How extraordinary," said Miller as we stepped into the courtyard. "It seems too unbelievable for words." He continued to talk about what Cecil McRae had done to Miss Archer; meanwhile, I remained silent and studied his profile. Certainly there was nothing in his physiognomy to suggest that he was hiding anything; in fact, his open expression and handsome features suggested nothing but a good, old-fashioned American wholesomeness, the kind I had encountered many times both at home in England and on my travels. Yet I knew that appearances counted for nothing.

"Sorry, I should stop talking about it, as I can see that it's distressing you a good deal," he said while we walked towards the ziggurat.

"Well, I am worried about what will happen to that young boy now," I replied. "Do you think he's the one who smashed up your camera?"

"I guess he must have been. Perhaps he thought that I had caught him looking at Sarah with an angry expression, or maybe he was just so cross about my flirtatious interchange with her on the top of the ziggurat."

"It will all come out when Forster questions Cecil again back in Baghdad," I said. I wondered how I could ask Miller a little more about his background without raising his suspicions. "But jolly annoying for you, having to buy a new camera."

"Yes. I'll have to go to Baghdad to put in an order," he said. "It will probably take weeks to arrive."

We started to climb the stairs up towards the first level of the ziggurat. "Have you always been a photographer?" I asked.

"I don't think I'm suited to do anything else," he said without a moment's hesitation.

"How did you learn?"

"I got the bug as a kid," he said. "I pestered my folks to buy me a Brownie and from that first Christmas I was hooked. I must have been about ten or eleven. I started to take shots of our dog, my grandparents, the trees in the park in winter, and then when I was sixteen I got a job on the local paper, the *Middleton Bulletin*. That was great training, let me tell you. I covered everything: crime, sports, personalities, local politics . . . It was a fast life but a hard one."

He didn't seem to be lying, but I knew that practiced or pathological liars sometimes came to believe their own falsehoods.

"It seems a bit of a jump from news photography to taking images of artifacts found in the desert sand," I said.

"Let's just say I had my heart broken," he said, turning away from me. "Anyway, I've talked too much about myself." He stepped closer to me. "I'd like to get to know you a little better."

"Ask away. I'm an open book." That was not entirely true.

Miller began to ask me some questions and I told him a little about my writing, my childhood, and my first marriage. He did not, thank goodness, ask about my disappearance in December 1926, an event in my life which had been on the front page of every newspaper. I also shared with him the feelings of guilt I felt about Rosalind: she blamed me for the breakdown of the marriage. It was important for me to show my vulnerable side to him if the plan was going to work.

"Sometimes I feel so alone," I said. "Of course, I have my writing, but often I think I only do that to tell myself stories because there's no one around to talk to."

"You don't have to be. Alone, that is."

"I know it's partly my fault. I'm not a terribly social being, I'm afraid."

"No, I didn't mean that exactly," he said. "You . . . you could always marry again."

"I don't think so," I said, laughing. "After all, who would want an old maid like me?"

Miller reached out and placed a hand on my shoulder. The touch was like a current of electricity through me. Although my mind felt detached—I knew exactly what I was doing—my body was a different matter. The photographer saw the effect his gentle caress had on me and, after looking into my eyes, felt emboldened to take a step closer. It had been so long since I had experienced anything like this. There had only been Archie. And then he gradually absented himself from our bed. He turned away at night, pleading tiredness. Then he started to spend more time away from home. There was business, he said; there was the golf. In truth, all along it had been the other woman in his life, Miss Neele, a woman who was now the new Mrs. Christie.

"Don't put yourself down—you're no old maid," whispered Miller. His hand moved from my shoulder to the small of my back and he drew me towards him. The sensation was a delicious one. I had to tell myself once more not to fall for his charms. There was something I needed to accomplish—to keep Miller away from his room long enough for Davison to search it. Davison and I had agreed on that much, but we had had different opinions on the actual methods involved. I could not risk telling my fellow secret agent what I intended to do in case he ruled against it. Davison assumed that we were going for a walk—nothing more than that. Of course it was a risk, but I thought it was one worth taking.

Miller moved his head forwards and bent down to kiss me, but I stepped away from him and looked around to see if anyone had spotted us. My reticence was all too real, and he simply interpreted my actions as those of a woman of my class and background.

"I'm sorry," he said. "I overstepped the mark."

"No, not at all," I replied.

"Perhaps we should get back to the house," he suggested, looking at his watch. "No doubt they'll be wondering what's happened to us."

I knew Davison would still be searching Miller's room. I had to try and delay him.

"I'm rather out of practice, I'm afraid," I said, blushing. "Since my husband left me, well, it's been . . ."

"You don't have to explain," he said, moving towards me again. He reached out and, with the tip of his thumb, touched my lips. He took hold of my hand and led me into a dark, shaded corner of the ziggurat where no one could see us. "Look, there's nobody around. You don't have to worry." As his face neared mine I inhaled traces of his expensive-smelling cologne. The aroma was deliciously heady and transported me away from the desert sands, but I had to remind myself that Miller was using it to mask something. The scent wasn't his true smell, and his name wasn't even his real one. What exactly was he covering up? I hoped Davison would be deep into the search of his room now.

"You seem distracted," he said.

"No, I was just thinking about—"

And with that he stepped away from me. "I really must be getting back," he said, coughing in embarrassment.

"Oh, dear," I said, starting to panic. "I hope I didn't give you the impression that I was . . ." I couldn't quite finish the sentence.

"No, not at all," he said, trying to smile.

"Perhaps we can go to the top of the ziggurat. We could admire the view from there."

"I'm not sure," he said. "I can see that the recent troubles have taken their toll. I wouldn't want to add to that."

"What do you mean?"

"Agatha, if I may speak plainly . . . ?"

"Of course. Please do."

"It seems to me that you're not ready to embark on a new romance," he said. "I think what happened with your husband is still preying on your mind." He started to walk away.

"But I do find your company very appealing," I said, feeling a flutter in my breast. "I can relax with you, something I haven't felt able to do with . . . well, with anyone since my husband."

"That's good," he said. "But I think we need to take this—what is it they say in novels?—at a slower pace, if only for your own sake."

Despite the evidence that seemed to suggest he was covering something up—perhaps something as evil as a murder—he was behaving like a gentleman.

He presented me with his arm and asked, "Shall I walk you back?"

It appeared I had no choice. I would have to think of some other way to slow his return. "Yes, that would be very nice, thank you," I said politely.

On our walk back to the house I asked him what he missed about America. He tripped off a list of seemingly trivial items—ice cream, the movies, the energy of a big city—before he mentioned one thing that I thought could be significant. "I suppose the idea that you can be whoever you want to be." The comment was a casual one, and he soon began to talk of skyscrapers and baseball and the grandeur of railway stations, but the phrase stayed with me.

I slowed my pace as I began to talk about my youthful dreams of being an opera singer, a concert pianist, a sculptor. I took my time describing each of these ambitions in turn, outlining the various hurdles that had stood in my way: my shyness, my horror at performing in public, my lack of talent. Miller did not want to offend by cutting my stories short, but I could tell a certain dullness had stolen into his eyes. As I waffled on, he stood there making appropriate facial gestures until finally he looked at his watch and said, "I'd love to talk more about all of that, but I really do think that—"

"Of course. I'm sorry if you find my stories boring," I said, pretending to be hurt by his decision to end our conversation.

"No, it's not that at all. It's just that—"

"I did think we had something in common," I said, trying to bring tears to my eyes.

"Oh, no, I've upset you," said Miller, stepping closer. "That's the last thing I wanted to do. Whatever it is I said or did not say, please forgive me."

Taking a deep breath, I steeled myself for what I had to do next. This was against my nature, my breeding, everything I had been told—imagine what my mother would have thought had she been alive!—but I had no choice. "No, it's you who should forgive me," I said. "I acted like a spoilt child." I grasped for half-remembered images from romantic novels I had read long ago. I ran the tip of my tongue over my dry lips and tried to open my eyes a little wider. I thought of something that amused me: What was it my grandmother had said about that curious woman in her sewing circle? Was it something about her having only one passage, like a bird? The memory made me laugh, and I felt a sparkle return to my eyes.

"What's so funny?" asked Miller.

"I was just thinking about what a fool I'd been," I said, placing a hand over his. "I get so nervous at times. I'm not used to male attention, you see, especially from a man as handsome and as nice as you."

Miller looked slightly taken aback. "Well, I—"

"I'd hate it if I've given you the wrong impression," I said, deliberately lowering my chin and raising my eyes so that I would appear a little more like a woman used to employing the dark arts of seduction.

"And what impression would that be?" he asked.

"That I was indifferent to your attentions."

He took another step closer to me and inclined his head in such a way that I could feel his hot breath on my face. But just then—just as he reached out his hand to caress me—I thought about what Davison might have found in his room. Proof of Miller's original name? Or something even more sinister that would link the American with the death of Miss Bell?

I tried to banish these thoughts from my head, but they refused to be pushed away. I caught a look of uncertainty in Miller's face that told me he had read something in my eyes. I thought again of what my grandmother had said about her sewing woman, but the spark of light amusement was impossible to rekindle. Miller's hand slowly retreated and, so as to not cause undue embarrassment, he pretended to brush a spot of dirt or sand from my shoulder before he stepped away from me and looked into the distance.

"But—"

"You're very sweet, but I can see that I was right," he said, smiling kindly. "Let's not hurry things. Now I really think we must be getting back. It looks as though there's a sandstorm coming."

"Could we not just . . ."

But Miller had already turned from me and started to walk briskly back to the compound. As I rushed after him I thought about falling, claiming that I had twisted my ankle. But by the time the notion came to me, Miller had reached the gates. Had he guessed that I had been trying to delay his return? I called out his name one last time, but I saw him disappear into the courtyard. I ran as fast as I could, but my skirts kept threatening to trip me up and send me crashing down into the sand. If I wasn't careful, my idea of hurting my ankle might actually become a reality. I felt my heart race and my face redden. Beads of perspiration broke out across my forehead, and then I felt something lodge in my left eye. I blinked and tried to rub the particle away with my finger, tears forming in my eyes as I did so. Miller had said that there was a sandstorm coming, and sure enough the horizon had disappeared, replaced by an ominous dirty brown mass.

I had no way of letting Davison know of Miller's imminent return. I only hoped that he had finished his search.

By the time I reached the compound I could not breathe. Feeling on the verge of collapse, I made my way to Miller's room. A stony-faced Davison stood in the doorway, holding out a handful of letters and other papers. Miller had pushed past him into his room, where he stood astounded and somewhat broken.

"So, Mr. Miller, may I ask what you are doing at Ur?" asked Davison. "Or should that be Mr. Conway?"

"I don't know what you mean," he said in a rather halfhearted manner.

"Mr. Harry Miller, as I'm sure you know, died in a car accident in 1925," said Davison. "And don't try and pretend that you are a different Harry Miller. It's a fairly common name, but you're not going to be able to get away with that."

Miller—or Conway, as he was—looked sheepishly at Davison, before he spotted me standing outside the room. His eyes shifted from Davison back to me before he realized the truth of the scenario that had just taken place.

"I expected better of you, Agatha," he said, picking up a stack of letters that Davison had left on his bed. "I thought we had something special." He sighed deeply. "Was that—I mean all that out there," he said, gesturing towards the direction of the ziggurat, "—was that just a tactic to try and slow me down so my room could be searched? Didn't you mean any of those things you said?"

I could not answer him.

He looked at me with disappointment and despair in his eyes. Then he sat on the bed, and let his head drop down, as if all the worries and problems of the world had suddenly been shifted onto his shoulders. A pallor now replaced his former healthy tan. "Okay, you've got me," he said. "I suppose I may as well confess."

23

"Do you want to go and get Forster?" asked the man I now knew to be called Conway. His voice was heavy with resignation, as if he didn't care what happened to him.

"No, I think we can handle this for the time being," said Davison. "Agatha, why don't you come inside and close the door. Let's hear what the man has to say for himself."

I stepped into Conway's room, took out my handkerchief, and wiped my face of dust. I studied the details of the room. The white walls were festooned with hundreds of photographs: pictures of street scenes in Baghdad; an image that looked almost obscene but which I realized was a close-up of the inside of a pomegranate; the craggy, lined faces of Arabs; dozens of views of the ziggurat taken at different times of the day and seemingly hundreds of representations of the undulating sweep of the desert sands. Here too were snapshots of some of the team at Ur. A smiling Woolley holding an ancient gold cup he had just removed from beneath the earth; Katharine Woolley with her cat; Father Burrows stooping over a cuneiform tablet, his brows knitted in concentration as he tried to decipher its secrets; and Lawrence and Cecil McRae at work on their drawings. One wall was completely devoted to images of the artifacts unearthed at Ur: daggers, earrings, bowls, cups, necklaces, rings, headdresses, cylinder seals, and cloak pins.

Davison walked over to a desk situated in the far corner of the room and picked up a maroon-colored photograph album that was lying underneath a pile of papers.

"Now, this is interesting," he said. I walked over to see what he had found.

As Davison turned the pages I saw image after image of Sarah Archer, photographs of her in every decent pose imaginable, together with close-ups of her neck, shoulder, wrists, and mouth.

"I know what you're thinking, but it's not like that," said Conway, standing up and reaching for the album.

"What is it like?" asked Davison, taking a step back.

"I liked the kid; of course I did," replied Conway. "She was beautiful. Everyone could see that. But I just wanted to try and see if I could capture that beauty."

"Are you sure there was nothing more to it than that?" asked Davison.

"What do you mean?"

"Well, unfortunately we can't ask Miss Archer about the nature of your relationship and what really passed between you, because she's dead," said Davison. The words were harsh if not a little cruel.

"You don't think that—" Conway could not complete the sentence.

"Think what, Mr. Conway?" Davison took a step towards him. "You see, we know now, thanks to these papers that I just happened to find, that your real name is not Harry Miller. That you stole that name from a dead man. My feeling is that if you could lie about that, you could lie about almost anything."

Conway turned to me, a pleading look in his eyes. "Agatha, surely you don't think that . . . that I had anything to do with Sarah's death?"

"I'm afraid I don't know what to think any longer," I said. "But you said you wanted to confess."

"Yes, but not . . . not to that," he said. He looked as though he might be sick.

"If not that, then what?" I asked.

He took a couple of deep breaths and began. "As . . . as you now know, my name is not Harry Miller. It's Alan Conway. Before I tell you any more, I must say, once again, that I had nothing to do with Sarah's death. I could never have hurt that girl. You do believe me, don't you?"

"If you don't tell us what you are doing here, then I'm afraid we have no choice but to suspect you of the murder of Sarah Archer," said Davison.

"But that boy, Cecil, he's already confessed to the crime," said Conway.

Davison thought quickly on his feet. "We have reason to believe that Cecil was not in his right mind when he made that statement."

"So he didn't do it?" asked Conway.

"No, we believe he didn't," said Davison. "Which means that unless you convince us otherwise, then—"

Conway, panicking now, interrupted him. "I know when the game is up." He ran a hand across his sweaty forehead. "You may as well know that I got myself into trouble back in America. I owed some money, some big money, to a couple of shady characters, the Solomon brothers. You know the type: men you cannot afford to mess with. You see, my printing business went under back in New Jersey. The banks wouldn't lend me a cent, and so I borrowed some money from the Solomons. That was the worst decision I ever made. But I couldn't see a way out. I had bills to pay. And if you must know, I had a wife and a child to support." He looked at me. "You've got every right to hate me, Agatha."

"My feelings are neither here nor there," I said sharply. "What matters is the truth. How did you end up here, at Ur?"

"It was the Solomons' idea. They had seen the splashes in the press, all the write-ups about the treasures being pulled from the sands and how much they were worth. One newspaper said one object alone was valued at something like a hundred thousand pounds. So they came up with a plan. They gave me the passport of this Harry Miller, who had been a photographer, and told me that I was going to take a job halfway round the world, in the Near East."

"You didn't object?" asked a skeptical Davison.

"Of course I did," he replied. "I tried to do everything to get out of it. I promised that I would pay the money back in installments. That I would find a job in America. But they were very insistent. I thought about faking my own death, but I guess they'd come across my type before. They threatened all sorts of things. What they said they would do to Mary and Tabitha—that's my wife and daughter—well, let's just say that I had no choice."

"So the story you told me about working for the *Middleton Bulletin* was a lie?" I asked.

"Yes, it was, but I had loved photography as a kid. I knew how to handle a camera—I'd done some photography during my work as a printer—so that part wasn't difficult. What was hard was what the Solomons asked me to do."

"Which was?" I asked.

He looked up at the photographs of the artifacts on the wall. He took another deep breath. "They wanted me to make copies of certain valuable pieces and ship the real treasures back to New Jersey. And I was to replace the originals with electrotype copies."

"But how on earth did you do that here without anyone realizing what was going on?" I asked.

"I thought it would be difficult, but it wasn't really," said Conway. "I did it in the darkroom. I could work there for hours without being disturbed. I had a lock on the door, which people thought was reasonable, because of course I couldn't have anyone just walk into the room in case the exposure to the light ruined the film. And when I was in Baghdad I would ship the artifacts back to America."

"How many objects did you manage to copy? And which ones?" asked Davison.

"I couldn't get my hands on that scarab or anything similar," said Conway, "but I didn't do too badly. A couple of gold necklaces and bracelets, a fine gold bowl, and a spectacular dagger."

"Which would be worth—what?" I asked.

"I suppose altogether between ten or twenty thousand bucks," he replied.

"And Mr. Woolley has never suspected?" asked Davison.

"I don't think so," said Conway.

"Well, he will have to be informed now," said Davison. "And the authorities will have to be made aware of it, too."

"Of course," he said, looking defeated. "In a way, it's come as a form of relief. I'd rather fall into the hands of the police than those brothers. The Solomons are incapable of mercy."

Davison and I looked at one another; perhaps we were thinking along the same lines.

"And what about your camera?" I asked. "Did someone else really smash it up or—"

"No, it was me," he said, looking thoroughly ashamed of himself. "I couldn't risk you seeing what was on the film, you see. I knew, because of your curious nature, that you'd want to see every single negative. And my game would have been up."

"And that day in Baghdad?" I asked. "When we first met?"

"I'm afraid that was all my doing, too," he said.

I turned away not so much in anger as in embarrassment and humiliation. To think I had fallen for his deceptive charms so easily. I felt my face flushing.

"But if you'll just let me explain," he said. "It wasn't because I was trying to hoodwink you."

"No, because I certainly do feel—"

"No, it was . . . well, because I'd spotted you earlier that day at the hotel. I was there visiting a friend when I caught a glimpse of you. I asked at the desk and they told me who you were. I followed you along Rashid Street and . . . well, I couldn't think of a way of introducing myself without it sounding corny."

"So you bribed a little Arab boy to snatch my handbag?" I remembered the look of hesitation and unease in that boy's eyes. "Just so you could pretend to be a hero?"

"You make it sound so sordid," he said, his voice rising in protestation.

I let his words speak for themselves.

"Look, the reason why I did that—and, yes, it was unforgivable of me—was because I'd taken a shine to you. I thought, stupidly, that if I came to your rescue you'd . . . well, that I'd stand a better chance with you."

The words were difficult to hear, but they must have been a thousand times more difficult to utter.

I was about to ask about Conway's wife and whether she knew anything about the relationship he had enjoyed with Gertrude Bell. But Davison said, "Would you excuse us for a moment? There's something I need to discuss with Mrs. Christie."

As we left Conway to contemplate his bleak future, he looked like a mere shell of a man, broken and hollow.

"Do you believe his story?" whispered Davison.

"Yes, I do," I said. "It was humiliating to listen to."

"Wasn't it just?" he said. "And it had that dreadful ring of truth to it. But listen—I'm sure you had the same idea as me? About using Conway in some kind of way?"

"I wouldn't put it quite like that, but, yes, I think there are a few things that he might be able to help us with. After all, I think he owes me a favor or two, don't you?"

"Indeed," said Davison, a mischievous sparkle lighting up his eyes. "Now, what did you have in mind?"

24

After having a long and detailed talk with Mr. Conway, all three of us walked back into the sitting room as if nothing untoward had happened. Fortunately, Conway was used to playing the part of Harry Miller, and we instructed him to carry on doing so. Of course, there was a risk that he might make a run for it, but we doubted that he would. Davison had confiscated his passport and warned him that if he did try to escape, then he would make sure that the authorities sought the heaviest sentence possible. The details of how to retrieve the stolen artifacts would have to be worked out later. There were more important things to deal with at the moment, such as the prevention of another murder.

"There's a sandstorm on its way, I'm afraid," Conway told the group comprising Mr. Archer, Father Burrows, and Miss Jones. "Looks like a pretty nasty one, too."

"A sandstorm?" asked Mr. Archer, standing up from the table. "But we need to get out of here. We've got to get Sarah to Baghdad. And that boy needs to go into custody."

"I don't think anyone is going anywhere for the next day or so," said Leonard Woolley as he entered the room. I remembered how Woolley had told me that once, after returning from England to the compound, one part of the house had been covered with sand up to its roof and it had taken his men three days to clear it.

"How bad do you think it's going to be?" I asked.

"I've just been up to the roof and it's sweeping in from the south," said Woolley. "We've had them before at this time of year. Luckily they're not as bad as the summer storms. It's nothing to worry about as long as we batten down the hatches. But obviously nobody can venture outside."

"But that's just impossible," said Archer, his face reddening. "I told you, Woolley, we need to get my daughter's body to Baghdad. She needs to be buried, you idiot. Don't you understand?"

"I'm afraid, Mr. Archer, if you go out there, within a few hours you'll find yourselves buried, too," said Woolley, who had clearly lost all patience with his former patron. "The sands are not discerning: they pay no attention to one's place in the world or how much money you have in the bank."

"I don't need to stand here and be spoken to like this." Archer looked at Woolley with contempt and walked away. As he left the room he turned and said, "I intend to leave this godforsaken place just as soon as I can. There's nothing but evil here, I can see that now. And to think I was going to invest in you. Thank goodness I didn't: it would have been like giving money to the devil himself."

Miss Jones jumped up from a chair after Archer stalked out. "Shall I go and get him, Mr. Woolley? Perhaps there's still time to try and salvage something from this."

"No, let him go," said Woolley, sitting down at the table and pouring himself a cup of tea.

"But what about our mission here?" she asked. "Just think about what his funds would do."

"Damn his money," said Woolley, before realizing what he had said. "Sorry, ladies." He took a sip of tea before he sprang up again. "I can't sit around here, not with this storm coming in. Burrows, Miller, Davison, would you mind coming with me so we can secure everything outside? I've already got some of Hamoudi's men on the job down by the dig, but there are still a few pieces of equipment lying around here and there. Mrs. Christie, Miss Jones, would you make sure all the windows in the house are closed and that the shutters have been secured?"

"Of course," I said. "But surely you're not going to let Mr. Archer venture out there? Not if it's as dangerous as you say."

Woolley walked over to the door and looked out at the sky, which was turning a sickly mix of sallow ocher, bright orange, and dusty brown. "No. By the time Archer's got his things together, he'll take one step outside and turn right around," he said.

The men left Miss Jones and me alone in the room together.

"It's quite frightening," I said. "The sandstorm, I mean. Have you experienced one before?"

"Oh, yes," she said blithely as we started to check on the windows and shutters. "The house feels like it is going to come crumbling down around you. Sand gets everywhere. It makes a terrible racket. But then it passes and life, well, it gets back to normal."

"But Woolley is right in saying that it would be dangerous to venture outside?"

"Indeed it would," she said. "I don't think you'd stand a chance, not against those sands. It's like an enormous tidal wave rolling in, only instead of water there's sand. I think the pressure would crush you—that or you'd die from taking too much sand into your lungs."

"It sounds terrifying," I said, drawing a deep breath. "I can't believe you're not more scared."

"I was the first time," she said. "I thought I was going to die of fright. I went to bed, but of course I couldn't sleep, what with everything rattling around me. It was as if an enormous giant had taken hold of the house and was trying to shake the life out of it. I had to keep singing nursery rhymes all night to comfort myself."

We went around the house, duly securing each of the windows and shutters, until we came to Katharine's room. I knocked gently on the door and a voice told us to enter. Mrs. Woolley was sat on a chair by the looking glass massaging some cream into her hands. She barely turned her head towards us as we stepped into the room. Despite the drama of the last few days, when she had been accused of the most terrible crimes, it was obvious that she still regarded herself as the queen of Ur.

"Would you please pass me that bottle of perfume?" she asked, gesturing with her hand in the direction of the desk. Her haughty tone of voice gave the question the air of a command more than a request. "It's just there, by my papers."

By some sheets of what looked like Katharine's novel in progress there was a beautiful black crystal perfume bottle with an enormous atomizing apparatus.

"Have you heard about the sandstorm?" I asked as I passed the perfume to her.

"Yes, we do get them from time to time," she said, spraying herself liberally with the musky aroma. "Very inconvenient, of course, but nothing to worry about."

"That's just what I was saying," said Cynthia.

"Mr. Archer seems intent on leaving," I said, "even though your husband has warned him against it."

"I wish that beastly man and his awful wife would go," said Katharine. "After what they put me through, I wish they'd step out into the sands and never be seen again."

"You don't mean that, surely," said Cynthia.

"Why not?" asked Katharine, turning to us, her eyes blazing. She had that manic look about her again, an unnatural, detached expression that frightened me. She stared down at her hands and seemed to recoil, as if she had seen something that repelled her.

"We've been told to make sure all the windows are closed and the shutters secure," I said, hoping to distract her from thoughts of Mr. and Mrs. Archer. "Would you mind if I check yours?"

Katharine did not respond but continued to gaze at her fingers and palms with revulsion. As I walked over to one of the windows that looked out towards the courtyard, Cynthia came to join me.

"Do you think she's all right?" she whispered. "Why is she staring at her hands like that?"

"I have to admit I am concerned for her," I said quietly. "As you know, she has a delicate constitution and she may still be in shock."

"What is that you are saying?" boomed Katharine.

"Nothing," said Cynthia, turning back towards her. "We were just talking about the approaching sandstorm and making plans for the cleanup afterwards." She turned to me and said, "You wouldn't believe how the sand gets into every nook and cranny in the house. It seems no matter how much you scrub, you simply can't get clear of it."

"The blood," murmured Katharine. "I can't wash it off."

I went to her and took her hand. "There's nothing there, my dear. Nothing at all. Your hands are clean."

As I raised them up for her to see, she dashed them down with a fury. "Get away from me," she hissed. "I can still smell it. It turns my stomach. I've got blood on my hands. I'll never be able to get rid of it." She started to moan, a horrible low sound that reminded me of the queer chant of the Arab workmen.

"I think we should fetch Mr. Woolley, don't you?" said Cynthia.

"Yes, I think that would be a good idea," I said. I tried to take one of Katharine's hands again, but she looked at me with poison in her eyes. It was obvious that I was causing her a great deal of distress.

"Perhaps it would be better if *you* went and found him," Cynthia suggested. "I can sit with her."

"Of course," I said.

Before I left the room, I glanced back. What I saw nearly broke my heart. I had thought that Katharine had been making such good progress, but here she was, muttering to herself, looking like an inmate in some foreign asylum being tended to by a kindhearted nurse.

I opened the door to a howling wind. This was no weather for a hat, and so I left it inside. The air was thick with dust and sand, and as I walked I had to shield my eyes and mouth with my handkerchief. It took me some time to find Woolley, who was down on a roped-off strip of excavated land, busy overseeing the collection of some odd pieces of equipment and tools. I didn't want to alarm either him or his men, so I called to him and asked if I could have a word. At first he could not hear me above the noise of the wind, so I had to shout. He noted the seriousness of my voice and the expression on my face and told the Arabs to carry on with their work while he stepped away for a moment.

"What's wrong?" he said.

"It's Katharine," I said. "I'm afraid she's having another one of her episodes."

"A headache?"

"No, something altogether more worrying. She's got this fixation that she . . . that she can still smell the blood on her hands."

"Oh, no," said Woolley, sighing. "I thought, what with Cecil's confession, that she might have put that to the back of her mind."

It was not yet safe to tell either him or anyone else in the compound the truth of Cecil's guilt or innocence. "Yes, so did I. But she does seem very on edge. In fact, I fear for her sanity."

Woolley returned to his men and shouted out instructions. On the way back to the house I told him something of what I had just witnessed, reassuring him that Katharine was being looked after by Miss Jones.

"That's all we need, just as this storm is coming," he said.

He must have seen the minute changes in my face—a small lift of an eyebrow, a sudden blink of the eyes—because he added, "Sorry, I didn't mean for that to sound cruel."

"It must have been difficult for you," I said, remembering what Woolley had told me about the state of their marriage.

"It seems the events here have proved too much for her," he said. "I should never have placed her in such a vulnerable position. Of course it's all my fault. I've been selfish, thinking about the contribution she made to the work here. I should finally face up to it. Perhaps it's time for Katharine to be taken somewhere safe, somewhere where she can be looked after properly."

"You mean—"

But before I could finish my sentence, Father Burrows came running out of the house. Panic haunted his eyes.

"Quick, Woolley!" he said breathlessly. "You've got to come!"

"What's wrong, man?"

"It's Mrs. Woolley! She's—"

Woolley pushed past him. I followed in his wake, running as quickly as I could across the courtyard towards Katharine's room. The scene that greeted me was even more disturbing than the one I had left. Cynthia Jones, her deathly white face streaked with tears, was already being comforted by Woolley. In the corner of the room, her head slumped forwards as if the life had been drained from her, was Katharine.

"What's wrong, Cynthia?" asked Woolley.

"It was awful. I can't tell you how . . . how awful it was," she said, sobbing.

Woolley looked over towards his wife. "Katharine . . . do you know anything about what happened?"

But she did not respond. I walked over to Katharine and knelt down beside her.

"Close the shutters," she mumbled.

I said gently, "We closed the shutters because of the storm. Don't you remember?"

"Thirsty," she said. "Water." As I poured her a glass I noticed that her pupils seemed dilated. After these few words she retreated back into unresponsiveness.

"I was only gone a few minutes," I said, walking towards Cynthia. "What happened?"

She took a few deep breaths and, encouraged by Woolley and me, began to tell us what had transpired.

"I thought that . . . that she would be a little calmer when you left the room," she said. "She was getting agitated by your presence, wasn't she? But almost as soon as you'd gone, she turned to me with that awful look in her eyes, like . . . like she wanted to do me some harm, some real harm. I told myself everything would be all right. After all, Mrs. Woolley had had these episodes before. But then, just as I was sitting there, trying to comfort her, she grabbed me. You can see how tight was her hold on me."

Cynthia raised up her right arm to reveal a reddish-purple mark around her wrist and lower part of her arm.

"I tried to free myself, but her grip was too strong. I told her that she was hurting me, but she just kept looking at me with those eyes—fierce, blazing eyes full of hatred. It was so painful that I started to cry. I heard some voices and called out for help. Thank goodness Father Burrows was nearby. But before he came into the room, Mrs. Woolley said to me in a whisper, 'Watch out—tonight . . .' "

Here Cynthia burst into tears once more. "Sorry," she said as she tried to compose herself. "But those words—you understand that they sent a chill straight through me. After everything that's gone on here . . ."

"What did she say, Cynthia?" I asked.

She hesitated for a moment, looked across the room at Katharine and took another deep breath. "She said, 'Watch out: tonight you're going to die. Tonight . . . I'm going to kill you.' "

25

Woolley led Cynthia, who was now so distressed that she was shaking with shock, out of the room. But then, just as I had given Katharine a glass of water and was guiding her to her bed, I heard a loud cry. I made sure that she was sitting down and that she could do no harm to herself before I ran towards the source of the noise.

I arrived in the sitting room to see Mrs. Archer in a state of hysteria, surrounded by her husband, Lawrence McRae, and Father Burrows. After alerting us to what had occurred between Katharine and Cynthia, Burrows, who shrank from arguments, had retreated to the relative calm of the main room, only to be faced with yet more conflict.

"I told you it was her all along," wailed Mrs. Archer. "If only you had all listened to me."

"I don't think that's helpful, not in front of Miss Jones," said Woolley, who stood in the corner of the room by Cynthia.

"Well, I'm afraid it's the truth," said Ruth.

Mrs. Archer must have only recently learnt that she could not leave the compound. This realization that she would be unable to take her daughter to Baghdad for burial was bad enough, but then she must have heard how Katharine Woolley had threatened to murder Cynthia. The combination had proved too much for the grieving woman.

"Woolley, you can't make excuses for her anymore," said Mr. Archer as he tried to comfort his wife. "You heard what Miss Jones just said: that your wife has got it into her head to kill her tonight."

At this, Cynthia started crying again and left the room, presumably returning to her own quarters.

"Where's Captain Forster?" demanded Mr. Archer. "We need to get him here to sort out this madness." He turned to find a servant and clapped his hands, but none came running. "Burrows, would you go and fetch him. Tell him it's an emergency."

Father Burrows stood there and, like a well-trained dog, looked to his master, Woolley, for guidance. Woolley no longer tried to defend his wife; after all, he had heard the words directly from Cynthia's mouth. "I think Captain Forster is with Hamoudi," he said to Burrows. "He's trying to make sure everything is secure before the sandstorm arrives."

"I can't believe we have to stay here," said Ruth Archer, looking at the sitting room as if it were a prison. "Not after what happened. Not with her."

"But you heard Cecil's confession," said Woolley. "All of us did."

"But how do we know Katharine didn't do it all along?" asked Lawrence McRae "She could have killed Sarah and then made Cecil take the blame for it. You know how suggestible he is and how forceful she can be."

"I doubt that very much indeed," said Woolley, trying to remain calm.

"And where is she now?" asked Mr. Archer. "Your wife, I mean."

"Mrs. Woolley is in her room," I said. "I left her resting."

"You left her by herself?" asked Ruth Archer, looking at me as if I were mad.

"She was lying on the bed. She seemed—"

But before I could finish my sentence, Ruth Archer pushed past me, quickly followed by Mr. Archer and Lawrence McRae. There was a dangerous spirit in the air now, as if the threesome were unified by the unruly emotions of grief and anger. They hurried towards Katharine's room.

"Really, I don't think there's any reason for you to behave like this," said Woolley as he ran after them.

"I think there's every reason," said McRae.

"Look here!" cried Woolley. "You can't go forcing your way into my wife's bedroom. This is completely outrageous. Stop right there! Stop, I say!"

But his orders were ignored. Mrs. Archer used her round form to push open the door and a moment later the three of them, shortly followed by Woolley, were standing in the room. They gazed at the bed. Katharine Woolley was exactly where I had left her, asleep. She had her hands crossed on her chest and there was something saintlike about her pose. Perhaps it was this—and the sight of her looking so peaceful—that made them turn away in embarrassment and shame and then walk out of the room. Woolley himself said nothing but gave them a stern look as they filed past him.

We left Katharine sleeping and returned to join the group in the sitting room. Mr. Archer was the first to speak.

"I'm sorry things got a little out of hand there," he said. "But, Woolley, you must understand why we feel as we do. Being unable to leave here, our poor daughter in that pantry, lying there like . . . like some slab of meat."

"Hubert, no. Please don't say that," said Ruth Archer, her face creasing with grief.

"I'm sorry, dear, but some plain talking is what's needed here," he said, reddening slightly in the face. He looked at us each in turn. "Don't you all realize that we're living under the same roof as her killer?"

"Yes, but he's under lock and key," said Woolley. "Cecil is not going anywhere. I can assure you that you're safe."

At this point the door opened and Father Burrows returned with Captain Forster, together with Davison and Conway, all of them looking distinctly weather-beaten. Their faces and heads were covered in a fine dust, and Forster asked for a glass of water to clear his throat.

"It's getting quite lively out there," he said, wiping some sand from the corner of his lips. "Nearly everything has been moved to safety. The last of the men, including Hamoudi, have gone and we won't see them now until the storm's passed. Now, what's this I hear about an emergency?"

Forster listened patiently as Mr. Archer explained the situation. As he outlined what had happened—how Katharine had threatened to kill Cynthia Jones later that night—he did not gloss over the fact that he had stormed into Mrs. Woolley's room, accompanied by his wife and Lawrence McRae. None of them came out well from the story, but Forster made no judgment on their behavior.

"Yes, I can see that you are worried," said the captain. "Especially since we are all going to be cooped up here in the compound tonight. But what we cannot allow to happen—what must be prevented at all costs—is any kind of descent into mindless savagery."

Various murmurs of encouragement and agreement came from Woolley, Burrows, Davison, and Conway, the man everyone still knew as Miller.

"So what I suggest is this," Forster continued. "In order for everyone to feel safe, I recommend that Cecil McRae and Mrs. Woolley remain under lock and key tonight."

At this, Mr. and Mrs. Archer and Lawrence McRae started to voice their objections, but Forster succeeded in shouting them down. "And then, in addition, a man—who will be armed—is going to be stationed outside each of the rooms. Now, who among the men here knows how to handle a gun?"

Woolley, Davison, and McRae raised their hands. "Thank you for volunteering, but I'm afraid we will have to discount Mr. Woolley and Mr. McRae, as they have what are clearly personal interests in the case," said Forster. "So, Davison, would you mind sitting outside Mrs. Woolley's room? And I will station myself outside Cecil McRae's. Of course, although the courtyard is protected to a certain extent, it's still open to the elements and we'll have to take certain precautions. Best to wrap ourselves up in blankets like Arabs, don't you think?"

Although it was clear Mr. and Mrs. Archer would much rather force both Katharine Woolley and Cecil McRae out of the house so that they could die in the desert storm, they had no choice but to accept Forster's decision.

"For those of you who haven't experienced one of these sandstorms before, I would just say this," Forster continued. "You should be safe enough crossing the courtyard, but please on no account step outside. Yes, the house may shake and you may think it's about to fall down around you, but it will pass. I suggest that you try to take your mind off it. If you can't sleep, then read, play bridge or patience, or catch up on your correspondence."

When Forster had finished his little speech, the group dispersed into cliques: Mr. and Mrs. Archer continued to whisper about Mrs. Woolley's instability of mind; Lawrence McRae still protested the innocence of his nephew to the man he addressed as Miller; Davison started talking to Forster about their forthcoming duties as sentry guards; Father Burrows questioned Woolley about the safety of the cuneiform tablets and the treasures of the *antika* room; and I, unnoticed, slipped away to go and check on Katharine.

I found her still sleeping, her arms still crossed. I walked over to her dressing table and selected two jars of cosmetics, as well as the pot of hand cream that she had been using earlier. I placed them carefully into my handbag and shut the door as quietly as I could. I returned to the sitting room, where people were discussing how they were going to spend the night.

"You can count us out; we're in no mood for frivolities," said Mr. Archer. "I trust all will be in order, Captain Forster."

"Indeed it will," he said. "I can guarantee that you've got nothing to worry about."

"Are you sure you don't want anything to eat before you go to bed?" asked Father Burrows, who, now that the servants had been dismissed, had been given the task of preparing a simple supper.

"No, we're not hungry," said Mrs. Archer. The couple said a plaintive good night and retired for the evening.

"Mrs. Christie, would you care to join us at cards? Bridge, perhaps?" asked Woolley, who seemed to be in remarkably good spirits, considering what he had witnessed at the camp.

"I would enjoy that, but perhaps a little later," I replied. "Mr. Miller has been promising to show me the basics of film development in the darkroom, and I rather think now might be as good a time as any."

"Oh, yes, of course," said Conway, acting on his cue. "There's really nothing to it, once you've got the mix of chemicals right."

A few eyebrows were raised, as the group must surely have picked up on the friendly, even at times flirtatious nature of our relationship. Perhaps they thought we were going into the darkroom to get to know each other a little better. Let them think that if they wanted. No, what we had planned was much more interesting. We were going to find out whether someone was being poisoned.

26

"Is there a light we can use in here?" I asked as we stepped into the pocket of darkness.

"Sure, just give me a minute," said Conway.

I felt him brush past me, and although I knew he was both a liar and a criminal, I still felt the leap of my heart and the quickening of my breath. Thank goodness the darkness hid my blushes.

"We can use an oil lamp," he said as he took out a flashlight to search for a box of matches. He drew out a match and lit one, and a moment later the lamp cast its gentle glow across the small room. "Now, tell me what you need." His tone was matter-of-fact, and although he was not rude, there was none of that easy charm that I had come to know and in some ways enjoy. Surely he was embarrassed by his recent exposure and humiliated by the way he had deceived me, but there was something in his manner which made me think I had behaved quite shabbily, too. I would never forget that look of disappointment in his eyes when he realized that I had been trying to delay his return to his room.

"So this is where you did . . . all your work?" I asked.

"Yes, that's right, so we probably have everything you could want for your experiment," he said, indicating a set of shelves on which stood various jars of salts and chemicals, a Bunsen burner, a number of trays, a set of pipettes, glass jars, funnels, bottles of water, and rubber pipes. Although Conway had kept the room locked, if a stranger had chanced to walk into it, then he would assume everything here had something to do with the process of developing camera film rather than the expert copying of ancient treasures.

"When we've got more time, I'd like you to show me how you went about it," I said. "But I suppose we'd better get down to the business in hand. Let's see. Yes, that Bunsen burner: if you could set that up . . . Firstly, I need to make some fuming nitric oxide." Fortunately, when I had been doing my nursing training, and in the dispensary in Torquay, I had always rather enjoyed the study of chemistry. All those lovely formulae, the way the elements could be combined to make something new; then there was the beautiful order of the periodic table. "I need some potassium nitrate and a little sulfuric acid; you have those? And a couple of flasks."

Conway scanned the shelves and placed everything on the table in front of me. I got to work mixing the various chemicals until the ghostly form of the gas rose up from the beaker.

"Now I need some potassium hydroxide, a three percent solution in methanol," I said.

Perhaps my knowledge of the wonders of the scientific world astounded Conway, because as I busied myself about the makeshift laboratory, working with the various chemicals and flasks, he looked at me as if he were seeing me in a new light. I was no longer the helpless woman he had rescued from the backstreets of Baghdad—a lady grateful for a gentleman's attention—but someone with a surprising skill. Little did he know of the true extent of my mastery of poisons, and I decided that it would be best to keep this to myself for the present time.

"Yes, that's working very nicely," I said. "All this is in preparation for the real test, of course. Have you heard of the Vitali color reaction?"

I was met by a blank stare. "Oh, a very interesting experiment, and so very pleasing when it works," I said. I stood back and checked that everything I needed was laid out before me. It was, in a way, a little like cooking. When one was making a roast dinner, there was little point in leaving everything—the roast potatoes, the joint, the bread sauce, the horseradish—to the last minute; the secret, as every good housewife knew, was in the preparation. So too with chemical experiments. Yes, everything was in order: the boiling water, various flasks containing the key ingredients, and all the equipment I would need. I took out Katharine's cosmetics from my handbag and spooned some of the pale cream into a flask. I then treated this with the fuming nitric acid, which was evaporated to dryness on the water bath. To this residue I added a small amount of the potassium hydroxide in methanol solution. As I did so, the color of the cream changed from white to bright purple and then red before fading to colorlessness.

"Yes, very interesting," I said as I watched the colors change.

"What's happening?" asked Conway.

"It's a positive result, just as I expected," I said.

"Of what?"

"Of hyoscyamine."

"Hyo . . . ?"

"It's a tropane alkaloid," I said. "Also known as daturine, found in the plants of the Solanaceae family."

"Sorry, I don't understand."

"Plants such as henbane, mandrake, jimsonweed, and deadly nightshade. Of course, it has its uses, but it is also very dangerous. Hyoscyamine can cause a dry mouth, blurred vision and eye pain, dilated pupils, dizziness, restlessness, nausea, headaches, euphoria, short-term memory loss, and, not least, hallucinations."

It took a moment or two before Conway began to understand the implications of my little experiment. "So you think that—"

"I don't think anything," I said. "Now I have proof—proof that Katharine Woolley is not mad. Her headaches were far from psychosomatic, as some people in the compound believe. Her visions were not those of someone who was deranged or mentally ill. Mrs. Woolley has been suffering in the most awful way possible. She was being poisoned."

"But how? Who by?"

"I cannot for certain answer your second question, but I do have an answer to your first one," I said as I spooned out a dollop of mixture from another of Katharine's jars so as to repeat the test. "Katharine Woolley was being poisoned by means of her face and hand creams. Each day, each night, she would anoint herself in the belief that the creams would help moisturize her skin in this dry climate, the potions going some way to help keep her looking fresh and youthful. But, unknown to her, the creams were driving her to the point of madness. More importantly, the poison that slowly seeped into her system affected her behavior in such a way as to give rise to the generally accepted notion that she was mad."

"You mean someone deliberately put this substance into her night cream?" asked Conway. "Into her hand cream?"

"Yes, and very effective it was, too," I said. "Someone wanted her to appear as though she were insane."

"So that's why she said that thing about threatening to kill Miss Jones," said Conway. "It was a hallucination brought on by that poison. But who would do that? Who would want to put poison in Katharine's face cream?"

I left the question unanswered and instead concentrated on the experiment. As I went through the steps of the procedure again—adding the fuming nitric acid to the cream, then the potassium hydroxide in methanol—I saw the mixture change its hue. For a brief moment it turned bright red, a shade that reminded me of the color of freshly spilt blood.

27

We returned to the sitting room to find Cynthia Jones setting the table for dinner. It was going to be rather a makeshift affair, she said; Father Burrows had told her that he was going to reheat some leftovers from lunch, together with a selection of cold dishes. She informed us that Davison and Forster had been given cups of tea before they had taken their respective positions outside the doors of Katharine Woolley and Cecil McRae.

"They were both adamant that they didn't want anything more than that," she said. "But I'll make sure to take them a little something else later, at least a little bread and cheese. It's going to be a long night for them."

As Cynthia placed some knives and forks down on the table, I noticed that her hands were shaking.

"You've no need to feel afraid," I said.

"Afraid?"

"I can tell you're trying to put a brave face on things," I replied. "But I doubt Mrs. Woolley knew what she was saying earlier."

"I have been trying to put it out of my mind, but I must admit it hasn't been easy," she said. "It's good to know that there's someone stationed outside her door."

Conway—who was pouring himself a generous measure of

whisky topped with soda water—asked her if she would like a drink, but Cynthia declined.

"I'll stick to my water," she said.

The table had been set for six, and over the course of the next few minutes we were joined by Lawrence McRae, Leonard Woolley, and Father Burrows, who came out of the kitchen bearing a tray of food.

"I can't make any great claims for the quality of the meal, I'm afraid," said Burrows as he placed the dishes on the table. "It's all been flung together at the last minute."

"We're very grateful for your efforts," said Woolley. "So, what do we have?"

Father Burrows guided us through the plates of vine leaves, creamed aubergine (which he warned us had been made with a great deal of garlic), a hot pepper spread, a chickpea salad, a minced meat stew, a plate of figs, and something that sat in a thick, congealed tomato sauce that I didn't quite catch. "I suppose the Arabs have been eating like this for centuries," he said. "One only has to look at the cuneiform tablets to see that. I've studied one tablet which gives two dozen recipes for a type of stew cooked with vegetables and meat, and of course they've always liked their spices and garlic, too."

"It's certainly an acquired taste," said Woolley as he dipped a little of the bread into the garlicky aubergine dish. "And it may be too much for some of the ladies here. Having said that, my wife has a fondness for strong-tasting Arabic cuisine, as did Miss Bell."

At the mention of Gertrude Bell's name, the table fell quiet and Conway looked down at his plate. Perhaps sensing that a spirit of melancholy was about to descend on the group, Woolley decided to lighten the mood by expanding on the story.

"I remember on one occasion when Miss Bell was here, she polished off one particular dish that was so hot and spicy, it brought tears to the men's eyes," he said, smiling. "We were all calling out for glasses of water after only a couple of mouthfuls, but she had a stomach like an Arab and finished it off as if it were a dollop of mashed potatoes or custard."

The statement presented me with the opportunity to ask a few questions, but I knew I would have to be very careful. "I remember many years ago, soon after I arrived in Cairo, falling very ill after sampling one of the local dishes," I said. "But I was very young and foolish. I could have done with someone like Miss Bell to show me the ropes."

"Yes, she would have liked you," Woolley said. "Don't you agree, Miss Jones?"

"Oh, yes, I'm sure she would have," said Cynthia, spooning a little of the minced-meat stew on to her plate. "Most women she regarded as—what was it? That's right: she called them 'dull dogs.'"

"I'm afraid I see myself as very dull indeed," I said. "Not like Miss Bell. So very clever."

"She was extraordinary in so many ways," said Woolley.

"Did you meet in Cairo?" I asked.

"Cairo?" Woolley looked askance.

I knew both he and Miss Bell had worked in intelligence in Egypt during the war—as had Katharine Woolley's first husband, who had died in Cairo, in 1919—but I could not reveal this.

"I can't remember exactly how I first met her," he said. "In fact, I think I might have read her work before I met her." He walked over to a bookcase in the corner of the room and ran his hands over the volumes before he found the one he was looking for. "Yes, here it is." Woolley blew some dust off its cover as he extracted it. "*Amurath to Amurath*, published in, let's see . . . yes, in 1911. Have you read it?"

"No, I'm ashamed to say I haven't," I said.

"Listen to this from its preface," he said. "'The banks of the Euphrates echo with ghostly alarums; the Mesopotamian deserts are full of the rumor of phantom armies; you will not blame me if I passed among them '*trattando l'ombre come cosa salde.*' "

"Treating the shadows as the solid thing," said Father Burrows. "*Purgatorio*, if I'm not mistaken."

"I see you know your Dante," Woolley remarked.

There was something to be said for Miss Bell's words; indeed, there was something about the environment, this dry desert full of mirages, half-truths and buried secrets, that called out for such a method. However, it was just as important, I thought, to treat solid things—so-called facts and seeming certainties—as if they too were as insubstantial as shadows. Nothing was what it seemed here.

"Miss Bell once said to me something I've never forgotten," Woolley continued. "We were at the end of a long day. We'd been digging in the heat of the sun. We walked up to the top of the ziggurat and looked out at the desert that stretched before us. She turned to me and said, 'I wonder, are we the same people when our surroundings, friends, and associations are changed?' I thought it a very interesting question, one I could not answer easily."

Just then a blast of wind hit the house, shaking it to its very foundations. From somewhere outside—the courtyard, perhaps—came the sound of a pot or a tile hitting the ground and smashing into fragments.

The noise made Cynthia Jones jump up from her chair, upsetting a glass of water by her side as she did so. "Oh, look—sorry," she said. "I'm so terribly clumsy."

"Here, let me," I said, taking up a napkin and blotting the water from the table.

"Thank you," she said, relieved. "I don't know what's come over me. It's not as though I haven't experienced a sandstorm before." She stared down at the food on her plate, most of which she had not touched. "Would you mind awfully if I retired for the night? I'm not much company, I'm afraid."

"Of course not," Woolley assured her, standing up. "It's been a long day for all of us. Now, will you need anything to help you sleep?" He looked at me for a response.

"Yes, I have a sleeping draught that you can take." As I said this another gust of wind and sand buffeted the compound with such force that the glasses and cutlery on the table vibrated.

"Thank you, but I think I'll be all right," she said. "I'll just take some water with me."

After Cynthia had said good night, talk returned to Woolley's question about identity.

Father Burrows believed that personality was something innate, something divine that one was born with, while McRae argued that surely it was formed by one's experiences. I'm afraid I sat on the fence and observed that it must be a combination of the two. Conway, who had remained quiet up to this moment, pointed out that the real issue at stake was not the source of one's personality but the extent to which it fluctuated when one was wrenched out of one's normal environment.

"I'm sure all of us felt it when we first came here," he said. "Looking out at the stretch of desert sands. Feeling the dry air on our faces. Hearing that incessant chant of the Arab workers as they dig up the ground." He talked with a passion which I knew came from personal insight. "It's enough to drive even the sanest of men a little crazy."

"Interesting you should say that, Mr. Miller," said Father Burrows, pushing his wire-rimmed spectacles back up on the bridge of his nose. "I see it almost as a test, as though each of us were feeling a little of Jesus's experience when he spent forty days and forty nights in the wilderness. I always think it would have looked something like this, like the desert."

Again the wind howled outside, shaking the house with an almighty force. "It's like God is trying to talk to us tonight, don't you think?" Burrows asked in a voice that rang with a false brightness.

"If God does exist, which I seriously doubt, he's certainly not here," said McRae, getting up from the table and helping himself to a large measure of whisky.

"Now, now, McRae," said Woolley, who went to join the architect by the drinks table. "There's no point in letting gloom set in. Certainly my father would never have allowed his spirits to sink in such a situation. He was a character, I can tell you."

Woolley started to tell a series of amusing stories about his father, a vicar first in Clapton and then in Bethnal Green, a man who had a passion for collecting porcelain and pottery, Minton and Copeland and so on. He described to us his big black beard and dark eyes and recalled how he had always insisted on taking a cold bath each morning. In the winter, Woolley said, his father would fill the bath the night before so that he could guarantee that it would have formed a crust of ice. "Discomfort was almost holy to him," he laughed.

Leonard was one of eleven children, he explained, and as a child he had been teased by his schoolmates that he was one of the flock of "Woolly sheep."

"But then, after a little reading, I discovered that the name Woolley actually came from 'Wolf's Lea,'" he said. "And one day, in front of the group of boys, I proudly announced that my brothers and sisters were not sheep but wolves in sheep's clothing!"

The comment made the group laugh, and Miller, McRae, and Burrows each revealed the names they had been called as children.

"And what of you, Mrs. Christie?" asked Woolley. "What were you called as a girl?"

I hesitated a moment—I never liked to reveal too much about myself—before I relented. "Well, my brother, Monty, used to call me 'Kid' when he was being nice and 'Scrawny Chicken' when he wanted to upset me," I said. "Of course, now I would do almost anything to earn the same epithet." The comment drew a laugh. "But I suppose we all had funny nicknames. For example, my sister Madge, or Margaret, we called 'Punkie." And my daughter, Rosalind, is sometimes known as 'Teddy' or 'the Tadpole.'"

As I thought of the nicknames I had chosen for some of the characters in my books something stirred at the back of my mind. It had been such a trivial, silly exchange, but I was sure something of import had been said. Silently, I ran through the conversation. A nickname. A term of endearment. A sobriquet. The question that Miss Bell had posed to Woolley, and which he had related to us, about whether one was the same person when taken out of one's normal environment. *A sheep in wolf's clothing. A wolf in sheep's clothing.*

Another wall of wind hit the house at full force.

"Mrs. Christie, are you all right?" asked Woolley. "You're looking a little pale."

I did my best to smile. "Yes, just a little tired, I'm afraid." I stood up from the table. "Would you mind if I went to bed, too? I think I'd like to try to sleep before the storm gets any worse."

"Let me accompany you to your room," said Woolley.

"No, I'm sure I can manage," I said.

"But even negotiating the courtyard might be difficult in this weather," he replied. "After all, we wouldn't want any more accidents."

"No, I'm quite confident, but . . . but thank you all the same," I said.

Instead of going straight to my room I went to see Davison, who was stationed outside Katharine's quarters. As I stepped into the courtyard I felt myself being sucked into a whirlwind of sand. Particles of grit covered my face and I felt the dry, deathly taste of the desert on my lips. I closed my eyes and felt my way forwards, using the edge of the wall as my guide. Just as I thought I was nearing the room I felt something by my feet. I opened my eyes but it was too late. As I fell I stretched out my hands and readied myself for the inevitable pain. I tried to imagine that I was surfing—oh, the fun I had

had surfing during that glorious tour around the world I had made with Archie back in 1922!—and that I was just crashing into the sea. I think the thought helped as I landed quite lightly, with only a slight crush of palm against stone and a slightly grazed knee. It had been a tin bucket that had brought me down.

I sat there for a moment, my hair whipping about my face in a wild frenzy, the air thick with dust and sand, and realized that I was afraid. A deep sense of unease crept over me. I felt sick to my stomach. I began to understand some of the evil that pervaded Ur. Despite the fact that Davison was here and that, if I so wished, I could spend the night making light conversation or playing cards with the people I had just left, I still felt desperately alone and exposed. A memory came to me then of a teacher I had had when I was young, at school in Torquay. During one of the lessons the teacher, whose name I could not recall, told us that, at some point in our lives, all of us would experience a crushing sense of despair, a feeling that there was no hope. She told us the story of Jesus in the Garden of Gethsemane and went on to talk about suffering and the importance of faith. I had to remember this. Without hope there was nothing. And yet I felt frightened, so terribly afraid.

I pushed myself up and made my way towards Davison. Not only was I a stranger in a desert land, but there was a murderer very near. Someone who I was sure would want to kill again.

28

After a brief conversation with Davison, I made my way back to my room and, despite my best efforts to stay alert, felt myself drifting off. I couldn't be certain how long I had been asleep, but the sound of a scream woke me with a jolt. I pushed myself off the bed, grabbed a scarf, wrapped it around my head, and ran into the courtyard. Visibility was next to nothing: all I could see was a whirling dervish of sand that danced in the air as if it were a malevolent spirit from the *Arabian Nights*.

I tried to shout, but the sand-filled blasts reduced my voice to a rasp. "Davison? Forster?"

There was no answer. Using strength I did not know I possessed, I moved forwards, battling against the power of the wind. Above and around me echoed the terrible sound of the sandstorm, a noise that suggested that the vengeance of the heavens was being visited on the earth. I listened for a scream. There was nothing. Had I been dreaming, or had I mistaken the high-pitched whine of the wind for a cry?

Then the scream came again; it was unmistakably that of a woman. Once more, using my hands to guide me, I edged my way around the courtyard until I came to its source.

"Help me! Oh, help!" cried the voice from inside.

Blinking through the sand, which stung my eyes, I saw the vague outline of a window. But the shutters were closed and I couldn't see inside the room. My fingers felt their way down and across against the mud-brick wall until I found the handle to the door. I grasped it and turned it, but it was locked.

"What's happened?" I cried. "Are you all right?" But there was no response. "Who's in there?"

I banged on the door, but this only prompted more unintelligible screams. I rattled the handle and pounded on the wood.

"Let me in!" I shouted.

"Please get help!" came the voice from the other side of the door.

I turned and edged my way around the courtyard until I came to what I thought was the main door to the house. I tried to open it, but it too was locked. Using my fist, I knocked on the wood with all my strength, and a few seconds later I heard the sound of footsteps and then the shifting of what sounded like a chair. The handle turned and a moment later I saw a sliver of light illuminate the inside of the frame. I pushed my way in.

"What the devil . . . ?" said McRae as I fell into the room.

"There's something wrong," I said, wiping the sand from my mouth. I felt like I wanted to gag, but it was important to get this out. "There's a woman . . . in there, in one of the bedrooms. She says she needs help."

"I told you to keep that door shut," said Woolley, making his way through the living room towards us. "What's going on?"

"It's Mrs. Christie," said McRae. "She's saying something's the matter."

"What?" asked Woolley.

"In her . . . her room," I gasped. "She can't get out."

"Calm down," said Woolley. "Take a deep breath."

"It's not Katharine, is it?"

"I lost all sense of whose room it was," I said. "She's in trouble. She says she needs—"

"McRae, Miller, come with me!" Woolley shouted. "Bring those flashlights. Mrs. Christie, you stay here with Burrows."

I ignored them and rushed out into the courtyard, followed by the plaintive cries of Father Burrows pleading with me to take shelter inside. Realizing that I was not going to change my mind, the priest shut the door to the house.

"Hello!" Woolley shouted into the storm. "Is someone hurt or in danger?"

He edged his way around the courtyard repeating the question. I followed the three men until we began to hear cries.

"It's coming from in there," said McRae, who seized the handle of the door to find it was still locked. "Can you get to the door?" he called to the person inside.

But his question was only met by another terrified cry.

"We're going to have to break it down," he said.

The men quickly organized themselves. "Stand back!" shouted Woolley. "Are you ready?"

The three men seemed to come together as one, using all their strength to run at the door. I heard the splintering of wood and a cry of pain from one of the men.

"Nearly there, but not quite," said the photographer.

"Let's give it another try," said Woolley.

They stood back, regrouped, and rushed towards the door once more. I heard something crack, the lock broke, and in an instant they forced their way into the room. A wave of sand followed them, making it hard to see inside. The wind unsettled a stack of paper and unused envelopes, sending them into a flurry of activity; the power of the storm even sent a pile of books crashing to the floor.

"Oh, dear God," said Woolley as the beams from the flashlights began to illuminate pockets of the room.

"What? What is it?" asked McRae.

I stepped into the room and closed the door behind me. The men were gathered around the bed. I pushed past them to see Miss Jones holding a glass, her face contorted in pain.

"What's happened?" I asked. "Cynthia, can you talk?"

She looked down at the bed with horror. A swirl of white fumes rose up from the bedsheet. As I bent down I noticed that there was a sharp smell that pinched my nose. On closer inspection I noticed that the patch by Cynthia's side seemed to bubble as if part of the mattress was beginning to dissolve.

"It looks—and smells—like hydrochloric acid," I said. I remembered Woolley telling me that the archaeologists used the chemical to clean the cuneiform tablets.

"What?" said Woolley. "Miss Jones—are you hurt at all?"

"The water—I went to take a drink," she said, stumbling over her words. "It was dark. I reached out for my glass by the bed, but . . ."

She started to shift her position, moving her legs dangerously close to the patch of bed that continued to fizz and dissolve.

"Don't move," said Woolley. "Cynthia, stay exactly where you are!"

"What?" she said, unable or unwilling to take in the horror of it all.

"It's dangerous," said Woolley. "There's acid on the bed. My God, look, it's eating away at the fabric."

Cynthia looked down at the sizzling mass beside her and then up at her glass. "I woke up with a dry mouth," she said. "I was about to take a drink and then I think the sound of the wind outside gave me a shock and I must have spilled it. I heard a fizzing noise. I felt something on my leg . . . and then pain. I managed to light a candle by my bed. That's when I saw this . . . that's when I started screaming."

I looked down to see a circular patch of redness above her left knee. It looked as though the top layer of skin had been eaten away by a splatter of acid.

"We need to see to that right away," I said, finding myself slipping into nursing mode. "Can you feel pain anywhere else?"

Cynthia shook her head.

"Miller, can you fetch me a pan of water and some clean towels?" Just as he was about to leave the room I called out, "And I don't suppose you have any ice?"

"I'm afraid not," said Woolley.

"Never mind," I said. "We can work with what we've got."

As I was studying Cynthia's burn, I heard her breathing become more erratic. Her face was white and she looked around the room with panic in her eyes.

"What would have happened if I had taken a drink?" she asked. She looked at the glass again.

"Try not to dwell on that," said Woolley. "Here, let me take that from you." He took a pillow from the bed, stripped it, and used the pillowcase to wrap around his hand and protect his fingers. "There we are," he said as he reached out and gently grasped the glass. "Let's place it over on the bedside table."

"To think that I could have swallowed it," she said. "How I would have suffered. With that . . . that acid burning its way through me." Cynthia burst into tears and covered her face with her hands.

McRae leant down and studied the glass. "The question is: How did the acid get into the glass and who put it there? Did you see anyone come into your bedroom?"

Cynthia looked confused, uncertain about what she had just been asked.

"What if . . . ?" said McRae to himself before he ran out of the room with no explanation.

"I nearly came head-to-head with McRae," said the photographer as he returned with a bowl of water and a pile of towels. "What's got into him?"

"We can't worry about that now," I said. I asked Cynthia to move to the other side of the bed, away from the nasty patch of acid on the mattress. "Please pass me the water and the towels." I placed a hand on Cynthia's arm. "Now, this is going to hurt, so you will have to be brave," I said. "Can you do that for me?"

Cynthia nodded her head as she tried to wipe away her tears.

"I'm going to clean the affected skin," I said, taking hold of a towel and dipping it in water.

I squeezed the towel over the acid burn so as to let some water drop onto the skin. Cynthia winced and automatically moved her leg away from me. As I began to dab and wash the site, she clasped the bedsheets with her hands and gritted her teeth with resolve.

"That's right," I said. "You're doing very well."

"I heard the knocking and the banging at the door, but I couldn't get out of bed," she said. "I know I should have got up and let you in, but I felt incapable of moving. I felt so afraid."

"Don't worry about that now," I said as I continued to clean the wound. "You were probably in shock."

I felt Cynthia's eyes on me as I dripped some more water onto her leg. I sensed that there was something she wanted to ask me. "This won't take much longer, I promise," I added.

Her eyes darted back and forth and she took a few deep breaths before she finally readied herself to speak. "Do you think this was Mrs. Woolley's doing?" she whispered. "After all, that's what she threatened to do. But I don't understand. She was being watched, wasn't she?"

At that moment McRae entered the room shouting.

"Davison's out cold," he cried. "He was supposed to be on guard. And Mrs. Woolley's door's unlocked."

"What?" asked Woolley.

"He's still breathing, but I don't know whether he's been knocked out or drugged or what," said McRae.

"Have you checked on Katharine to make sure she is all right?" Woolley asked.

"No, but I—"

Woolley cut him off. "Stay here and look after the women," he said, pushing past the architect. "I'll go and see what's happening. What about Forster?"

"Yes, he's all right," McRae said. "At least, I think he is. I called out to him and I heard him answer."

"Why didn't he come earlier when I was calling?" I asked.

"Perhaps he fell asleep," McRae offered. "That, or he didn't hear you because of the noise of the wind."

With Woolley out of the room, McRae began to tell us his hypothesis. It was obvious who was behind all of this, he said. There was only one name under suspicion: that of Mrs. Woolley. Had Katharine drugged Davison at some point that evening? Could she have persuaded him to open the door and then slipped something into his tea? Or had she simply hit him over the head?

"She would stop at nothing, of that I'm certain," he said. "With Davison unconscious, all she needed to do was walk across the courtyard. Nobody would have seen or heard her with the sandstorm raging. Then she stole into Miss Jones's room while she was sleeping. She simply replaced Cynthia's glass of water with one containing the acid and then slipped back to her own room."

"I don't understand," said Cynthia. "What about the door? I locked it before I went to bed and it was still locked when you broke in."

"Perhaps she has a spare key," said McRae, "which she used to open the door and then lock it again from the outside."

"But why? Why would she want to do this to me?" asked the terrified woman.

"Maybe you saw something," McRae suggested. "Or perhaps you overheard a snatch of conversation that incriminated Mrs. Woolley in some way—something that connected her to the murder of Miss Archer."

"I don't know," she said, and started to cry once more. "I'm so terribly confused."

"Think!" insisted McRae. "You must have seen something. Even if it seems inconsequential, trivial."

"I don't know . . . I . . ."

"Look, Woolley will be back soon and you may not get another chance," said McRae. "You know what he's like."

"But surely not Mrs. Woolley? We've always been friends. She would never do anything to hurt me!" Cynthia insisted.

"You may like to think that, but she's obviously lost her reason," said McRae. "What other explanation could there be? I'm certain that Cecil would never have hurt Sarah Archer. And if he didn't do it, then who did? The answer is obvious, isn't it?"

"But what about the boy's confession?" asked Conway.

"Just a smoke screen," said McCrae in a dismissive manner. "That, or as I've said before, it was forced out of him by that fool Forster. No, as far as I see it, the killer has to be—"

"You were saying, McRae?" said Woolley, stepping into the room. "Who is the killer?"

McRae did not even hesitate. Instead, he walked towards Woolley and faced him head on.

"Your wife!" shouted McRae. "That's who!"

"We've been through all this before," said Woolley. "The accusation is ridiculous."

"Can't you see what is right before your nose?" McRae exclaimed. "She herself said as much earlier. She told Miss Jones that she would try to kill her, and lo and behold, what happens?" He turned to each of us in turn, pausing for extra effect almost as if he were an actor on a stage. "The poor woman wakes up with a glass of hydrochloric acid by her bed!"

"I'm sure there is some explanation for this," said Woolley. "Let's see . . . Perhaps, Miss Jones, you, you picked up the acid by mistake from one of the workrooms where the cleaning of the cuneiform tablets was taking place."

Cynthia look bewildered. "No, I don't think so," she said.

"Or you . . . perhaps you experienced an episode of sleepwalking," Woolley posited. "I've heard it's more common than people think."

"Really?" replied McRae. "Is that the best you can do? It's pathetic."

"I will not have you speak to me like that," said Woolley, reddening in the face. "Do you hear me?"

"What are you going to do about it?" McRae took another step closer to him. "What?" he shouted, his spittle spraying the older man's face. "Are you going to get your wife to try to kill me, too?"

On hearing that, Woolley clenched his fist and readied himself to strike. I could bear it no longer. "If fight you must, can you please take yourselves elsewhere?" I said.

The sharp remark brought both men to their senses. "Of course," mumbled Woolley. McRae did not respond but turned away from the group in anger and no doubt embarrassment as well.

"How was Katharine?" I asked.

"She was sleeping," said Woolley. "Looks like she's been in bed for hours. But it's true, her door was unlocked."

My second question was about Davison.

"Yes, out like a light," he said. "Slumped in the chair outside her room. Mighty queer business. I can't make head or tail of it." Bafflement was written across his face. "I think it's best if I talk to Forster and tell him . . . well, tell him about Davison and also what's gone on here."

"And what about your wife?" asked McRae. "You can't just leave the room unguarded." Although his tone was more polite now, it was obvious that the architect still had his misgivings about Mrs. Woolley. "If nobody else is prepared to go and sit outside her room, I will do it myself." He walked to the door and, just before he left the room, turned back to face us to say, "I don't know about all of you, but I have no wish to be murdered in my bed."

29

Just as the storm began to ease outside, the pressure inside the house intensified.

Before he was due to take his place outside Katharine's door, McRae raised Mr. and Mrs. Archer from their beds and informed them that there had been an attempt on Cynthia Jones's life. Someone had swapped the secretary's customary nighttime beaker of water for a glass of hydrochloric acid. Miss Jones was now in her room, where she was recovering from a minor burn to her leg and the shock of the experience. He also told them that Davison, the man in charge of guarding Mrs. Woolley, had been rendered unconscious and had been carried back to his room. He pointed the finger of suspicion at the woman they had originally blamed for the death of their daughter: none other than the clearly deranged Katharine Woolley.

In the meantime, Woolley had given the facts of that night's events to Forster. Although he tried to remain impartial and pronounced that it was important to wait for the appropriate evidence to come to light, it seemed that Forster too suspected Katharine Woolley. McRae appealed to the captain to let him see his nephew, but the policeman was adamant. Nothing would be decided that night, he said. Instead, he thought it best if he took both Cecil McRae and Katharine Woolley back to Baghdad the next day for questioning.

The storm should clear by first light and they would set out, together with the Archers and their daughter's body, in the morning. He guaranteed that he would get to the bottom of it all. He asked everyone to keep calm. It would be best, he said, if we all retired to our beds and tried to get a good night's sleep before we met the next day. He suggested we pull together to help clear up after the storm and then meet for breakfast. After that, he would set out for Baghdad, where he was certain that justice would be done.

I had my doubts. Not only was there a very real possibility that the rule of law was in danger of being corrupted, but an innocent person would suffer in the most appalling way possible. If I did nothing I knew what would happen.

It was time for me to act.

I pretended to say good night, but instead of going to bed I slipped into Davison's room.

"Davison, it's me, Agatha," I whispered. "It's safe."

I saw his body stir on the bed and a moment later he sat up.

"What's happening?" he asked.

"Just what we thought would happen," I said. "The Archers and McRae are baying for blood. Katharine Woolley is one step away from being hanged, or whatever barbaric form of punishment they choose to inflict upon her out here."

I walked over to his bedside table and used a match to light a candle. "Did you enjoy your beauty sleep?" I asked in a deliberately mocking tone.

"Pretending to be asleep is actually strangely exhausting," he said, swinging his legs over the edge of the bed. "And I must say, having to be carried around like a sack of potatoes is most undignified."

"Did you hear anything?"

"Nothing of any import," he said. "Just the usual grumblings about Woolley and his wife. Now, what's the next step?"

"We haven't got much time," I said. "What with the storm beginning to ease off, Forster has said that he plans to set off for Baghdad in the morning."

"Do you think anyone suspects?"

"No, I don't think so," I said. "But maybe that's a bad thing."

"What do you mean?"

"We know what's going on, but we still need proof," I said.

Davison looked at me with a concerned expression. "You're not proposing to . . . ?" He hesitated. He knew from past experience how far I would go in the search for truth. "Please, Agatha. You're beginning to worry me."

"It is a risk," I said. "But I cannot for the life of me think of another way."

"What?" he hissed. "Tell me what you've got in mind."

Slowly and as calmly as I could, I outlined my plan to catch the killer.

30

During the night, as the screaming of the storm lessened to a howl and then a mere whisper, we finalized the scheme. Just before dawn I crept out of Davison's room and retreated back to my own to wait for first light, when everything would be exposed.

At dawn I made myself a cup of tea and stepped outside. The early morning sun caressed the desert with a delicate beauty that nearly brought tears to my eyes. I watched the ever-shifting sands turn from purple to violet and rose to yellow ocher, and finally towards something that approached a delicate shade of apricot. I breathed in the clean air and steeled myself for what was to come.

I listened as the house came to life and Woolley began to direct a superficial cleanup after the storm.

"I should think the servants, together with the rest of the workmen, will return from the village in a couple of hours," he said. "Hamoudi will tell them when he thinks it's safe to make the trek across the desert. After one of these storms, one always has to be mindful of sand rivers and sinking sands. It can be quite perilous for those who don't know how to navigate the territory."

Conway began to sweep up great piles of sand that had amassed in the corners of the courtyard. After making sure that Katharine could not escape, McRae left his position outside her room to climb onto the roof to fix some tiles that had come loose. Father Burrows had been given the job of preparing a substantial breakfast for all of us, and from inside the compound came the delicious smell of baking bread and the cooking of fatty meat.

By seven o'clock everyone had started to drift into the main room for breakfast. When Davison appeared, he was questioned about the events of the night before. What could he remember? Had someone bashed him over the head? Had he ingested something—perhaps a tincture or tea laced with some drug—that had made him feel drowsy?

In response to the inquiries he said, "I'm sorry, but I cannot for the life of me remember anything about it. I woke up this morning feeling a little groggy."

"Perhaps you had too much sun," said Father Burrows as he placed a pot of coffee on the table. "I did notice that you went out without your hat at one point yesterday."

"Yes, that could well have been it," Davison agreed.

It was then that Hamoudi knocked on the door. He said a string of sentences in Arabic which I think were related to the storm and then took out a letter and gave it to Davison. Apparently it had been sent express from London but had been delayed due to the weather. My friend did not open the message but made his excuses and said he was still feeling a little out of sorts. He retreated to his room, where I joined him a few minutes later. Both of us were a trifle nervous about reading the contents of the letter. We had been waiting for some information to come from London. Would the missive prove our theory or reveal that we were completely off the mark?

"Why don't you open it?" asked Davison.

"No, it's addressed to you. It could be anything—something personal."

"I doubt it . . . Here," he said, passing the letter to me. "It looks like it's from the department."

I carefully opened the envelope and took out some documents, together with a photograph. My heart did not flutter so much as almost stop when I saw what lay before me. Here was the link to the past that had been eluding me.

* * *

On my way back to the sitting room I encountered Captain Forster in the courtyard and asked him whether it was possible to have a quiet word with him.

"I wonder if you'd mind bringing in Mr. and Mrs. Archer, Mrs. Woolley, and the young McRae," I asked.

"I'm not sure about the Archers—they may have chosen not to come to breakfast after everything that's happened—but as far as the other two are concerned, they are still held under lock and key," he replied.

"Yes, I understand, but it is terribly important that everyone is here," I said.

"As soon as Hamoudi tells me that the men have cleared a path to the station, I plan to take Mrs. Woolley straight from her room under guard," he said. "Of course, it's going to be difficult for the Archers, traveling with their daughter's body in the same vehicle as her suspected murderer, but I can't see any other way. Anyway, just time for a spot of breakfast before we set out."

As he turned away from me to go back inside, I placed a hand lightly on his arm. "Captain Forster, I have to tell you that Katharine Woolley is not responsible for the murder of Miss Archer," I said.

"But surely, what with the incident with Davison, who must have been drugged while guarding Mrs. Woolley's room . . . ," he said. "I can't see any other explanation: the culprit has to be Mrs. Woolley herself."

I gave a little understated cough. "If you'd be so kind as to go and gather everyone and bring them into the sitting room, I will furnish you with all the details," I said, almost as if I were about to run through a complicated travel itinerary or a particularly tricky recipe for a fruit cake.

"I'm really not sure that—"

Davison, who had silently stepped out into the courtyard, cut him off. "Forster, please do as Mrs. Christie says. She's the one who has been working on the case since she first arrived here at Ur. She is about to explain everything."

Forster looked at me as if seeing an example of some exotic species for the first time, then flushed, no doubt embarrassed at the public wounding of his male pride. "Of c-course, yes," he said, stumbling over his words. "W-whatever you say, Davison."

The captain left us alone. Davison's eyes were full of concern for me. I smiled gently at him, a smile that spoke of the depths of our friendship.

"You are quite certain of this," said Davison softly, "of what you intend to do?"

"Yes, quite certain," I said. "In fact, it's the only course of action."

"But what about the documents—the photograph?"

"It's something, but not enough. We need more."

Davison looked at me in a new way, almost as if he were a visitor to a museum and I were one of the ancient marble sculptures on display. "Why are you looking at me like that?" I said lightly.

"I'm just wondering how you became so brave, so fearless," he said.

The comment made me laugh. "I'm neither brave nor fearless, but good at pretending to be so," I said. "And you're forgetting my books."

"Your books? What have they got to do with anything?"

They were not works of great literature; I knew that. But they had fast-moving plots that people could lose themselves in, and characters who showed a great deal of pluck and courage. These were men and women who fought for truth and justice. Some of them were detective figures, of course, but others were ordinary enough individuals who found themselves in quite extraordinary circumstances. I saw myself in the same light. Although in the grand scheme of things I was nobody very special, I recognized that I did have a talent for rooting out evil.

"Everything," I said. "Now, what do you say to a spot of breakfast?"

31

We need some more chairs," Davison said as we walked into the sitting room. "And some extra places, too."

"What for?" asked a rather harassed-looking Father Burrows as he busied between kitchen and table.

"Mr. and Mrs. Archer are joining us for breakfast," Davison replied. "As well as Mrs. Woolley and Cecil McRae."

The mention of the two names sent a ripple of anticipation that stilled the low murmur of voices.

"But I thought that—"

Father Burrows was interrupted by Captain Forster, who appeared at the door like someone stepping onstage right on cue.

"Mr. and Mrs. Archer, please take your seats at the breakfast table," said the policeman. "I'll go and fetch . . . well, the rest of the party."

The Americans looked wretched, pale, and worn-out. Mr. Archer had tried to shave, but a series of nicks and cuts around his jawline suggested that the experience had been an unpleasant one. Mrs. Archer had pouches under her eyes and it appeared as though she had dressed in haste, as her blouse was creased and a little dirty around the cuffs. Neither of them seemed to understand what was about to happen or that they were going to be joined at the table by the woman they blamed for the death of their daughter.

"Did you manage to get much sleep?" asked Woolley as the couple took their seats.

The archaeologist did not receive an answer, and perhaps it was this that made him feel he should continue to talk over the awkward silence. "At least the storm is over now," he said. "Terribly inconvenient, I suppose, but 'theirs not to reason why.' "

I whispered the rest of the Tennyson couplet to myself, " 'Theirs but to do and die.' "

Understandably, everyone looked miserable and downcast, and Woolley realized at once he should have chosen a different line. "Beautiful sky, though," he said as he tried to ameliorate the situation. "I don't know if anyone saw the dawn. Quite extraordinary colors cast over the desert: such a very pure quality of light."

The comment drew a few murmurs of assent as people began to take their places at the table. Cynthia Jones chose a seat by Mr. and Mrs. Archer. I sat down opposite them, between Davison and Conway. Leonard Woolley waited for the arrival of his wife, and Lawrence McRae stood by the door, ready to welcome his nephew. Father Burrows continued to place plates and dishes on the table. People started to make small talk about storms, the sands, the possibility of other ancient sites lying buried under the surface of the desert. Yet, apart from Mr. and Mrs. Archer, who still seemed to be trapped in some kind of daze, everyone's real attention was directed towards the door as we awaited the arrival of the two people who had been accused of murdering of Miss Archer. The air of expectation may have been invisible to the eye, but it was certainly palpable in that room.

As the minutes passed and the conversation ebbed and stalled, I wondered what could be keeping Forster. All he had to do was unlock the doors and accompany Mrs. Woolley and Cecil McRae from their makeshift prisons to the sitting room. I hoped the boy had not done anything stupid. We had tried to tell him that his imprisonment was just a temporary measure and that he was being kept in the room for his own safety—that he was in no way a suspect in the investigation into the death of Sarah Archer. But I knew he was in a terribly vulnerable state. His erratic behavior when he had pointed a gun at Mrs. Woolley and me and contemplated killing himself illustrated the unbalanced nature of his mind. I would never forgive myself if he felt he had no choice but to end it all. As I saw an image of him hanging from a length of sheeting, I felt the familiar bird of panic flutter in my chest. *Please, no . . . please, not that.*

Just then I heard the sound of approaching voices. Captain Forster entered the room, followed by Katharine Woolley and Cecil McRae. The two made very different impressions. Katharine was immaculately turned out, dressed in her favorite shade of *vieux rose.* She greeted the room as if she were the star attraction and smiled demurely as Woolley walked forwards and pulled back a chair for her. The boy, meanwhile, was unshaven and unkempt and appeared to have aged a good ten years. He could not meet anyone's eye, and as he walked he stooped as if he feared the ceiling would collapse on him.

The sight of Mrs. Woolley and Cecil McRae wrenched Mr. Archer out of his stupor. "What is the meaning of this?" he demanded of Forster.

The captain did not answer.

"Woolley, do you know what the hell is happening?" asked the American. But he received no answer from the archaeologist.

Mrs. Archer reached out and grabbed the hand of a pale-looking Cynthia Jones. "And to think that woman nearly succeeded in killing you," she said. "After what she did to poor Sarah, I don't know how she's got the cheek to sit at the same table."

"We must all remain calm," said Forster. "There's an important matter that needs to be discussed—something that has come from quite unexpected quarters."

"Don't be a fool," said Archer. "I appreciate the gesture of offering us breakfast before the journey, but if that means sharing a table with the likes of this . . . this *creature*, then you can count me out." He stood up to leave. "It's a long way to Baghdad, and in case you've forgotten, we have to bury our daughter."

"Please sit down, Mr. Archer," said Davison.

"And who are you to tell me what to do?"

Without a moment's hesitation Davison said calmly and with a matter-of-fact tone, "I'm with His Majesty's Government; more than that you need not know. Now I'd like to invite Mrs. Christie here to say a few words."

"Mrs. Christie?" asked a clearly appalled Mrs. Archer. "I don't think we're in any mood for frivolity. As you heard my husband say, we—"

But Davison cut her off. "What Mrs. Christie is about to tell us is far from frivolous," he said. He paused for maximum effect. "In fact, Mrs. Christie was sent by the British government to accompany me to Iraq. And now she is about to reveal the real identity of your daughter's killer."

"But we thought . . . ," said a bewildered-looking Mr. Archer.

"Yes, you thought that Mrs. Woolley here was the killer," I said, standing up. "And in many respects it looked as though she must be the person responsible for the murder. After all, she was there at the scene of the crime. She was discovered kneeling by the body with blood on her hands. She was, people said, jealous of Sarah Archer's youth and her beauty. And the two women had had a disagreement only minutes before Sarah stormed off into the night, soon followed by Mrs. Woolley. But, more importantly, Katharine Woolley's behavior was already—how shall I put it?—somewhat erratic. In effect, she needed little motive to kill Sarah; it was genuinely believed that her madness was enough of an explanation. Of course, she was known to have quite an unusual, dominant personality, but she started to complain of seeing things, hearing voices. Other people in the camp became understandably fearful of Mrs. Woolley and her strange ways. Many of you also believed that she had killed her ginger cat too. But I can tell you that she did not kill that poor animal and neither did she murder Sarah."

I had the attention of everyone now. I took a deep breath and continued. "For a number of months Mrs. Woolley has been subject to a most terrible form of poisoning."

The revelation produced a series of gasps from around the room. I opened my handbag and took out one of the jars of night creams I had taken from Katharine's dressing table and tested.

"Mrs. Woolley was in the habit of using a number of creams, some to moisturize her hands, others which she rubbed into her face last thing at night," I said. "It's a habit common to many of us women. And with this very dry climate out in the desert, it was almost essential. However, in the creams there was one ingredient that was responsible for Mrs. Woolley's strange behavior: hyoscyamine."

"But how do you know?" asked Cynthia Jones.

"I tested them," I said. "You see, during the war I not only trained as a nurse but also worked in the dispensary of my local hospital. I learnt a good deal about poisons, and the knowledge proved very useful indeed—and not just for my books. You see, hyoscyamine produces a range of symptoms, such as headaches, blurred vision, dizziness, disorientation, euphoria, short-term memory loss, and, most importantly, hallucinations. Katharine Woolley experienced many of these symptoms—symptoms which some of you believed were indicative of her mental instability."

Katharine looked like she was too afraid to let herself believe what I was saying; after all, for months she must have thought that she was going insane.

"She may have had this . . . this substance in her beauty creams, but why does it then follow that she is innocent of murder?" asked a clearly skeptical Mr. Archer.

"A very good question, Mr. Archer," I said. "One must learn not to take anything at face value. Let me explain." I took another deep breath. "As you now know, I did not come to Ur as a mere tourist. I came to investigate the death of Miss Gertrude Bell."

"Miss Bell?" asked Woolley.

"Yes. I'm sorry for the deception, but I had to keep my real motives hidden. You are all aware that Miss Bell died in Baghdad in July 1926. There was an air of mystery surrounding her death, but the official line was that she died due to a weakness of her system after an episode of pleurisy and then an attack of bronchitis. However, the doctor who examined her body discovered that she had died due to an overdose of Dial, a sedative similar to veronal."

"This is all very interesting, but what's it got to do with the death of my daughter?" asked Mr. Archer.

"Absolutely nothing," I said.

"Nothing?" he replied. "Then why are you telling us all of this?"

"Quite recently two letters which seemed to have been written by Miss Bell came to light which stated that she had been in fear of her life," I said. "She added that if she were to die, then it was likely that her killer would be found at Ur. But—and this is important—there is no connection whatsoever between the deaths of Miss Bell and your daughter. The truth of the matter is simple: one was a case of suicide or an accidental overdose—I suppose we may never know—and the other was a cold and heartless murder."

"Then why are you bringing it up here?" asked Mrs. Archer, who had taken a handkerchief out of the sleeve of her blouse and started to wring it between her fingers. She looked first at her husband and then at Cynthia Jones. "I don't understand."

"The killer thought they were being very clever, you see," I continued. "They laid the foundations of the case thoroughly, skewing one's perception of it from the very beginning. You see, someone took advantage of Miss Bell's death. They wanted it to be seen as a murder, when in fact it was nothing of the kind, just a rather wretched end after a life full of achievement."

"But who would want to do that?" asked Father Burrows, who looked hot and exhausted after cooking a breakfast that no one was looking at, never mind eating.

"Indeed, who?" I asked, looking around the table. It always fascinated me how the innocent appeared the most guilty, while those who had committed the worst sins often seemed guileless.

"And what of Cecil?" asked Lawrence McRae. "Surely it's time to clear the boy's name. He was foolish, wrongheaded, but he's suffered enough. Look at the state of him."

Cecil could still not meet my gaze. It was time to tell the truth.

"What Cecil McRae did was unforgivable," I said. The boy flushed red in the face and, as I spoke, began to squirm in his seat. "He threatened Mrs. Woolley and me with a gun and we were in fear of our lives." I paused. "However, he acted in the mistaken belief that Katharine Woolley had killed Miss Archer. In a fit of adolescent passion he took it upon himself to try to enact some kind of revenge. Luckily for us—and for him—he had more sense than to let his hotheaded nature get the better of him."

In fact, I believed it was Cecil's lack of courage that was behind this, but he was in too delicate a frame of mind to hear such an ungarnished interpretation of his behavior. I could see the next question almost forming itself on the lips of my small audience, and so I preempted it. "And now we come to the matter of Cecil's confession."

"Yes, why did the boy confess to a crime he didn't commit?" asked Mrs. Archer.

"That was a necessary deception, I'm afraid," I said. "And I'm sorry, Cecil, that you've been locked up against your will for all this time. But really we had no other choice."

"Locking up a vulnerable lad like a savage beast . . . It's criminal!" exclaimed Lawrence McRae. "If we were so minded, we could bring—"

"Yes, I can see your point, Mr. McRae, but if you'd be so kind and let me explain," I said in a calm and steady voice. "After all, I'm sure Mrs. Woolley here could easily pursue the matter herself if she so chose."

The comment silenced McRae and I continued. "The real killer of Miss Archer wanted to point the finger at Mrs. Woolley. That had been the overarching motive from the very beginning. Everyone had to believe that it was Katharine who had killed Sarah Archer. After all, she had been found literally red-handed next to the girl's body. But what the killer had not expected—what no one could have predicted—was the way that Cecil McRae behaved after hearing the news of Sarah's death." I addressed the boy directly. "You truly loved that girl, didn't you?"

As Cecil nodded, a tear slipped down his cheek. He did not need to say any more.

"The killer panicked when Cecil threatened to shoot Mrs. Woolley," I explained. "You see, the person behind all of this did not want Mrs. Woolley to die. They wanted Katharine to suffer much more than that."

"Suffer more than death itself?" said Woolley, looking at his wife with tears in his eyes.

For her part, Katharine listened to my account with a certain regal dignity, almost as if she occupied a different, higher plane. Although she had suffered, she would not let the group know quite how much she had endured. It was a trait that one had to admire.

"And so you see, after explaining the complex situation to Captain Forster, we fashioned a confession from Cecil in which he took responsibility for the crime," I said. "It seemed as though the motive was a clear one. He said he had been driven to kill Sarah Archer out of misdirected love. They had quarreled that night on the ziggurat.

He had reached out to touch her, but there was an unpleasant scuffle and Miss Archer fell back and hit her head. Seeing what he had done, Cecil decided he had to kill her and then went on to frame Mrs. Woolley for the crime. This of course was absolute fiction. He played no part in Miss Archer's death. But Cecil's false confession was essential to drawing out the killer. I suspected that the person behind all of this would make a mistake. And Cecil's confession to the murder of Miss Archer forced the killer to make their first error."

As I approached the final moment of revelation—a moment when anything could happen—I was conscious that my heart was beating faster than normal. My mouth felt dry, and even though I took a sip of water—water I had brought with me from the safety of the kitchen—the liquid did nothing to ease my discomfort. All eyes were on me.

"What was the error?" asked Forster.

"The killer acted in such a way that they revealed their true identity," I said as I tried to clear my throat.

"So who is it?" demanded Mr. Archer, looking around the table. "If it's not Mrs. Woolley and it wasn't the boy McRae, which one of us is the murderer? I demand to know who killed my daughter!"

32

"I don't think I can stand this much longer," said Cynthia Jones, standing up from the table. "I think we could all do with a fresh pot of tea, don't you?"

The spinsterish woman shuffled off into the kitchen. "Yes, a very good idea, Miss Jones," I said as I continued to look around the table at the increasingly uncomfortable faces before me. "To begin with, it seemed we had our man. I discovered someone at Ur who was not who he said he was. Mr. Miller—or should I say Mr. Conway—could you please stand up?"

"Is this really necessary?" said Conway.

"Please do what Mrs. Christie asks," insisted Davison.

The photographer pushed himself out of his chair and nervously rubbed his mustache with the fingers of his right hand.

"Miller?" asked an astounded Woolley. "What is this? What does Mrs. Christie mean?"

Conway took a deep breath and on the exhalation began to make his confession. "It's true," he said. "I'm not who I said I was." I nodded to signal that he should explain a little more. "My name's not Harry Miller. I'm . . . I'm Alan Conway."

"And tell everyone about your job," said Davison. "Your real purpose at Ur, I mean."

Conway gave me a look that pleaded with me to intervene. I had once had feelings for him, but I knew that it would be wrong to let my emotions stand in the way of justice.

"I think you owe Mr. Woolley an explanation, don't you?" I said, perhaps more harshly than I intended.

"I'm . . . I'm here because I've been copying some of the treasures," he said in a quiet voice.

"You've been doing *what*?" cried Woolley.

Conway described how he had been using his cover as a photographer to make electrotype copies of valuable objects so he could then ship the real artifacts back to America. As he listened to Conway's account, Woolley's face drained of color. Quite understandably, he wanted to know the specifics, but while Conway was in the middle of detailing how he had made the copies and outlined who was behind the plan, Mr. Archer lost patience and interrupted him.

"I don't care two hoots for you and your trinkets!" he shouted. "I still want to know about my daughter. Who murdered my Sarah?"

"Yes, of course," I said. "I was just coming to that. As I said, I did have my suspicions about Mr. Conway here, purely because of the evidence that showed he was operating under a false identity. But then something happened which proved beyond a doubt that—"

"Now who would like some tea?" asked Miss Jones as she returned to the table with a tray.

"Can't you be quiet, woman!" shouted Mr. Archer.

Miss Jones looked shocked and upset. "I'm sorry, but I just thought we could all do with—"

"Mrs. Christie was about to tell us the name of the man who murdered my daughter," he said.

I took another deep breath. The time had come for the final revelation. "It was not a man," I said.

There was a collective gasp and more than a few cries and exclamations, some of them quite earthy. Katharine Woolley placed a gloved hand over her mouth. Mrs. Archer looked as if she was going to be sick. Father Burrows seemed so shocked, he did not know what to do with himself. And Woolley was struck down by a strange paralysis, like one of those poor men at Pompeii whose bodies had been covered in volcanic ash all those hundreds of years ago.

"Yes, I'm sorry to say that the person behind all of this is a member of the so-called fairer sex," I said. "I may as well name her as she is standing before us. Have you anything to say for yourself . . . Miss Jones?"

Cynthia looked at me with a mix of innocence, amusement, and astonishment. "I really don't know what you're talking about."

"Come, now, you know very well that there's no point in pretending any longer," I said. "Yes, you've been very clever, particularly at the beginning of your plan, because you knew that Mrs. Woolley already suffered from terrible headaches. You believed that people would think that Mrs. Woolley's other symptoms—which we'll come to shortly—would simply be an extension of her illness. But you've also been so very wicked. How could you kill that poor cat? You knew that Mrs. Woolley adored that creature. What did you do? Did you give it a special little something in its food? And I suppose you must have drugged Katharine at that time. She would have had to be sedated, because you took something sharp to her arms to make it look as though the cat had scratched her. Is that what happened?"

"This is completely absurd," she said. She looked around the table at her friends for signs of support. "You must be out of your mind."

"And, of course, you were the one who was responsible for spiking Katharine's creams with the hyoscyamine, weren't you?"

"The hyo . . . the what?"

"You know very well what I'm talking about. But I'll explain more in a moment."

"I think you've been reading too many of those silly detective stories—that, or writing one," she said, pretending to laugh.

"I think this particular tale—and your involvement in it—is beyond anything even I could have dreamt up," I said. "Let's start at the very beginning, Miss Jones"—I could no longer bring myself to call her by her Christian name—"with the letters that Miss Bell wrote to her father: unsent letters which described how she feared for her life; documents in which she said that if she were to be killed, the authorities should look to Ur for her murderer."

"But what's that got to do with the murder of Sarah?" asked Mrs. Archer.

"Forgive me, but to understand Sarah's death, we need to take a step back in time," I said. "It was perfectly natural that when those letters came to light, the first line of inquiry would be to follow up Miss Bell's suspicions. And so that's why I was sent here: to investigate the matter."

I paused for a moment as I cleared my throat. "I always thought that there was something odd about those two letters and the accompanying drawing of the Great Death Pit at Ur, with Miss Bell's initials placed next to one of the stick figures. It was strange that they were never sent, that they were just waiting around for someone to find them, almost as if someone had placed them in that seed box, where the gardener would at some point come across them. And, despite the detailed nature of the letters, my first reaction was that they were forgeries. Yet apparently an expert had compared the handwriting of the letters to Miss Bell's own hand and declared them to be one and the same. But then one night, during what seemed like a perfectly innocent conversation, I heard a comment that caused me to think. Do you recall what it was?"

Miss Jones did not answer.

"I thought not. Do you remember, Father Burrows?"

The priest looked bemused. "No, I'm afraid I don't," he replied.

"Let me refresh your memories," I said. "It was a conversation of all things about learning the cuneiform script. Father Burrows, you very kindly offered to teach me how to write it, and in an aside you said . . . yes, this was it: 'When I first met Miss Jones, she was a complete novice like you, and yet she picked it up very quickly.' You added, 'Quite the natural, weren't you, Miss Jones?' That got me wondering. If you could master a script like cuneiform with such ease, perhaps you were a natural at copying the handwriting of others. Not only that, you were a close companion of Miss Bell's and you would have been privy to certain pieces of information that she would have shared only with a very good friend. But I kept these thoughts in the back of my mind. You see, at that point it was still very early days. Everyone, I suppose, was a suspect."

"Everyone knows I was a friend of Gertrude's, and, yes, I did pick up cuneiform easily—but so?" asked Cynthia, looking at Mrs. Archer for support. "That means nothing."

"And, Mrs. Christie, aren't you forgetting that poor Cynthia here was herself the victim of the killer?" asked Mrs. Archer. "She could have died by drinking that acid."

"Thank you, Mrs. Archer," said Cynthia. "At least somebody has some thought for my feelings. Now, why don't we all have a cup of tea?"

I watched as, with a steady hand, she lifted a large teapot and began to pour. There were, I noticed, eleven cups in total. But there were twelve of us in the room. Cynthia walked around the table, placing the cups before everyone apart from Katharine Woolley. I knew, when challenged and presented with the evidence, that Cynthia would plan something—and I had deliberately allowed her to go into the kitchen when she said she was going to make tea—but I could never have imagined that she would dream up such a wicked scenario.

As people lifted the cups to their lips I said, "Don't touch the tea.

Please, whatever you do, don't drink it. It's poisoned." The group froze as if trapped in a grotesque tableau.

It was in that moment that I saw Miss Jones show her true colors. She turned from the shy, retiring spinster—the kind of woman who would not say boo to a goose—into something else, something purely evil.

"Look at the cups," I said. "Look at where she's placed them. Each of you has one—including Miss Jones herself—everyone, that is, but Mrs. Woolley."

"So?" said Cynthia, a darkness burning in her eyes.

"It's the death pit, isn't it?" I said, remembering the eerie place of human sacrifice that Woolley had shown me soon after I first arrived at Ur. "You were going to poison everyone—including yourself—and leave Mrs. Woolley alive. When the authorities came they would find everyone dead apart from Katharine. No matter how hard Mrs. Woolley tried to explain what had happened here, her account would be taken as nothing more than the crazed rantings of a madwoman. Katharine Woolley would be surrounded by eleven bodies—all victims of poisoning—and she would be the only survivor. Of course she would have to be the killer. No other explanation would make sense."

"But why would Miss Jones want to kill herself, together with the rest of us, but leave Katharine alive?" asked Woolley, pushing his teacup away from him.

The hatred that had festered for so long in Miss Jones's breast began to show itself now. "Just look at her, sitting there as if she were better than the rest of us, like some kind of queen." Cynthia seemed to spit the words as she looked at Katharine. "If only you knew the truth about her."

At this, Katharine started as if woken from a dream.

"Yes, that got your attention, didn't it, Mrs. Woolley?" continued Miss Jones. "Or should I say Mrs. Keeling?"

The mention of Katharine's first married name brought an expression of horror to her eyes.

"Why don't we talk a little of Mr. Keeling and your love for him—or should I say your lack of love?" said Cynthia in a horrible, mocking voice.

"Oh, please no," begged Katharine. "Please not that."

"Is there something you'd like to keep secret?" Cynthia continued in her nasty tone. "People have always wondered why your husband killed himself after only six months of marriage. He shot himself, didn't he? At the foot of the Great Pyramid of Cheops. All very dramatic."

"Cynthia, please, I'll do anything—anything you ask," said Katharine, who had started to sob now.

"Stop this immediately!" shouted Woolley. "I will not have you upsetting my wife!"

"Your wife?" replied Cynthia. "Are you sure about that?"

It was then that Katharine reached for her husband's cup and, so slowly as if to make the action almost indiscernible, began to lift it towards her. She brought it closer to her lips, and just as she was poised to take a sip, I said, "The tea! Don't let her drink it."

Woolley was quick to respond and dashed the cup from her hands, spilling the dark liquid across the table.

"I can't bear it," cried Katharine. "Oh, why didn't you let me end it all? I wish I were dead!"

"It's an interesting point," I said, trying to sound as detached and unemotional as possible. Although I wanted to go and console Katharine, who was sobbing now, I had to steel myself to remain strong. "Miss Jones could have killed Mrs. Woolley at any time. After all, she had many opportunities. She was being poisoned over time with the small doses of hyoscyamine in her cosmetic creams, and it would not have been hard to give her a fatal dose. Indeed, she could have been the one to die that night out on the ziggurat instead of your daughter," I said, addressing Mr. and Mrs. Archer.

"And by the sounds of it she could have died drinking this damned tea," said Forster, who went to stand guard by Miss Jones. He cast a look of warning in her direction. "Let's clear this lot up. Burrows, would you be so kind as to take the tea things away? Don't throw anything away, though: we'll need to test it for poison."

Slightly taken aback at being treated like a common servant, Burrows placed the cups, saucers, and teapot back on the tray and then carried them back into the kitchen. I waited for Father Burrows to return before I continued.

"As I was saying, Miss Jones took advantage of what she thought were the perfect circumstances in which to commit the crime. It was nighttime. The situation was chaotic. Her two victims—because there were two victims here, not just one—came together like two planets in an unholy alignment. There had been an argument between the two women, and it was clear that Mrs. Woolley did not care for Sarah Archer. Miss Jones saw Sarah rushing down the steps and then realized that, if she were to smash that rock over her head, the girl would collapse and be discovered by Mrs. Woolley. Yet even she could not have envisaged the scene that followed, with Katharine falling down by the girl's body, besmirching her hands in Sarah's freshly spilt blood."

Mrs. Archer looked at Cynthia Jones as if seeing her for the first time. No doubt she was forced to reassess the moments of friendliness and quiet intimacy that had passed between them. It had all been a sham, a performance. This quiet mouse of a woman was her daughter's killer. In addition, this unassuming spinster had prepared a pot of tea that had the capacity to kill everyone in the room, including Mrs. Archer herself. As she came to this realization hatred, emanated from her eyes.

"Miss Jones wanted to exact a revenge that went beyond murder," I continued. "At the moment I merely want to set out the facts of the case; we'll come to the motive in a little while. When Katharine Woolley was discovered next to the body of Sarah Archer, it seemed as though she must be the killer. After all, everyone in the camp believed Mrs. Woolley to be unbalanced, if not insane. And so the stage was set. It looked as though Katharine Woolley would be hauled back to Baghdad, where she would receive a terrible punishment for her crimes and, crucially, her reputation would be ruined.

"But then something happened which skewed Miss Jones's plan. When Cecil 'confessed' to the crime, I knew the real murderer would have to do something desperate. And indeed, Miss Jones was forced into a corner. First of all, there was the scene in Mrs. Woolley's room the night of the sandstorm. Katharine had started to behave oddly. She was convinced that she could smell Sarah Archer's blood on her hands. Then she lashed out at me. I went to find Mr. Woolley, but as I was speaking to him Father Burrows shouted for help. I returned to Mrs. Woolley's room to discover Miss Jones in a highly distressed state. Her wrist and the lower part of her arm were all red, as if someone had twisted her skin, and she told me that Katharine had threatened her with the chilling words 'Watch out: tonight you're going to die. Tonight . . . I'm going to kill you.'

"The evidence seemed to suggest that Miss Jones was the victim. After all, Katharine Woolley was behaving very oddly. It looked as though she had attacked poor Miss Jones and had gone so far as to say that she was going to murder her. Then, later that night, we heard screaming coming from Miss Jones's room, and after breaking down her door we discovered that someone had swapped her nighttime water for a glass of hydrochloric acid. The conclusion was simple: Mrs. Woolley had indeed tried to follow through on her threat to kill Miss Jones.

"And yet . . . were there any other witnesses to the conversation between Miss Jones and Katharine Woolley? No, there were not. The account came entirely from Miss Jones herself. In addition, just before the episode when Mrs. Woolley started to behave oddly, she had been massaging cream into her hands—one of the creams which I now know had been tampered with. I noticed that her pupils were dilated and she said she was desperately thirsty—both symptoms of hyoscyamine poisoning."

Woolley could not take in the enormity of what I saying. He had been betrayed by the man he knew as Miller already and that had hit him hard. I could see the desperate look in his eyes: *Please let this not be true . . . Please let the murderer be anyone but dear old trusted Cynthia.*

But it was Lawrence McRae who spoke up first. His suspicions of Katharine Woolley had not dissipated. "What of the marks on Miss Jones's skin?" he asked. "And the acid burns on her legs?"

"I'm afraid to say they were self-inflicted," I said. "Recognizing that Mrs. Woolley was suffering from hallucinations brought on by the hyoscyamine in her creams, Miss Jones could do and say almost anything in front of her without impunity. My guess is that, while in Mrs. Woolley's room, she repeatedly twisted and pinched the skin on her own wrist and arm until it became red and raw."

"But what about the business with Davison here?" said McRae. "He was sitting outside Katharine's room. She must have drugged him so she could escape from her room and place the glass of hydrochloric acid by Miss Jones's bed."

Davison stood up from the table; it was time for him to speak. "I must admit to a little deception on my part, too," he said. "You see, before I went to take my position outside Mrs. Woolley's room, I was given a cup of tea by Miss Jones. I took the drink with me, but in the courtyard I poured the tea on the ground, as I knew it was likely to contain some substance that would make me go to sleep. And so, later that night, when Miss Jones came to check on me, I was actually wide-awake."

He turned and looked directly at Miss Jones. He related what he had then witnessed. "Although I appeared to be dead to the world, I did indeed see you turn the key in the lock and open the door into Mrs. Woolley's room before you then made your way back to your own quarters. I stayed there, outside Mrs. Woolley's room, all night and I can tell you that the lady never stepped outside."

"So you see, Miss Jones, we have incontrovertible proof of your terrible crimes," I said. "There is no escape. Do you have anything to say for yourself?"

Just at that moment, as Captain Forster reached out to arrest her, Miss Jones started to cry like a little girl. Tears streamed down her face and she began to sniff. She searched the sleeves of her blouse for a handkerchief and looked distraught at the prospect of not having one to hand to wipe her eyes and nose.

"Oh, dear," she said. "I appear not to have a . . ."

At that moment Ruth Archer stood up and came towards her, proffering a handkerchief.

"Thank you for—" said Miss Jones, reaching out for the square of white cotton embroidered with forget-me-nots.

But before she could finish her sentence, Mrs. Archer charged at her with the fury of a mother set on avenging a recently murdered daughter. All her pent-up aggression and anger found expression in that moment. With the handkerchief in her right hand, she pushed the fabric hard into Miss Jones's open mouth. A muffled noise came from the secretary, as if she could not breathe. She clawed at her face, her eyes stretched wide in panic, but Mrs. Archer pushed the cotton farther in.

Captain Forster and Davison were quick to act. Forster separated the two women and Davison reached into Miss Jones's mouth and extracted the handkerchief. Miss Jones took in great gulps of breath and fell back into a chair.

The words dripped from Ruth Archer's lips like poison. "You deserve to die for what you did to my daughter!"

Nobody could argue with her. "But w-why?" Ruth was hysterical now, shouting and crying at the same time. "Why did you want to kill Sarah? What had she ever done to you?"

After she had recovered her breath, Miss Jones sat down in a chair and said in a quiet voice, "Do you really want to know?"

"Of course I want to know," replied Ruth Archer. "I still don't understand . . . What was it all for?"

"It was a shame Sarah had to die, because I actually quite liked her—mainly because she stood up to that stuck-up bitch over there." Miss Jones glared at Mrs. Woolley. "But her death was convenient."

Mrs. Archer was appalled by the secretary's choice of word. "*Convenient*?"

"Yes, convenient," continued Miss Jones. "She was in the right place at the right time, that's all."

"So you're admitting to the murder?" asked Captain Forster. "That you killed Sarah Archer?"

"Yes, I suppose I am," said Miss Jones.

"But why?" pleaded Mrs. Archer. "Please tell me why."

" 'In a land of sand and ruin and gold,' " said Miss Jones. " 'There shone one woman, and none but she . . .' "

That was obviously a reference to the regal Katharine Woolley. But was it not also a line from a poem. Who was it by?

" '. . . I wish we were dead together to-day,' " she continued, " 'Lost sight of, hidden away out of sight . . .' "

"What's she talking about?" asked Mr. Archer. "Has she lost her mind?"

Even in the grip of insanity, there was a part of her that was able to tap into the poetry she had once learnt. I recognized the lines from Swinburne's "The Triumph of Time."

" '. . . Forgotten of all men altogether,' " she whispered, " 'As the world's first dead, taken wholly away, / Made one with death, filled full of the night.' "

She gazed at some imaginary point in the distance, and in that moment she seemed to glow with a kind of inner happiness. I knew then what she planned to do.

"Captain Forster!" I shouted. "Davison! Watch her! . . ."

But Miss Jones was too quick. She took out a small vial from her pocket and pressed it to her lips. As I ran towards her I smelt the slight aroma of bitter almonds. I knew my poisons. It was cyanide. The chemical started to do its sinister work quickly. She tried to quote another line from the poem, but as the life force ebbed away from her, she could only whisper a few words. And so, as I stood over her body and watched her die, I completed another, more fitting couplet from the same poem which could serve as her epitaph.

" 'At the door of life, by the gate of breath,' " I said, " 'There are worse things waiting for men than death . . .' "

33

Cynthia Jones's body had been taken away from the sitting room and both murderer and her victim, poor Sarah Archer, were hauled onto the same carriage that would soon take them back to Baghdad for burial. Alan Conway—the man who had pretended to be the photographer Harry Miller—was handcuffed and led away by Hamoudi. Davison and I would put in a good word for him—the American had helped us with part of our plan—and I hoped he would serve his sentence in his home country.

I had a quiet word with Cecil McRae, and during a tearful confession he apologized again and told me how his parents had died. His father, in a fit of rage and jealousy, had shot his mother and then turned the gun on himself. The boy, who adored his father, had not wanted to reveal the sordid truth of the crime and had chosen to remain silent, leading to suspicion that he had been involved. I told him that I understood and how noble I thought he had been.

Samples from the teapot would be taken and sent off to an expert in the capital for further testing, but Forster, Davison, and I had all smelt the noxious brew that Miss Jones had prepared and we were certain that it too carried the distinctive whiff of cyanide.

Cynthia Jones's suicide left many questions unanswered, of course, and I had to fend them off like flies around a decaying corpse.

The main one was the issue of motivation: Just why did Miss Jones want to frame Katharine Woolley? The line from the Swinburne poem echoed through my mind again: "In a land of sand and ruin and gold . . ." In this case the "ruin" did not refer to the traces of ancient structures and temples found among the desert sands but the destruction of a reputation. That was at the root of the case.

What was left of our little group remained in the sitting room, and the time had come for me to finish the story.

"In order to see the whole picture, we have to take a step back in time once more," I said. "Before Katharine married Mr. Woolley here, she was married to a Lieutenant Colonel Bertram Keeling." I opened my handbag and took out a cutting from the *Times* newspaper. "This is a brief report about his death, which doesn't give us very much detail about the manner in which he died, but we know that the unfortunate man did indeed commit suicide at the foot of the Great Pyramid in Giza, just outside Cairo, in September 1919."

At this Mrs. Woolley began to show signs of agitation. "Do you really have to go into all of this?" she asked. "Is it really necessary?"

"Yes, my dear, I'm afraid it is," I said. "Before his marriage to Katharine, Colonel Keeling had had a sweetheart, someone he had met while studying at Cambridge. That woman was a Miss Edgecombe, the daughter of one of his professors there."

I could see Mr. Archer looking at me with impatience; no doubt he thought what I was saying was nothing more than a needless digression. "Please bear with me, because this is the key to the whole mystery," I said as I opened up my handbag once more. "Please pass this photograph around. It's a picture of Colonel Keeling and Miss Edgecombe, taken in a punt on the river Cam."

Woolley squinted at the picture. "I'll be damned . . . sorry," he said. "It's—"

"Yes, that's right, it's Cynthia Jones, in younger and no doubt happier days," I said.

"I can barely recognize her," said Katharine, taking hold of the snapshot. "She looks—I don't know—so different. She was quite pretty, really. Nothing like . . . well, you know what I mean."

"Grief and hatred and bitterness can eat up a person, masking whatever beauty they once possessed," I said. "But I also think Miss Jones went some way to disguise herself. I often wondered why she made herself so plain, taking little pride in her features. Then, Mr. Woolley, do you remember that story you told about your name? How you were a wolf in sheep's clothing? The phrase started me thinking: What if someone was pretending to be meek and mild, but in reality they were vicious and cruel?"

"I knew Bertie had a girl before me, but he didn't talk about her, and I certainly never saw a photograph of her until today," said Katharine. "Where did you find this?"

"My colleague Mr. Davison here did a bit of digging for me," I said. "It really was a matter of trial and elimination. I had an inkling that the past was significant in this case. But it was like a shadow always out of view. Each time I tried to get a fix on it, it seemed to slip away. At one stage, Mrs. Woolley even thought that her first husband might be still alive and that he might have disguised himself. I quickly established this was highly unlikely. When I suspected that someone was trying to make it appear as though Mrs. Woolley was mad—and then frame her for the murder of Sarah Archer—I thought about possible motivations. Of course, one's immediate suspicions always turn to the husband."

"Me?" said an astonished Woolley. "You really didn't think I would do anything to hurt my wife, did you?"

I thought it best that the conversation I had had with Woolley—about the lack of intimacy between the couple and his thoughts on divorce—remain private. I also decided not to reveal that I had made inquiries into the beneficiaries of the wills of Sarah Archer and Cecil McRae's parents. "Please forgive me. It's just that husbands—or wives, for that matter—are so often to blame for this sort of thing," I said. "But once I had ruled that out, I had to think of other possibilities. I asked Mr. Davison whether he could use his contacts back in London to do a thorough check of Colonel Keeling's background. It was the very helpful men back in England who discovered that the colonel had had a sweetheart. Although by then I had a clear idea of the identity of the murderer, the photograph, which only arrived this morning, confirmed my suspicions."

"So it was all because Miss Jones was . . . what? Jealous of Mrs. Woolley?" Lawrence McRae sounded unconvinced. "Because Katharine had stolen her boyfriend?"

"Not quite," I said. "You see, I think Miss Jones blamed Mrs. Woolley for Colonel Keeling's death. Of course, she was not pleased by the fact that Katharine had taken away her lover. But that wasn't enough."

Katharine blinked as if to warn me off the subject.

"She blamed Mrs. Woolley for forcing Keeling to take his own life. In her own twisted way, she got it into her mind that Katharine was somehow responsible for his suicide. And so she wanted to make Mrs. Woolley pay for the death. As I said earlier, she did not want to simply kill Mrs. Woolley: that would be too easy, and the suffering would be over too quickly. What she dreamt up was something much more wicked than plain murder. She wanted to bring about Mrs. Woolley's downfall and ruin her reputation."

"What a truly terrible thing to do," said Mrs. Archer. The sentiment was echoed by Father Burrows and Captain Forster, who was busy scribbling everything down. The American woman got up, walked over to Mrs. Woolley, and said, "I think I owe you an apology."

Katharine, no doubt remembering how Mrs. Archer had treated her, simply nodded her head and held out her hand as if she were a queen forced to endure the pathetic attentions of a lowly subject.

"And I, in turn, need to beg for your forgiveness, dear Agatha," said Katharine, suddenly turning to me and flooding me with the light of her eyes and the brightness of her perfect smile. "Would you mind coming with me? I have a small token I'd like to bestow on you."

"Of course," I replied.

As we entered her room and closed the door, she turned to me and apologized. She did not have a present for me—this was a ruse to get me away from the others—and she also said she was sorry for behaving so regally back in the sitting room. I understood that, for a great deal of her life, she too had been playing a part, a role that sometimes restricted and imprisoned her. But what she said next surprised me.

"I do have to thank you for so many things," she said. "One, for saving my life. Two, for sorting out all this awful business with Cynthia. And three—and most importantly—for not telling quite the whole truth in there."

I did not respond.

"But you do know, don't you?"

"Not the full story, by any means," I said.

"I think I owe you an explanation, then," she said.

Katharine sat me on the bed and told me, as calmly as she could, the reason why her first husband had taken his own life. They had married in March 1919, but the wedding night had been a disaster. She did not quite know why she had been fooling herself, but she must have been blinkered, like one of those poor horses you see at the races who jump to their deaths. She'd had little expectation of that side of things, she said; her mother had said nothing to her about intercourse. After a few months of sleeping in separate bedrooms, Bertie insisted she go and see a doctor for a full mental and physical examination. She tried to avoid talking about the subject, but finally, in Cairo, there was a terrible bust-up. Either she had to see a doctor or he would call an end to the marriage on grounds of non-consummation.

That September, she swallowed her pride and submitted herself to an examination. She felt a chill descend on the consulting room. The doctor, a horrid, ratlike man, looked at her as if she were some kind of freak. After she had got dressed again, he told her the awful truth. And then he insisted on telling Bertie about it, too. She pleaded with the doctor not to, but the medico said it was a husband's right to know.

The words were too terrible to hear.

"Your wife here will never have a child," said the doctor.

"Is that all?" exclaimed Bertie, his face lighting up. "There are ways around that. We can always—"

"It's not just that," the doctor interrupted. "Your wife is not—in the strictest sense—a woman."

"What do you mean?" Bertie's face drained of color.

"It's a very rare condition," he replied, "where a person shares certain aspects of the male with certain aspects of the female."

"What the hell are you saying?" Bertie looked as though he might be sick. "Y-you're saying that—that I've married a m—"

And with that, Katharine had fainted. The next thing she knew, she had woken up in her bedroom. She felt groggy, as if the doctor had given her something to make her sleep. She tried to get out of bed but was unable to move. When she woke up again, she was presented with the news that her husband had shot himself.

"That must have been awful for you to hear," I said, placing my hand over hers.

She nodded. "It was, but what I still don't understand is how Miss Jones knew about it," she said.

"Perhaps your husband, the colonel, wrote a letter to her before he died," I suggested. "No doubt he was feeling full of regrets and shame. It would have been natural for him to seek out the one person who said she had loved him all along—his first sweetheart. He probably poured his heart out to her and told her what the doctor had related to him. It must have been awful for Miss Jones to receive that letter, no doubt days or weeks after first hearing the news of Bertie's death. In her view the colonel killed himself because he considered that his reputation had been ruined; he could not bear the shame of continuing with the marriage, and so he took his own life."

"And her name—or names?" asked Katharine. "Miss Edgecombe . . . Miss Jones?"

"Oh, that. Quite easy to establish: the information came from Somerset House, a birth certificate which arrived this morning. Although she was born Cynthia Edgecombe, Jones is her mother's maiden name. She simply started using that when she began work out here."

Katharine swallowed nervously. "And w-what are you going to do with all this information now?"

The final pieces of information began to fit into place. I remembered the phrase that Betty Clemence, that overbearing woman on the Orient Express, had used when she described Katharine Woolley to me: "She's not all there," she had said. At the time, I had assumed that she had meant that Mrs. Woolley was not quite right in the head. Had she been referring to something else entirely?

"Of course, the police will have to be told about your connection to Miss Jones, but I can assure you there's no need for them to know about . . . well, about your own personal history and background."

"And you don't think other people suspect?" she asked.

How had that old cat Betty Clemence guessed at the truth? Perhaps Cynthia Jones had initiated a vicious campaign of gossip, another weapon in her arsenal designed to destroy Katharine Woolley's reputation. "No, of course not," I said. "How could anyone suspect such a thing? No, we'll keep this strictly between ourselves."

"I don't know how to thank you," said Katharine flatly. But then a thought occurred to her which brought life back into her face. "I've got the most perfect idea!" she said, sounding like a schoolgirl. "Although I've been enjoying working on my novel, I realize that I'm never going to make it as a proper author: I haven't got your talent. But one day, when I'm dead, perhaps you could write a book about what happened here and tell the whole story—like one of your mysteries."

"I'm not sure whether I would be up to it," I said demurely.

"I can see it now," she said. "It's got everything—murder, secrets, suspects—and all set against the backdrop of an archaeological dig. I've even got a title for it: *Death in a Desert Land*. What do you think?"

I thought about it for a moment before I replied yes, that might work very well indeed.

Epilogue: The Facts

- The body of the writer, traveler, and archaeologist Gertrude Margaret Lowthian Bell—who helped found the modern state of Iraq—was discovered at her house in Baghdad on July 12, 1926. She appeared to have taken an overdose of Dial (diallyl barbituric acid), a sedative. While the two letters that open the novel are fictitious, some of the details contained in them are authentic and come from Bell's archive held at Newcastle University: http://www.gerty.ncl.ac.uk. I also drew on the excellent Gertrude Bell biography *Gertrude Bell: Queen of the Desert, Shaper of Nations* by Georgina Howell (Farrar, Straus and Giroux, 2006).

- In the autumn of 1928, after her divorce from Archie, Agatha Christie traveled by herself on the Orient Express to Istanbul and then by another train to Damascus. From there she journeyed across the desert to Baghdad in a bus organized by the Nairn Line, a trip that took two days. She then took an uncomfortable train south to Ur, where she met Leonard and Katharine Woolley and Father Eric R. Burrows, a Jesuit priest and an expert on cuneiform tablets. "I fell in love with Ur," Agatha writes in her autobiography, "with its beauty in the evenings, the ziggurat standing up, faintly shadowed, and that wide sea of sand with its lovely pale colors of apricot, rose, blue and mauve changing every minute." Although Agatha acknowledged that Katharine could be a divisive figure, she remained friends with the Woolleys and she went on to dedicate her 1932 Miss Marple short story collection *The Thirteen Problems* (*The Tuesday Club Murders*, 1933, in the US) to the couple. It was in 1930 in Ur that the Woolleys introduced Agatha to the archaeologist Max Mallowan, who was indeed suffering from appendicitis during her first visit to the site in the autumn of 1928. The couple married in Edinburgh in September 1930. Christie's experience at Ur—and subsequent visits to the Near East—inspired her 1936 novel *Murder in Mesopotamia*, which features Louise Leidner, an archaeologist's wife who bears a striking similarity to Katharine Woolley.

♦ Leonard Woolley led a joint expedition at Ur organized by the British Museum and the University of Pennsylvania between 1922 and 1934. He worked in British Intelligence during the First World War and was stationed in Egypt. It was there that he met Gertrude Bell, who also worked for the intelligence services. He met Katharine Keeling in the spring of 1924, when she came to Ur as a volunteer, and the couple married in April 1927. On their wedding night, Katharine locked him in the bathroom until he promised that he would not try to sleep with her. Leonard Woolley contemplated divorce but thought that the scandal would ruin his career. For more information about the lives of Katharine and Leonard Woolley—including the detail of the boyhood taunt of Leonard being a "Woolly sheep"' and his subsequent retort that he was actually a wolf in sheep's clothing—see H. V. F. Winstone's superb biography *Woolley of Ur: The Life of Sir Leonard Woolley* (Secker & Warburg, 1990). A good online site is: www.penn.museum/blog/museum/adventure-calls-the-life-of-a-woman-adventurer/.

- According to Max Mallowan, Gertrude Bell regarded Katharine Woolley as a "dangerous woman." (*Mallowan's Memoirs: Agatha and the Archaeologist,* William Collins, 1977, paperback reissue, 2010, p 36). She was born Katharine Menke in June 1888 in Worcestershire but grew up in a German-speaking family. She dropped out of Somerville College, Oxford, after two years due to ill health. On March 3, 1919, she married Lieutenant Colonel Bertram Francis Eardley Keeling, at St. Martin-in-the-Fields, London. Six months later, on September 20, 1919, thirty-nine-year-old Colonel Keeling—who had also worked for British Intelligence during the First World War—shot himself at the foot of the Great Pyramid of Cheops, Cairo. There have been a number of theories surrounding the suicide of Colonel Keeling, but according to one report he killed himself after a meeting that he had with a doctor who had been called to examine his wife. According to Henrietta McCall, author of a biography of Max Mallowan (Agatha Christie's second husband), Katharine may have had what is now known as complete androgen insensitivity syndrome, a condition which meant that although she was born genetically male, she was insensitive to male hormones and therefore appeared female. In 1929, John Murray published Katharine Woolley's novel *Adventure Calls*, about a young woman, Colin, who disguises herself as her twin brother to travel through Iraq. The quote in Chapter Eleven is taken from page 99 of *Adventure Calls*, a copy of which I read in the British Library. Katharine Woolley died of multiple sclerosis at the Dorchester Hotel in London in November 1945.

- Many of the spectacular treasures of Ur unearthed by Leonard and Katharine Woolley can be seen on display at the British Museum, London.

- One large grave site at Ur was named the Great Death Pit because it contained the remains of sixty-eight women and six guards or soldiers, together with four musical instruments, including a silver lyre. It was here that Woolley unearthed evidence of human sacrifice. As he writes: "Each man and woman brought a little cup of clay or stone or metal, the equipment needed for the rite that was to follow. There would seem to have been some kind of service down there, at least it is certain that the musicians played up to the last, then each of them drank from their cups a potion that they had brought with them or found prepared for them on the spot—in one case found in the middle of the pit a great copper pot into which they could have dipped—and they lay down and composed themselves for death. Somebody came down and killed the animals (we found their bones on top of those of the grooms, so they must have died later) and perhaps saw to it that all was decently in order—thus, in the king's grave the lyres had been placed on the top of the bodies of the women players, leant against the tomb wall—and when that was done, earth was flung from above, over the unconscious victims, and the filling-in of the grave-shaft was begun" (Woolley, quoted in Winstone, page 153).

Acknowledgments

The British Museum's Mesopotamian rooms are places of wonder, and so I'd like to thank the curators and staff of this wonderful institution.

I would like to thank my fabulous agent and friend, Clare Alexander, as well as the whole team at Aitken Alexander Associates, in particular Lisa Baker, Lesley Thorne, Steph Adam, Geffen Semach, Anna Watkins, and Monica MacSwan.

At Simon & Schuster in the UK, I would like to acknowledge Ian Chapman and my fantastic editor, Suzanne Baboneau, both of whom have supported me throughout the writing of this series. In addition, I would like to thank Bec Farrell, Jo Dickinson, Anne Perry, UK copyeditor Sally Partington, Justine Gold, Dawn Burnett, and the marketing department, Jess Barratt, Harriett Collins, Gemma Conley-Smith, and everyone in publicity, Gill Richardson, Claire Bennett, Richard Hawton, Rhys Thomas, and the super-enthusiastic sales team. The cover was illustrated by the talented Mark Smith and was designed by Pip Watkins.

In the US, I would like to thank the wonderful staff at Atria, particularly my editor, Peter Borland, as well as Sean Delone, Daniella Wexler, and David Chesanow.

Thanks too to all the Agatha fans, scholars, and academics who have embraced the series, particularly Dr. John Curran, Mike Linane, Dr. Jamie Bernthal, Scott Wallace Baker, Tina Hodgkinson, Emily and Audrey at the Year of Agatha blog, and many more.

Lastly, I would like to thank all my family and friends and Marcus Field.